BESTSELLING AUTHORS PRAISE
AWARD-WINNER SHIRL HENKE!

"Shirl Henke is one of the brightest stars in romance. Her engaging characters and talent for storytelling grip readers from first page to last!"
—Katherine Sutcliffe

"A riveting story about a fascinating period. I highly recommend *Paradise & More.*"
—Karen Robards

"A grand and glorious novel....I couldn't stop reading."
—Bertrice Small on *Paradise & More*

"*Return to Paradise* swept me away!"
—Virginia Henley

"A romantic romp of a Western. I loved it!"
—Georgina Gentry on *Terms of Surrender*

"*White Apache's Woman* is a fascinating book...an absolute must read for anyone who loves American history."
—Heather Graham

"Fast paced, sizzling, adventurous...with a hot-blooded hero who will set your heart on fire."
—Rosanne Bittner on *A Fire in the Blood*

"A fascinating slice of history...with equally fascinating characters. Enjoy *Love a Rebel...Love a Rogue!*"
—Catherine Coulter

BAD BUSINESS

Sky Eyes backed Max across the floor of the empty saloon toward the door. From the corner of her eye she caught the motion when the barman started to raise a shotgun. "I wouldn't," she said coolly. "I mean to talk with your friend." When his thumb reluctantly slid back toward one of its hammers, Sky cocked the hammer of her rifle. The standoff was interrupted by the creak of floorboards at the top of the stairs leading to the second floor bordello. Keeping her rifle trained on Stanhope, she glanced quickly up, then back to her prisoner.

The small, round woman dressed in a pink wrapper looked old enough to make her coal-black hair improbable. "You mean to hurt 'em?" she asked.

"No, I won't hurt him," Sky said. "I only want to discuss private business. He seems inclined to be stubborn."

Rosie chuckled. "Honey, Max is stubborn, or he'd spend most of his time conductin' private bidness with half the females west of the Mississip. 'Pears yore bidness ain't that kind." She paused for a moment, then said, "He stays in room seven of that flea bag across the street."

"Thanks." Sky uncocked her rifle and pushed her quarry out the door.

Rosie waddled down the stairs, bursting into laughter. "Lordy, Max Stanhope, 'The Limey,' 'Scourge of the Bad Men,' 'The Hangman's Hound,' dragged out of a whorehouse with a rifle in his gut—by a young gal, no less! Damned, if I wouldn't like to be a fly on the wall fer that conversation."

SHIRL HENKE

in collaboration with
Jim Henke

PALE MOON STALKER

LEISURE BOOKS   NEW YORK CITY

For Pam and Bob Voit,
from the river to the Rockies, friends forever.

A LEISURE BOOK®

November 2008

Published by

Dorchester Publishing Co., Inc.
200 Madison Avenue
New York, NY 10016

ISBN 10: 0-8439-6112-0
ISBN 13: 978-0-8439-6112-6

The name "Leisure Books" and the stylized "L" with design are
trademarks of Dorchester Publishing Co., Inc.

Printed in the United States of America.

10 9 8 7 6 5 4 3 2 1

Visit us on the web at www.dorchesterpub.com.

Authors' Note

All right, I know and accept my place in this literary universe. I am the collaborator, the menial who comes up with imaginative story concepts and outlines plots, does research, creates characters and frequently writes the more hilarious and exciting scenes in our books. However, Shirl is the primary author—the sun that illuminates and enlivens this fictional universe; the moon that casts a silver glow over its dark recesses and softens any somber shadows. I thank my lucky stars to be able to add my humble offerings to this glorious act of creation. (What a crock of drivel!)

Now, I don't want to sound bitter. Hey, I can acknowledge when Shirl really does improve my writing. I'm big enough to do that! For instance, I labored over a crucial action scene. Then, she rewrote it. At first, I was a trifle annoyed, only a trifle, mind you, given my natural humility. However, the more I read her scene, the better I liked it. Hers was not only more exciting than mine, it was more realistic. See. I can admit her superior insights.

But why does she have to muck up *my* superior insights? I wrote another scene in which Sky Eyes subdues the Limey, Max Stanhope, physically. Friends, it was funny. You would have loved it. But Shirl took the good stuff out. When I asked why, she said, "It's not realistic." Not realistic? All Sky did was apply a jujitsu technique that used leverage to create painful pressure on a part of Max's anatomy. (Not the part you think.) I pointed out, reasonably, that I was the one who had taught judo professionally. Those green eyes of hers started sliding sideways back and forth, like she always does when she's thinking up an excuse.

She said, "If Sky did that to Max, female readers just couldn't respect him anymore." Good grief! A variation of the old insulting male cliché about reluctant females saying, "You won't respect me in the morning." When I pointed this out, she started her eye-slide, then said, "Sorry, but your version was too *precious.*" That did it. "Precious! Do I knit dollies? Do I look like I wear a tutu under my jeans?" The next morning when I was getting dressed, I found them. I don't know where she got Fruit-of-the-Loom tutus! You have no idea what I endure for your sake.

Jim,
who refuses to knit

Second Author's Note

Ah, the fragile male ego. Poor baby. Any time I disagree with a character's motives or visualize a scene differently, he goes into a snit. Well…more of a temper tantrum, actually. And to think I used to believe as a naive young bride that I really was his sun and moon. Janice had it right, the real metaphor from the male point of view is "Ball and Chain." It's a good thing women have greater intestinal fortitude than men—not to mention infinitely greater patience. But he is correct about his contributions to research, plotting and characterizations.

His collaboration just sort of evolved over the years. Outside of choreographing the fights in my first two books, he never read them. But during the writing of the third one, I caught him sitting up late one night perusing the manuscript pages that my best friend and former collaborator, Carol Reynard, had typed, edited and returned to me. "Ah, ha! I thought you didn't like romances," I challenged. Jim fixed his turquoise gaze on me (how's that for a romance writer's description?) and replied defensively, "I was afraid I'd hate what you wrote and then what would I say?" "But you like this story?" I asked, noting that he'd read at least a dozen chapters of *Capture the Sun.* "It's really pretty good," he admitted. I could hear the grudging tone in his voice, but let it pass. As I said, women possess infinitely greater patience than men.

After that, he joined our collaboration. Mostly his help remained blocking out action and fight sequences, but he also started to come up with some very funny quips for the verbal sparring between heroes and heroines. Remember the old cliché about letting the camel get his nose under the tent? By the time I wrote *Terms of Love*, he insisted he could write a love scene! The gall of the man! But when he finished a draft, Carol and I both thought it was so good that we not only used it—we ran a contest for readers to guess which one was his.

Writing this has given me an idea—not a contest to guess which love scene Jim wrote in *Pale Moon Stalker*, but which "crucial action scene" I rewrote. You see, we had a real donnybrook over one in particular, until Jim finally, finally admitted that my version was better. Pick the scene and submit your choice at my website, www.shirlhenke.com. We'll take all the entrants and place them in a drawing for prizes. And after that, just to show how magnanimous to Jim I am, I'll post both scenes on the website so you can decide for yourselves which one is better. If more of you say I should've used his scene, I'll defer to him more often (I'm talking writing, friends, just the writing).

Shirl,
willing to risk her ego

Chapter One

"You're going to kill a man for me."

A strident female voice dragged him back to consciousness. For a blurry moment Max forgot where the hell he was. Rosie's joint? He looked up, eyelids feeling as if they'd been shaved with a dull razor, and recognized the battered chairs and tables strewn like discarded dice across the beer-soaked wood floor. Yes, Rosie's. He was collapsed on his own table in the farthest corner of the room where nobody could get at his back. Her bartender Ben had a shotgun that would keep off the jackals.

Then who was the harpy standing next to him? Exhaustion combined with whiskey made considering the question too difficult. With a guttural grunt he dropped his head over his arms and returned to oblivion.

"I said you're going to kill a man for me. Wake up, you drunken sot!"

Max looked up and tried to focus on the source of the voice. Damn, he was bone weary. Twenty hours of hard riding could do that to a man—and that was after two weeks on the hunt with almost no sleep whatever. Once more he lowered his head.

"I said wake up, and this is the last time I'll tell you." There was a tight desperation in her tone now.

He should have paid attention to that. Ordinarily he would have. His head barely touched his arms before he felt her hand seize a fistful of his hair and yank backward until he thought she'd broken his neck. Why hadn't Ben blown her to hell with his twelve gauge? Because she was female, Max guessed. Damn the softhearted bastard! He struggled to open his swollen eyelids when she suddenly released her grip on his hair.

"Put your head down one more time and I'll kick the bottom of this table till your brains rattle like beans in a gourd."

To make her point, she gave one leg a stout kick, nearly overturning the table. He rubbed his burning eyes and looked at her for the first time. Yep, a female all right, even though she was dressed like a man in buckskin pants and a shirt that laced up the front. The generous curve of her breasts strained against the lacing. No doubt she was a she. His eyes swept down her body, which was a very good one indeed.

A narrow waist gave way to the gentle swell of hips followed by long legs. She stood with her back to the door, silhouetted in the morning sun so that he could not make out her facial features beneath the low-crowned, flat-brimmed plainsman's hat she wore. Some sort of old Winchester was clutched in her right hand, barrel to the floor.

"Well, Sleeping Beauty, looks as if you're finally waking from your drunken stupor."

He struggled to unglue his furry tongue from the roof of his mouth, then said, "Look, lady, I'm not a hired gun. I don't kill men for money."

"If you're the one called 'The Limey,' reports say otherwise."

"I genuinely dislike that epithet. My name is Maxwell Stanhope. If you must address me, call me Maxwell, Stanhope, even Max. And I repeat, I am *not* a gun for hire."

"Well, Mr. Stanhope, I take issue with that. You hunt men for bounty, specializing in murderers. I've heard you've brought back over twenty men . . . and eight came back facedown across a saddle. I call that killing men for money."

She possessed a clear, deep voice—but it was beginning to

grate on his overtaxed nerves. "Lady, I don't give a damn what you call it. I'm not for hire."

"I think you'll want this job," she said, grabbing his ear in her left hand and twisting it forward and down. At the same time she pulled him out of his chair so quickly that the table almost tipped over. A shot glass and the half-empty bottle of Rosie's best, which wasn't all that good, crashed to the floor.

"Ouch!" He cut loose with a string of oaths. "That's not a damn handle!" He was rapidly coming awake now. Her grip was strong as steel and he could see the hard gleam in her brilliant blue eyes. "Are you crazy?" Max reached down for the Smith & Wesson in his holster.

It was not there. Then he saw it lying on the floor in a puddle of whiskey beside the table. The damned female must've tossed it away just as she grabbed his ear. Mortifying! That never would have happened if he were not insensate with exhaustion. He swatted at her hand and the pain in his ear intensified for an instant. Then she released him and raised the Winchester to his gut.

"You're going to listen to what I have to say . . . and we're going to talk in private. Do I make myself clear?" It was a rhetorical question.

Sky Eyes backed him stumbling across the floor of the empty saloon, heading for the door. From the corner of her eye she caught the motion when the barman started to raise a double-barreled shotgun. "I wouldn't," she said coolly to the dapper little man. She prodded Maxwell Stanhope's midsection with the barrel of her modified Winchester '66 "Yellow Boy."

"The Limey" teetered, nearly falling backward, then groaned, clutching his gut. "Lady, unless you want me to christen those fancy buckskins with the contents of my stomach, I wouldn't do that again." His voice was raspy and he coughed as he righted his balance.

With one eye on the barkeep, Sky said to Max in a low,

emotionless voice, "Be quiet." To the man with the shotgun she said, "I mean to talk with your friend." When his thumb reluctantly slid back toward one of its hammers, Sky cocked the hammer of the Yellow Boy. The metallic click seemed loud in the large room. The bartender froze in nervous confusion. Sky waited unblinking. *Probably hates the thought of shooting a woman . . . even one like me.*

Their standoff was interrupted by the creak of floorboards at the top of the stairs leading to the second-floor bordello. She watched the barman's eyes lift. Keeping her rifle trained on Stanhope, she glanced quickly up, then back to her groggy target.

The small, round woman dressed in a pink wrapper looked old enough to make her coal black hair improbable.

"You mean to hurt 'im?" she asked. Her voice seemed incongruously young coming from a decidedly middle-aged female.

Sky hesitated for a moment, then asked in a flat voice without challenge, "Why do you care?"

"Max is my friend, honey."

"No, I won't hurt him," Sky said. "I need him fully functional—to discuss private business. He seems inclined to be stubborn."

Rosie chuckled. "Well, honey, Max is stubborn, or he'd spend most his time conductin' 'private bidness' with half the females west of the Mississip. Still, 'pears your bidness ain't that kind." She paused for a moment, as if considering, then said, "He stays in room seven in that fleabag 'cross the street." She shook her head at Ben, who very slowly slid his shotgun back under the bar and carefully brought up his empty hands to rest them on its scarred surface.

Sky uncocked the Winchester. She pushed her quarry out the door while he continued growling obscenities.

After they had banged through her front doors, Rosie waddled down the stairs, bursting into laughter. "Lordy, Max

Stanhope, the darling of news rags from Chicago to San Francisco, 'The Limey,' 'Scourge of the Bad Men,' 'The Hangman's Hound,' dragged out of a whorehouse with a rifle in his gut—by a young gal, no less!" she chortled. "Damned if I wouldn't like to be a fly on the wall fer that conversation."

Outside, Sky considered the Englishman who spoke with the perfectly clipped accent of an aristocrat. Small wonder he'd been dubbed the Limey by ordinary citizens out West. The irony of an upper-class Brit being given a pejorative name did not escape her. Neither did his physically imposing appearance.

He topped her own five-eight by four or five inches. She'd had no idea her bounty hunter would turn out to be a perfect male specimen, tall, lithe and sinuous with curly silver blond hair a London belle would kill to have. Lord, it was pale as moonlight! Small wonder so many women wanted to conduct "private bidness" with him. Even filthy with sweat and trail dust, his sun-bronzed face was as patrician as one of those old oil paintings she'd seen in museums back East. The nose was long and slender, the mouth wide, the jawline chiseled.

But it was Stanhope's eyes that held her attention. Even after one brief confrontation with him in the bar, she would never forget those eyes. Framed by arched silvery eyebrows, they were dark green, slitted and ice-cold. This was a dangerous man. She'd been blessed lucky to get him this far. She imagined his trail fatigue had more to do with it than her skill. He was killingly angry at her, but somehow she would convince him to go for her proposition. She absolutely had to.

After their short trip across the dusty street, Sky Eyes Brewster and her charge entered the lobby of the Angel's Rest. The scruffy old hotel's small lobby was devoid of any furnishings except for a scarred desk, unmanned. Behind it on the wall keys hung from pegs. "Grab number seven," she instructed him.

In spite of his obscene protests, he stretched one long arm

across the desk and retrieved his key, squinting through bloodshot eyes. "Now what?" he asked in an arctic voice.

"We go to your room and have our private talk, what else? Do you think I find you so irresistible I'll molest you at rifle point?" He shook his head. She wasn't certain if it was to disagree with her, or simply to clear out the cobwebs.

"At the moment, I am so limp . . . from fatigue, you could not 'molest' me at cannon point, dear lady."

"Your virtue is safe with me, Mr. Stanhope," she said tersely, motioning with her rifle toward the stairs.

Max climbed the creaking wooden steps and fumbled with the key until he got the door open. Once inside, he made a flourishing bow, gesturing with his hand, as if to welcome her. "My humble hovel, ma'am." Sky stepped inside, backing him over to a straight-backed chair in the corner.

"Sit down," she commanded, much relieved that he complied. In truth, he looked ready to drop to the floor with exhaustion. She quickly surveyed the shabby quarters—besides the chair, a bed with a lumpy mattress, a washstand, a chipped pitcher and a bowl were the only furnishings. In one corner a Winchester '76 with a checkered pistol grip and special target sights leaned over carelessly tossed saddlebags, his only personal possessions. If he made a fraction of the reward money reported in the newspapers, he certainly wasn't spending it in Bismarck.

"Why do you stay in a dump like this?" she couldn't help asking.

"Central location, close to Rosie's . . . oh, yes, and my friend Mort Hersh runs the place. He'll be along shortly, I rather imagine, so you'd better make this 'conversation' quick," he said dryly.

"All right." She whipped off her hat and tossed it on the bed, then moved over to the door, holding her rifle on him as she turned the lock. "At least I'll have some warning before anyone intrudes."

"I could use some water," he said with a cough.

"After all that whiskey, I imagine you could. And probably a chamber pot as well," she said tartly. Filling the basin with brackish water, she turned suddenly and threw the contents into his very surprised face.

Max gasped and choked. Sky calmly looked on as he shook his head like a dog emerging from a river. "Now you should be alert enough to comprehend what I have to say."

Max was indeed alert. He was also coldly furious. "Look, miss—"

"Missus . . . Mrs. Sky Brewster. I'm a widow."

"Well, Mrs. Brewster, I'm sorry for your loss—"

"I didn't come for condolences, Mr. Stanhope. I'm here to hire your skills with a gun. I want you to track down and kill the man who murdered my husband."

Max sighed. Damn, the woman had a head as thick as a brick. Best to hear her out, then get rid of her so he could collapse on the bed—that was if Hersh didn't arrive first. Rosie probably had Ben out looking for him now. One way or the other, he needed to lie down and sleep, preferably for about a week.

"Why should I be interested in taking this 'employment'?" he asked, leaning back in his chair. "So far the only inducements you've offered have been indignities." He detected a faint flush in the widow's cheeks.

The Limey examined her carefully now that his head was starting to clear and she was fully visible in the light pouring like butterscotch from the room's lone window. Mrs. Brewster was one of the most stunningly beautiful women he had ever met. She was tall, with a mass of very long, glossy black hair done in a braid as thick as a man's wrist. Judging by the faintly dusky hue of her complexion, he would assume she had some native blood, but damn little.

Her features were cameo delicate, with a mouth that had slightly puffed lips as if swollen by kisses, a small straight nose, pointed chin and arched black eyebrows that framed the bluest eyes he'd ever seen. He'd been right about her body, too. It was slender with high, pert breasts that pushed against her loose shirt, and legs—lord, what legs—long and shapely in fitted buckskin breeches. She wore moccasins instead of boots. She also wore a gun belt strapped around those shapely hips and in the holster rested a Merwin & Hulbert, ivory-gripped revolver, likely a .38-caliber piece. This was a formidable female.

Sky watched his cool green eyes sweep over her, head to toe. Those eyes had seen a lot of death. "Do I pass muster?" she asked dryly.

He nodded. "I've always suspected beautiful women know they do."

"The same could be said of beautiful men," she snapped, then bit her tongue as his eyebrows rose slightly at the backhanded compliment.

Stanhope chuckled. "A beautiful bounty hunter? A most novel oxymoron. It even alliterates."

Sky bristled. "Let's focus on a not-so-novel idea—you killing a murderer."

"Look, Mrs. Brewster, if a man killed your husband, get the courts to try him. See him hanged. You shouldn't require my services."

"Unfortunately for both of us, I do. You can see I have mixed blood. I'm Ehanktonwon—Yankton Sioux. My husband was a missionary, an Episcopal priest, who championed the rights of Indians. He was a thorn in the side of every sleazy Indian agent and local bureaucrat in the region. Are you so naïve as to expect justice for a psalm-singin' preacher who didn't understand 'all Injuns is semihuman, murderin' trash'?" she asked, emphasizing the last words with a nasal twang.

Max could hear the roughening in her voice and recognized that she was suppressing tears. She was right. Any white who took the natives' side, much less married a mixed blood, was fair game. "I've lived out West long enough to know how people here feel about the native population, but I don't go after men unless the law's on my side. I take it that the authorities don't agree that your husband was murdered."

"No," she said coldly, "they don't, and it isn't because I haven't tried to use the courts for the past year. It all began when Will and I were on the northern border of Yankton lands. We came across a man flogging a young girl with a riding quirt. God knows what that animal was doing there. I never did find out. My husband never carried a gun in his life, but he was a big man. He jumped off his horse and grabbed the quirt away from the little bastard."

She paused to compose herself, then continued. "The coward tried to pull his six-gun, but my husband grabbed it and tossed it away. Then he took the man by the scruff of his collar and used his own whip on him until he'd cut through the fellow's pants and blistered his ass." Sky swallowed, then said in a low, flat voice, "Will made two mistakes. He turned his back on the snake and he never let me carry my weapons. I could have stopped what happened next . . ."

Max finished for her. "This child-beater had a hideout gun? He shot your husband from behind?"

She nodded. "Then the girl he'd hurt started screaming. We . . . we both went for him barehanded, but he'd emptied his gun into Will. He jumped on his horse and rode away. The sheriff and the courts concluded it was self-defense," she said bitterly. "Even though everyone knew Will never owned a gun and he was shot in the back. The only ones to protest the verdict had the wrong color skin."

He looked at the Merwin & Hulbert .38 in her holster, then at the Winchester Yellow Boy. "Why don't you kill him yourself? You look capable enough."

Sky bit her lip. "Before he died . . . Will made me swear I wouldn't kill his murderer. He was a priest . . . and a far better Christian than I'll ever be."

"I assume he didn't specify that you could not hire it done?"

"I suppose, in a way, I'm still breaking my oath, but when I learned more about what kind of animal his murderer was, I couldn't let it rest. I want that killer dead."

Max sighed. "Hell, I'd like to help you, but there was a letter waiting for me when I returned this morning." He glanced over at the drawer beneath the washstand. "I have some very pressing business that must be resolved back in England. I truly am sorry, Mrs. Brewster. I hunt men, but I don't set out to kill them."

"I don't believe you'd have any qualms about killing this one—if you're the man called the Limey."

She seemed so sure of herself. "You know I am. But what would make me agree to your offer? Surely not your delightful interviewing skills," he could not resist adding.

Those huge blue eyes flashed triumphantly. "A few weeks ago, you were in a card game with a man, cleaned him out. He was a bad loser and tried to draw on you. You had him beat by a mile, but like a damned fool, you didn't squeeze the trigger. The man left the bar, got on his horse, rode sixty or seventy paces down the street, unbooted his rifle, and shot your horse, which was tied at the hitching rack. Shot him in the belly."

Max turned pale under his suntanned skin. "Johnny Deuce shot Rembrandt . . . my Remmy, the bravest, most intelligent, most beautiful paint pony I ever saw. If he's the son of a bitch who killed your husband, you'll get what you want. Sooner or later our paths will cross again. I assure you that he'll be as dead as you could wish him."

Sky shook her head. "That's not good enough. I want him dead at my feet, and I want him dead now! I've already waited for over a year fighting for justice in courts that don't know the meaning of the word. I can pay you seven hundred dollars to do what both of us want. Kill Johnny Deuce."

Max stared at Sky intently while thinking about the news he'd received that morning. A crazy idea flashed into his brain. Wildly improbable, but it just might work. She could be the solution to his dilemma . . . if he handled the matter deftly. The shock of learning about his uncle Harry's death had not yet worn off. Hell, it probably never would. That was why he'd sought the oblivion of liquor. Harold Stanhope, Baron Ruxton, was the only family he'd ever cared about . . . and now he was gone.

He absently gazed at the drawer in which he had placed the letter from his uncle's London solicitor. He had to return . . . and soon. "What if I make you a counterproposal?" His mouth curved ever so slightly at the double entendre only he understood.

One of Sky's finely arched black eyebrows rose. Heaven above, when the man smiled that way, she didn't have any idea what to expect. "What kind of proposal?" she asked suspiciously.

"Why, of marriage, naturally," he said with a perfectly straight face.

Sky almost dropped her rifle. She did lean it in front of her, using the stock to support her suddenly unsteady legs. "How much *did* you have to drink?" was all she could manage to say.

"I am quite sober, thanks to you—and deadly serious, I assure you."

"Why would an Englishman want to marry a mixed-blood woman, much less one he's just met—and not under the most ideal circumstances, as you've repeatedly reminded me?"

He made a dismissive gesture with one elegant hand. "Back in England, your Sioux blood, what little there is of it, wouldn't signify. I have just come into an inheritance, but to claim all of it, I must present to my solicitor in London a suitable wife. The intent, I believe, is for me to wed and fertilize a delicate 'English Rose.'" He spit out the phrase as if it were a slice of lemon. "But there may be another option . . . with no fertilization required. You're educated, Church of England, and to make it believable, attractive. You fit the requirements admirably," he added, amused at her stunned expression. She looked as if she had just seen George Armstrong Custer leap out of his grave, yanking arrows from his body.

Sky finally gathered her wits. "You're rather crudely proposing what I believe the English call a marriage of convenience. Is that right?" At his nod, she attempted to gather her wits, unable to believe such a bizarre bargain. "I assist you in claiming your inheritance and you kill Deuce for me in return?"

"Precisely so. We can have the marriage annulled once we return to America. Then I'll track down Deuce and—"

"No! First you kill him, then I marry you and sail to jolly old England," she countered stubbornly.

Max rubbed his burning eyes, cradling his head in his hands. This wasn't going to be easy. *She* wasn't going to be easy. "It can't work that way. It might take weeks, even months, to track him. I haven't the luxury of time. I have inherited my uncle's title, but if I don't return immediately, I'll lose his unentailed fortune. Worse, my gutless little bastard of a cousin will receive it in my stead. Cletus allowed my elder brother to die when we were children. If not for that . . . I doubt I'd go back."

"You don't want the money? The title?" she asked, amazed.

"I don't give a damn for any of it. I am not unlike what some would unflatteringly call a remittance man. My uncle has sent me money, which has been piling up in a New York bank for the past five years. Couldn't talk the old boy out of it, so . . ." He shrugged, then looked away, staring with those cold green eyes into a time and place far away.

"So, you let this money sit untouched and made your own

way with a gun," she supplied. The man was an enigma. What would cause him to do such a thing? Sky intuited that it would not be wise to ask. Then he stood up and advanced a step toward her. Now he was grinning at her like a lobo wolf . . . a very dangerous male animal. She did not back away but stood her ground.

"That is one of the tools of my trade," he said, gesturing to the .45-70 Winchester in the corner. "By the by, that Smith & Wesson double-action you left basting in whiskey at Rosie's was custom-made to my precise specifications. If it's damaged, the cost of a replacement will come out of your share of the inheritance."

"I have not agreed to marry you—and if I did, it wouldn't be for money," she replied, caught off guard by his sudden shift in mood. "Anyway, it . . . it wouldn't be proper. Will's only been dead a little over a year."

"Do you want me to kill Deuce or not?" He studied her keenly, trying to gauge what lay behind those incredible eyes. Would she help him?

"Yes, I do, but if I go through with this sham marriage, will I have to accompany you to London?"

"I'll book adjoining staterooms. You may lock your doors against me," he said dryly.

Sky considered her options. With every passing week, Deuce's trail grew colder. She had learned he'd left Dakota Territory almost immediately after the last in a series of mock trials left him a free man. He was afraid of what she would do. Rightly so. "How could you find him months from now after we return from England?"

A good sign. She was not rejecting his terms outright. "It's what I do. Track wanted men," he replied simply.

She barely shook her head. "Why would you ask me to form this alliance? Surely you could find any number of women who'd give their eyeteeth to marry a titled Englishman." *One handsome as sin like you.*

"I want the liaison to end amicably. What I don't want is a woman who covets being a baroness so much that she'll raise a fuss about an annullment. Your speech and manners—in spite of your rather unorthodox dress—indicate that you're well bred. I'm quite certain you do not want to remain my baroness. But can you act well enough to fool my solicitor, hmm?"

"You are presumptious, arrogant and altogether too glib . . ." She allowed her voice to fade away, placing one slender finger to her cheek, making him wait. "In spite of that, yes, Maxwell Stanhope, I'll marry you." The moment she spoke the words and saw the triumphant gleam in his hard green eyes, Sky wondered if she had just made the worst mistake of her life.

St. George's Episcopal Church, Bismarck

"I now pronounce you man and wife," the priest said solemnly. "You may kiss the bride." The latter was added with a gentle smile as the elderly clergyman looked from Sky to her husband.

My husband, Maxwell Livingston Stanhope, Baron Ruxton. Sky felt her throat tighten with uncertainty as she looked up at his face, trying to read any emotion. There was none discernable. At least he wasn't gloating, thank heavens, but at the prodding of Father Granton, he did lower his head and give her lips a chaste brush. She felt an odd frisson of . . . something pass over her fleetingly. Then, before she could identify the feeling, it evaporated. She resisted the urge to touch her lips with her lace-gloved fingertips.

Looking around the ornate brick church with its gold-trimmed altar, she considered how different this was from her first marriage to Will in a tiny wooden chapel on the Ehanktonwon reservation. She had worn a white buckskin tunic lovingly embroidered with beads and quills, made for her by the women of her tribe. Her whole family was there . . . and so was love. Now she had just wed a dangerous stranger after making a frighteningly cold-blooded bargain.

As they left the church, Max sensed her restiveness and knew she was having second thoughts. "Repenting our bargain so soon?" he asked.

"No . . . that is, it seemed wrong to make vows before a priest that we don't intend to keep—not that I want a real marriage," she quickly amended.

Max chuckled. "If I thought for one moment you did, I'd be the one having second thoughts. But I explained why it had to be a Church of England marriage."

"A civil ceremony wouldn't be sufficient to satisfy the requirements of your uncle's will," she replied, trying to convince herself.

"You're still in love with your dead husband, aren't you?"

The question surprised her. Of course she would always love Will, but what business was it of his? Composing herself, she replied, "I adored Will from the moment I first saw him standing at the foot of the gangplank of my brother's sternwheeler."

"You have a brother?"

Sky nodded. "Yes, Clint Daniels from St. Louis."

"That's where your white family lives?"

"No, just Clint and his wife Delilah and their children. Clint is my adopted brother. He married my sister Teal and became one of us . . . until she was killed . . ."

"Sorry to bring up unhappy memories," he said.

"It was a long time ago. Clint brought me to St. Louis and saw to my education so that I would be able to return to my people and help them in their struggle against the whites."

What an enigma she was. "You speak about the whites as if they're your enemy. Is that why you didn't ask your brother for help when your husband was killed?"

Her face became shuttered. "Clint doesn't know about Will's murder. I never told him. He would have sought vengeance . . . and that would stain his soul."

Max considered her words. *But mine is so black already, what matters another smudge or two?* For some inexplicable reason the implication hurt.

When they reached New York, Max reserved a suite in a fine hotel with a sitting room separating their bedrooms. They had one evening before their ship sailed for London. Sky had mentioned reading about Delmonico's in the heart of New York's "Tenderloin District." He intended to surprise her by taking her to the famous restaurant.

Sky stood in front of the mirror in her bedroom, imagining what Max was doing at the moment. No doubt he was dressing, humming tunelessly as he had so often done on the long rail trip from Bismarck. It seemed a lifetime since she'd lived with a man. Will had always been thoughtful about simple courtesies, assisting her in and out of carriages or opening doors for her, but his touch had been gentle and familiar . . . comfortable.

When Max did the same things, she felt completely different. There was a strange tension between them. She almost thought he was angry with her for some fault she did not understand. Now that they were so close to embarking for his homeland, did he regret marrying a woman of mixed blood?

She checked her appearance again in the mirror. The deep rose silk gown dipped low in front, revealing more of her breasts than she would have chosen as the wife of a clergyman, but it was the height of fashion for ladies of quality—or so the saleswoman had assured her. She wore her mother's cameo on a slim gold chain around her neck.

Since childhood, she had carried the treasured memento with her everywhere, but the engraved gold wedding band from Will she had placed in a shabby black velvet pouch. Removing it from her finger when she made her bargain with Max Stanhope had felt like a betrayal. She glanced down at the heavy gold ring that the Englishman had placed on her hand. There were no words of love etched on the inside of the band. It felt heavy . . . and cold. Like her new husband's eyes.

A tap on the adjoining door interrupted her troubled thoughts. She walked across the room and opened it. Max looked every inch the English lord in a dark blue wool suit, his white shirtfront winking with emerald studs. His tall, lean body was made to wear custom tailoring. He'd been to a barber and his curly hair was fashionably tamed, the sideburns silvery blond against his bronzed skin. For an unbidden moment, she caught herself wondering if his body was as pale as his hair. Appalled at the thought, she quickly suppressed it.

"You look quite splendid, m'lord," she said with an insouciant curtsey.

"Even more so, you," he managed as his gaze swept from her lush black hair, braided in an intricate crown atop her head, to the soft curves of her hips revealed by the tempting concoction in silk that clung so lovingly to her body. His attention was drawn back to the deep vee of her cleavage where a simple oval of carved ivory nestled. Fortunate cameo! "Is that a family heirloom?" When she reached up and fingered the cameo, he felt his throat tighten, wanting desperately to touch those soft mounds.

"It belonged to my mother. The only thing she managed to hide from her Pawnee captors."

Max struggled to find his voice, then said, "It's as lovely as you."

Sky was delighted by Delmonico's. After sharing a bottle of excellent champagne, they both began to relax. He enjoyed watching her study the haughty socialites and powerful Wall

Street businessmen surrounding them. "Many of the men and women you see here are as powerful as any earl or duke in England."

Sky made a moue of distaste. "They exploit Indian land and prey on the poor of every race."

He smiled at her. "You would be a daunting reformer. Even the likes of Gould and Fisk might back down if you jabbed your Winchester in their fat guts."

"A thought worthy of consideration," she said dryly. "But not in such a lovely place. The meal was incredible. Thank you, Max, for bringing me here."

"My pleasure," he said, and it was, indeed. He signaled a waiter for the check.

Outside, the night was warm and the moon full when they stood on the street awaiting a hack. When an open carriage approached, he hailed it.

The driver, a small fellow with slicked-back dark hair and an ingratiating smile, asked, "Would you folks enjoy a ride through Central Park? Perfect night for it."

"I'd appreciate some fresh air," she said to Max. "It's been seven years since I lived in a large city and I don't like the smell or closed-in feeling of being surrounded by so much brick and stone."

"The park it is, then," Max said, then asked, "Are you homesick?"

She shook her head. "No. I need time away from the memories back in Dakota lands. But eventually I'll return there to live out my life."

And find a real husband. The thought rankled. He pushed it aside. "No interest in St. Louis?"

"It was a good place to learn what I needed to know."

"Yes, how to outwit the wily white-eyes," he said wryly. "Tell me more about what you studied in St. Louis. Healing arts? Teaching?"

"We have a doctor and several missionaries who care for

our ill and teach our young. No, I read law with one of the most successful attorneys in the city." She watched that silver eyebrow rise just as she'd expected it would.

"I might have to let go our family solicitor. Poor Jerome."

"You'd be unwise to dismiss him," she said with the hint of a smile. "I know nothing of English law."

"That's a relief. Jerome Bartlett's been with the Stanhopes for decades. Quite a decent chap."

Suddenly, their carriage came to an abrupt halt in a tree-shrouded grove. Sky was thrown against Max's shoulder. She could feel his arm reaching inside his jacket for the .32-caliber Hopkins & Allen pocket revolver she knew he carried.

"Stay down," he commanded as the driver jumped from his perch and vanished into the darkness.

Sky had learned her lesson well the day Will died in her arms. She never again went anywhere unarmed. As Max looked from side to side for an approaching thief, she plunged her hand into her small beaded reticule and extracted her Colt Derringer just as a shot rang out and her husband cursed.

"Are you hit?" she whispered.

"No," he muttered, sliding from the carriage when he detected a figure emerging from the bushes. He palmed the .32 so that it would be invisible in the gloom, and raised what appeared to be empty hands. "Don't shoot. I'll give you my money—"

A harsh guttural laugh echoed in the darkness. "More'n that, I'm thinkin'," the thief said as he raised his pistol and took aim.

Max's arm came down lightning fast and he rolled to the ground. From a prone position he fired as the startled thief's finger closed on the trigger of his gun. He missed. The Limey did not.

Sky held her Derringer level, watching their assailant crumple. Max stood up and walked over to the man on the ground, kicking his weapon away. Suddenly, a slight movement caught her eye from the side of a large tree. "Max, watch out!" she shouted, firing at the man taking aim. She knew she was out of range, but the shot did the trick. The thudding of footsteps pounded away from them as he crashed through the undergrowth.

"Are you all right?" she asked, struggling to alight from the carriage in her slim skirt.

"No. Blasted suit's ruined," he replied calmly, holding up his left arm to reveal a tear in the sleeve from a bullet.

"You can afford a new suit. New arms are difficult to come by, even for a baron. Consider yourself very lucky," she said in a chiding voice.

"I always have been . . . so far." There was a darkness in his voice before he shifted his attention to the unconscious man, who moaned softly. "Bastard was a frightful shot."

"Why would he try to kill you when he thought you were willing to give him your money?" she asked, looking down at the man lying on the ground. A rough customer, probably from New York's infamous slums. "Our driver was part of the robbery setup."

"Most certainly—and I was stupid, not suspecting it." *Stupid because all I was thinking about was a carriage ride in the moonlight with my beautiful wife.* Sighing, he knelt and checked the injured man for weapons, pulling a knife from his belt and slipping it into his pocket. Then he hoisted the man over his shoulder. "Maybe the police can break up a ring of thieves if this chap starts talking."

Sky watched him carry the thug to the carriage and deposit him beneath the driver's seat. The fellow had to outweigh him by a good twenty pounds. This was a feat Will could have easily accomplished, but she would never have believed it possible for the lithe, slim Englishman. He turned to her then with a harsh smile.

"I didn't thank you for shooting at the second thief." He looked at her reticule as she dropped the Derringer into it. "Do you always go to dinner armed, Lady Ruxton?"

"Always," Sky replied in a flat voice. She did not smile.

Chapter Two

London daunted Sky from the moment they arrived. New York was large and bustling, but . . . raw and new, filled with the frenetic energy of a young nation. This magnificent ancient city was far larger, the very center of the greatest empire the world had yet seen.

"Nervous?" Max asked as the driver drew in the reins and stopped the carriage at the front entrance of the Ruxton City house, a lovely three-story edifice constructed of pale aged brick replete with ivy tendrils trailing like green lace across the front. "The servants will adore you, especially Baldwin, the butler. He's the one who's really in charge of the household."

Sky swallowed for courage. "Yes, to be honest, I'm more frightened now than I've ever been—even when I walked into Miss Jefferson's Academy my first day at age fourteen."

"No one here bites," he said with a grin.

She smiled. "Lucretia Mottly did, quite viciously, as a matter of fact."

"Why is it that I suspect you gave as good as you received?" he asked dryly.

"I didn't bite her back, if that's what you think," she replied in mock indignation. "I put a large black spider in her bedcovers. She all but screamed the dormitory down!"

He grinned at her self-satisfied chuckle. "I detest spiders. Remind me never to bite you," he said.

The double entendre was not lost on her as he slipped easily from the hack and offered her his hand. She could feel the thrill of contact the moment she placed her fingers in his palm, in spite of the fact they both wore gloves. "A few of the other girls at Miss J's bit and did other things far more heinous than I could ever have imagined," she said, attempting to cover her reaction to his touch.

"Henderson, my uncle's cook, had a dog when I left for America. Smart mutt was known to take a nip or two when he disliked someone—but his only victim was my cousin Cletus."

"The one you dislike so?" she asked, but before he could reply they were interrupted.

"Welcome home, m'lord," a small, frail looking man said as he climbed down the front stairs. He was amazingly spry, possessed of a booming bass voice . . . and completely bald. His shrewd gray eyes crinkled at the corners with pure joy as he looked Max over from head to foot. "America has certainly agreed with you, if I may be so bold as to say."

"So happy for your approval, Baldwin, although I know you wish I'd never left 'civilization.'"

"But then, m'lord, you'd never have found such a lovely lady," the butler replied with a cheeky grin. He bowed handsomely to Sky while Max made the introductions.

She had worried about the welcome she might expect from the longtime retainers of Harry Stanhope, Max's beloved uncle. This warm greeting was a good omen. Although she did have to stifle a tiny smile at the shiny-pated man's name. "You are most kind, Baldwin. I feel welcome, in spite of the sad circumstances that have brought us here."

A fleeting expression of deep sorrow crossed the old man's face, but was quickly banished as he replied, "His lordship will be sorely missed. He was a fine man who lived a long and full life."

"Baldwin was with my uncle for most of it," Max said as they entered the foyer, where a line of servants stood expectantly on the polished marble floor.

Sky took in her surroundings, feeling like those first Native

American chieftains must have when summoned to the Great White Father's "lodge" in Washington D.C. A staircase wound upward to the second floor, and a glittering chandelier of breathtaking crystal hung suspended from the twenty-foot ceiling. Vases of fresh cut flowers were placed about the large space, their summer fragrance vying with the succulent aromas wafting from the kitchen at the rear of the house.

All the cooks, maids and footmen appeared respectful to her, hiding any curiosity about her racial background quite well except for one young lad who stared in rapt awe as if she were a goddess from another planet. As Max greeted them, each by name, and introduced his lady to them, all exhibited genuine joy at his return. He must have indeed been his uncle's favorite nephew.

Her husband had explained that Harry Stanhope had been devoted to his wife Lodicia and never remarried after her death at the tender age of five and twenty. The couple was childless, so after her untimely passing, Harry had devoted his life to amassing a huge fortune in trade, acquiring vast estates, woolen mills and other manufacturing interests. He also dabbled in railroads and shipping.

Harold Stanhope, the sixth Baron Ruxton, had inherited a minor title yet become one of the wealthiest men in England. He would have given it all in exchange for his beloved wife's life. The sad tale only served to make Sky ache for her own loss of Will . . . and feel an unidentified stirring deep in her innermost heart for Max. She quashed it, knowing that any hope for a love match with the new baron was foolish . . . and disloyal to Will's memory. But her curiosity remained about why a man so beloved by his uncle and all these people would leave his home in the first place.

Max puffed slowly on an excellent cigar offered to him by Jerome Bartlett's assistant and surveyed the lavishly appointed office of the family solicitor. "Business must be very good, indeed," he murmured to himself as he waited for his uncle's old college chum. Jerome had sent profuse apologies via his assistant for being detained at a luncheon engagement.

The delay amounted to less than a quarter hour. Bartlett, a pudgy man of medium height with watery blue eyes and thinning tan hair, rushed in breathlessly. "Please forgive me, Max, or should I now address you as m'lord?" he asked as the two shook hands heartily.

"Why on earth since you always called my uncle Harry and you've known me since I was in knee britches?" Max replied.

"Very well, Max. So sorry about the delay. Some beastly old harridan of a widow, who shall, of course, remain nameless, has set her cap for me. Since her deceased husband, poor sod, was one of my best clients and I must see to her estate, there is little to do but humor the old bat."

Max barked a laugh. "I thought you had moved up in the world as soon as I arrived at your new office. Quite impressive."

"I owe a good deal of my success to Harry, God rest his soul. We prospered together." Bartlett's shrewd gaze swept over Max. "You've changed since leaving for America . . . even more than you did in the army—"

"I would prefer not to discuss ancient history, Jerome," Max interjected. "I have here my marriage lines, as you will note, duly signed by a Church of England cleric, albeit an Episcopalian one in America. Now, let us turn to the matter at hand. Fulfilling the terms of my uncle's will and keeping that bastard Cletus from receiving anything more than the law absolutely allows."

Bartlett nodded. "Please, be seated and I will go over the will with you . . . in some detail." There was the faintest hint of a smile in his expression as he rummaged about his large desk, extracting a sheaf of documents. "As you will see, your uncle made a few changes since last you saw the will."

"I don't give a fig about the title or the unentailed money. You know that."

"Indeed," Bartlett replied, adjusting a thick pair of spectacles over his narrow nose. "Rumor has it that your wife is quite a beauty."

"Rumor travels quite fast, considering we only reached London this very morning," Max said, uncomfortable speaking about Sky and the way he was using her. As to his other feelings for her . . . he suppressed the thought.

"My widow client far exceeds the telegraph when it comes to gossip. You had only to disembark for word to spread that the infamous 'Limey' had returned with a lovely American wife. And that she has, perhaps, a touch of exotic Red Indian blood."

Max bristled. "Does her pedigree signify?" he asked in a baronial tone.

Bartlett chuckled wryly. "Good heavens, please don't go all lordly on me, Max. You know me well enough to understand I meant no offense. If she's half as beautiful as word has it, the two of you will produce very striking offspring for the Stanhope line."

"I have no particular desire to turn myself out to stud, Jerome. I intend—"

"Oh, I believe I understand quite well what you intend, young man. Your marriage was rather hasty," he said, glancing down at the date on the papers Max had given him. "The ink must scarcely have dried before you set foot aboard ship for home."

"You have no way of knowing how long Sky and I were acquainted prior to our marriage, not that it matters in regard to the will."

Bartlett extracted a single sheet from the pile of papers on his desk and handed it to Max with a twinkle in his eyes. "This is a codicil to your uncle's will, written after we filed the original document. It . . . rather changes the provisions of inheritance, as you shall see."

The wily old man was positively gloating. With growing unease, Max began to skim down the page. By the time he'd finished, he was cursing. "I thought Uncle Harry had some regard for me, even though I went to America and refused to live on his stipend."

"Harry Stanhope loved you dearly, Maxwell," Bartlett said in a stern voice. "The day you received the Victoria Cross was the proudest of his life. You were the son he and Lodicia could not have."

"Then why this?" Max asked, honestly bewildered.

"Harry feared you were losing your way. Recall, we heard the American news stories about the Limey and your infamous reputation. You see, he charged me with keeping track of you from the day you left the army. All you did was exchange one dangerous profession for a far more dangerous . . . job, for want of a better word."

"I did what I'm best at doing. Hunting and killing men," Max said bitterly.

"Yes, quite so," Bartlett replied quietly. "And precisely the reason Harry hoped that these terms would force you to end your self-destructive odyssey. With not only a wife—but a child as well—you would be forced to settle down. He knew you cared nothing for his money or the title. In truth, since Lodicia passed, he cared little for either himself."

"Yet, if I don't produce the heir, the money and the rest pass to Cletus," Max gritted out.

Bartlett chuckled. "Harry was not so medieval as all that. As you can plainly read, there is no provision that your offspring need be male. And no time limit, as long as you are cohabiting with your wife and trying to start a family. Considering that he and Lodicia were childless, he was well aware of how painful such a problem could be."

He paused, now somber, and studied Max. "Harry understood perfectly how you felt about Cletus. Indeed he shared your aversion to the worthless sot—"

"Hell of a way to show it, offering him a fortune to squander," Max said bitterly.

"He knew you better than you know yourself, Maxwell. You will do your duty and settle down, if for no other reason than to prevent Cletus Stanhope from laying waste to an immense fortune." Jerome consulted the documents before him. "Several million pounds in factories, railroads, shipping—"

"I understand enough about my uncle's varied financial interests," Max said with a dismissive wave of his hand. "Does Cletus know he may well be the next Baron Ruxton and heir to millions?"

Bartlett shook his head, then adjusted his spectacles before replying. "As far as he is aware, his settlement amounts to twenty thousand pounds with an additional four thousand pounds annual living allowance for the rest of his life. I've arranged matters so that this last codicil your uncle requested is 'buried,' so to speak. It would take another quite keen solicitor to discover it. Only you and I and two legal witnesses—friends of mine—are aware of Harry's deathbed changes."

"So, if I fail to produce an heir and predecease Cletus, my cousin will inherit the title as well as the fortune." Max made this a flat statement, not a question. He looked as if he'd just sucked on a very sour lemon. "He's responsible for Edmund's death, dammit! Both Uncle Harry and I agreed."

"Your brother's drowning was rather suspicious, I certainly concur. The river was shallow, Edmund was a strong swimmer, and Cletus apparently was found standing on the bank in dry clothing . . ."

A hard, cold light came into Max's green eyes. "Well, one thing is certain. Uncle Harry was right. I will do anything to prevent Cletus from becoming the next baron."

"Even starting a family with your lovely bride?" Jerome could not resist asking.

Max did not give him the satisfaction of a reply, but instead asked the well-connected solicitor to draft a will for him as the new baron . . . and to make some discreet inquiries.

Propriety demanded that no formal entertaining be done during the year of mourning for the late Lord Ruxton, but family gatherings were expected, especially when the heir returned from abroad with a new wife. Sky let Baldwin and the housekeeper arrange all the details for the evening meal, a simple repast for four—the baron, her and the only other remaining Stanhopes. She felt nervous about the confrontation between Max and his detested cousin Cletus, but it was a formality that could not be ignored. The last guest was his second cousin Phillip. Like his father before him, Phillip managed the Ruxton country estates for the family.

She had just finished inspecting the dinner table with its daunting assortment of crystal and flatware at each place setting when her husband returned from his day's outing in an exceedingly foul mood. "You look as if you've just swallowed a live skunk," she said when he glowered at the chair with a card for Cletus set discreetly beside the wine goblet.

Max looked at her, studying her as if he'd never laid eyes on her before in his life. "I can assure you, my indisposition has nothing to do with diet, but much to do with my 'skunk' of a cousin. Damned if I know why I agreed to let that little drunken bounder darken my door."

"He is your cousin, no matter his faults. Baldwin claims that I must be presented to him and to your cousin Phillip . . ." Her voice faded as a disquieting thought flashed through her mind. "You're not . . . you aren't worried about my Sioux blood, are you?" Was he ashamed of her now that they were in London and faced with meeting the Stanhopes?

For a moment, he simply stared at her, seeing a startlingly

beautiful woman even in her black silk gown which shone almost as richly as her gleaming raven hair. Then he realized what she had asked and vehemently shook his head. "Don't be absurd. I would never have offered marriage if I felt you weren't quite perfect as my baroness."

His reply sounded stiff and unnatural to Sky. "You must truly detest Cletus," she said, to cover her own unease at his peculiar distraction. The sooner they settled matters here and returned to America to track Johnny Deuce, the sooner they could go their separate ways. *That will be for the best.* Why didn't she believe her own thoughts? "Did things go well with your solicitor?"

"I've had more enjoyable confrontations with cold-blooded murderers," he gritted out as he spun on his heel and stalked from the room.

Sky stood rooted to the floor, stunned at his vile temper. What must have happened to cause this sudden shift in his mood? Had Jerome Bartlett done something amiss? This afternoon when he'd left for the solicitor's office, Max had appeared resigned if not exactly overjoyed with the family gathering. In fact, he'd been quite concerned about her feelings regarding the introduction to his cousins. He'd even assured her she would be the perfect hostess.

She stewed as she waited for Max to change, rechecking her own appearance in a sitting room mirror to make certain she was presentable. The heavy crown of gleaming braids and elegant mourning gown made her complexion appear startlingly pale by comparison. Her normally bright blue eyes appeared washed out. Smudges had suddenly appeared beneath them.

What have I gotten myself into?

Her troubling ruminations were interrupted by Baldwin as he announced the arrival of Phillip Stanhope, the family estate manager. From what Max had told her about his second cousin, the fellow was an affable chap, competent and hard-working. When the tall, rather raw-boned man with the trademark Stanhope silver-gilt hair entered the room, she felt the warmth of his smile.

After they had introduced themselves, she murmured, "I must say, you do bear a striking resemblance to my husband."

"You are most kind, Lady Ruxton, but I'm just a poor country bumpkin cast adrift in the big city," he replied with a winsome smile. "Max has always been the charmer. How else could he have won such a lovely bride?"

"Now, who's the charmer?" she teased, instantly liking him. "Please Phillip, call me Sky, if I may be so bold as to address you by your Christian name."

"Most certainly, Sky," he replied warmly.

"I've seen the portraits of your uncle Harry and Max's father. Do all the Stanhope men look so alike?"

Phillip appeared to hesitate. "Not all," he replied vaguely as the front door again opened and Cletus was announced. The moment he entered the sitting room, Sky knew why Phillip had not wanted to discuss family resemblances. Cletus Stanhope was short and pudgy with a dough-soft belly. Narrow bloodshot eyes of a color difficult to discern squinted at her from beneath the bush of his heavy red eyebrows. His complexion, no doubt owing to copious quantities of alcohol, was bright red, several shades darker than the faded, thinning strands on his scalp.

"So, yer Max's new lady," he said by way of introduction, scarcely giving her a nod before he sauntered toward the sideboard, where an assortment of liquors were set out in glittering crystal decanters.

"Chivalrous as always," Max said from the doorway, scowling at Cletus, who scarcely turned to acknowledge his host as he filled a snifter with French brandy. "Phil, how are things going down in Kent?" Max asked as the two men shook hands.

Sky could see they shared not only hair coloring and sundarkened skin but also callused hands. They were both men who worked and lived outdoors. She listened as they discussed the family estates and was surprised to learn how much Max appeared to know about agriculture and livestock.

"I've met your lovely wife, Sky," Phillip said, drawing her into the conversation. "You are to be congratulated, coz. The lady is a true beauty."

Max regarded her with those hard green eyes. "Yes, she most certainly is," he replied thoughtfully.

A ripple of unease swept over her. Whatever had set him off this afternoon must have been troubling in the extreme. Her worried thoughts were interrupted by Baldwin, announcing dinner.

"About time, before Cletus becomes so inebriated that he attempts to eat his soup with a fork. He's done it before," Phillip murmured to her as they filed into the dining room, with their portly cousin bringing up the rear, brandy glass clutched in one meaty fist.

Sky smothered a chuckle.

By the second course, Cletus indeed was having difficulty getting food to his mouth without spilling spots of consommé and slices of fish on his shirtfront. Somehow he managed never to spill the brandy or wine, which went directly down his gullet. Between swallows and bites, he prattled on about various influential people in high social circles with whom he hobnobbed.

Just before the fowl was served, he raised his glass and cleared his throat, garnering their attention as he sneered, "A toast to our dear uncle Harry, wretched pinchpenny that he was. Leaving me only a measly twenty thousand with a yearly pittance of four while the fair-haired Maxwell inherits everything." He burped in the stone silence of the room, then blustered on, "But you were the hero of Rorke's Drift, weren't you, coz?"

Phillip leaned toward his cousin and placed a restraining

hand on his arm. "Clete, old man, you're foxed and unfit for decent company. Our uncle left me the same inheritance, a tidy fortune, and I'm exceedingly grateful. So should you be." When Cletus subsided and sullenly stuffed nearly half a quail in his mouth directly from the tray the server held before him, Phillip turned to Max and asked, "Would you mind if I used part of my inheritance to buy some land adjacent to Ruxton Manor? I could manage all the property easily from Kent—that is, if you don't object?"

Max nodded, forcing himself to ignore Cletus. "Certainly, Phillip. I was hoping you'd want to stay on."

"Always so generous is our Max," Cletus interjected.

Seeing her husband was nearing the end of his patience, Sky spoke up. "Sir, you call twenty thousand pounds measly?" she asked the drunken man, then turned to Phillip and inquired, "What would twenty thousand pounds be worth in American dollars?"

Phillip stroked his jaw, considering, then replied, "The last exchange rate I recall was one pound sterling to a bit more than four dollars. Four fifty-eight, if memory serves."

Her face flushed with amazement as she calculated. Max watched her with a sudden burst of amusement. He had a suspicion Cletus was about to receive a verbal thrashing—far preferable to his beating the imbecile to death and leaving a gory mess for the servants to clean up.

"That's more than ninety thousand dollars! And you have the audacity to call your uncle a pinchpenny?" she asked incredulously. "That's a fortune! In America it would take a skilled physician a lifetime to earn that much money."

"My dear, I am an English gentleman, not a skilled physician," Cletus replied contemptuously.

"Cletus, you are not a skilled anything," Phillip interjected, eliciting a chuckle from Max, for whom the evening had just taken an amusing turn.

"And most certainly not a gentleman either," Sky found herself blurting before she thought better of it. Now Phillip joined in the laughter.

Tossing down his unused napkin, Cletus glared at her. "Well, m'lady, I don't see that your husband is any different, except for receiving a Victoria Cross for killing a bunch of bloody wogs."

"Here, Cletus! Watch your language," Phillip remonstrated.

When Max stood up, Sky reached over and took hold of his hand, pulling him back into his seat. "He's drunk," she said.

"And stupid," Phillip added cheerfully.

She turned to him and asked, "What are wogs, Phillip?" although she already had a pretty fair idea.

Max's cousin looked exceedingly uncomfortable, casting a glance at Max, who nodded for him to reply. "I fear Cletus is referring to the Zulu people of Africa, one of the largest and fiercest warrior groups inhabiting a sizable portion of the continent."

Sky turned to her husband and inquired in dulcet tones, "Would you say, Max, that the Zulus are analogous to the Sioux Nation?"

Suddenly the conversation had taken a most unpleasant twist he'd never anticipated. He swallowed hard and nodded silently.

Sky turned to Cletus with glittering eyes and addressed him in a harsh burst of alien language. "That was Sioux, Mr. Stanhope. I called you an offal-licking, lizard-lipped miscreant. Now, I'll tell you in the English of which you are so proud, that if you ever dare to enter my home again, I will use a Sioux scalping knife on the pitiful remains of your scraggly red hair—and if I ever encounter you on the street, I'll employ it to geld you to prevent you from contaminating the stock of your much-loved English nation! Leave this house this instant." The last words were delivered in icy cold command.

Cletus Stanhope overturned his chair in his haste to escape.

He stumbled for the door to the hallway and crashed against the walnut frame, then careened into the foyer, where they could hear him bleating when he slipped on the marble floor.

"He's probably crawling out the front door on hands and knees," Phillip said gleefully.

Sky found her rage suddenly dissipated after Cletus's ungainly retreat. She had behaved like the uneducated savage "wog" that odious man believed her to be. She glanced apprehensively over at Max . . . expecting censure. If he had not already, he surely regretted his hasty marriage now.

Chapter Three

Sky sat frozen, not daring to meet her husband's hard green gaze. Until the sound of clapping broke the sudden silence after Cletus's exit. Her head jerked up and she saw Max smiling at her as his hands applauded her treatment of his detestable cousin. Phillip, too, joined in the accolade. She was speechless. They suddenly broke into laughter, slapping each other on the back as Max informed her, "Lizards don't have lips, love."

"Egad, but it does alliterate! You both do!" Phillip joined in with a hearty guffaw.

Max nodded. "She has a gift for alliteration and oxymorons." He smiled at her.

Not noting the byplay, Phillip continued with glee. "I've been waiting for years for someone to take Cletus down for his egregiously drunken behavior, but never in my wildest imagination did I envision it done to such a splendid turn!"

Sky smiled at Phillip and expressed her gratitude for his support, but her husband's reaction to her outburst was of far more import. She tried to read behind those mysterious dark eyes, now crinkled with laughter. Was he truly pleased by what she had done? With Maxwell Stanhope, one could never be certain . . . least of all if one was his wife.

Later that evening, Max and Phillip retired to the study to go over some estate bookkeeping matters. Sky excused herself, as was the English custom, and went upstairs to the adjoining bedrooms she and Max were using. After her maid assisted her in getting the elaborate gown and undergarments off, she dismissed Polly with thanks, glad for the time to herself to consider the most disconcerting evening. She could never be comfortable surrounded by servants, all eager to do her bidding.

"A good thing I won't be Lady Ruxton for long," she murmured to herself as she sat brushing her own hair before the mirror in her dressing room. She studied her reflection, noting the dusky tinge of her complexion. She knew Polly had been shocked that evening when she'd prepared a bath for her mistress and saw that the lady's skin was not merely bronzed by the harsh American sun, but a natural tan over every inch of her body.

"Perhaps she thinks I sunbathe nude," Sky speculated, not really interested in what the servants' gossip would be on the morrow. They would remain unfailingly polite as befitted their station. If the beloved Lord Ruxton chose to marry a "wog," they would never complain, even if they speculated below stairs about why he'd done it.

Phillip, too, appeared to readily accept her, although, as the steward of Ruxton estates, it would have been unlikely he'd openly disdain her. He seemed genuinely pleased by her set-down of Cletus, but that might owe as much to Cletus's vile personality as to any genuine fondness for a woman of mixed blood.

She really did not give a fig for family or servants or, for that matter, the whole of London's approval. Then why on earth did Max's approval mean so much to her? They had a business arrangement. Pure and simple. It would end once the Limey had done his job—tracked down and killed Johnny Deuce. The thought of Max riding away from her squeezed her heart, catching her off guard. She forced aside the pang of longing and turned to brushing her hair its usual hundred strokes, angrily counting as she plied the brush. *Why am I acting like a lovesick schoolgirl? I'm a widow in mourning!* she reminded herself.

From beneath the doorway between their rooms, Max saw a pale crack of light. Sky was still awake. For some self-torturing reason he refused to examine, he turned the well-oiled knob silently and watched her. She brushed that gleaming mass of ebony hair, hanging her head forward so the heavy weight fell over her breasts. He could see the slender outline of her spine through the sheer silk of her black lawn night rail. Mourning clothing, worn as tradition dictated down to the most intimate garments, made most women look washed out, faded and gray.

Not his Sky. Her rich coloring and vivid blue eyes were brought to life by the somber wardrobe. Since when was she *his* Sky? He cursed silently, reminding himself that he had not yet decided whether he wanted to make the marriage permanent. He could do as he'd done years ago. Simply walk away from the land, money and title, go back to being the Limey. Let Cletus have the whole of Harry's fortune to squander.

Then he smiled sardonically. Even if he decided he wanted to fulfill the terms of his uncle's will, would Sky agree? He could well imagine her furious reaction if he broached the idea. Sky had obviously been devoted to her first husband, probably loved him still. She had been willing to make a devil's bargain to see justice done for his murder. Which brought him back to the practical matter at hand. He looked down at the note just delivered from Jerome Bartlett's assistant.

He broke the silence. "May I come in?"

Sky turned, nearly dropping her brush, then tangled it in her thick hair. "You move as quietly as a Pawnee raider," she accused, trying to cover her reaction to him as he stood in the doorway between their quarters. He wore a black brocade robe belted carelessly around his narrow waist. The lapels gaped open, revealing far too much of a thatch of pale silver-gilt hair on a hard, muscular chest. Below his neck, his skin was as pale as she had imagined. Sky wondered how he kept from sunburn, spending so much time in the broiling heat of her native land . . . and in Africa.

"Sorry, I didn't intend to disturb you, but when I saw the light, I assumed you were still awake." He admitted nothing of watching her for several moments before announcing his presence. "I have something I thought you'd like to see."

She glanced at the note in his hand. "What is it?" she asked, trembling as she disentangled the brush from her hair.

He stepped closer and she turned to face him, letting her hair act as a curtain covering her breasts beneath the sheer night rail. It was all Max could do not to reach out and brush the hair back so he could feast on the proud, upthrust mounds hidden beneath all that ebony luster. But if he did that, he knew he would not be able to look without touching. And that would violate their agreement.

What bloody self-punishing instinct made me open that door? He cursed silently as he handed her the note, but could not keep his fingers from brushing hers. When she flinched and withdrew her hand, he could see that she was trembling. Bloody hell! So was he! At least she was not as indifferent to him as she attempted to make him believe she was.

Filing that thought away, he said, "Upon my request, Jerome Bartlett has unearthed some information that will help us track the Deuce."

She quickly scanned the lines, then asked, "How does knowing his identity here in England help us? I already knew he was an Englishman. He's in America now, disowned by his family."

"Ah yes, but a family that still remits funds to him to keep him across the Atlantic."

"How can you be certain this Jonathan Framme, third son of an earl, is Johnny Deuce? Just because of the first name—"

"You didn't finish the report. Allow me to summarize. Young Framme was banished back in eighty-one for the last in a series of indiscretions. He enjoyed using a riding crop on young girls. Tolerable as long as he contented himself with prostitutes and serving wenches. But he made one unpardonable error—he plied his whip on the daughter of an MP."

Sky nodded. "The actions certainly seem to fit, but it's not conclusive."

"Framme's middle name is Ducelin, a male version of his grandmother's name, Ducelina. And she was the one who raised the spoiled darling. She's also the one sending the remittances."

"Deuce from Ducelin. It makes sense. Can you trace where she's sending the money?"

He smiled harshly. "Always keen witted, m'lady. Being connected with the banking establishment, Jerome requested a few favors from clients and learned that one firm discreetly sends the remittance to New York. From there, the money is forwarded wherever our prey chooses. The most recent place is Denver."

"Denver is a large city," she said, doubtful yet daring to hope.

"I have a friend there named Blackie Drago who knows every unsavory secret in the city. If anyone can learn where Deuce is currently skulking about, it's Blackie. I'll wire him in the morning to begin the search. My affairs here will be settled tomorrow. We'll leave the day after."

"Then you have the title and fortune secured from Cletus?" she asked, shuddering at the memory of the odious little toad. An oddly guarded expression veiled his face.

"I've done all I can in London. Yes . . . I believe it is," he added on a more positive note.

When he turned to leave, Sky said quietly, "Thank you, Max."

"No thanks necessary. Remember Remy." He paused at the doorway and murmured, "Sky, you did well setting down Cletus tonight. You made me proud, m'lady."

She watched him step through the doorway and close the

walnut door. When she turned back to the mirror and picked up her brush, she was startled to see a look of shy pleasure wreathing her face.

Sky found it difficult to sleep in her elegant bedroom that night. Whether her insomnia was caused by the unsettling experience with Cletus at dinner or Max's earlier ill humor after returning from his solicitor's office, she did not know. After tossing and turning for an hour, she threw back the coverlet and rose, then turned up the gaslight.

Just as she began scanning the books in a case against the wall adjacent to Max's room, she heard the sound of Max's voice. The tone was soft, indistinct at first, but there was an anguish in it that had her straining to hear what he was saying. Then his voice grew louder. He appeared to be issuing orders.

"Form the company here, backs to the redoubt!" He let loose a string of curses. "I don't give a damn if there are a million of them—follow my commands and you'll survive. Do not fire until I give the order." His tone was precise, cold, deliberate now.

Sky found herself reaching for the heavy brass knob to the door separating their rooms. It felt clammy in her grip, but it was not locked. Too preoccupied to consider why neither of them had thought to take that simple precaution, she opened the door and peered inside. A sliver of moonlight trickled into the large room through the draperies. His hair shimmered like a pale halo, framing his stricken face.

Max sat upright in his bed, eyes wide open. Yet she was certain that he was not awake. His hard gaze was fixed on something only he could see. He raised his right arm in the air, bent at the elbow. His right fist was closed with the index finger curled and the thumb upright . . . as if he were holding a pistol. Very slowly his thumb moved back, cocking his weapon.

Suddenly he extended his arm and shouted, "First rank, preeesent," drawing out the last word before he commanded,

"Fire! Second rank, preeesent. Fire! Third rank—" He stopped abruptly, making a choking sound and squeezing his eyes shut. His arm dropped. He fell backward onto the mattress, mumbling to himself, a garbled mixture of oaths and horrible descriptions of "blood, so damned much blood . . . rivers of the filthy red stuff . . . bones are still white, shining through it . . . bloody hell! That's right. This is hell . . . bloody flaming hell . . ."

Sky stood transfixed for another moment as he gradually quieted, tossing in a restless, exhausted sleep. She silently withdrew, closing the door and locking it from her side, then leaned against it to quell her shaking. Max could never know she had spied on him. If he thought for an instant she had witnessed his midnight battle, the proud Englishman would be humiliated beyond bearing. No wonder he did not want to speak of his earlier life. What had he witnessed?

What had he done . . .

He had been an officer in some distant and bloody war. Cletus had mentioned Rorke's Drift and the Zulu warriors of Africa. Was that the battle Max had been reliving in his nightmare?

He could not have run from the fighting or left the army in disgrace. No, something else had caused his alienation from his family, his coming to America. She had witnessed first-hand his coolness under fire. He'd become a bounty hunter, for heaven's sake—scarcely the occupation of a man who had won the Victoria Cross.

Then another thought occurred to her. He only hunted murderers, even though the bounties for bank and train robbers were usually much higher. What if he risked his life bringing killers to justice as a means of atonement? What had he done that he must atone for?

In two days they were booked on a steamer bound for America. Because their suite had a sitting room separating their sleeping quarters, Sky had no idea if his nightmare recurred during the crossing. She had heard no further outbursts during their brief sojourn in London. Now aboard ship, the mystery continued. She felt loath to ask him about his experience in Africa, or the battle which had earned him the highest military honor bestowed upon a British soldier. Thinking of butchers like Custer and Chivington in America, she found it difficult to imagine her husband being cut from that cloth.

Without knowing anything about the battle at Rorke's Drift, she had no way to judge, other than by his terrible nightmare. Maxwell Stanhope was a man riven by guilt and bent on atoning. She intended to understand why before they parted.

The nearer they drew to New York, the more Max stewed about his dilemma. Should he make a permanent commitment to Sky? Would she be willing to accept such a cold offer? She obviously cared nothing for money or the trappings of English society. He had watched her standing at the ship's railing when they embarked. She looked not at the receding coastline of the Old World, but rather, gazed eagerly to the West. She was going home.

Oddly, he realized for the first time that so was he. America, brash, crude and dangerous as it could be, had become his true home. The time spent in London had only served to sharpen his perception of how far he had drifted from English propriety. A life of serving in parliament, hosting formal dinners and attending Ascot filled him with claustrophobic dread. Maxwell Stanhope had the pedigree, but no longer the predilections for being a baron—if, indeed, he'd ever possessed them. He longed for the clean, harsh wind of the High Plains, the babel of languages and races, the teeming promise of the New World.

A place where a man could begin again . . .

But did that mean begin with the added responsibilities of

a wife and family? Even if he decided to chance a permanent marriage, that still left Sky's feelings to be considered. How could he approach her? "Bear me a child and be tied to me for life just to spite Cletus Stanhope?" Doubtful that would win her over! But there was that undeniable frisson of sexual attraction that sizzled between them at awkward and unexpected moments. He could seduce her . . .

She could scalp him, too, once she learned why he'd done it. He smiled wryly.

By the time they landed in New York, Max was no closer to figuring out what he should do than when they'd left London. He brooded in his stateroom, pacing as a steward loaded his steamer trunks and carried them away. A light tap on the open door broke into his reverie.

Sky stood dressed in a soft blue suit with a jaunty little hat perched on her head, her lush hair caught in a heavy bun at her nape. She looked good enough to eat—and he was very hungry. "Everything packed and ready to go?" he asked before he blurted out his thoughts or something equally stupid.

"They took the last of my things," she replied. "I know it's customary, the mourning clothes, but I'm glad you didn't want to continue wearing black for the year. It always did seem a foolish idea to me."

"Uncle Harry abhorred it. He would've wanted to see you in clothes to match your eyes, not your hair. He would've approved of you, you know." What had made him say that?

She appeared to digest the remark, uncertain why he was flattering her. The marriage was a sham, and Uncle Harry certainly wouldn't approve of that! She practically thrust the telegram she'd been holding at him as she explained, "This just caught up with me. You know I've been keeping my family in Dakota Territory informed of where I've been this past year. My father worries—in fact he's worried so much about our marriage and trip to London that he took it upon himself to have a wire sent to my brother."

"Clint Daniels in St. Louis?"

Sky sighed with frustration, waiting until the steward wheeled Max's trunks from the cabin, leaving them alone. "Yes. And Clint, being the protective elder brother he is, found out when our ship was arriving—don't ask me how—and sent this wire, demanding to meet you."

"Imperious fellow," Max said with a hint of a grin. "Resourceful, as well. You mentioned he was in the river trade, dabbled in real estate. Does he own stock in the Pinkertons as well?"

"Quite possibly, but one thing I know for certain. If we don't detour to St. Louis for a family visit, he'll track us down." She bit her lip and looked out the porthole at the busy wharf.

"What is it, love? We can spend a few days in St. Louis, then take the train directly west to Denver. It's not so out of our way." Max knew there was more to her relationship with Daniels than she'd told him. "Do you and his wife not get on?"

Sky smiled sadly. "Delilah's my best friend in the world. I've missed her as much as Clint."

"Then what?" He waited.

Sky met his keen gaze, knowing she would have to explain some family secrets she did not want to reveal. "You asked why I didn't have my brother avenge Will's death for me . . ." she began.

"And you said you neglected to tell him it was murder. That if he sought vengeance it would 'stain his soul.' Something you were quite certain wouldn't bother mine . . . if I indeed possess a soul. Some reason for doubt on that score."

"I didn't intend to hurt you, Max," she said earnestly.

He studied her, then nodded. "No, I believe you didn't. I assumed there must have been a good reason you feared for Daniels. Perhaps he simply isn't capable of killing, like your first husband. Or not proficient with firearms. I'm certain you'd not risk his life—"

"Clint is more than proficient with guns, knives, war lances, any weapon you can name," she said abruptly. "I was surprised you didn't make the connection with his other name . . . upriver they called him the White Sioux."

"Lightning Hand?" he asked as Clint Daniels's name finally clicked into place in his mind. "Good lord, the Pawnee Killer!"

"Don't ever use those names," she snapped, then sighed. "I'm sorry, but that part of his life ended long before he met Delilah. Now they have a family and a prosperous life in St. Louis. When Will died, Delilah had just had a miscarriage. So they didn't travel upriver after the funeral as they otherwise would have. Then, I fobbed them off with a series of excuses, saying I was traveling to get away from reminders of Will, things of that sort, which were true in a way. They never learned the circumstances of his death. I've written and wired a lot, but I haven't seen them since six months before Deuce shot Will.

"I'll do anything to keep my brother from returning upriver where he earned his reputation. He . . ." She appeared to grope for words. "He changes . . . reverts to the man who slaughtered all those men indiscriminately. I don't ever want him to know why I came after you in Bismarck . . . Please."

A man who slaughtered other men indiscrimately. Max shuddered. What would she think of him if she knew how he'd won that damned Victoria Cross? "Your reasons for marrying me will remain our secret, Sky. But that does present a problem if we're to visit them in St. Louis."

Her hand closed around the telegram, crumpling it into a tight ball of paper. "You mean, we'll have to pretend to be . . . to have . . . to . . ."

He forced a chuckle. "Yes, we'll have to pretend this is a real marriage. I fear I'll be sleeping on the floor during our family visit, thanks to your charmingly American custom of single bedrooms for husbands and wives. Never fear, we'll pull it off handily, then be on our way to Denver."

In spite of his good-humored reply to her floundering, Sky detected a flash of alarm . . . or was it pain in his eyes? Surely it was just the light from the porthole playing tricks. She was becoming frighteningly attuned to his moods. "We must agree upon a story about how we met. Clint wouldn't for a moment believe I married you for a title or for your money."

"Then it must be for love . . . love," he replied as that same haunted expression passed quickly over his face once more and vanished.

Sky was too preoccupied to notice his disquiet. They had argued furiously when he'd told her he'd had Jerome Bartlett draw up a will leaving the Stanhope fortune to her. She told him firmly that she didn't want any part of his money—and that they would soon no longer be husband and wife. It was irresponsible of him. But he'd replied that he cared nothing for the money, only that Cletus did not get it. Then he'd blithely suggested she could donate it to charity. The debate had ended in a stalemate.

St. Louis was a bustling river city at the nexus of the mighty Mississippi and Missouri, with railroads and warehouses crowding its urban core. Clint and Delilah Daniels lived outside the hectic center of commercial activity in a lovely new residential district called Lafayette Square, facing on a large park filled with strolling pedestrians. Luxurious carriages moved around the park, picking up and dropping off well-dressed passengers.

The Daniels home was one of the newest and most elegant, a three-story frame row house with mansard windows on the top floor peering down like eyes on the picturesque scene below. The house was painted a deep cream-gold color with various shades of chocolate brown trim on the elaborate window sashes and doorway. To the side, a wrought-iron fence and arched gate covered with ivy led to a formal garden, complete with gazebo.

Sky could see Delilah's rich brown hair glint red in the sunlight as she pushed a swing with a squealing little girl in it. Her heart clutched, watching mother and child lost in a moment of joy. Then a piping young voice called out, "Look, it's Aunt Sky!" Young Rob, the eldest of the three Daniels children, came dashing from behind a lilac bush and through the gate. He practically barreled into her as Max helped her from the hack they'd hired at Union Station.

Sky knelt and hugged young Robert Horace Daniels with a pang of joy. She and Will had tried in vain to have children. Rob was named after Delilah's beloved uncle Horace Robert Mathers, who had insisted they reverse his given names so as to prevent "the odious appellation of Horace from being inflicted upon yet another generation of our estimable family."

"Father said you were coming, but we didn't expect you so soon," Rob babbled excitedly.

"The trains now are quite fast," Max said.

The towheaded boy looked up abruptly at the imposing man with the distinctive accent. "Are you Aunt Sky's new husband? Why do you talk so funny?"

"Robert! Mind your manners," Delilah admonished. She was a striking woman with deep reddish brown hair and cat green eyes, tall and slender as Sky, but with the fair complexion of a city lady. While she embraced her dearest friend, her eyes were not on her son. Rather they studied the tall, pale-haired man standing beside Sky. "You must be Maxwell Stanhope," she said after she and Sky had hugged fiercely. A maid stood a discreet distance away, holding little Dorcas in her arms while a second boy hid behind her skirts, peeping out at the Englishman.

Max bowed over Delilah's hand gallantly, but he had

caught the guarded expression on her face before she smiled. "Guilty as charged, Mrs. Daniels. I do hope you forgive me for whisking your husband's baby sister away to England before we paid our respects to you."

"Well spoken," Clint said as he walked down the steps from the front stoop. The shallow yard facing the street allowed him to reach the rest of the group in a few long-legged strides. He was of an equal height with Max, lean and hawkish looking with pale blue eyes and straw-colored hair. "When we received my sister's wire saying she'd remarried in May, we were somewhat surprised. It was rather sudden."

"There's a lot I couldn't explain in a telegram, Clint," Sky interjected, reaching up to hug her brother.

"Well, we certainly aren't going to hear it standing in the middle of the street," Delilah said as the hack clopped away. "Come inside and we'll have a cool libation. St. Louis may not be London, but we are civilized here . . . well, mostly." She gave Max a polite smile and added, "Please, call me Delilah. We are family now, aren't we?"

He detected an undertone, not exactly of mistrust, but certainly of caution. "Yes, we are, and I'm Max to family and friends."

"And the Limey to folks out West," Clint said, his pale gambler's eyes fixed on his new brother-in-law. In spite of his sardonic comment, he extended his hand.

Now Max understood their guarded reaction to him. "I hope you won't hold my past against me," he replied, shaking Clint's hand. "Sky has changed my life since the day we met." Nothing could have been more true!

As they entered the foyer of the lovely house, Sky said, "What my husband means is that he's a peer of the Queen's vast realm now. And I am officially a lady—and don't you dare snort, Clinton Daniels," she added with mock severity.

"Wouldn't dare. You'd take a scalping knife to me," he deadpanned, studying her, then returning his gaze to Max.

"Yes, I would. I said 'officially,' not truly, Clint," Sky retorted with a sassy grin.

Delilah led them into the front parlor and rang for refreshments. When everyone was settled, she instructed the maid to take her daughter and the two boys upstairs for afternoon naps. Rob and his younger brother Jacques protested, but were quickly overruled. They trotted obediently up the steep steps in the long hallway outside the wide parlor door, peeking from between the wooden rails at the fascinating stranger their aunt had married.

Below, their father and uncle continued to take each other's measure. "So, you've come into a title," Clint said as they faced each other, seated in two elegant wing-back chairs while the women occupied the green brocade sofa. "That the reason for the quick trip to London? I was rather curious when Sky sent her cryptic telegram," Clint said.

"So, like any good brother, you had me investigated," Max replied good-naturedly. "I'd do the same in your place. We did have some papers to sign in London to make me officially a baron. The uncle who raised me died without heirs."

"Oh, please accept our condolences," Delilah said.

Max nodded. "Harry detested mourning clothes. We only wore them in England. He wouldn't have wanted to see Sky draped in black, even though the color favors her."

Butter wouldn't melt in his mouth. Sky felt her cheeks heat beneath his warm gaze. She knew they had to convince Clint and Delilah that they were truly married, but the ruse was painful for her. She had always had a difficult time concealing anything from either of them.

Max explained how he'd become heir to the title and that his uncle had bequeathed him an unentailed fortune besides, hoping the knowledge of Sky's being well provided for would quell some of the Danielses' concerns about his shady past. Heaven forbid they should ever learn of the cold-blooded proposition she had broached to him that day in Bismarck . . . or his counterproposal.

As they had anticipated, Sky and Max were given a spacious guest bedroom—with one large bed as its focal point. After Delilah had left them to rest and freshen up for dinner that evening, Max walked around the room, inspecting the accommodations. "Well, that chaise by the window might work tolerably well," he said doubtfully.

Imagining his feet hanging over the edge, Sky shook her head as a far more disturbing image flashed into her mind—his lean muscular body stretched out on that big bed, covered by nothing more than a sheet. There would be neither walls nor locked doors between them tonight. Her voice took on a breathless quality that she tried to cover with a slight cough as she replied, "You're too tall. I'll take the chaise. You sleep in the bed."

Max studied her flushed cheeks with interest. He had learned that despite her complexion, when his wife was perturbed, a faint hint of peach-pink tinged her skin. "Rather unchivalrous if I were to allow that, don't you think, love?" he asked with a grin. "Never fear, Sky. We shall deal with each other's sensibilities. Be grateful your brother's new home has a private water closet adjoining our room."

"Frankly, I'd prefer a good screen of sagebrush to squat behind," she said, trying to match his light tone. "Would you consider sleeping in a nightshirt?" The last thing she needed was to watch him stride naked across the room to the WC in the middle of the night!

Max threw his hands in the air. "Now that is pushing English chivalry to its utmost limits. I hate the bloody things. I don't even own one. Besides, you know how hot and sticky the nights are in this river valley in summer."

"Well, since Delilah has confided that my brother does not

use them either, I suppose you will just have to keep your robe close at hand during the night."

"I could wrap a sheet about myself like a Roman toga," he suggested, amused by her odd mixture of primness and earthy practicality.

Ignoring the absurd idea, Sky said, "I'll work out a schedule for our baths."

"Won't that make your sister-in-law a bit suspicious? She seems quite keen-witted, as does Daniels."

"She was a professional gambler before she married Clint." She loved the way his narrow eyes widened at that sally. "She won Clint's stern-wheeler from him in a poker game, and then the clothes right off his back. He turned the tables on her by stripping right in front of her and a crowd of people aboard the boat."

Max threw back his head and laughed. "I stand warned. A most formidable pair."

"Oh, and you'll meet Uncle Horace tonight at dinner. He was the one who taught her to play cards. He's sort of adopted me, too. Best shot I've ever seen with either long or short arms."

"Good grief, a white Sioux, a lady gambler and now a deadly shootist. I can scarcely wait," Max replied with a resigned sigh. "It doesn't seem fair, love. You only had to face lizard-lipped Cletus."

Sky's husky laughter filled the room.

Juggling bathing schedules proved easier than anticipated. The family had added a second tub room at the end of the hall since Sky's last visit. She returned to their room, swaddled in a long robe and flushed from a refreshing bath in tepid, scented water. "The new maid is refilling the tub for you," she said, trying not to look at him as she fussed with the gown lying spread across the bed.

Max could smell the essence of herbal fragrance that was

her unique signature. Her waist-length mass of damp hair fell like spilled ink over her shoulders, as if inviting a man to bury his fingers in it. He fought the impulse to tear the soft cotton cloth open and pull her against him in a fierce, passionate embrace. *How the hell am I going to get through a week in this room with her?* But sanity prevailed and he replied, "I'm on my way."

Her husband wore that same black brocade robe he'd purchased in England, still gaping open to reveal his pale, muscular chest with the thick pattern of gold hair enticing a woman's hands. His feet were long and narrow with high arches. She'd never seen them bare before. His beard stubble, glowing silver-gold in the evening light, she already knew. She began to fantasize about how scratchy it would feel if he kissed her, brushed his lips over her body . . . *Stop it!*

Max interrupted her disturbing thoughts, saying abruptly, "I'll give you half an hour to dress." With that, he walked past her and out the door.

After it closed behind him, she began putting on her chemise with trembling hands. *How will I survive a week with him in this room?*

Chapter Four

As they descended the steep straight flight of stairs from the second story, Max offered Sky his arm gallantly. "Watch you don't fall," he leaned down and murmured in her ear. "By the by, you look quite ravishing tonight, m'lady."

Sky fought the unexpected wave of pleasure that shot through her at his whispered compliment and protective arm. She wore the deep rose silk gown she'd purchased in New York since the clothes she'd worn in England had of necessity been black. Being home with Clint and Delilah and their children made her feel like celebrating, not wearing a reminder of why she was here with this man under false pretenses.

"Thank you, m'lord," she replied with an air of insouciance. "Oh, I forgot to mention that Clint and Delilah allow young Rob to eat with the adults since he turned six. I know it's not the English custom—"

"I've lived in America for years, love. I know the customs. I believe I can manage one six-year-old boy," he said dryly.

"You haven't seen Rob in action," she replied with a chuckle.

As they entered the parlor, a tall, cadaverously thin man with stooped shoulders and an elongated face well seasoned by time turned and smiled at Sky. She rushed into his open arms, crying, "Uncle Horace! How I've missed you! How long has it been?"

"Nearly three years, child." He held her at arm's length and inspected her, saying, "I, alors, merely dodge the slings and arrows of outrageous fortune, while you remain as fresh and lovely as a newly cut rose."

Then, he turned his shrewd black eyes on Max. "And this is your English bridegroom, I presume?" he asked, offering his hand in welcome. "My felicitations on your recent nuptials, even if they were somewhat precipitous. I know this young pup"—he gestured to Clint—"would have fancied giving away the bride. For that matter, as the senior member of this family, so would I." His eyes were crinkled with mirth.

"Deelie was the one who nearly had a case of the vapors, wanting to plan a big fancy weddin'," Clint said, giving his wife a teasing wink.

"I have never suffered 'a case of the vapors' in my life, Clinton Daniels," Delilah shot back. "Besides, Sky has a mind and will of her own. She's quite capable of deciding where and how she chooses to get married."

Clint threw up his hands in mock surrender. "I'm surrounded by females with minds and wills of their own, Lord deliver me."

As everyone chuckled, Sky enjoyed the easy camaraderie of her brother and his wife. She and Will had shared that . . . if not the sudden flaring of passion she occasionally detected between Clint and Delilah. Her first marriage—no, she corrected herself—her *only* marriage had been one of deep love and devotion, gentle and enduring . . . until Johnny Deuce ended all her dreams. Forcing the painful past from her mind, she concentrated on the present, watching Horace and Max laugh together at Clint and Delilah's antics.

Sky was relieved that Max's reputation had not put off her adopted uncle, who was a keen judge of character. Perhaps dinner would go well after all, and they could survive this visit without mishap.

Perhaps pigs could fly . . .

The adults enjoyed mint juleps and canapés in the sitting room, making small talk about various joint business ventures between the Danielses and Mathers. Sky glossed over how she and Max had met and married in Bismarck, then traveled to London to ensure his inheritance and title. She made certain that she gave the impression they had known each other for several months prior to his proposal.

Shortly, dinner was announced. Feeling they had just cleared the first hurdle, Sky and Max followed their hosts and Horace into the beautiful dining room, where a low arrangement of bright summer flowers adorned half the length of the table. The maid ushered young Rob in from the hall door. His face was pink and cherubic, but a bit of perspiration dotted his forehead. Like any proper gentleman, he wore a starched high-collar shirt and summer suit, albeit it with knee britches and high stockings.

Upon seeing Max, his big hazel eyes lit. "Uncle Max, I spent the afternoon reading all about England while my baby brother and sister were sleeping."

"Most commendable," Max said gravely, giving a nod of approval. "I trust you've not neglected to study the history of your own great nation as well."

As she seated her son next to her, Delilah said, "He was supposed to be napping, too, but I fear he's been far too excited about your visit for that."

"I'm too old for naps," Rob replied with a hint of stubbornness. "I've read all about the Revolutionary War. It started when England poisoned our tea," he pronounced as the soup course was served.

Horace arched an eyebrow. "Pray, elaborate, young sir."

Rob took a slurping sip of the consommé, then said, "Well, the Patriots dumped all that English tea in Boston harbor, so it must have been poisoned." He looked from his uncle Horace to his uncle Max for confirmation.

Both men attempted to keep their expressions serious. Horace gave Max a nod, as if to say, "You handle this. It's your country being inadvertently maligned."

"Well, it's a bit more complicated than that, Robbie," Clint interjected with an indulgent chuckle. "It was really about taxes the English king and his followers placed on the tea."

Not to be placated, Rob looked back at Max. "Aunt Sky says you're a baron in England. Is that like being a king?"

This time Max did smile. "Not quite. In fact, a baron is at the bottom of the ranks of noblemen, after dukes, marquesses, earls and viscounts. Only baronets are below us."

The child's face fell for an instant, then brightened again. "But you still get to chop people's heads off if they don't bow to you, don't you?"

Max choked on a mouthful of soup. Delilah looked alarmed. "Robert—"

"Please, Delilah, no harm done," Max quickly said. He turned back to the boy. Damn, could he be the victim of a send-up by a six-year-old? "Well, Rob, I fear head-chopping-off has been declared illegal in England. What your father and uncle are too polite to tell you in my presence, since I'm an Englishman, is that another reason for the Revolutionary War was that the English wanted to treat Americans like Englishmen." He waited expectantly.

The lad did not disappoint. "Oh! I see, Uncle Max. They wanted to chop the heads off Americans. Gee, that would *really* start a war, wouldn't it?"

Stanhope nodded with a broad grin. "Intelligent lad."

Horace, attempting to suppress his own grin, commented to Sky, "My dear, your husband has a bright future in scribbling penny dreadfuls, I fear."

Max smiled at her, charming her with a twinkle that she had never seen in those normally cold, green eyes. *He actually likes children.*

But Rob wasn't done yet. "Uncle Max, if you're a nobleman, you must be a knight. Where's your armor? And your lance? Did you ever slay a dragon like the knights in my books?"

"Rob, you're being far too inquisitive," Delilah remonstrated. "I fear we've read him too many fairy tales."

"I'm too old for silly fairy tales," Rob protested.

"I don't mind explaining, if it's all right with you," Max said to his hostess. When she returned his smile and nodded, he turned to Rob. "It's been a long time since noble knights wore armor or slew dragons. In fact, all the dragons died out, so you might say we've been put out of work."

The child looked puzzled for a moment, then blurted out, pleased with himself, "So when the dragons died off, you came to America to kill bad men." He nodded, pleased with his reasoning.

This time Max not only choked on his soup, but some of it spewed out of his nose, quickly trapped by his napkin. He coughed and gasped as his wife thumped his back. Over the commotion a confident Rob explained to his mother what he had overheard. "Daddy told Uncle Horace that he checked up on Uncle Max, and he found out Uncle Max hunted down bad men out West—and got paid for it."

"Robert, you know you are never to eavesdrop!" Delilah said sharply, her face flushed with embarrassment.

This time it was Horace who coughed up a bit of soup as he eyed Max apologetically, but Clint coolly handled the matter. "There's a reason for your mother's rule, Rob. Boys don't always understand grown-up matters, so it's better to leave them to the adults. Do you understand?"

Rob knew that tone of voice when it came from his father. He nodded dutifully, even though Max caught a curious glance from the boy indicating that he understood more than the adults wanted him to.

Rob subsided while the meat course was served, struggling to cut his slice of juicy pink ham, resisting his mother's attempt to assist him. The conversation turned to the Stanhopes' plans for the future.

"We intend to stay in America, mostly," Sky said. "First a visit to Denver where Max has an old friend he wants me to meet, then, who knows? Perhaps San Francisco. I've never been to the Pacific."

"A city of grace and beauty, San Francisco. Truly the jewel of the West Coast," Horace averred, raising his wine glass in a toast. "To a safe journey."

"Here, here," echoed around the table.

By the time the lush triple-layer cake with freshly churned ice cream was served, Sky began to relax, noting that Max seemed to be handling her family with his usual smooth charm. All was going well until the dessert plates were being cleared and the adults rose to adjourn to the side porch for coffee and brandy, where the men could enjoy their cigars. Sky and Delilah did not follow custom and leave the men to their vices. Instead they intended to join them for drinks, even though they did not indulge in tobacco.

Delilah turned to Rob, saying, "Why don't you help me tuck in your sister and brother before you go to bed?" She extended her hand.

Not usually a disobedient child, Rob was fascinated by his new uncle—and perhaps a bit refueled by the sweet dessert. He'd had two scoops of ice cream. He shook his head and seized hold of Max's coattail. "My daddy was in the army. Were you in the army, Uncle Max? Did you kill any enemies?"

"Robert Horace Daniels!" Delilah cried, aghast.

Sky felt Max tensing. This time she intervened quickly. "Yes, your uncle was in the British Army. He was very brave, as was your father. But neither one wants to brag about it. They did their duty, Robby."

Max knelt down beside the boy, indicating with a gesture to Sky and Delilah that it was all right. "Rob, a wise person once told me that killing leaves a stain on your soul. I hope you never have to stain yours."

Sky covered her mouth, not knowing whether to be upset or honored by his using her words to explain to the boy. She stood mutely as Max continued speaking to Rob.

"Now, be a good lad and go with your mother. I bet she'll need your help corralling those little ones for bed," he instructed gently, tousling the boy's thick shock of straw-colored hair.

"Will you be here in the morning?" Rob asked eagerly.

"Yes, I will. Maybe we can even have a bit of a history lesson, eh?"

When Rob reached around Max's neck and gave him a hug, Sky could see he was taken aback for an instant, but quickly recovered and hugged the boy in return. *Another conquest for the Limey.*

Preparing for bed with the two of them sharing a single room could have been an ordeal. To forestall the problem, Sky excused herself early, saying the train trip from Chicago had tired her and she wanted to get a good night's rest. By the time Max entered their room, she was covered head to toe in a night rail and robe, making up a bed for herself on the chaise.

"I expected you'd be sound asleep by now—in the bed," he said, nodding to the large mattress with the coverlet turned back.

"And I thought you agreed that you'd never fit on the chaise," she replied, then quickly changed the subject. "I hope Rob didn't upset you. He's such an inquisitive boy and quite taken with you."

Max tossed his suit jacket on a chair and began to remove his shirt studs. "He is bright as a new penny. My elder brother never had that kind of devilment in him, but according to Harry, I did. I was forever asking questions of the, er, impolitic sort. Let us hope our nephew will turn out better than his black-sheep uncle."

Sky's mouth was dry as ashes, watching him peel off his shirt, but she managed to mutter an agreement to his remarks. He had his back turned so she could admire the flex of hard muscles beneath his skin. As she had imagined, where his body was untouched by sun, it was indeed pale as his hair. Scars, some of them indicating quite serious injuries, dotted his sides and shoulders. She wanted to run her fingertips over that broad back and touch them.

To suppress her wayward thoughts, she said, "You did very well with Rob. I never would've suspected you liked children."

He turned around and looked her in the eye. "There are a great many things about me you would never suspect," he said with an enigmatic expression on his face. Without another word, he strode over to the chaise and lay down to test it.

Sky stifled the urge to stamp her foot. "You can't fit. See?" she said when he stretched out—and his feet dangled so far over the end that they nearly touched the floor.

"Well, considering your height," he replied, his eyes sweeping from her head to her feet, "neither will you. I propose a simple solution. Share the bed."

She recoiled. "Are you deranged? We're supposed to get an annulment."

He arched one eyebrow and gave her a cheeky grin. "Does that mean you find me so irresistible you'd ravish me in my sleep, love?"

"Don't be absurd." She could feel the heat stealing into her cheeks and prayed for a cool breeze from the open window. "Far more likely you'd take advantage of me . . . or," she added grudgingly, "nature would take its course for both of us. I'll sleep on the floor." She pulled the bedding from the chaise and knelt to make a pallet beside the bed.

"Stubborn female," he gritted out, kneeling beside her. "I'll sleep on the floor. Now, get in that bed or I'll drag you onto it. Neither of us would want that . . . would we, love?"

The taunt worked. Sky leaped to her feet and practically

bounded onto the mattress, then sat glowering down at him. "Please turn down the gaslight before you totally disrobe," she said primly.

Both of them lay in the darkness staring at the ceiling for hours, too acutely aware of each other to sleep.

After breakfast, Clint had a business meeting down at the levee. When Rob's tutor sent a note saying he was ill, Max, against Delilah's better judgment, insisted he would spend the morning entertaining the boy while the maid wrestled with the two younger Daniels children. That allowed Sky and Delilah freedom for a ride into the countryside.

"There is a farm for sale up in the old Spanish Lake area, on the Missouri River bluffs. It would be a lovely place for a summerhouse. I'd like your opinion on where we should build," Delilah explained to Sky.

"A ride out of the city sounds heavenly. I haven't been on horseback in what seems like ages," Sky responded.

Soon the women were off, riding astride in split skirts, their gleaming hair and faces bare beneath the hot summer sun. The arbiters of St. Louis's highest social circles were scandalized by such behavior, but no longer surprised by it. Delilah Daniels had come to town as a professional gambler and then married a former bordello owner. She and Clint had first spent a summer making their fortune in the Fort Benton river trade. They did not require social approval, but lived as they pleased.

Sky, the daughter of a Sioux Indian chief, had found even less acceptance. She was not only of mixed blood but also Clint Daniels's adopted sister, a most unnatural female. University educated, she'd even read law under one of the most successful attorneys in the city.

The two friends set out on the warm breezy morning, riding two fine geldings from Clint's large stable of prime horseflesh. Patting the neck of the paint she rode, Sky said, "Max once had a beauty like this one. Named him Rembrandt."

"Rembrandt the paint instead of the painter. I like that. Your husband has quite a sense of humor. I like him, too." Delilah reached over and squeezed Sky's hand. "I confess I was worried when we received your wire about the marriage. After . . . well, after all the tragedy you've endured, I just want you to be happy. Now that we've met Max—a peer of the realm, no less—Clint and I are reassured . . . you are happy, aren't you, Sky?"

"His being the infamous Limey doesn't worry you?" Sky asked, evading the question.

"It did when Clint first had him investigated, but when he learned that you were en route to England, that the Stanhope name was so highly respected, well, that put a different light on matters. I know it's none of my business, Sky, but why did an English nobleman come to America and become a bounty hunter?"

Sky wished she knew the answer to that very question herself. She could only extrapolate and hope to convince Delilah. "He was a soldier in Africa. He doesn't want to talk about it, just as Clint never wanted to talk about what happened to him during the war of the rebellion," Sky added, knowing how bitter her brother's experiences, first as a Confederate, then as a galvanized Yankee, had been.

"So, he came to America to start over. Did his family approve?"

"He wasn't a remittance man, if that's what you mean."

Delilah smiled at Sky's knee-jerk defense of Max, finding it a good sign. "No, that isn't what I meant." *But there's something not quite right about your relationship.* "It's difficult to envision such a charming Englishman tracking killers through the wilderness for a livelihood," she said, fishing. "Considering Clint's past, I'm scarcely in a position to cast the first stone, Sky, but Max is so . . . please forgive me for saying this, but he's so utterly different from Will . . ."

"Yes, he is," Sky replied at length. She'd anticipated that deceiving her family would be very difficult, but she'd never realized just how painful. Swallowing for courage, she said, "I suppose opposites attract. You and Clint certainly started out with nothing in common. At least Max and I already agree about the West. He prefers America to England." That much was true. She desperately did not want to lie to her best friend.

Delilah kept her reservations to herself. It was obvious that Sky did not wish to discuss her hasty marriage and unlikely bridegroom. She was not with child, for which Delilah thanked heavens. Most marriages made because of pregnancy did not do well. But she had an intuition that there was something amiss between the baron and his lady. Not a lack of physical attraction. The sexual tension hummed between them like a tuning fork hitting high C. No, it was something she could not put a name to . . . yet.

The sharp crack of a shot instantly put an end to her troubling reverie. A bullet tore through the sleeve of Sky's windblown shirt, leaving a smear of red on the pristine white cotton. Both women ducked low against the necks of their horses and kicked them into a gallop, veering off the wide open trail toward a stand of scrub hickory and oak a dozen yards away as a second shooter burst from the honeysuckle-choked underbrush and raised his rifle, taking direct aim at Sky.

Seizing the paint's mane in her left hand, Sky slid over the opposite side of her mount, using the heel of her boot to anchor her body while she pulled her .38 Merwin & Hulbert pistol from the pocket of her riding skirt. She fired under the neck of her horse. Even though she was out of range, the startled assassin dived for cover. His companion, hidden on a rocky hillside directly ahead of them, opened up once more and a second shot whizzed by her head.

Please don't shoot this beautiful horse! Surely it couldn't be Johnny Deuce. Sky and Delilah reached the trees as both men continued firing. When the third shot narrowly missed Sky, it was apparent she was their target. Both women had freed the rifles from the scabbards on their saddles and knelt to return fire.

"We're lucky they're rotten shots," she said to Delilah.

"But they have the advantage of high ground and who knows how much firepower," Delilah replied, moving the muzzle of her rifle barrel slowly, searching for any telltale movements above them.

"How isolated is this place? Won't some farmer hear the shooting and investigate?" Sky asked.

As if answering her question, two more shots rang out, one immediately following the other. They could hear the guttural cry of a man mortally wounded. Then the ugly bearded fellow who'd burst through the brush at Sky crashed down the hill and rolled to the road, landing faceup with a bullet hole in the center of his forehead. A second, smaller man, bald and pockmarked, tumbled after him. He, too, had been shot cleanly in the center of his forehead.

"What on earth is happening?" Delilah murmured, still holding her rifle level.

"Look, up there," Sky said, clutching her rifle but raising the barrel as she motioned ahead of them.

A diminutive woman dressed in an elegant gray traveling suit followed the two men down the hillside. Calmly, she stepped over the dead men's bodies, blowing smoke from the barrel of a large revolver. Her face was concealed by a gray veil hanging from the brim of her stylish hat. She tipped her head courteously toward Sky, as if acknowledging unspoken thanks, then turned around and sauntered away.

Close by, Sky and Delilah could hear approaching hoofbeats. Then an expensive closed carriage drawn by two perfectly matched black horses materialized from around the bend in the road. A small swarthy man with a heavy mustache and oiled black hair tied in a queue reined in the great beasts. Another virtually identical foreigner leaped from inside the carriage and held the door open for his mistress after she handed him her pistol.

Before Sky or Delilah could utter a word, their rescuer and her assistant climbed inside the vehicle and the driver snapped the reins smartly, sending the blacks off in a cloud of dust. The carriage vanished over the next hill before the women could lead their horses back to the road. Both animals shied at the smell of blood.

"Who were they and why were these river rats trying to kill you?" Delilah asked, looking at Sky as if she should know the answers.

"I have no idea," Sky replied, gazing down at the bearded thug and his bald companion. "I've never seen these men or that woman before in my life."

"She might have been English," Delilah ventured. "I think her style of dress was English, and her mannerisms were rather regal, especially considering the circumstances."

"Regal," Sky scoffed. "I've never seen a woman in a coach gown swagger before. I bet that female could strut sitting down."

In spite of their near brush with death, Delilah chuckled at her sister-in-law's description. "She was, er, a bit cocky."

But Sky was no longer listening to her friend. Instead she was remembering the bizarre attack in Central Park. After killing Max, might that killer from Five Points have turned his gun on her? An icy chill ran down her spine on the hot summer day.

"Sky, what aren't you telling me?" Delilah asked suspiciously.

Ignoring the question, Sky started walking toward the hill. "Their horses must be tethered nearby. They surely didn't walk from the city—and they don't have the look of good old country boys to me. We can tie them to their saddles and take them to the authorities for identification."

"Somehow I doubt we'll learn who our mystery lady is," Delilah said darkly.

"Pete Griesner and Hammet Aimes would hire on to bushwhack a baby if the price was right—and their price was always cheap as rotgut whiskey," Clint said as the two couples sat in the gazebo that afternoon, out of earshot of the children.

"Thank God," Max said fervently. "If whoever hired them had paid premium price, Sky could well be the one lying dead in the road." He looked at her arm, clearly concerned about the shallow slash left by the bullet intended for her heart.

"I think it's about time you laid all your cards on the table, brother-in-law," Clint said, his pale blue eyes steady on Max. "This has something to do with that inheritance of yours, doesn't it?"

"You've obviously been talking to Delilah," Sky interjected. "She's convinced our rescuer was English. I have no idea who she might be and nor do the police."

Max leaned back and sipped from a tall glass of iced bourbon, then nodded. "Sky told me you were once a gambler by profession. Very well. I will lay my cards out, but don't expect to learn much from them." He sighed and combed his fingers through his hair. The tale had to be edited most carefully, not only for Delilah and Clint's benefit, but for Sky as well. "On our way to England we spent a night in New York . . ."

When he had finished telling them about the attack in the park and the situation with his distasteful but cowardly cousin Cletus, he concluded, "Much as he would love to see me dead and inherit the money, I can't imagine Cletus would bestir himself to come to America—or dare risk hiring someone else to do so. But now it would appear that someone wants both me and my wife dead. The attack was clearly on Sky, not Delilah," he said to Clint.

"You must've made a lot of enemies over the years," Daniels said neutrally.

"As I told Sky, an occupational hazard, I fear. But now that this enemy has decided to punish me by killing her, I intend to entrust her to your safekeeping while I find out who the devil—in America or England—the bastard is."

Sky set her glass down with a harsh click against the wooden table. "When, pray, did you intend to share this plan with me?" she asked sharply. "I won't have it, Max. We need to watch each other's backs." Her eyes communicated far more than she dared reveal to Clint and Delilah.

"I wouldn't sit at home and let Clint ride off with a target painted on his back," his wife said flatly, but her cool green eyes studied the interplay between Sky and Max. Whatever was going on, it had become apparent to her that Sky would not talk. Neither would Max. No, they certainly had not laid all their cards on the table. They were holding back all of the aces and half of the face cards.

Clint was not the only card shark in the Daniels family.

Late that night, when the household was fast asleep, Sky and Max sat in their bedroom, glaring at each other across a small rattan table as they held a whispered argument.

"Flaming hell, Sky, your brother is Lightning Hand. He can protect you. You've already been shot once," he hissed in frustration.

"This is only a scratch. I admit I was lucky, but now we're forewarned. I won't be careless again. We can be pretty certain that attack in the park was intended for both of us. Whoever is trying to kill you is also trying to kill me—and I very much doubt it's some kin of one of the men you captured or killed for bounty. If not Cletus, who? Phillip? Your solicitor?"

Max scoffed. "You're a frightful judge of people if you

think Phillip capable of such perfidy, and as to Jerome Bartlett, he's been with my family since I was a boy. Not only are they good men, but neither has anything to gain if I die. Only Cletus."

"But I must die as well," she said calmly. "I've been doing a bit of reading in my brother's library. On English law. In spite of the fact I told you I would not accept it, you had a will drawn up leaving everything you own to me. Of course, I can't keep the title, but the bulk of your fortune is not entailed. Cletus or Phillip or Bartlett—or all three together—must have me dead, too. If you die, Cletus will be Ruxton right enough, but with little to show for it.

"The settlement your uncle gave him is forfeit. Your will supersedes it now. You've told me that twenty thousand pounds a year is all the title's entailed estate yields. We already know what a 'paltry sum' he believes that to be. No, Cletus wants me dead, too. Perhaps one or both of the others could be in this, too, for a share of the fortune."

"Cletus is too indolent and cowardly to think of bribing them," Max said, unconvinced yet acknowledging that she was still in danger. "I could always disinherit you, love. Give all my uncle's money to charity."

"A sensible idea but it would still leave you in the bull's-eye. We go to Denver together . . . love," she added, daring to use his casual endearment. She was not his love. Yet when he'd seen the bloody gash on her arm this morning, the look in his eyes had stolen her breath away. Sky forced herself to think rationally. He merely felt guilty, that was all . . . wasn't it?

"I could give the money away now. I never wanted it in the first place," he said, knowing it was not yet his to give. But he was quite certain this was a poor time indeed to explain Harry's devious codicil to her.

"I only have six hundred dollars left to pay you for Deuce," she said, wondering how he would react. Was their bargain over?

"You still thirst for vengeance for your priest, don't you, Sky Eyes of the Ehanktonwon?"

She stiffened. "It isn't vengeance. It's justice. Deuce is a monster who'll kill again and again if he's not stopped—and who knows how many innocent girls he'll torture along the way?"

Max shrugged rather too casually. "Forget the six hundred. You've already paid my price. All right, you win. We go to Denver together. But you'll remain the beneficiary of my will." *And stay safe with my friends in the city while I track Deuce.*

Chapter Five

$\mathcal{B}$eing a close friend of Steve Loring, a Denver railroad magnate, had its advantages. When Max had wired Blackie to begin tracing Deuce, he'd also wired Loring and asked if one of his custom cars might be available for the trip. What he had not realized was that the convenience of a real bed still meant that he had to share the spacious railcar with his wife. They slept separately but he feared that his nightmares, dormant since London, might resurface on the train. So far he'd managed to hold his demons at bay . . . with a bit of help from overindulgence in alcohol.

On the third evening, Sky ordered her usual bath. While he listened to the sounds of her humming softly behind the large silk screen at the rear of the car, his mind conjured up visions of her naked in the tub, her dusky smooth flesh slick with bubbles, glistening in the flickering lights. Every splash of water was like a jolt of lightning.

How much more of this could he endure? Normally, he excused himself while she bathed, but the afternoon had slipped by too quickly and he had already consumed half a decanter of brandy when two youths arrived and quickly filled the tub.

They were to have dinner in their car that evening, at her suggestion. Perhaps because of the way he had begun drinking? Max wondered what she would think if she knew why he was behaving so badly. Damn, he would be soused before the braised quail was served if he did not stop. Drinking would solve none of his problems . . . but passing out just might.

He shoved the glass away, disgusted with his self-indulgence. The sounds of soft cloth rustling behind the screen indicated that his wife was finished with her bath. He raised his head and watched as she emerged, her hair pinned in a haphazard topknot with wispy tendrils touching her flushed warm skin.

"You look damp and refreshed," he said, his mouth going dry at the sight of her.

"And you look as 'soggy' as dear cousin Cletus." She smiled wryly when Max's hand halted halfway to his ear, a habit he'd developed since they'd met. "I may have to wring both of your ears this time."

"If you twist my ear again, I'll be tripping over it," he said irritably.

She inspected him, taking in his bloodshot eyes and the amount of brandy left in the decanter. "Pity I don't have another basin of cold water to dump over your head. Then, again . . ." Her eyes scanned the elegantly appointed private car's furnishings, settling on the dry sink below a rounded mirror where shaving utensils had been laid out.

"Are you considering the basin of water or the razor?" he asked.

Sky smiled, tightening the belt of her embroidered yellow silk robe. "Well, it certainly wouldn't do to have you bleeding all over this lovely Turkish carpeting, or even to stain it with water, so I'll allow you to have a cool bath the same as I."

He inclined his head. "Ah, 'the quality of mercy.' "

Ignoring his attempt at levity, she ran her hand over the satiny teak trim on a brocade settee. It stood facing two leather chairs with a heavy brass tea table in the center of the grouping. "You have very wealthy friends in Denver. I expected you to know saloon denizens, but not rail tycoons."

"Steve and Cass Loring have been friends for some time.

You'd like her. She built her father's freighting business into the largest in the Rockies before she was twenty years of age."

"I'm impressed. Also rather surprised that you'd admire such independence in a mere woman."

He looked at her, studying the strong, beautifully sculpted shape of her face. "I've always admired independent women. Why do you think I didn't choose a simpering English schoolgirl to wed?"

"I seem to recall something about your desire for a woman willing to relinquish her title once the will was adjudicated," she replied with a lightness she did not feel. His gaze was unsettling in the extreme. As if . . .

He grunted as he rose unsteadily to his feet and pulled the cord summoning the porter. "Bugger the title," he muttered beneath his breath.

Before Sky gathered courage to ask what he had just said, the porter tapped on the door and Max ordered a bath before their evening meal, which was to be served at the small dining table by one of the large windows in their car. In moments the tub behind the screen had been refilled. Perhaps he could sober up enough so that he would not pass out during the first course.

While he was bathing, Sky admitted a host of men in white jackets who quickly set the table with fine linens and china, then wheeled in a long cart with heated sterling chafing dishes on it. Dinner was ready whenever they chose to eat.

She thanked the stewards and dismissed them, then took a seat at the table, as far away as she could get from the sounds of Max's bath. Willing her mind to focus on anything besides her husband's naked body, she gazed out at the countryside, watching the mountains on the far horizon. It had been two days since the jagged Rockies appeared, yet they seemed no closer, only a hazy promise beckoning from the west.

Eager as she was to return home again, it had been difficult to say good-bye to Clint and Delilah. She hated deceiving them and feared that Delilah suspected something was amiss with her marriage. *What will she think when she finds out my relationship with Max has been a sham?*

Sky pinched the bridge of her nose with thumb and index finger, trying not to think of how hurt her sister-in-law and Clint would be. At least Delilah would understand why Sky had wanted to keep Clint out of her quest. But her brother would be furious that she had made such a cold-blooded arrangement and brought a stranger into their home under false pretenses just to "save him from himself."

"Deep thoughts?" Max asked as he took a seat across from her. He, too, was damp from his bath and wore a dressing robe to the table. A bottle of French Margeaux sat between them, cork lying beside it. He noted that Sky had already taken several sips from her glass.

She looked up, wakened from her troubling reverie. "No deep thoughts," she replied. "I'm just impatient to reach Denver and get to work." She turned from his unnerving gaze and studied the sagebrush and scrub pines of eastern Colorado that seemed to whiz past the speeding train.

He studied her profile. Lord, she was beautiful! After sharing a bedroom in St. Louis and now a private railcar, the proximity was driving him half mad. At least they each had a comfortable bed and did not have to pretend marital bliss for the porters, but it was small consolation.

Women had always been easy for him. He knew his looks and the money his family possessed helped. He'd never had to do anything special to have females falling at his feet, from simpering society belles to sharp-eyed harlots. After a succession of mistresses through university and during his tenure in the army, he'd decided that he did not possess the temperament for faithfulness. Besides, women tended to become demanding of time and attention he did not want to give.

In America, he'd availed himself of high-priced prostitutes, content to slake his lust and move on to the next city or town, always rootless, searching for new adventure—or trying to outrun old demons. Now, thanks to Harry, here he was saddled with an enigmatic wife who still fancied herself in love with her dead first husband. Sky was set on avenging his death so she could put her own demons to rest. *Ah, love, you may find that once justice has been served, the demons refuse to rest . . . or allow you to rest either.*

Ever since that day in Jerome Bartlett's office, he'd wrestled with the question of whether he wanted to consummate the marriage and have a child with Sky Brewster Stanhope. How would she react if he told her why he required an heir? The proposal of marriage had been mercenary enough without involving an innocent babe. She'd probably take that nasty little .38 pistol and shoot him in the heart. He could scarcely blame her.

But he still desired her. She was like no other woman he'd ever known—keenly intelligent, fiercely independent, intensely loyal . . . and a most sensual creature, although he was virtually certain she was unaware of it. Married to a priest. They had probably made love in the dark, both wearing nightshirts! Did they say grace before . . . *Flaming hell, what an obscene bastard I've become!*

In spite of his foul humor, he was sure she was aware of the sexually explosive chemistry between them. Each time they touched, he could feel the tension humming. Max knew women and those signs were unmistakable, even with one like Sky. He was certainly unlike her first husband in every imaginable way, he thought wryly as he poured himself a bit of the wine.

He raised the round crystal bowl in a toast. "To Denver and our quest," he said.

Sky raised her glass and nodded, saying nothing as the soft tinkle of crystal echoed over the steady hum of the rails beneath them. Each was lost in private thought.

Max wondered what she was thinking as she helped herself

to a bowl of clear golden broth flecked with fine herbs. Could they build a relationship that would allow them to raise a child? He'd seen far too many marriages among the English aristocracy where children were ignored as much as the vows their parents had taken. His own mother and father had gone their separate ways after Edmund and he were born.

The only love match he had ever known had been that of Harry and Lodicia, which ended tragically after such a brief, bright run. Now past his thirtieth year, Max still doubted such constancy as his uncle had exhibited ran in his soul. Before he even thought of truly making Sky his wife, he had to sort that out. Then, if he decided it was possible for him, he would have to consider the best way to approach her with a new and even more unsettling proposal . . .

Idly fishing for some clue about her plans for the future, he asked, "Will you resume your role as legal protector of the Ehanktonwon once Deuce is dead?"

The question startled her. Before she could stop herself, she said, "I've honestly never considered . . . that is, all I've been able to think of since the courts let him go was getting justice. After that . . ."

"Best to consider the 'after,' love. To borrow a Shakespearean conceit from your uncle Horace, 'The evil that men do lives after them; the good is oft interred with their bones . . .'"

"There is no good in Johnny Deuce," she snapped, closing the lid over the roast quail with a sharp clank.

"I only meant that ghosts have a way of returning to haunt one." His eyes were darkest green, distant and hard for an instant before he turned away.

"You believe I'll regret being responsible for Deuce's death?" she asked. *As you're haunted by whatever you did in Africa?*

Max shrugged. "I'm just saying that you should think of the future. Consider what you want to do with your life. After your quest ends, then what? You can never go back to the way things were before. I should know."

"Why did you leave England in the first place?" she asked. Now he smiled, that slash of white teeth in his darkly tanned face making him almost boyish—but only for an instant. He took his time, serving himself quail and wild rice, before he replied. Sky sensed he was stalling, gathering his thoughts.

"Boredom," he finally replied. "My university classes were dull, carousing and drinking had lost their charm. My chances of inheriting the title seemed remote and I was glad of that. You see before you a man who has ever shirked family obligations."

"But when your brother died and your uncle never remarried . . . you were next in line."

"Whoever could've imagined that Harry would mourn the rest of his life," he asked almost rhetorically. "I fully expected him to marry a beautiful young woman and set up his nursery." He slowly chewed a piece of the juicy meat without tasting it, then studied her expression, looking deeply into her eyes. "You won't shun remarriage, having a family, will you? It's a waste, Sky. A misplaced loyalty your Will would not have wanted."

She dropped her fork, startled as if a barb had just pierced her heart . . . and in a way it had. Swallowing hard, she blinked away tears. "The promise not to kill Deuce wasn't the only one my husband exacted before he died," she said quietly.

"He urged you to marry again."

Her head jerked up in surprise. "How did you . . . oh, I suppose it would be the logical thing to imagine a selfless man like Will doing. We . . . we never had children and he knew how much I wanted them."

Oddly, Max had never considered that she might be unable to provide him with the heir he required. Even more odd, he now realized that he did not care. He remained quiet, waiting for her to continue, the food on their plates now forgotten.

"He felt guilty about it . . . while we worked in the reservation hospital during an epidemic of measles, he contracted the disease and nearly died. He ran a very high fever and . . ."

"I've heard that can render men infertile," he murmured.

"I told him he was doing God's work and we had a whole village filled with children to love and care for. They're still waiting for me. I will return once I've seen our bargain through," she said, almost defensively.

He took her hand and raised it to his lips, barely touching her fingertips in a chaste salute. "Who are you trying to convince, Sky—me . . . or yourself?"

She jerked her hand away angrily. "I neither require your permission nor want your advice regarding my future," she snapped, shoving back her chair before she relented. "That sounded churlish. I—I'm sorry."

Max rose, too, and smiled at her, a crooked grin. "You nearly choked on that apology. Please, let me make my own for intruding into your private affairs. I have no right."

She could feel those green eyes probing her. He was standing much too close. The car was much too confining. "Considering you are my legal husband, most people would argue otherwise," she replied lightly.

"A marriage of convenience doesn't make me your husband, Sky." His voice was low, the accent less clipped, the tone warm.

"Surely you aren't arguing for a change in our agreement?" The moment the words escaped her lips, she stepped back, stunned at her monumental stupidity. *How could I have asked that?* "What I mean is . . . this conversation has become far too personal. You were right. Let us change the subject to our course of action when we reach Denver."

Max nodded as she walked over to the two leather chairs facing each other. "I'll ring for coffee," he replied.

After the porter removed their mostly uneaten meal and poured two cups of thick black coffee, Max laced his liberally with golden cream. Sky preferred hers black. "You'll have to forgo the luxury of that stuff on the trail," she said.

"I've had to forgo many things since leaving England," he replied enigmatically.

They discussed what information the saloon owner might have about Deuce and how they'd track him down. But in the back of his mind, Max turned over thoughts about how she'd withdrawn her hand from his with a flash of heat in her eyes, the startled confession he'd elicited about her desire for children, and the way she'd blurted out her confusion over whether he wanted a real marriage. All things considered, the signs were pointing to Lady Ruxton's willingness to renegotiate.

But two questions still remained unanswered. Did he want a wife and family? And, would she accept his proposal once she learned about the codicil?

Jump one hedgerow at a time, old chap.

Sky stayed up and read for a bit after Max retired. He was drinking too much and it worried her. Would his tracking skills suffer? His hand had to be steady enough to keep him alive when he faced Deuce. She set aside the book, not having understood a word she read and admitted the real reason she was worrying about him. Her attraction to Maxwell Stanhope had grown over the weeks they'd spent together. Damn the man, she thought as she removed her robe, then lowered the lamps and climbed into her bed, which was separated from his by a high screen to afford her maximum privacy.

She lay awake, staring at the ceiling, praying for the car to rock her to sleep. But sleep would not come. Thoughts of Max filled her mind instead. He was far more than a well-educated and heart-stoppingly handsome man. Wit, courtesy and gentleness were not traits she would have assumed the Limey would possess. His mysterious nightmare and the way he avoided speaking about his past gave him an aura of vulnerability, adding to his appeal. He was still a hard, dangerous man with a bloody past, utterly different from Will. More like her brother Clint. Small wonder the two of them had quickly moved from wariness to friendship in a few short days.

She was just drifting off when Max stirred restlessly. Then the harshly issued commands and orders to fire on the advancing enemy again rasped out. He was having the nightmare. Sky lay with her fists clenched in the covers, trying to decide what to do. In London he had abruptly stopped and fallen back into bed. Would that happen again? Or, would he awaken and know that she had heard him?

Making a snap decision, she threw back her covers and darted around the partition between their beds before he began talking about the blood and gore. If she could either awaken him quickly or get him back to restful sleep, perhaps he would never know he'd revealed anything damning. "Max, Max, you're having a bad dream," she whispered fiercely.

Once again, he was sitting up, his hand holding the imaginary pistol. The bedsheet lay tangled around his hips, more off than on his body. In the moonlight streaming through the window, she could see the contrast between his darkly tanned face and neck and the pale skin of his hard chest and flat belly. Gingerly, she perched on the edge of his bed and reached for his hand, lowering it and murmuring in his ear, trying to soothe him out of the nightmare. If only she could get him to lie back and go to sleep without awakening him!

Sky pressed her palm against his bare, hot chest. The feel of his hard male flesh, the swift hammering of his heartbeat, the crisp texture of his chest hair sent a jolt of sexual awareness racing through her body. Now it was she who cried out. But she quickly bit her lip and leaned over him, willing him to lie down. Slowly, he dropped backward onto the pillows. Still, she could not seem to remove her hands from his chest. Instead, she laid her head over his heart and listened as the frantic thudding began to slow to a regular rhythm. It had been over a year since she'd felt the steady soothing beat of a man's heart close beside her.

I could lie this way forever. What was she thinking? Comparing her calm, loving Will with this cold, dangerous mercenary? Sky straightened up and started to slip from the bed, but suddenly his long, elegant fingers encircled her wrist tightly. She tumbled back onto his chest, her hair spread like spilled ink over his shoulders.

"Smelled your perfume," he murmured against her ear. The tip of his tongue darted inside the small shell, sending a shiver of delight coursing through her. "I must be dreaming, Sky Eyes." His warm breath caressed her face as he tangled his hands in her hair, moving her head so her lips met his.

He brushed his mouth ever so softly over hers. Then, with a guttural oath, he deepened the kiss, his tongue plundering. Sky had never imagined this searing bliss—that something could frighten her and at the same time awaken her to such passion. No, this was wrong, a violation of their agreement! It would mean heartbreak when he left her, as she knew he would.

He was a killer. He was the infamous Limey! She tried to hold that disquieting thought in her mind . . . but it would not stick. Sky pressed her palms against his chest, trying to break free, but he rose up and cupped her head in one hand, holding her fast while he continued the breath-stealing kiss.

"I've wanted to do this since the first day we met," he whispered harshly as his mouth moved from hers to her jaw-line, then down her throat to find a tiny pulse that had leaped to life at her collarbone.

"Let me go, Max," she said softly, too softly for him to hear above their rough breathing. Sky could not seem to catch her breath to speak louder, nor to push harder. In fact, her fingers seemed to dig into the muscles of his shoulders, holding on to him. His arm wrapped around her waist in an iron grip while his other hand left her hair and slid around, entering the sheer lawn of her night rail, sending buttons flying as his callused fingertips grazed one nipple, then the other.

"Nooo," she murmured, then gasped at the sharp tingle of intense pleasure from the delicate caress.

"Yes, oh, my lord, yes," he crooned, cupping one pert breast and suckling the rose brown nipple until it puckered even more tightly. Then he turned his attention to the second breast, which hung suspended like a piece of ripe fruit, his for the taking. Sky was his for the taking. His wife. For the rest of his life . . . if he continued. Max could not have stopped if Queen Victoria herself stood at the foot of his bed and cleared her royal throat in disapproval.

No, the only thing that would stop him was Sky's protest. But rather than pushing him away, she now clung tightly to him, digging her nails into his body, thrusting those luscious breasts toward his mouth. It was all the encouragement required to render him mindless of consequences. He kicked away the tangled bedsheet and rolled over, pulling her on top of him so their legs entwined. Then he peeled the sheer batiste night rail from her breasts completely and continued his sensual assault.

Sky could feel the air on her back and the faint scratching of his hair-roughened legs as they rubbed against her smooth ones. His mouth was hot and wet on her breasts, his hands everywhere, caressing her skin as he slipped one of her arms free of her night rail, then the other. Through the haze of desire burning her, she could feel the probing insistence of his staff pressing into the ruched-up tangle of soft cloth. That thin layer of batiste was all that lay between her and him . . . and the consummation of a marriage neither had intended to be real.

She should roll away, run back to her bed and leave him to his own private demons, but feeling the heat and hardness of his erection rubbing between her thighs, Sky could think of nothing but the power of his lean, hard body and the ache of long-dormant desire he had ignited. When his hand sought her soft petals, she knew they wept with wanting. He grabbed the hem of her gown and slid it upward so their lower bodies were flesh on flesh. No more barriers remained between them.

The pull began deep in her belly and spread downward. Of their own volition her thighs clamped over his staff as if urging him to hurry, to fill her. In answer, his hips arched and he emitted a low, feral growl of raw male hunger. His hands with their elegant long fingers, positioned her hips above him, raising them so the head of his phallus teased her aching core, gliding back and forth for a moment, as if prolonging the inevitable.

Her slick moisture told him that she was ready, eager for what was to come. He plunged deep inside her and then held her hips immobile, struggling to keep from spilling his seed like a virgin schoolboy. She was so hot and tight and wet, as if untried, even though he knew she had been another man's wife. He gritted his teeth, trying to hold on.

"My sweet love, you've driven me mad with wanting you for so very long," he whispered, his voice as raw as his emotions.

Sky heard his words, but did not truly comprehend them, only that he wanted her and his passion was as great as hers. Her body, unaccustomed to intercourse for the past year, slowly stretched, glorying in the feeling of being tested and filled with such heat. But she wanted more, much more. Greedily, she rolled her hips and felt him shudder. Her body accommodated his hardness as it penetrated even deeper.

"Now, please," she begged, unaware she'd even spoken aloud.

Max could not resist her breathy plea. He started to move again, setting a slow steady rhythm, guiding her so as to help him maintain control of his wildly raging body . . . and hers.

Unbidden, she locked her knees tightly to his sides so she could take him deeper, harder. Before he lost control, he rolled her over onto her back and commanded harshly, "Wrap your legs around me, love." When she complied, he sped up the pace.

Sky matched him, each thrust met by her keening cries and arching hips. She had never felt so utterly abandoned in passion, lost to everything but the pale-haired man above her. He rose up on his elbows and looked down into her eyes. She could see the predatory gleam in their green depths. Unable to bear the intensity of his gaze, she closed her eyes and clawed at his back, pulling him down for another hard kiss. His weight pressed her into the mattress, flattening her breasts against the hardness of his chest. Rather than frightening her, it only served to inflame her passion even more.

All of this was so new . . . wild . . . mindless . . . forbidden. Then every fragmented vestige of thought fled as a fiercely sweet contraction began deep inside her quaking body. But instead of flaring and dying out as she expected, it built, growing stronger, multiplying into a series. She opened her mouth to cry out his name, but he smothered it with another soul-robbing kiss. When his whole body stiffened and shook, she could feel his staff thicken even more. Through her own continuing ecstasy, she felt him spill himself high and deep inside her in pulsing waves that at last satiated her own seemingly boundless need.

When he collapsed on top of her, burying his face against her neck, Sky stroked the silver-gilt curls of his head and held him fast. His arms embraced her, buried in the tangle of her hair. They lay that way for several minutes, utterly spent. Then their breathing slowly began to return to normal. Max pressed a soft kiss against her throat and murmured indistinctly, "I've wanted this for so long . . ."

His last words were unintelligible to her, but Sky realized that what she'd taken for hostility and embarrassment over having wed a woman of mixed blood had perhaps been the simple desire of a man for a woman, a woman in close proximity. She knew she was attractive, even beautiful some said, although she was not vain enough to believe that. Among the Sioux, her delicate features and lighter complexion were a liability. Among the whites, her dusky skin and straight black hair were a stigma. She had never found her place in either world . . . until Will Brewster had fallen in love with her.

Will! How could she have forgotten him so quickly? To lie with the gunman she'd hired to kill Deuce—it was unthinkable, unforgivable. Bad enough she'd made a devil's bargain with the Limey to obtain his inheritance in exchange for bringing justice to Will's murderer. Now she'd betrayed the memory of the husband she'd meant to avenge.

Max felt her body stiffen beneath him, even detected the slightest hint of a hitched breath. "Regrets again, love? I have none," he murmured, nuzzling her neck. When he spoke the words, he realized they were true. His decision was made. Sky was well and truly his wife now and he wanted to continue that way . . . but did she?

Chapter Six

When Max rolled to his side, allowing her to sit up, Sky clutched the night rail bunched at her waist and quickly covered her breasts, holding the ripped cloth up to her neck. "Well, I suppose I have my answer," he said softly.

If she had not been so embarrassed and guilty, Sky might have noted the hurt in his voice. But all she could think of was that she'd betrayed Will.

"So, you're still in love with your priest," he murmured, sliding off the bed, quite splendidly naked, and unconcerned by that fact as he reached for the robe tossed across a chair and put it on. She damn well wanted his body, if nothing else of him. Let her look!

"I'm . . . confused, Max," was all she could manage. Just looking at his backside made her desire him again. Why did he have this . . . this *physical* hold on her? It was something she'd never felt before. And that, too, was a betrayal of Will.

"Your first husband is dead, Sky. He wanted you to marry again, to—"

"No! He never intended for me to marry a man like you!" The moment she said the hateful words, Sky wanted to call them back. This time she could see the hard gleam in his eyes, the way a mocking smile covered the pain she had inflicted. "I didn't mean—"

"I rather think you did. 'A man like me'—don't you mean a killer? Poor trade, this, a man of war in exchange for a man of peace. Do you want to cry off our agreement now?" Max was surprised to realize he was holding his breath, waiting for her answer.

She swallowed, trying to regain control of her senses, to think rationally. "Even if I wanted to end our bargain, I could not. I'll not compound the sin of lying in church by lying to a bishop for an annulment."

"We could always get a divorce. Of course, when you found that *noble* replacement for me, getting married again in church would present a bit of a problem." He stressed the word "noble" mockingly, angry and wanting to lash out at her, to wound as he had been wounded.

"There'll be no 'replacement' for Will, noble or otherwise," was all she could think to say.

He watched her slide from the mattress, still clutching the ridiculous flimsy nightclothes in front of her like a shield as she stood facing him across the tangled bedcovers. "First you feel guilty for not consummating our vows. Now you feel guilty because you have. Sky, have you any idea what in bloody hell you do want, love?" He did, but he was damned if he'd confess it to a woman who chained herself to a 'holy ghost' rather than be wife to a man with such a sinful soul as his.

"Don't call me your love!" she snapped. "We don't love each other. We do, however, still have a bargain to fulfill. I've done my part for you in England. Now you do yours for me in America."

Max walked deliberately around the bed, his eyes fixed on hers, waiting to see if she was actually so ashamed of what they'd done that she'd run from him. "You mean do what I do best . . ." he drawled as he stood in front of her.

He was stalking her like a sleek, deadly mountain lion. Sky knew it would be cowardly, not to mention a tactical error, to back down. She stared up into his harshly beautiful face and replied in an equally cold tone of voice, "Yes. Kill Johnny Deuce."

No longer a raw gold rush boomtown, Denver had grown into a formidable city by 1884. Nattily dressed Eastern businessmen brushed by Jewish rabbis and shabby dirt farmers on the bustling sidewalks, each intent on his own task. In the streets, burly sweating teamsters cursed and wielded their bullwhips over teams of mules while Chinese immigrants dodged through the heavy traffic.

Though it had been bypassed by the Transcontinental, other rail lines had come to Denver in the preceding decade. The town had become a bizarre mixture of Gothic brick edifices still skirted by wooden shanties. Opera houses and sporting houses existed within shouting—or singing—distance of each other, even if the music was of varying quality. Only in a city such as Denver could the fanciest bordello and the largest Methodist church have been designed by the same architect.

Everyone agreed the American House was the finest hotel, having hosted a ball for the Russian Grand Duke Alexis back in 1872. Max had wired ahead for a suite. When their carriage pulled up and the doorman unloaded their luggage, Sky swept inside to check the registration while Max remained behind. Since the passionate interlude on the train and its ugly aftermath, they had spent the final day of their journey studiously avoiding each other. She had stayed behind the screen in her bedroom area, packing. He had sent a porter to attend to that chore for him while he sat brooding in a vacant coach seat, staring out at the mountains but not seeing them.

At least the sleeping accommodations in a luxury hotel would allow real privacy. She would not be able to hear his nightmares and he would not be able to seduce her, Sky thought angrily. But there was an ache in her heart that denied what she had said to him that night. Some small kernel of hope buried deep inside her would not relinquish its hold.

But her guilt would not relinquish its hold either.

As she climbed the winding staircase to the second floor, Sky considered how she would survive being alone with Max on the trail. They would have to share a campfire, though they would have separate bedrooms. Perhaps Deuce would not be far off and the hunt would end quickly. But then what?

Breaking into her chaotic thoughts, the bellman opened the door to the suite with a flourish and ushered her inside, saying, "If there's anything you need, please ring, Mrs. Stanhope." With that he was gone.

Mrs. Stanhope. She was Max's wife. He had said he didn't regret consummating the marriage, but that didn't mean he wished a lifetime commitment. Maxwell Stanhope had made it very clear from the beginning that the last thing he wanted was to be saddled with a wife. He merely wanted her body . . . and she wanted his. Simple, yet so very complicated.

"I'll just have to uncomplicate it. We have a murderer to bring to justice," she said as she closed the door to her bedroom firmly and began to unbutton her yellow silk suit jacket. Shortly, she heard Max enter the sitting room, then close the door to the opposite bedroom. A small, bitter smile curved her lips. "Let's get on with it, m'lord Limey."

Max quickly stripped off his civilized clothes and dug out his trail gear. If Blackie Drago had been able to get a line on Deuce, there were at least six hours of daylight left. He could find out what he needed to know and be on his way, leaving Sky behind while he fulfilled his promise to her. After that . . . damned if he had any idea.

With an oath, he checked the action on his Smith & Wesson and slipped the weapon into its well-oiled holster, picked up his Winchester '76 and strode to the door leading directly into the hall. He yanked open his door and almost collided with Sky. She stepped away from the hallway wall and stood directly in front of him, dressed in trail gear.

He rubbed his ear, remembering the first time he'd seen her

in those tight buckskin breeches and the plainsman's hat with her fat plait of hair hanging down her back. The Yellow Boy lay cradled comfortably in her arms. He'd had more pressing matters on his mind in Bismarck than examining the rifle. Now he could see how Daniels had customized it for his sister. It had been shortened and refitted with a new butt plate, and half the magazine underneath the barrel had been removed. It had less cartridge capacity but the modifications made a light-weight weapon perfect for a skilled woman to handle.

Sky met his level gaze with one of her own. Daring him.

"Dammit to bloody hell, get it through your beautiful but very dense skull—I'm going after Deuce. You're staying here. I'll bring his body to you if you don't trust me to kill him."

"That wasn't our deal, Max. I'm going with you," she replied calmly.

He let loose a volley of oaths, but she remained unmoving, blocking his way to the stairs. "At least leave the damned rifle behind. Blackie Drago's my friend."

"As far as I've seen, you don't seem to make friends. Besides, we're going to a saloon. If you'll recall what happened in Bismarck, you don't do very well in saloons." Sky was gratified to see him flush angrily beneath his tan.

"I was exhausted that day."

"So exhausted you almost drowned in a shot glass and lost that fancy six-gun," she replied, eyeing the weapon in his holster.

He could see the fierce, stubborn light in those blue eyes and knew it was useless arguing. He hadn't been able to convince her to stay in St. Louis. He probably wouldn't have any more luck keeping her here either. It would do no harm to take her to see Blackie. Maybe the wily Irishman could charm some sense into her . . . or lock her in one of the upstairs rooms with his madam, Junie Walsh, standing guard.

"You don't need that rifle at Blackie's place," he said.

"From here on, where I go, the rifle goes. I can handle it faster and shoot better than most gunmen. My brother taught me."

"Flaming good thing your brother wasn't in the artillery. We'd look damned silly rolling a howitzer down Cherry Street," he muttered. "Let's get on with it, then."

Smiling grimly, Sky followed his angry strides down the stairs.

The Bucket of Blood had not changed since the last time Max had visited Denver. Drago's saloon and bordello had been legendary in the city for nearly two decades now. It was an enormous place, gaudy and noisy, with a three-foot-high beveled glass mirror running the length of the bar. The floor was polished oak and the walls were covered with red flocked paper imported, according to the proprietor, all the way from France. Two pianos plunked out a verisimilitude of harmony while satin-clad ladies of the line swished between rough-looking teamsters and miners.

The clientele was not socially prominent, but they had plenty of cash to spend. A big man, bald as the Ruxton butler, stood behind the bar polishing glasses. Seeing Max enter, his mouth split into a wide grin, revealing several missing teeth. "Good afternoon, Odd Job," Max said, walking up to the bar.

Sky slipped in silently behind him, moving sideways and positioning herself against the wall, taking stock of the room and its occupants. The Yellow Boy dangled casually from her right hand, barrel down.

"Good to see ya, Max. Boss man got yer telegraph right 'nough. You still drinkin' the usual?" Odd Job inquired, pulling a bottle of stout from beneath the bar as Max nodded.

Sky listened to the two men, then decided that Max was indeed among friends. She stepped up to the bar and laid her Yellow Boy on it. Her manner remained watchful.

"Hey, purty l'il breed, why so cloudy-faced? Reckon I cud

cheer ya up," a tall skinny teamster suggested with a drunken hiccup.

Sky cocked the rifle without removing it from the bar. Its barrel was pointed in the direction of the teamster. "I'm 'cloudy-faced' because I can almost hear the thunder now . . . and the lightning's gonna flash very soon after."

Max barely turned toward the drunk. "If I were you, old chap, I'd move further down the bar and leave the lady alone. That way you might live to crack your whip another day," he said conversationally, nodding to the coiled bullwhip hanging from the teamster's thin shoulder. "If you work for Cass Loring, I'd hate for my wife to make her shorthanded."

Through the glaze of alcohol coating his eyes, which suddenly widened in recognition, the teamster stammered, "No offense, Mr. Limey. No offense." He backed away, stumbling over his own feet and crashing in a tangle against two of his companions, who shoved him away and guffawed as they swilled more whiskey.

The proprietor of the establishment descended the stairs overlooking the bar, calling out, "Well, boyo, not dead yet, I see, but still drawin' trouble like nectar brings bees." The Irishman wore an austere black suit, but his diamond shirt studs, rings and a large diamond stickpin in his crimson cravat winked beneath the bright lights of the crystal chandeliers overhead. "It's that glad I am to see your pretty limey face."

Max walked over to the stairs and they shook hands, slapping each other on the back in male camaraderie. "You haven't changed your ways either, Blackie. Still wearing enough jewelry to make Queen Victoria salivate with envy."

"Me sworn duty, as a good Irishman," the little man said, bouncing forward on the balls of his feet as he chuckled, and flexing his fingers so the large diamond rings flashed brilliantly. Drago stood barely five foot five and did not affect heels on his shoes. The dapper little man sported a neat mustache and a thick head of hair, the ebony color well flecked with gray.

"How long has it been, three years now?" Max asked.

"And we're both still alive," Blackie said with an amazed chuckle. "I'd been hopin' you'd quit the manhuntin' business, but when you sent that wire, I knew better. A smart fellow like yerself could find another line of work, boyo." His gravelly voice held a note of concern.

"Your hopes aren't entirely in vain, Mr. Drago," Sky said, coming up behind Max. "My husband has a new line of work—if you can call it that. He's in the m'lord business since becoming a baron."

Max rounded on Sky. "Dammit, woman, do you number a town crier among your antecedents?"

Drago threw back his head and burst into laughter. "So, it's a bloody baron ye are now, boyo—and married to boot! You don't deserve the likes of this beautiful lady."

Max quickly regained his composure and tilted his head to gaze at her. "Nothing could be more true," he replied gravely. "Blackie Drago, may I present my wife, Sky. Sky, this is my old friend Blackie. Nothing happens in this fair city without his knowing of it."

Waving away Max's compliment, Blackie observed Sky with interest and appreciation. "You've the divil's own luck, boyo." He stepped forward and extended his right hand to salute hers with a kiss.

Forgetting the Winchester, she reached her right hand out, then flushed in embarrassment. *I'm an idiot!*

With his left hand, the little Irishman gently took the rifle by its stock and set it aside. Then with his right hand, he raised hers and kissed it gallantly.

"It's honored I am to meet you, m'lady." He then returned the Yellow Boy to her as if it were merely a glove.

Sky felt her cheeks heat and without looking at Max, could

feel his gloating delight at her gaffe. "My husband speaks most highly of you, Blackie. I hope we can be friends in spite of this awkward beginning. Max does have a way of drawing trouble like a lame deer draws wolves."

"Yers is the more apt way of describin' his problem," Blackie said with a twinkle.

"I've managed to stay alive for over thirty years without aid from anyone," Max replied smoothly as his eyes fixed on Sky.

Blackie quickly covered the tension by saying, "Let us adjourn to me office for a hearty lunch, not to mention some dacent liquor. I'm thinking the two of you will have quite an interestin' tale to tell."

"I hope you have some information for us in exchange," Max replied, not relishing the prospect of explaining his marriage to anyone, even an old friend.

"How soon do you think Blackie will find out what rock Deuce has crawled under?" Sky asked Max as they entered the sitting room of their hotel suite.

He shrugged, frustrated that his old friend did not already have a solid lead for them, but there was no sense in striking out blindly when Blackie might well be able to furnish a direct link. In a few days a freighter who drank with Deuce was due to return to Denver The two men had departed together. The teamster owed Drago a gambling debt. Blackie would collect it in information. "This Longerman chap's wagons are scheduled to return any day."

"In the meanwhile, we just wait," she said, pacing like a caged cat.

"Much as you wish our agreement terminated, I fear you'll just have to be patient, Sky."

She looked up, meeting his disturbing gaze. What went on behind those hard green eyes? Did he actually care for her? She bit her tongue to keep from asking. No, he merely desired her, as she did him. Scarcely the stuff upon which to build a real marriage. But she'd spurned him, saying cruel things she had not intended to say, did not mean. He was, in spite of everything, an honorable man. "I . . . I said some things after we . . . after . . ." she stammered, flushing.

"After we consummated our vows," he provided helpfully, then stood very still, waiting for her to continue.

"I said things I didn't mean . . . things you didn't deserve. I was wrong, Max. And I apologize." She stood, mute with misery, too confused by her stumbling confession to reveal any more.

He walked slowly across the carpet and lifted her chin in his hand, studying her eyes, as if trying to read her mind. "Apology accepted, love. Do you think—"

A sharp rap on the door interrupted whatever he was going to ask. Max dropped his hand, muttering in frustration. Sky stepped back, her heart suddenly racing. She desperately wanted to hear him out, but a voice from the other side of the door broke the spell. "I know you're in there, Max, so you might as well answer."

"Loring, you have the most abominable timing of any man alive," Max said, but a grin split his face when he opened the door.

A tall slim man, about Max's height, stepped inside. Sky studied him as he and her husband greeted each other warmly. He wore a perfectly tailored suit as if born to wealth and had patrician features with a thin white scar across one cheek adding a dramatic effect. His hair was a sun-streaked light brown faintly flecked with gray, and his skin was almost as dark as Max's, indicating he spent a good deal of time outdoors. Eyes of golden brown studied her with keen interest. So this was the mysterious Steve Loring with the bullwhip-wielding wife.

"We owe you thanks for providing us with the beautiful private railcar, Mr. Loring," she said, offering her hand. If the elegantly attired man was put off by her buckskin breeches and gun belt, he gave no indication. After all, his own wife carried a whip, Sky thought.

Smiling broadly, he shook hands with her. "I understand congratulations are in order, Mrs. Stanhope, or should I address you as 'm'lady'?"

"Please call me Sky. Neither Max nor I have any interest in titles."

"As a mere baron, the title isn't even used in formal address in England," Max said dismissively. "How are Cass and the children?"

"Kylie's in charge of the inventory at the main office, Billy's finally grown enough to ride that buckskin you gave him and Padrick's at the age where all he does is ask questions." Steve paused, filled with fatherly pride, then said, "And Cassie has just presented me with another little Loring."

"Well, congratulations are in order all about the place, old chap," Max said delightedly. "Did you get the daughter you were hoping for this time?"

Steve nodded. "We named her Victoria—after Rhys's wife, not your Queen. And speaking of my imperious wife, she demands that you and your bride come for dinner tonight. No excuses accepted."

Max looked at Sky, then said, "We'd be delighted, but are you certain Cass is up to it if she's just given birth?"

"You know how Cassie is when she wants something, and she's dying to meet the woman who finally captured a lobo wolf like you. She's up and about. Couldn't keep her down unless I tied her to our bed," Loring said with a rueful chuckle, then turned to Sky and sighed. "I'm sorry. I didn't mean to speak crudely in front of a lady, Sky."

She smiled, liking the man instinctively, as she gestured to the trail gear she was wearing. "I may officially be a titled lady, but I'm really a fake. No apology required."

"Then you and my wife will be fast friends," he said, laughing. "We'll see you at seven."

The Loring family owned a large brick mansion just outside the city. A breathtaking view of the Rockies served as a backdrop with a glorious sunset gilding the windows so they sparkled in welcome. Sky fretted about yet another masquerade, deceiving Max's friends just as they'd deceived her family. In spite of that, she had to admit she was curious about the woman who had run a freighting empire since the age of seventeen.

In spite of having had a baby a scant week before, Cass Loring looked radiant and vibrantly energetic. She was tall and slim with pale copper hair and unfashionably sun-darkened skin that complemented her wide-set amber eyes. Cass's beauty was not conventional either. Her features, though delicate, were strong, as befitted a woman of business. Cass wore a vivid green silk gown and had her gleaming hair piled in a tumble of curls atop her head. Sky was glad she'd chosen the sapphire blue velvet and taken the time to plait her hair in a crown of braids. This appeared to be a formal evening.

But Cass walked down the front steps and greeted Max with an affectionate hug. Then she turned to Sky with a wide grin. "At last! A woman has tamed our lone wolf. I'm so happy to meet you, Sky," she said warmly.

Sky felt a strange, sudden longing to be the woman who had tamed the Limey. Under different circumstances, she and Cass might have been friends, but once the truth about her marriage came out, that would be impossible. Would her quest for justice over Will's death cost her everything? She wondered how Clint and Delilah would feel as well. "Thank you for your kind hospitality. I'm always happy to meet my husband's good friends."

"Then you'll be glad to know Blackie's coming to dinner, too," Cass said. "It usually takes some arm-twisting to pry him away from his saloon, but he really likes you, Sky."

Max had mentioned that Cass did business with Drago, but considering the Lorings' social position in Denver, she was surprised to learn Blackie was a visitor in their home. Most proper people would never allow the owner of a sporting house to darken their door. Of course, neither would they invite a woman of mixed blood to table, but she sensed no hesitation when Steve had issued the invitation, or from Cass as they met.

This time, the gathering was somewhat more relaxed than the meal they'd shared with her family in St. Louis. The children asked no embarrassing questions of her as Rob had of Max. No one objected to the way Max had chosen to earn his living, although it was evident that Steve and Cass, like Blackie, worried about his safety. Now everyone seemed reassured that he'd "settled down."

Sky felt like a fraud.

But her feelings of guilt and deceit evaporated as lively conversation around the table held her attention. At fifteen, Kylie was a younger replica of her mother, and just as business minded. Billy, going on twelve, and his seven-year-old brother Pat hero-worshipped the English gunman. Both boys peppered Max with questions about where he'd been, what bad men he'd captured of late and what it was like being an English nobleman.

Again, Sky was struck by how he enjoyed children, teasing them, even joining Blackie to charm Kylie, eliciting blushes and giggles over a young clerk at the office who was smitten with her. *What kind of a father would Max be?* Instinctively, she knew he'd be a very good one . . . if he wanted to settle down. A big "if." She wondered again what he had intended to say when Steve had interrupted earlier at the hotel.

No use worrying about what it might be. If he asked her to stay, what would she answer? Sky felt torn in two. Dismissing her troubling thoughts when she noticed Cass studying her, Sky turned her attention to the discussion at the table. Blackie had diverted his hostess with a question about a shipment for his saloon, due to arrive any day.

"Those teamsters and miners split up chairs and tables like kindling wood, they do. I can't be turnin' me back for more than an hour without a fight breakin' out."

"According to my invoices, the new furniture is hard maple. I expect it'll withstand quite a lot of punishment."

Blackie snorted. "Would you be knowin' how hard miners' heads are?"

"Cass changed factories last month," Steve said. "She had other complaints about soft pine and miners' heads."

"I went with a new company that only uses hardwoods. They have maple, walnut and oak kiln dried back East, then shipped by rail to Omaha, where their workshop is located," Cass said.

"Shipped by a rail line Steve owns, no doubt," Blackie said with a chuckle.

Cass looked at her husband fondly. "Of course. That way, we both get the best rates."

"It won't be long until the rails put horses and wagons out of business," Steve said. "Then Cassie'll be cracking her whip over the boiler of a locomotive."

Cass let out an inelegant snort. "There will always be places where rails can't be laid and wagons will be needed to haul in goods, but I've been reading about some French and German scientists who're experimenting with small engines to fit carriages. Petroleum will run them."

"Horseless carriages?" Sky said, amazed by the image.

"Yes," Cass replied, warming to her topic as her husband rolled his eyes and said, "Don't get her started on that subject unless you plan to spend the night."

Everyone laughed good-naturedly when Cass launched into a description of the various experiments on the continent to make a working internal combustion engine that could propel a carriage. By the time Kylie excused herself to escort her brothers up to bed, it was apparent to Sky that the Lorings had the same kind of relationship as Clint and Delilah.

Sky had always believed her brother and his wife were a unique pairing—a man willing to accept an independent woman as his equal in a business enterprise . . . and in marriage. Her relationship with Will had been one of mutual respect, but she had been a clergyman's wife. Her role was secondary to his and quite prescribed by convention. Even when she traveled to the capital to use her legal talents on behalf of her people, her husband had always accompanied her. His had been the advice legislators and judges weighed, even though the ideas were hers.

When Steve, Blackie and Max headed to the library for cigars and brandy, Cass said to Sky, "Would you care to join me while I take care of Victoria? Perhaps get a little practice in before you have a baby of your own?"

"That would be lovely," Sky said woodenly. Would there ever be children of her body for her to love? *Max's children* . . .

Cass led her up the stairs to the second-floor nursery adjoining the master bedroom. A buxom nurse held a tiny bundle with delicate pink arms waving as the infant cried lustily. "Ms. Vicki's gettin' a mite fussy fer her late night feedin', ma'am," the older woman said.

Cass introduced Sky to Lucinda Austin as she took her daughter. "I can see my little one is hungry, isn't she?" she cooed at the baby, then turned back to the nurse. "I'll change her and put her to bed when I've finished, Cinda. You get some rest yourself now."

"Don't'cha over do, now, ma'am." With that stern admonition, she nodded at them and left.

Cass sat down in a comfortable rocker beside the beautifully carved wooden crib, and motioned for Sky to use the large leather chair beside her. "That's Steve's chair. He likes to sit and talk with me while I perform motherly duties," she said with a soft smile, unfastening the buttons at the bodice of her gown.

Sky watched the baby nurse blissfully and felt a keen pang of envy. She so wanted children of her own. As if intuiting her thoughts, Cass said her, "Max loves children. I can see you do, too . . ." She left the sentence hanging, her shrewd amber eyes sweeping over Sky's flushed face. When Sky made no reply, Cass said baldly, "You can tell me about your marriage if you wish. I sense something's not quite right, and I'm a sympathetic listener."

Somehow, Sky believed her. Why not tell her the truth that she dared not share with Delilah and Clint? "Our marriage isn't exactly conventional," she began haltingly.

"What marriage ever is? Especially if it's a good one," Cass replied.

Sky smiled bitterly. "You and your husband appear to have worked things out admirably, but our situation is quite different. I dragged him out of a saloon with a rifle jammed in his back . . ." She looked up at Cass expectantly, wondering how she'd receive that startling pronouncement.

Cass threw back her head and laughed. "You got the drop on the Limey?" Upset by her mother's sudden shift in position, the baby fussed until Cass soothed her by caressing the cap of pale copper hair on her head.

Sky swallowed hard and pushed ahead. "I offered him a deal. Then he made me a counteroffer. We agreed upon a marriage of convenience so we could both achieve our goals."

"Well, at least Max had a vote. Steve didn't. I bought him for three hundred dollars, two cans of peaches and a bottle of tangle leg whiskey." At Sky's startled look, Cass elaborated. "I sent Kyle Hunnicut, a gunman friend of mine, to pick him out of a tumbleweed wagon. Steve was bound for Fort Sill. He had two choices—marry me, or hang."

Sky's jaw dropped. "But why . . ."

All the amusement faded from Cass's eyes. "My father's will dictated that I marry or lose everything to a distant cousin—a *male* cousin. Neither of them were very nice people."

As comprehension came, Sky was struck by the similarities in their situations. "You wanted a husband you could control."

Cass nodded, warmth once more returning to her eyes. "It didn't exactly work out that way," she replied dryly. "We had epic battles. I rather imagine you and Max will fight the same way. What were the terms of your propositions to each other?"

As Delilah would say, trust your gut and bet everything if it feels right. Sky metaphorically shoved the whole pile of chips across the table. "I wanted him to kill a man for me. He needed a wife to claim his inheritance." She waited for a shocked reaction, but received nothing more than Cass's patient nod, urging her to elaborate. "My hus—my *first* husband was an Episcopal priest on our reservation. A piece of scum shot him in the back, then walked away from the trial because Will was an Indian lover."

"And Will made you swear you wouldn't kill his murderer," Cass said softly.

Sky's breath hitched. "How did you know? Max figured it out, too, but it took him a bit longer."

"He's a man," Cass replied, as if that explained everything. "But he's lonely and very lost, I think," she said softly, studying Sky. "Would you hold her while I fasten my dress?" She offered the baby.

Trembling, Sky took the wee one. During the years she and Will were married, she had ached to hold her own baby this way, but always, it was another woman's offspring. "Do you really think Max would want a family?"

"Yes, I do. It's obvious the two of you strike sparks off

each other, but because of the way you married, things aren't right. Give it time, Sky. Once you see justice done for your first husband, put the past behind you and begin again with Max."

"Do you know why he came to America? Became a bounty hunter?" Sky asked.

Cass shook her head. "There are some dark secrets a man will only share with the woman he loves. He'll tell you . . . when the time is right."

Chapter Seven

There are some dark secrets a man will only share with the woman he loves . . . when the time is right.

Cass's words rang in Sky's mind as she rode by Max's side in the carriage back to their hotel. Did she dare ask him? No, it would have to be his decision, as Cass had said, when he felt the time was right. If only she knew what he had started to say before Steve knocked on the door. Could she ask him that? Sky glanced furtively at her husband as they passed beneath Denver's bright streetlights.

He appeared preoccupied, gazing outside the carriage window, seeing nothing. Was he rehearsing a speech for her? Her throat suddenly felt bone-dry. She cleared it, then blurted, "The Lorings are a wonderful family." No, that was not what she'd intended to say, but it was what came out.

"So are the Danielses. But for pure devilment, I'd bet on Rob over Billy and Padrick combined," he said with a grin. Then his expression sobered as he studied the play of light and shadow on her beautiful face. "What did you and Cass plot while the men were innocently smoking and drinking brandy?" He had a feeling Cass had caught on to their subterfuge. Perhaps Delilah Daniels had as well. Bloody hell, this was getting complicated!

"You were going to ask me a question just as Steve interrupted us this afternoon," she murmured, forcing herself to meet his eyes.

"So I was," he replied, stroking his chin contemplatively. "You made a handsome apology, Sky. Did you truly mean it?"

"Of course," she said reflexively.

"I know I'm no paragon of virtue. And I admit I never intended to marry or take on the responsibility of a family . . . but now that we are married, I find myself willing to risk it. Would you?" His eyes held hers. When she did not answer immediately, he asked, "Or are you still bound to memories of a better man?"

Sky struggled to breathe. Would she always be haunted by Will? Or was it simply that Max was such a different man—a difficult man? "I . . . I don't know, Max," she replied at length. "You and Will are nothing alike—but that does not make him a 'better man.' You live by a different code. He was a clergyman. You were a soldier. But they're both honorable professions."

Max winced. "Yes, I was a soldier, right enough," he said grimly.

"Whatever happened then is just as much in the past as what happened to Will. You were the one who told me we had to go on living."

A faint, haunted smile flitted across his face, then vanished. "Does that mean you'd give up your quest to see Deuce dead?" He heard her breath hitch and knew he'd struck a nerve. "Ah, I thought so. Ever the bloodthirsty avenger. Must be the Sioux in you, tiny bit that it is."

If he intended to hurt her as she'd hurt him, it worked. In white society, people such as the Danielses and the Lorings were rare. Sky had spent her life in cultural confusion, enduring prejudices from both sides of the racial divide. Will had bridged that gap with his gentle love, but now he was dead, in part because of her. "I want justice for Will. Then he can rest in peace. Maybe once Deuce is dead, I'll have some peace of my own. You intended to kill him anyway, once you'd thwarted Cletus. You have what you want, Max. I don't."

"Fair enough. I'll give you what you want, Sky." There was a tightness in his voice as he leaned over and took her hand in his, pulling her into his embrace. Sky did not resist when his mouth slowly lowered over hers. The thick black fans of her lashes swept down. He could not read what was in those huge blue eyes, but her body's response was clear and strong.

Sky felt his lips, hot and seeking, pressing against hers, his tongue demanding she open for him. She complied eagerly. Her hand moved up, burying her fingers in his pale hair, pulling him closer as he cupped her breast through the heavy fabric of her gown. Then that swift, clever gunman's hand insinuated itself inside the low-cut bodice, teasing one nipple, then the other until she whimpered unintelligibly against his mouth.

Her free hand returned the favor, sliding between his shirt studs, palm splaying against his chest. His heartbeat accelerated just as hers did. They were scant moments from losing all control when the carriage abruptly slowed as they neared the hotel. Max raised his head, breathing heavily as his glowing green eyes stared into her blue ones.

"Best to repair yourself, love," he said in a hoarse voice. He scooped up two emerald shirt studs from the seat cushion and placed them casually in his pocket, then reached up and smoothed the bodice of her gown, covering her breasts once more.

Sky could feel the pins in her hair digging into her scalp and knew the heavy crown of braids was badly askew. Nothing for it but to pull the whole thing loose. With the flick of several pins, the two heavy plaits fell below her shoulders. She was grateful when Max covered her and the loose braids with her cloak, securing the tie at her throat with trembling hands.

He helped her from the carriage, handing the driver a generous amount of cash, then took her arm and whisked her through the door and toward the stairs. In moments he was sliding a key into the lock of his bedroom door. When he swung it open, Sky realized this was not the sitting room. Before she could say anything, he scooped her into his arms and kicked the door closed behind him.

When he let her body slide down the length of his own, still holding her tightly, they stood beside his large bed. "Shall we continue where we left off, love?" he asked as he unfastened her cloak and let it drift to the floor.

Sky clung to him, speechless. All she could do was nod, then bury her head against the hardness of his chest. She felt his hands unplaiting her hair until it fell loosely down her back. Quickly, he turned his attention to the button loops at the back of her gown, unfastening them with surprising deftness, considering how labored his breathing was. His fingers were warm against her flesh as he lightly grazed the delicate vertebrae, sending frissons of pleasure humming through her.

Seemingly of their own volition, her hands began to slip the remaining studs from his shirt and cuffs, stuffing them clumsily into his coat pocket as he had done back in the carriage. *This is what you want. Don't deny it.* The relentless voice inside her head repeated the litany as she slid both jacket and shirt from his broad shoulders. He obliged her by swiftly yanking them off and tossing them behind him.

The drapes had been drawn closed, bedcovers turned back and the lights dimmed. All Sky could see was the glistening pale flesh of his chest and shoulders. Her fingers sank into the silver-gilt hair on his chest, tracing the cunning pattern as it narrowed at the waistband of his pants. She hesitated for a moment, but then he thrust his pelvis against her belly and she could feel the hardness of his erection.

"Do it, Sky," he commanded harshly.

She fumbled with the belt buckle and buttons of his fly, freeing his staff. Just as her hands glided over it, eliciting an oath of pleasure from him, her heavy gown fell around her waist. Already he had her chemise straps down and her breasts free. His head bent to suckle one and she arched her back, offering herself to his hot, seeking mouth. After giving each nipple a tingling tug of pure bliss, his lips swept up to her collarbone, then pressed soft, wet kisses on her throat. She rubbed her aching nipples against his chest, crying, "Yes, oh, yes . . ."

Max could see the blue-black sheen of her hair falling down her back like a midnight waterfall. He held her trembling in his arms, but she held him equally a prisoner with her soft hands caressing his shaft. He'd explode if she didn't stop. Gritting his teeth, he reached down and pried her fingers away, then worked her gown and petticoats over her hips. Now she wore only the chemise bundled about her waist, her silk stockings and shoes. The rich cream color of the chemise made her skin gleam like honey.

His breath caught when she again caressed his sex. He picked her up and laid her on the bed, then stepped back. Stockings and soft kid slippers emphasized the length and perfection of her legs. Such an incredibly erotic picture. "You're a witch, casting a spell over me with your beauty," he murmured, tearing his eyes away from her golden body and the great splash of inky hair spread over the snow white sheets.

Sky watched him pull off his shoes and stockings, kick away the last of his clothing and then stand over her like some Norse god, gleaming in the soft light. But there was nothing soft about Max Stanhope. He was all planes and angles, his face hard in its masculine beauty, the narrow lips a slash below those incredibly green eyes that seemed to bore into her very soul. His flexing muscles and scarred skin attested to the dangerous life he'd led.

A man she did not know . . . yet knew so very intimately.

"Come to me, Max," she whispered, opening her arms.

He sank onto the bed and embraced her, inhaling that delicate scent of sweet herbs and Sky, his Sky, his wife. He devoured her mouth like a starving man, savoring the way she returned his ardor. Her body twisted and arched beneath him as he seated himself at the apex of her thighs. When she opened herself, her stocking-clad legs clamping around his hips, he plunged deep inside her and rode hard.

Sky gave in to the unbelievable pleasure, matching him thrust for thrust, crying out his name and other incoherent things . . . things she might later regret but now did not even realize she spoke. She tossed her head from side to side, awash in mindless passion. Her hunger was so great she could not have controlled the swiftness of culmination even if she'd known how to do so. The contractions swept over her like an avalanche of molten lava, burying her in sheer blind ecstasy.

Like his wife, Max let go all control, even though he'd had considerably more practice at holding off. This time he did not want to. Perhaps, if he had been coherent enough to think, he would have realized he could not have stopped their frenzied ride any more than she. Her silky sheath squeezed his shaft, causing it to swell and spill in glorious release.

And still he could not get enough of her. He lay on top of her, his fingers interlocked with hers, their arms stretched above their heads. Perspiration slicked their bodies in the cool night air. She maintained her leg-lock around his hips. He stayed buried deep inside her, unwilling to relinquish what he now claimed permanently. *I'll never let her go.* With that thought, he began to move again, this time very slowly, very gently . . .

At first Sky could not believe this was possible. He'd spent himself. So had she, utterly. But she had read some rather salacious books, sneaked in by older girls at her boarding school, and eavesdropped on the women in the Ehanktonwon village as they whispered and exchanged boasts about their men. So such things were possible. She felt Max once more begin to stoke the fire that he ignited so easily in her. But this time it was not a wild, mad hunger, over so swiftly. No, this was unbearably sweet . . . almost as if . . . as if he loved her, rather than merely desired her. Could that be true? Did she want it to be true?

Sky didn't know, but very quickly all her chaotic thoughts tumbled into the abyss of renewed passion. She held tightly to his hands, letting him guide her down this new and intricate labyrinth of pleasure. After a long, slow while, he rolled them over, placing her on top, tugging on her hair, bringing her mouth down to fuse with his, then kissing and suckling her breasts. She used her teeth on the hard tawny nub of one flat male nipple and was rewarded by a guttural oath of pleasure. They turned and twisted, arched and thrust, gave and took from each other until the bedcovers tangled around them and came loose from the mattress.

Finally, they reached the end of their endurance. Sky felt the slow, delicious fulfillment envelop her and keened her pleasure, urging him to join her, to swell and spill deep inside her. As he did, she cried out his name and held him fast.

They lay on their sides, facing each other, legs and arms still entwined, bodies intimately joined. Feeling his eyes on her, Sky opened hers and met his level green gaze. A tender, almost wistful expression seemed to fill them as he reached up with one hand and brushed a straight lock of black hair from her cheek. He tugged on the end of a sheet and used it to gently wipe the dots of perspiration from her face, then rubbed his own dry.

"We'll have no need to lay a fire, no matter how cold the winters," he said with a lopsided grin of utter satisfaction. "That was incredible, love . . . and addictive, if a bit uncomfortable after the fact."

Sky looked nonplussed as he reached down between them and pulled one of her slippers from beneath his ribs. It was only then, when she saw the red mark made by the heel of her slipper, that she realized she'd made love with her shoes and stockings on! And lost one in the midst of their lusty bed sport. "Oh, I must look like some fancy house female," she said, stricken, trying to untangle herself from him.

"You look delectable—and completely innocent, albeit alluring as hell." He encircled a slender ankle and removed the other slipper, tossing both of them from the bed. When he sat up and removed a garter, then peeled down her silk stocking, she resisted.

"You are utterly depraved. Surely you can't . . . we can't . . ."

Max threw back his head and laughed. "Utterly depraved I am, but I fear you've quite wrung me out, love. And if we tried, neither of us would be able to walk tomorrow . . . not that the thought of spending the day in bed with you isn't tempting," he said. He waited for her reaction.

Sky's face flushed with heat, but she forced herself to meet his eyes. "You need not ask if I have regrets this time. I don't. I wanted this. We desire each other. Can that be enough . . . for the present?" *If you tell me you love me, I'll be lost, Max.*

He nodded slowly. "For the present, I'll be content if you share my bed," he replied simply. "In time, I hope you'll want to be my wife as I want to be your husband." He made no declaration of love, sensing that it would drive her away from him. It was too soon. She was too confused about Will.

But if there was one thing the Limey had learned over hard years on the hunt, it was patience . . .

Sky awakened to the fragrance of coffee and blinked her eyes. She sat up and looked at the tangled bedcovers. She had spent the night in her husband's arms. Memories of their lovemaking filled her mind, leaving it spinning. The pillow beside her bore the indentation of his head, but when she placed her hand on it, it was cool to the touch. Then she heard him directing a bellman to leave the breakfast tray on a table in the sitting room.

She swept the covers away and swung her legs over the side of the mattress, only to be appalled that she was completely naked . . . and incredibly sore. Every muscle in her body screamed as if she were an untried schoolgirl, instead of a woman used to hard exercise. A foolish smile curved her lips. Well, she had certainly participated in some very hard exercise last night!

Looking at the tangled covers, she took a sniff of her body and knew she desperately needed a bath. Best to consider practical matters, not think of the larger implications of what they'd said and done . . . and not said. At that moment Max appeared in the bedroom doorway. His hair was rumpled and silver-gilt beard stubble covered his tanned face. He wore a green silk dressing robe, belted casually so his chest was revealed, giving her a tantalizing view.

He held a cup of steaming coffee in one hand and her blue dressing robe in the other. "I thought to wake you, slugabed. It's nearly noon." He was pleased that she did not look away from him, although she did casually drape a corner of the sheet over herself.

"Noon! I can't believe I've slept away the whole morning." The moment she blurted the words, Sky blushed. They both knew perfectly well why she'd overslept.

"You needed the rest, love." His tone was neutral as he handed her the cup.

"Is that black, I hope?"

"Certainly. I know how you like it," he said in a low voice. "I've arranged for a bath to be brought to your room, and a hotel maid will be up to press a dress for you after breakfast, which awaits us in the sitting room."

She took a sip and regarded him over the steaming rim of the cup. "You're most accomplished as a valet, m'lord. Did you ask Baldwin for instruction?"

Max chuckled and shook his head. "Baldwin would have an apoplectic seizure if he saw me waiting upon anyone, even my wife." With that he held up the robe for her. She placed her cup on the table beside the bed, then stood and turned her back to slide her arms into the robe. She felt his hands gently tugging her hair from the neckline.

"Don't get too close. I stink like a badger," she said, bending down to retrieve her cup.

"Badgers never smelled so good, wife. This scent is of us." His tone was intimate now.

Sky knew she had to turn and face him. Boldly, she did so, saying, "I suppose you're right. I only hope you've arranged a bath for yourself as well. Others might be offended, even if we aren't."

Max laughed. "Not offended. Aroused, perhaps."

And her heart lurched at the joyous sound of his voice.

By the time Sky had finished relaxing sore muscles in her bath, it was afternoon. She threw on a fresh robe, then plaited her damp hair into one thick braid and entered the sitting room. Max awaited her with a note in his hand. She'd heard a knock on the door only a few moments ago.

"What is it?" she asked.

"Blackie sends his regards. It would appear Mr. Longerman has returned to Denver a bit earlier than expected, and was more than eager to sell out his erstwhile companion."

Sky seized the piece of paper and noted the small, neat script of Drago's handwriting. Somehow, it fit him. She scanned the lines, then said, "So Deuce is in some silver boomtown in southwestern Colorado—or, at least, that's where Longerman parted company with him. How soon can you be ready?" she asked Max, turning to her bedroom door, eager to dress and hit the trail.

"Let's not move so precipitously, love. Note that Blackie says he's wired one Frances Simmons in Leadville. She may know precisely where Deuce is. Before we start a mad dash through mountain terrain where we may have no access to telegraphs, it would be wise to confirm his location. Also, I just sent a telegram to Jerome Bartlett in London regarding an investment that Steve thinks is an excellent idea."

"How long will we have to wait for your London lawyer and this friend of Blackie's?" she asked impatiently.

Max shrugged. "It won't take Jerome more than a few hours to reply. He's a great believer in American railroads for profitable returns over the long run. Mrs. Simmons might reply today, or take a bit longer. That depends on what she knows, or can find out for Blackie. As the owner of the finest parlor house in a city of some twenty odd thousand souls, I imagine she'll prove resourceful."

"A parlor house? Isn't that just another name for a bordello?" she asked.

Max smiled at her naïveté. "For a woman raised on the frontier and educated at university, you lack certain, er, shall we say, basic information. A first-rate parlor house is a place where men pay women of varying degrees of refinement and beauty, frequently simply for conversation and nonphysical companionship. Say to attend a play or lavish dinner, even a picnic."

Sky looked skeptical. "You're making that up. White men out West, just wanting to talk with a female?"

"Not all men—even whites—are animals, Sky. Many, far from home, long for mothers, sisters, lost sweethearts . . . or some facsimile thereof, even if they must pay for female companionship. Often the less educated clients ask parlor house ladies to write letters to their families or sweethearts back East."

"I suppose in some strange way that makes sense, but I can't imagine a man like Deuce writing home, which he could do for himself. And I doubt he'd be interested in genteel conversation," she said bitterly.

"He was forced to leave England. Blackie said this Mrs. Simmons is English and properly educated. Who knows?"

He shrugged, rather too casually, arousing Sky's suspicions. "Have you ever visited a parlor house?" she asked, then could have bitten her tongue when he grinned, showing off those beautiful white teeth of his.

"Jealous, love?"

She resisted the urge to stamp her foot. "Don't be ridiculous. I was merely curious. Besides, from what Rosie told me in Bismarck, it's obvious the Limey has never lacked for female companionship, physical or otherwise," she snapped.

Max cocked his head, studying her narrowed eyes. "Ah, but when you, er, introduced yourself to me that memorable day, I didn't have a wife to provide female companionship of any variety."

"Now you do," she replied, nervous under his scrutiny. "But what about friends, family? England was your home. Don't you ever think of it?"

"Oh, I think of dear Cletus often, but with Uncle Harry gone . . . I'll never go back again," he said bleakly. "Jerome Bartlett will handle business matters for me. I trust him implicitly."

Sky could not understand why Max should feel so alienated from his own people. "I could never imagine closing out my family—red or white, not needing to see them again or go home to my father's ancestral land."

Max sighed and tugged his ear. "It's been a lifetime since I knew what home was . . . if I ever did."

"Your uncle provided you a home," she said hesitantly. "Yet in spite of loving him, you left."

"I did what I had to do, Sky." His voice was suddenly cold, final.

This conversation was closed. Frustrated, Sky said, "I'm going to get my things together, check my weapons again. You might do the same."

He nodded. "I already have. You forget, love, this is the way I've earned my living for some years."

As she turned toward her door, she could feel those hard
green eyes boring into her back. She had touched a raw
nerve. Whatever dark secrets drove him, he was far from willing to share them with her. *Will he ever be?*

Jerome Bartlett, as Max had anticipated, replied within a few
hours. The investment was an excellent idea. He would handle everything. Then around the time they were preparing to
go out for dinner, Blackie knocked on their hotel room door,
waving a telegram. "Thought you'd be wantin' to read this
the minute I had it in me hands." He doffed his hat and
smiled at Sky, who had changed into a simple day dress of
pink muslin with a high-buttoned collar.

Max glanced through the message, then handed it to Sky,
saying to their friend, "Blackie, now I insist you consider
your imaginary debt to me paid in full."

"I owed you for catching that scum who savaged me girl
Alice. Just you take care of your lady here, boyo, and we'll stay
even."

Sky looked up from the wire. "In spite of my foolish reaction yesterday, I'm normally able to take care of myself.
Johnny Deuce won't be kissing my gun hand. But I am most
grateful for this information." She turned to Max and said,
"Now we know where Deuce has been within the past
week or so. He might still be there! Can we travel by rail to
Leadville?"

"Steve owns stock in General Palmer's narrow gauge line.
For the likes of you, I know he'll be happy to send a special
car tonight," Blackie replied. "Just have a care, colleen.
Johnny Deuce has a reputation black as the divil's own."

The train began to slow for a water stop early the following
day. Sky paced like a caged lioness after a restless night, then
forced herself to calm down. Running on pure nerves would
not keep her sharp enough to outwit a back-shooting killer

like Johnny Deuce. She looked out the window, watching the sun gild the western horizon, drawing strength from the old Sioux ritual.

Max was already up, dressed and gone in search of coffee. Although she and her husband had shared a bed in their private car, he had not attempted to make love to her, but neither had he experienced terrible nightmares. For that she was grateful. He did not remember having the horrid dream the night they'd consummated their marriage. As far as Max was aware, his wife knew nothing of his demons.

Although the nightmares held the key to his past, she was not certain she was any more prepared to unlock that door than he was . . . at least for the present. Cass had cautioned her to give their relationship time, to build mutual trust. After hearing how the Lorings' marriage had begun, Sky supposed she and Max had a chance.

Her ruminations were interrupted when the sound of strident curses and the meaty thunk of fists striking flesh came from outside. She crossed to the end of the car and peered into the gloom through the small window in the door. The private railcar was positioned at the end of the train, so she had an unobstructed view.

Two men were dragging a kicking and yelling girl toward a small wooden shanty near the water tower. A third scruffy-looking man in trail gear was unbuttoning his fly with the obvious intent of raping her once they had her inside. A fourth man lay crumpled on the ground near the water tower. The girl's husband or protector? Were none of the men aboard the train going to stop this? Then she realized that only her proximity to the crime enabled her to hear over the engine's noise.

Sky quickly put on her robe and slippers, then reached for her Yellow Boy, ready to leap from the moving car if necessary, but she was thrown off balance when the train lurched to a complete stop. She yanked the door handle open. Two of the three miscreants had taken their victim inside the shack and the third had dragged the unconscious or dead man's body behind them. The woman's cries fell silent. Had they beaten her unconscious or stuck some filthy rag in her mouth to keep her from yelling for help?

Not waiting for reinforcements, Sky climbed noiselessly down the metal steps of the rear platform and crossed the ground to the now closed door of the shanty, listening to the sounds of drunken male voices inside.

"Hold 'er still, dammit, Hank. I ain't fixin' ta git my pecker kicked!"

"Her gambler feller's comin' round, Mr. Zeb. Yew want me ta kill 'im?" a second voice asked deferentially. Zeb must be the leader.

Sky kicked in the door with a loud crunch and moved against the wall so all three of the brutes were in view. "I wouldn't advise that, Mr. Zeb." She could see them in the murky light filtering through a westward-facing window.

Startled, one of the men holding the woman dropped her feet but the other looked to Zeb and continued holding her arms. "Shit, it's a Injun gal, boss. With a rifle," he said stupidly, as if that were not readily apparent.

"I got eyes, Cary," Zeb replied, facing Sky without bothering to button his fly. He had a pockmarked face with cruel colorless eyes protruding above loose pockets of skin that lay on his sunken cheeks. Gray hair, greasy and thinning, hung over his high forehead, which was crinkled with anger. "Wall, lookee here. We got us 'nother 'un fer the pot. Not bad, one dressed red, the other *is* red. Injun stew and real tasty lookin'." He chuckled viciously at his bad jest.

"Let her go," Sky said calmly, the barrel of her rifle pointed at Zeb's cadaverous body, even though the one called Hank held her arms.

"Why should we do thet? They's three 'o us . . . one 'o

yew," Zeb replied with a leer, motioning for Cary to move toward her.

"You can count. More than I would've given you credit for," Sky replied calmly, blasting a chunk of the dirt floor directly in front of the advancing man's feet, taking part of one boot toe off.

Cary screamed and bent over, hobbling around as he held his injured foot in his hands. "She done shot me, boss! Shot my big toe plumb off!"

The barrel of the rifle returned to Zeb instantly. "My next shot cripples Hank's right arm. Still think you'll have that Injun stew, Mr. Zeb? I think I'll shoot off your little pecker and leave your filthy bleeding hide for the coyotes to chew on— if they'll have it."

"She isn't bluffing, gentleman," a sardonic voice said from behind Sky.

When Hank saw Max's Smith & Wesson pointed directly at him, he dropped the girl and shuffled back. "We wuz jest funnin' . . . didn't mean no harm."

"I could see damn well what you were doing and it wasn't fun for her," Sky snapped, half angry Max had interfered, half glad to have his backup.

Zeb sneered. "She's jest a whore, hangin' on with thet card shark," he said, jerking his head toward the flashy-looking man moaning in the corner. "Nobody in the car we tuk 'em out 'o gave a shit. Whut da yew keer?"

"Maybe it's the idea of three big men beating one girl . . . or maybe it was the part about having 'Injun stew' that raised my hackles, you filthy white trash."

"Yew damn breed, yew can't talk ta me—"

Sky spun the stock of her rifle and smashed Zeb's mouth with it so swiftly, the motion was a blur. Before he hit the ground, cursing through broken teeth, she had the barrel of the Yellow Boy again leveled directly at his crotch. She glanced at his two men, Hank cowering against the back wall, Cary squatting down holding his injured foot. Their bloodshot eyes were wide with fright. She dismissed them. "You aren't worth the bullets," she said, "but you, Zeb . . ."

"Yew know who I am, Injun bitch?" he roared, spitting broken pieces of bloody teeth across his chest. "I own the Z-Bar, biggest spread in the state. Fuckin' gov'nor jumps when I fart. Yew kill me 'n he'll hang yew!"

Her lips smiled but her blue eyes were ice-cold, narrowed with hate. "Might just be worth it to see you burn in hell. Watch the devil struggle to find that shriveled little pecker of yours to stab it with his pitchfork."

Max could see she itched to pull the trigger. She was remembering Deuce with a beaten and helpless Sioux girl, and the tragedy that had followed. "Do what you must, love. I certainly won't say you nay, but what would Father Will want you to do? If you don't give a damn, we shall cleanse the world of all three pieces of offal and be on our way."

Both of the cowhands trembled, white-faced with fear, but Zeb just glared at her through hate-filled eyes. Max held his breath, waiting. The rancher needed killing, but Sky must not be the one to do it.

Chapter Eight

*A*fter what seemed an eternity of standoff between Sky and Zeb, she turned to Max. Tears of frustration and fury clouded her vision. "Damn you!"

Max nodded sadly as she shoved the rifle at him. "Conscience may not make cowards of us all, but living with one surely is a bitch."

When she stormed out into the dawning light, he murmured, "The problem is, if you killed them like this, you'd never be free of them. No train can travel that fast or that far. I'm an authority on the subject." He looked at Zeb, who was barely conscious now that the object of his hatred had left; his two hirelings cowered when they saw the hard expression in the Englishman's eyes.

"If you'd be so kind as to remove your weapons, gentlemen?" he said. Hank and Cary could not divest themselves of their sidearms quickly enough. "Now, your employer's Colt." Hank obliged, very gingerly tossing the expensive six-shooter at Max's feet. He kicked all three guns aside and instructed Hank, "Drag your boss up. Then all of you, outside." His pistol never wavered as he cradled Sky's rifle in his left arm.

Cary struggled to his feet and hobbled out. Hank hoisted his boss from the hard-packed earth. Zeb's mouth was bleeding so profusely it had soaked the whole of his shirtfront as red as the girl's dress. Max followed them out, calling to the engineer. "Mr. Berry, I require some assistance. Send two of your stokers to aid me, if you'd be so kind."

The engineer knew the Englishman was a personal friend of Mr. Loring. He took in the situation, then yelled for the stokers to come on the double.

Sky stood trembling in the shadows, fists clenched as the past washed over her. She was a little girl again, picking berries with her sister when three big, blue-coated soldiers attacked them savagely. Then her mind shifted abruptly to that child Deuce was beating and Will, falling into her arms, dying . . . yet begging her not to kill but to forgive.

"No, no, no . . ." Then the sounds of sobbing brought her back to the present ugly reality. Another injured girl lay inside the shack. She watched as two railroaders tied up Hank and Cary, then hoisted them and their unconscious boss into a freight car just behind the engine.

Gathering her wits, she reluctantly stepped through the doorway and knelt by the injured girl. "Can you sit up?" When the young woman nodded, Sky helped her.

There was little doubt she was a prostitute. But, good lord, she was young, probably no more than sixteen, although those had been hard years. She was dressed in a garish red satin gown, cut low in the front. Her lips were painted bright red, the color smeared from her struggle with her attackers. The kohl ringing her eyes ran in black rivulets as tears poured down her rouged cheeks. Hennaed hair that clashed horribly with her clothing hung in a frizzy mass around her shoulders, pins dangling from it. She might have once been pretty.

"You're going to be all right," Sky said. "We'll need some cold towels for that cheek." A large ugly bruise was already forming on one side of the girl's face.

"That old bastard, just 'cause he's got money, 'n I'm a whore, that don't give him no right . . ." She broke down in hiccupping sobs. The man on the floor groaned again. "Oh, Jimmy, you all right, baby?" she asked, starting to crawl toward the gambler, whose once fine suit was torn and dirty. His face was a mass of bruises and Sky could see a goose egg beginning to form at his receding hairline when he sat up. He appeared to be several decades older than his traveling companion.

Jimmy touched the swelling, grimacing as he worked his jaw experimentally. "I'll live, Ginny." He looked over at Sky, his cool gray eyes calculating as he took in her dressing gown and air of command. "I'm James Cavendish, and this is Ginny Mars, missus . . . ?"

"Stanhope, Sky Stanhope," she replied as Ginny helped him to his feet. The two of them, beaten and bloody, stood together. "You both need to have your cuts and bruises treated," Sky said. "If you'd like, I can help for now. When we reach Leadville, I'm sure you'll be able to find a doctor."

"Gee, thanks. We'd sure—"

"No, er, that is, I think it would be wise for us to get off the train at the next stop," Jimmy replied, silencing Ginny, who immediately hung her head and said no more, deferring to the older man for guidance in spite of his failings as her protector. "Zebulon McKerrish is a nasty fellow to have as an enemy."

"So is my husband. He'll see to it that Zeb and his men are locked up when we reach the next town," Sky replied.

"Won't do no good," Ginny said with a weary shrug. "Jimmy's right. No sheriff'll be able to keep McKerrish in jail. None of them passengers in our car tried to stop him when he had his men drag me off the train. Only Jimmy."

"If you press charges—"

"It would be bad for our health," the gambler said with finality. "We thank you for your help, but Ginny and I are going to disappear. You and your husband might want to do the same, unless you got some pull in Denver." He sounded dubious.

A bitter smile touched Sky's lips. "You might be surprised. We aren't afraid of McKerrish . . . but I do wish my husband hadn't talked me out of killing the bastard." Turning to Ginny, she said, "At least let me treat your injuries. We have a private car where no one will see you."

The girl looked at the gambler, who nodded. "I expect it'd be a good idea to stay out of sight until we can slip off the train. Maybe McKerrish will forget about us."

Unspoken was the fact that the cattleman would not forget the mixed-blood woman who had smashed in his face with her rifle butt. And because of her, the Limey had another enemy to add to an already long list.

True to his word, James Cavendish took young Ginny and slipped off the train when they reached the next town. Sky gave them money to purchase a couple of horses so they could disappear. Max returned to their railcar shortly before the train once more got under way.

"Well, are they in jail?" she asked, already guessing the answer.

"It would seem Mr. Zebulon McKerrish is a very important landowner, a veritable American earl. The sheriff flatly refused to arrest him or his lackeys. And, since their victims have refused to press charges . . ." He shrugged in disgust.

"He just let them go then." Her voice was flat.

"No, Cary and his boss were both in need of a doctor, thanks to you, love. At least with McKerrish unconscious, he won't be sending gunmen after that girl and her companion for the present."

"He'll come after us. Bet on it."

Max nodded. "Your brother wouldn't take odds against it, but by the time McKerrish is able to issue orders, we'll be long gone, too."

"He'll find out who you are. You've just made another vicious enemy."

"He'll have to wait his turn. The queue is already quite long," Max replied dryly, as he poured two cups of coffee and laced them generously with whiskey, then handed her one. "We're after bigger game than McKerrish, love. Forget about him." He studied her over the rim of his mug, fearing she might be right, but not wanting her to second-guess her decision that morning.

"When he wakes up, do you think he'll send someone after Ginny and her gambler?" she asked.

"No. And I doubt he'll try me either. I made certain he knew who I was before we left town."

"What if you're wrong?"

He smiled sadly at her and took a swallow of the hot black liquid. "Then I suppose I shouldn't have talked you out of killing the lot of them."

She set aside her cup without taking a drink. "I've become someone I don't even recognize anymore."

"You're seeing that little girl who Deuce brutalized . . . and Will Brewster. I recognize you, Sky Eyes of the Ehanktonwon. You aren't a cold-blooded killer. In fact . . ." He set down his cup and walked over to her, taking her chin in his hand, tilting her face up to his.

Sky held her breath as he lowered his mouth to hers and gave her a soft kiss. "Sometimes we can't forget the past, love. We have to live with it." His eyes held hers until she nodded. "You did the right thing, Sky. If McKerrish causes trouble down the line, I'll handle him."

He left a taste of coffee-flavored whiskey on her lips and a burning warmth spreading through her body. *He's offering me comfort . . .*

When she reached up and encircled his neck with her arms, he picked her up and carried her to the bed . . . and the oblivion of passion.

The following day the train pulled into Leadville. Sky sat at the window, already dressed in one of her best traveling suits, a gray linen with narrow white stripes and black piping on the jacket. She'd arranged her hair into a bun at her nape and wore a small gray hat perched at a jaunty angle on her head.

The veil on the headgear reminded her fleetingly of the mysterious woman who'd rescued her and Delilah back in Missouri, but before she could dwell on her identity, the train lurched to a complete stop.

Max entered the car in a three-piece suit with gold watch fob glittering in the late afternoon sunlight. He inspected her appearance with appreciation. "You'll be the most elegant lady in Leadville."

"Somehow I doubt that would be difficult."

"Don't sneer. The population is around thirty thousand souls, or so I was told. Quite a boomtown, filled with rich men and beautiful women."

"If Blackie's friend has information on Deuce, I don't care if she's ugly as Medusa," Sky replied, trying not to flush with pride at the way he admired her. With the passing of each day—and night—it seemed their marriage grew to be more genuine . . . more permanent. His reply brought her back to reality.

"I'm certain Mrs. Simmons will be reasonably attractive, considering her work, but Blackie's never mistaken about a source. We'll find out where Deuce has gone to ground."

"Good. I hope he's here in town."

"In case he's already overstayed his welcome, I saw to stabling for the horses Steve lent us. If we have to ride after Deuce, we'll require camp supplies, but that shouldn't be a problem in a mining town."

"At least you're not still insisting I stay behind any longer. Thank you, Max."

Her earnest expression caught him off guard. Did it mean that she trusted him and only wanted to watch his back . . . or did she still need to see Johnny Deuce die at her feet? He hoped it was the former, not the latter. "You're welcome, love. What man can stand against a determined woman—especially one who's a dead shot with a Yellow Boy?" he asked as he helped her from the train steps to the crowded platform.

Sky looked around her, amazed at the stark scene. Leadville was a huge, sprawling mining town plunked ten thousand feet above sea level, yet surrounded by snowcapped mountains. "Why would so many people want to live in this cold, isolated place?"

"Hot or frozen, gold has its draw, love. And the men who run the mines want their pleasures close at hand."

Suddenly a shot rang out nearby. Max shoved Sky behind him and crouched, his double-action Remington pocket pistol drawn from his jacket with blurring speed. He tracked the shooter, then slipped the stubby revolver back into its hiding place. A drunk in a plaid flannel shirt had just taken a potshot at a jackrabbit and missed. The critter's white tail bounced across the open brushy landscape and vanished while the man cussed.

Then a second shot erupted from down the street leading into town. He again reached for his pistol, but quickly stopped himself when he saw another miner lower a rusty old Colt that he'd just fired in the air while yelling, "Whoopee! Drinks on me, boys. I struck 'er rich tadday!"

A crowd of eager takers converged on the celebrant, following him into the saloon, appropriately named The Hot Shot. Sky looked at the crowds of people walking, riding horses or driving carriages up and down the muddy streets. "Where are all these people going? This is busier than New York City!" Then, when another random shot rang out, she could sense Max flinch.

"Small wonder they call it Leadville. Whoever sells ammunition here probably makes more than the silver kings." He took her hand and tucked it around his arm, then hailed a carriage to take them to their hotel.

During the ride to the Clarendon Hotel on Harrison Avenue, the gunfire continued sporadically. Sky could see it was unsettling to Max. For a man who earned his living with a veritable arsenal of firearms, she found it difficult to understand, until she realized that stalking a murderer and capturing or killing him required few shots to be fired. A protracted battle, however, was quite a different matter.

Max must be reliving his war experience. Now she wished desperately that she'd found the time on their journey to visit a library and read about the battle at Rorke's Drift. How long must it have gone on? Knowing the details might help her better understand the enigma that was her husband . . . and the ghastly nightmares that still held him prisoner.

"Instead of going straight to the hotel, why don't we call on Mrs. Simmons at her parlor house?" she suggested to Max, thinking such a practical matter might take his mind off his ghosts. "It is on the edge of the city, isn't it?"

He smiled at her. "Patience, love. Although her establishment is nearby, the lady is doubtless occupied marshaling her staff for this evening's business. If we wish her goodwill, it would be wise not to disrupt her schedule. I'll send a note requesting a visit after we've checked into the Clarendon. They're reputed to have a splendid dining room."

Sky harrumphed her dissatisfaction, but said grudgingly, "I suppose we'd be wise to wait until it suits her."

The hotel was indeed quite impressive, a three-story brick building located next to the Tabor Opera House. It stood like some medieval castle overshadowing the peasantry milling about below. "A bit garish, but it will do. Has done for men with titles far exceeding my paltry one," he said as they entered the front lobby. Their suite was spacious and overlooked the front of the building from the second floor.

Before dismissing the bellman, Max ordered baths for both of them and requested dinner reservations for seven that evening. He watched as Sky pulled the pearl hat pin from the frilly concoction on her head and tossed the hat and its lace veil on a pier table. He moved silently behind her and reached up, unfastening her hair and letting his fingers comb the heavy mass down her back.

"Mmm," he murmured. "It's so thick and shiny, but I imagine carrying all that weight about one's head is a trial . . . one I am most happy you endure."

She leaned her head backward, letting his caresses soothe the tension from her body. Then another series of shots rang outside the windows and she felt him tense. *I should be the one soothing him.* She turned in his arms and kissed him softly. It was not an embrace of passion, but rather one of solace.

Max inhaled the sweet scent that was so uniquely Sky and felt his frayed nerves calm. He was becoming addicted to having her in his life. If only it could last. He closed his eyes and held her fast, burying his face in her night-dark hair. Their tender moment was interrupted by a rap on the door.

"Bathwater, yer worship," a voice with a thick Irish brogue called out from the hallway.

Sky dressed in her finest blue silk gown and wore a sapphire necklace and earrings Max had given her while they were in St. Louis. "You look luscious enough to eat. Perhaps we should forget about dinner and adjourn to the bedroom," he said when she twirled around, holding the train of the frothy gown out so it floated like a bright blue cloud.

"You promised me a gourmet dinner, sir. I will have that . . . first," she replied with warmth in her eyes that stole his breath.

And a gourmet feast it proved to be, beginning with smoked oysters on garlic toast points, followed by a rich beef consommé and then a rack of lamb in a marsala wine reduction sauce. The dessert was a pastry concoction filled with chocolate and whipped cream.

"I'm so stuffed you may have to carry me back to our room," she said, pushing away her rich dessert, half uneaten.

"Madame does not like ze puff pastry?" their waiter said in a heavy French accent, with one silver eyebrow raised haughtily.

"Oh, no. I've not had such a feast since Delmonico's in New York," Sky replied with a smile that disarmed him.

"Zat is no accident, madame." He puffed out his chest. "I myself accompanied ze chef from Paris to America, where we were employed at Delmonico's—until ze Clarendon brought us here to honor its guests with the finest cuisine in ze world."

Max raised his linen napkin and smothered a chuckle at Sky's look of amazement. "As I said, love, silver barons can enjoy the best of everything right here in the Rockies."

After leaving the crowded dining room, they requested coffee and cognac in their suite. Sky watched Max lace his coffee with heavy cream. When a burst of gunfire erupted down the street, he splashed a bit of it in his saucer and muttered an oath. "Damned if we'll be able to sleep tonight. I've heard stories about this place, but I must say it far exceeds its unenviable reputation."

"Well . . ." she replied, pausing until he turned his head and gazed at her, "We shall simply do something to tire us so we sleep soundly . . . that is, if you don't object to making love with a fat lady?" She patted her stomach and elicited the laugh she hoped to receive.

"Come, my plump pullet, and allow me to perform maid's duties," he said, rising and extending his hand to her.

"Only if you'll allow me to be your valet," she replied as he led her into the large bedroom, where the lights had been dimmed and the coverlet laid back by efficient hotel servants.

"Even more chocolate on the pillows," he said, holding up an exquisite chocolate rose resting on a small silver dish.

"The last thing I need is another bite of chocolate," she said, moving into his arms.

They took turns, slowly peeling the layers of formal clothing away, her silk gown, his linen suit, kicking off shoes, rolling down stockings, then with soft wet kisses, removing undergarments. "Not quite sporting," he murmured. "Men have so much less to unfasten than ladies."

"Ummm, all the better. I can taste your skin more quickly and it's more delicious than the chef's dessert," she whispered, nuzzling his chest.

When he had slipped her lace chemise over the sleek curves of her hips, she started to pull him toward the side of the bed, but he stopped her. "Not this time," he murmured, leading her to the foot of the mattress. "Sit down, if you please, love," he commanded softly.

Puzzled, Sky complied. Then he gently pushed her onto her back and raised her legs over his shoulders as he knelt in front of her. He began nibbling her inner thighs, his lips drawing closer and closer to the heat of her body's core. "No, you can't—" Her protest died on a gasp of raw pleasure.

"Yes, I can . . . and I will," he said, bringing his head to the silky black curls at the apex of her thighs.

Sky had never imagined making love this way. The heat of his mouth and the tip of his tongue worked blistering magic, leaving her too breathless to protest, or to think any more. He cupped her derriere in his hands and raised her hips like some pagan offering.

"Before dinner, when I said you looked good enough to dine upon . . . I was being quite literal, love." His voice was low and husky, brushing against her nether lips as she writhed in ecstasy.

Her hands, which at first had tried to push him away, now cradled his head, urging him to continue, her fingers buried in his pale curling hair. This was mindlessly sweet and yet scorchingly passionate at the same time. She moaned, feeling the wild contractions beginning to hum from that tiny bud, radiating through her whole being. Just as she cried out, unable to bear it another instant, he stood over her. Lifting her legs up on the bed, he plunged deep inside her, stroking hard and fast to prolong her pleasure.

But when she finally passed the crest, he stopped, making a deliberate effort to do so. Instead, he began kissing her breasts, caressing the soft curves of her body, nuzzling her throat while he held his weight on his elbows, gazing down at her face. Sky looked up into his eyes, so green, not cold now, not harsh, but mirroring the same wonder as her own. Had they just crossed some new threshold in their strange and confusing relationship? She had no time to ponder the question, for he started to move inside her again.

She responded by placing her hands on each side of his head and lowering his mouth to hers, as if sealing some unspoken bargain with the kiss. He tasted of her. But instead of offending her finishing school sensibilities, the intimacy sent a thrill quivering through her body. She locked her ankles behind his back and arched into his strokes with renewed abandon, glorying in the muffled sounds of endearment he made as his staff swelled even harder and larger inside her.

Now! The waves of culmination began within her once again, increasing as she felt him joining her in the unspeakable pleasure. Her own murmured words of love blended with his as they reached the summit together. Outside, gunshots echoed in the night and violence ruled, but joined together in their own private heaven, they were safe from its ugliness. Here was true beauty. And both of them sensed it as they lay side by side, holding each other fast, even though neither spoke a word.

At length, when their breathing returned to normal, Max pulled the covers over them to ward off the chill night air of the mountains. They lay beneath linen and brocade, locked in an embrace as they drifted off to sleep.

Toward dawn, a renewed burst of gunfire erupted near their hotel. Max turned restlessly and sat up, his nightmare beginning again as he raised his arm into firing position and issued commands. Feeling the loss of his body heat, Sky came quickly awake and reached out, taking him in her arms. She pulled him down beside her and crooned low in his ear, "Sleep, my love. I'll not let them have you."

Gradually, the sound of her voice, the softness of her touch, soothed him. She could feel the tension drain from his body as his head fell against the crook of her shoulder. Max Stanhope never awakened, but slept peacefully through the gunfire for the rest of the night, his nightmare banished.

Sky lay awake, staring at the ceiling, wondering what new direction her life was going to take as his wife. If he would have her, she was his to keep for the rest of their days . . .

Chapter Nine

$\mathcal{M}$ax awakened to the sound of gunfire, but knew that the loud reports were not the reason his sleep had ended. Sky's body was no longer beside him. He could feel her warmth lingering on the pillow. She had just arisen. He quietly looked about the room and saw her belting a blue satin robe that matched her eyes. When she felt his gaze, she looked over at him and smiled shyly. He knew what they had shared last night was the most precious memory of his life. But how could he express that to her? Did he dare?

"I'll ring for coffee. Or, would you prefer tea?" she asked.

"Coffee's fine, love," he said, sitting up. Why in flaming hell were they both acting so awkward? Of course. He realized that her first husband had most certainly never made love to her the way he had last night. Did she feel guilty? If so, her soft smile gave no indication of it, only faint embarrassment. That was good.

Then he also remembered how edgy he'd been since arriving in this accursed town of trigger-mad drunks. A disturbing thought occurred. "Did I—that is, did the shooting keep you awake?" *Did my raving nightmares frighten you to death?*

Sky shook her head. "No, I slept as peacefully as you." A lie, but one she could live with.

He watched her hips sway as she walked from the room and felt desire stir once more. A slow smile spread across his face, replacing the strained lines around his mouth. Insatiable lust for one's own wife was far from the worst thing in the world, he thought wryly as he climbed out of bed and reached for a robe.

The coffee arrived shortly and they placed an order for breakfast. While waiting for their poached trout and eggs Benedict, they perused the *Leadville Herald*. Sky read a review of an opera, then smothered a chuckle. "The Tabor Opera House next door enjoyed a rather unique performance of *Faust* last night. It seems the lady in charge of the production, a countrywoman of yours, one Miss Emma Abbott by name, inserted the old hymn, 'Nearer My God to Thee,' in the middle of the opera!"

"Well, this Miss Abbott certainly must've breathed new life into that rather depressing opus," he said. "I wonder if her addition came before or after Faust sold his soul to the devil?" He lifted an eyebrow and was delighted when she burst into laughter. "You're fabricating that. No self-respecting English actress would even consider performing *Faust*. Let me see that page."

Sky handed him the theater reviews, smirking. "Oh, Miss Abbott hasn't only produced her version of that odious German opera, but your beloved Bard as well. *Romeo and Juliet*—with a few embellishments, such as adding a trapeze to the balcony scene."

He scanned the page. "Egad! I can see it now, Romeo swinging across the stage into his true love's arms, accompanied by hoots of encouragement from the great unwashed in the audience." He shifted his normally cultivated English tones to a fair imitation of an uneducated Western twang. "'Wal, Mater Nose, didja like Shakespeare last night?' 'Shakespeare? Hell, never seen the feller, but I done bagged me a Romeo flying through the air.'" Max pulled an imaginary six-gun from his hip and took aim at the ceiling. "'I warn't sittin' by whilst some sissy in tights insulted a sweet lil' gal, askin' 'er, where fart thou?'"

Sky convulsed, doubling over and holding her sides. She

barely managed to correct his literary license. "You've mangled Juliet's line. Now stop before I die laughing."

He, too, was laughing so hard it almost hurt. Then their eyes met and the laughter abated. "We could be good for each other, m'lady, were we to make this permanent," he said softly.

"Perhaps we could, m'lord," she replied solemnly. When the smile reached his eyes, he was so very easy to love. Did she love him? Did she dare? *Would I be able to erase the darkness inside you? What of the darkness inside me?*

Sky had no answers. The waiter brought their breakfast before she could consider the disturbing questions further. They ate the superb meal in relative silence, each lost in dreams they dared not share.

Just as they finished dressing, a bellman delivered a note from Mrs. Simmons, saying that she would be delighted to receive them at one that afternoon. Scanning the missive, written on expensive vellum, Sky noted the lovely penmanship. "Well, judging from this, she certainly is qualified to write to miners' mothers and sweethearts back home."

"She's probably from a good family fallen on ill times. Perhaps immigrated to America hoping to better her lot," Max said as he stood before an oval mirror expertly straightening the short Western tie he'd chosen to wear with his black suit.

"How sad," Sky replied, "being so far from home, without family."

"Family isn't always a blessing such as yours, love. Many people are only too happy for the opportunity to begin over again. Judging from the quality of her stationery, she's done quite well."

"I applaud her success, then." She cleared her throat nervously and asked, "Is that how you felt about the Stanhopes— I mean besides your uncle Harry? What of your parents?"

He hesitated for a moment, then said, "I scarcely knew

them. We're a standoffish lot, we English, none more so than the Stanhopes. My parents packed my brother, then me off to boarding schools while we were younger than your nephew Rob."

"That's horrible. Didn't they want children?" Among her father's people, children were considered the greatest treasure of a family.

"Oh, if one is a member of the upper class, one always requires heirs, but it is not necessary to suffer them underfoot. After my parents managed the requisite 'heir and a spare,' they went their separate ways. In spite of our age difference, Edmund and I were close. Harry was largely responsible for that, inviting us for holidays at his country house. Our parents never attended."

"What of Phillip? Have you any other cousins—besides that horrid Cletus?"

Max shrugged. "I seldom saw Phillip as we were growing up. He and my brother were of an age. When his father died, running the Stanhope estates fell to him. As to other cousins, a couple of much younger girls, one elderly bachelor uncle on my maternal side . . . not much else. I never spent time with any but Phillip, and that was only because we saw him when we visited Uncle Harry. As for Cletus, after his father died, no one else wanted anything to do with him."

She walked up behind him and placed her head against his back, her arms wrapping around his waist. "In spite of everything else, I've been blessed with a wonderful family. You had your uncle. I'm glad he was there to give you a home. Perhaps after he lost his wife, you were his consolation."

Her words stung, even though he knew she did not mean them to. Some consolation he'd been. "I was a spoiled, wild boy, grief stricken over my brother's senseless death, then an indifferent student at university who rejected the career path dictated by family custom. I was not destined for the army, but the church."

"The church? You—a priest?"

He turned and looked at her expression of utter incredulity. Smiling wryly, he said, "You see the obvious problem inherent in my fulfilling family expectations."

"But you were a fine soldier and you served with the highest distinction." Sky stopped herself when she saw his eyes harden. Now was not the time to press him about his nightmares. Instead, she changed the subject, looking down at the yellow muslin day dress she'd chosen. "Will this be suitable for such an English paragon of erudition as Mrs. Simmons?"

He, too, was more than happy to shift the conversation. "It's quite splendid. Let us only hope that Frances Simmons possesses more erudition than Emma Abbott," he added with a chuckle.

They set out for the parlor house in a hired carriage whose driver was an ancient black man so wizened he appeared to be approaching the century mark. But Eustace Freeman handled his spirited horse with calm competence in spite of the incessant gunfire.

"Is Mrs. Simmons's place by chance near the red-light district?" Max inquired.

Eustace laughed, revealing several gold teeth and the fact that driving a hack in a city filled with nouveau riche miners was lucrative indeed. "Capt'n, this here whole town be one big red-light distric' with a sprinklin' 'o lee-gita-mite bidnesses here 'n yonda." As he held his horse in check when another burst of shots erupted down the street, he remarked, "A couply lawyer mans hang out they shingles hereabouts. Doan know how they keeps from starvin', bein's most folks settle things with guns."

Sky shivered and looked at Max's drawn face. "Are all boomtowns this prone to violence, Mr. Freeman?"

"Been in some bad 'uns. This be the wors' eveh, missus."

With that unsettling pronouncement, she cast about for a distraction, then saw a pharmacy on the right side of the street and read a large advertisement in the window. "Look, The Great English Remedy, a wonder elixir." She scanned the claims for what it cured as the carriage passed by, then burst into laughter. "Max, we must buy some of that for you," she said, pointing to the sign. "It is English, after all."

He read, " 'Cures loss of memory, lassitude, nocturnal emissions, noises in the head, dimness of vision and aversion to society.' " He then leaned closer to her and whispered, "If it cured my 'aversion to society,' it might also deprive you of my 'nocturnal emissions.' Best if we don't risk it, love."

"You are a vulgar lout, m'lord." Sky pouted with mock reproof, but squeezed his arm, delighted that she had succeeded in easing his tension. They rode to the edge of town, where the gunfire grew distant and the houses more lavish. Finally, Eustace pulled up in front of a grand-looking two-story place made of gray stone with a large turret jutting above the steeply pitched roof. A spacious porch stretched from the tower around the front to the opposite side of the house. Comfortable-looking rockers and swings flanked small tables, perfect places to enjoy afternoon tea. The white picket fence and meticulous yard completed the picture of homey elegance.

"It's like something from a small town in Ohio, Max. Not at all what I expected."

"I told you Mrs. Simmons's enterprise would be quite different from the Bucket of Blood," he replied with amusement as he helped her from the carriage and asked Eustace to wait.

"Happy to oblige, Capt'n," the little man said with a broad smile. If he was curious about why an English gentleman was taking his lady to a parlor house, he gave no indication.

When Max used the ornate brass door knocker, a large man whose formal dress did not conceal the fact that he was employed as a protector as well as a butler opened the door. His face was creased from sun and wind, his manner wary but polite. When Max offered him his card, saying, "We have an

appointment with Mrs. Simmons," the man bowed and ushered them inside.

"I'll give this to the lady. Please wait in there," he replied,
gesturing to a beautifully appointed sitting room immediately
off the foyer. It contained lovely oak furniture and a settee
and chairs upholstered in pale blue silk. The wallpaper was a
rose floral pattern with several oil paintings of excellent quality spaced neatly around the room. Sunlight filtered through
lace curtains.

"Mrs. Simmons could teach some Colorado millionaires a
thing or two about good taste," she said to Max.

"Thank you, Lady Ruxton. I do fear many in England—as
well as America—confuse opulence with garishness," said a
tall blonde woman with angular features and shrewd gray
eyes who stood in the doorway.

Max stepped forward, bowing as he saluted their hostess's
hand. "A pleasure to meet a countrywoman so far from home,
Mrs. Simmons."

As Max introduced his wife and they exchanged pleas-
antries, Sky noted the cultivated tone of Frances Simmons's
voice and her confident self-possession. She possessed excellent taste in clothing as well as home décor. Her simple day
dress of pale gray linen was only adorned by pearl buttons
running from the high-collared neckline to the waist. It was
well tailored and elegant, just as the lady herself.

"Please seat yourself and I shall ring for tea. I have it imported from London, a special blend. Would you prefer cream
or lemon?"

"Cream for me, lemon for my wife, if you please," Max
replied.

Seconds after she used the bellpull, a young maid curtsied
at the door and was instructed to fetch the beverage and freshly
baked scones. "A proper English tea is never complete without Marie's scones and marmalade."

"A touch of home," Max said with a nod of appreciation, although he'd grown to prefer coffee and sourdough bread.

Sky and Frances made small talk until the heavy sterling tea tray was brought in and the maid dismissed, closing the door behind her as instructed. As their hostess poured for them, she asked, "Now, shall we indulge ourselves in the deliciously crude American habit of speaking directly to the point?"

Max smiled grimly. "Yes, that would be best, considering why we're here."

Sky sat silently, her earlier animation stifled. She merely listened as Mrs. Simmons spoke.

"I have been given to understand by my friend, Mr. Drago, rapscallion Irishman that he is, that you are seeking Jonathan Framme, commonly known as Johnny Deuce. May I push crudeness to the limit and inquire why?"

"I intend to kill him," Max said calmly.

"Capital idea," Frances Simmons murmured, taking a sip of tea.

"Then you've met the man," Sky said, her mouth dry.

The older woman nodded. "Yes, I've had that misfortune. Had he not been born into a family of consequence, he should have trod the boards of the Drury. Such a superb actor when first we met, lamenting the absence of stimulating conversation in the barbaric American West. After interviewing the vile little rodent, I felt confident in introducing him to one of the young ladies in my employ. After all, he is an Oxford scholar and the son of an earl."

"Son of an earl, yes, but scarcely a 'scholar,' our Johnny. He was sent down from university after a fortnight and banished on remittance from England by his own father," Max said.

"Considering his abominable behavior here, I am not surprised. He attempted to molest my employee. Please understand, Lord and Lady Ruxton, my home is a respectable place where only polite conversation and musical diversions are offered. Nothing of a more . . . personal nature is permitted—ever," she added sternly.

While Max doubted the absolute veracity of that statement, he did not show it, but only nodded.

Sky gasped. "What happened to the poor young lady?"

"She was distressed, but unharmed. You may have noted when my assistant, Mr. Laughlin, ushered you in, that he is a large and most capable man. He ejected that scurrilous vermin before he could do more than tear one of her gowns and threaten her with a small quirt he had concealed inside his suit coat."

"I hope Mr. Laughlin gave him a sound thrashing," Max ventured and Frances nodded. "Do you know where he went to lick his wounds?"

"I have it on good authority that Framme, or Deuce as he is more appropriately called, spent several days recuperating in a house of ill repute near the center of town, on State Street, I believe. But he was ejected from there when he beat a young serving girl with that selfsame riding instrument. He then set out for the Indian Nations, announcing that no one would say him nay if he treated 'squaws' as he wished." She shuddered with revulsion. Then noting Sky's narrowed eyes, she quickly added, "Please forgive me, m'lady, for repeating his vulgar and racially repugnant language. I do so hope I have not offended you."

Sky nodded and managed a smile. "No offense taken, Mrs. Simmons. Going someplace where he can beat and torture Indian girls is exactly what I would expect of Johnny Deuce."

The following morning they rode out of Leadville. Sky observed the way Max calmed as soon as the incessant sounds of gunfire faded in the distance. His grip on the reins to their packhorse loosened and his posture in the saddle relaxed as he moved as one with the splendid gray gelding from Steve Loring's stables. She marveled at his natural horsemanship. He was as good as the finest Sioux warrior.

But then, he had been a warrior, too, in a far distant place. Pushing aside troubling thoughts about his nightmares and his unwillingness to share his past with her, Sky said, "I suppose you learned to ride as a boy in England."

He turned in the saddle and looked at her. She was clad in those same soft buckskins she'd worn the day they met. The wide-brimmed hat shaded her face from the bright morning sun. She wore a gun belt on her hip and her custom Yellow Boy was secure in the scabbard on her saddle. "Riding English is quite different from riding out West, but, yes, I did my share of jumping hedgerows as a boy, chasing after my brother."

"Did you hunt foxes?"

"My parents were keen on the hunt, but I never acquired a taste for killing innocents—animals or people."

She could see a fleeting look of pain in old memories, but he quickly turned ahead and kicked his mount to a slightly swifter pace as they started to climb a steep hill. When they crested the ridge, they paused to rest their winded horses and surveyed the panorama of jagged, snow-covered mountains dotted with golden aspens and deep green pines at the lower levels.

"I never tire of this," he said thoughtfully, removing his hat and wiping the perspiration from his forehead. The sun glinted on his hair, so pale against the bronzed skin of his face and neck. "Quite a remarkable country."

"Do you want to spend the rest of your life out West?" she asked. *Do you want to live here with me?*

"I've finished with the Queen's empire and don't much fancy Eastern American cities. Yes, I'd like to live here. This is a magnificent land, as yet not totally spoiled by the hand of civilization." He pronounced the last word with mockingly soft English sibilance.

"Whites have poured West, lured by free land, the quick riches of gold and silver, the desire to conquer the wilderness . . . and destroy its original inhabitants," she said.

"You say that, yet you're more white than Sioux. Where do you choose to belong, Sky Eyes? Do you want to return to Dakota Territory when we've finished our business?" he asked, not certain if he would ever be free of Will Brewster's shadow there.

"My father's family accepts me. You've seen how most whites treat me, not quite certain of my origins, whether I'm a 'squaw' or a lady."

"You are your own woman. Better than any 'lady' I've ever met. Don't try to be anything but true to yourself."

"Does being true to myself mean giving up my search for Deuce?" The words came as a knee-jerk reaction, spoiling the tender moment. She regretted them the instant they left her lips.

Max simply shrugged, his expression unreadable. "Only you know what will give you peace." With that he turned the gray about and headed down the ridge . . . ever closer to Johnny Deuce.

Sky followed the packhorse, deep in thought, feeling more confused by her conflicting emotions than ever.

They reached the Nations after nearly a week on the trail, during which time they shared camp chores and slept beneath the stars, making love in their blankets while lying on the hard earth. No more was spoken about giving up the quest to kill Deuce . . . or what would happen to their marriage after the deed was done.

If it could be done. They rode through a nameless host of squalid settlements composed of mud huts and ragged tents. Crude wooden saloons were the most substantial structures, serving dusty cattlemen who stopped on their way from Texas to the railheads in Kansas. Life here was cheap, violent and short. Outlaws from everywhere fled to the isolated no-man's land known as the Indian Nations. No single tribe owned the land and no government kept order. It was not an organized territory, but rather a vague jurisdiction contested by Kansas farmers, Eastern railroad barons, Texas cattlemen and the scores of tribes of Indians herded there by the Great White Father in Washington.

No one recalled an Englishman with a fetish for whipping "Injun squaws." As they neared the Red River, the boundary line with Texas, the tension growing between Max and Sky drew close to the boiling point. How long could they continue? Had Frances Simmons's information been wrong?

Max's nightmares roused them both from sleep repeatedly. When she attempted to soothe him, he withdrew, walking into the darkness far from their campfire, unwilling to speak of the demons eating away at his soul. Often he would not reappear until dawn. Then, haggard and sullen, he would pretend nothing had happened during the night. They would break camp and resume their journey.

At times, Sky wondered if she, too, would end up seeing the face of Johnny Deuce in nightmares for the rest of her life. Will had told her killing his murderer would destroy her life. Perhaps he had been right. Was she throwing away a chance to redeem not only Max's life but also her own because of her thirst for vengeance?

When they rode into the town of Tumbleweed, it appeared little different from a dozen before it, rough, dirty and mean-spirited, as evidenced by a trio of drunks who surrounded a wizened Indian man in the dusty street. They had pulled him from his horse and were shouting curses as they punched and kicked him.

Sky and Max exchanged glances and rode toward the fracas, both noting that none of the men or whores standing on the sidelines appeared the least sympathetic to the old man's plight. The residents simply watched the "show."

"Back me up," he whispered harshly as he dismounted. "Watch the crowd in case anyone tries to interfere." With that he walked up behind the tall, lanky bully rearing back for another kick at their victim. The Limey's Smith & Wesson came from his holster with blurring speed. He quickly brought the barrel down across the back of the man's head, dropping him to the ground, out cold.

Then the weapon pointed levelly at the unconscious man's two associates. One, overly fond of biscuits and gravy judging by the size of the paunch overhanging his belt buckle, touched the handle of the Colt Thuer Conversion revolver in his holster. "I wouldn't do that, old chap," Max said conversationally.

Behind him Sky sat on her horse, the Yellow Boy's barrel moving back and forth in warning. The hammer of the Winchester was cocked. "Are you going to shoot him, Limey?" she asked, mimicking his casual tone.

The fat man jerked his hand away from his Colt as if it were the top of a red-hot cookstove and raised both arms so quickly one filthy flannel shirtsleeve ripped, revealing a malodorous hairy armpit. "Are you the . . . *the* Limey?" he croaked.

Max nodded, revealing a flash of white teeth. The smile did not reach his stone-cold green eyes as they swept over the fat man and his squat companion. "Just so."

"Oh, shit, this ain't good, Ralphie," the smaller man whispered. Like a bird mesmerized by a rattler, he was too frozen with terror even to turn his head from Max to his friend.

The fat man observed Max's wolfish grin and started shifting from one foot to the other, his Adam's apple bobbing up and down beneath the fatty pouch hanging from his jawline. "Lookie, please, Mr. Limey, they ain't no wanted posters on me er Winnie er Peetie neither," he said, gesturing to their companion sprawled in the dirt, moaning.

"Is that a fact?" Max replied as if dubious.

"Don't believe him, Limey. He looks like a killer to me. Look at those piggy little eyes," Sky said, still watching the crowd, trying to gauge their mood. So far they appeared to be amused, but she knew that could change in an instant.

So did Max, as he said, "I believe you gentlemen should meet my, ah, associate." He nodded to Sky. "This is Calamity Jane, trained by the prince of pistoleros, James Butler Hickok himself. She can shoot out a gnat's eyes at fifty feet."

"She don't need to demonstrate on us," Ralphie pleaded. "We wuz jest tryin' to find out where this here ole Injun got hisself sech a good piece of horseflesh. Bet he stole it."

"Yeah, he gots to have stole it," Winnie echoed hopefully, eyeing the tall old man who was now picking himself up from the ground and dusting off his bare arms and buckskin leggings.

Beside him stood a handsome mouse-brown gruella with a gleaming black mane and tail. "A fine specimen, indeed," Max concurred. "Perhaps we should ask him whether or not the horse belongs to him."

"H-he don't speak no English," Ralphie volunteered.

"By the sounds of it, neither do you," Sky said pleasantly as she dismounted and stepped forward. Her expression was icy. "I suggest we shoot them, Limey."

"B-b-but he's jest a Injun," Winnie interjected, as if trying to appeal to the Limey's white sensibilities.

Max could sense Sky's anger without looking at her. "Bloody hell, I was hoping to walk away without killing you, but now you've put the pot to boil. You see, gentlemen, the reason my partner is so furious is that she's part Indian herself."

Both Ralphie and Winnie gulped in unison, blanching white as flour. "We didn't mean no offense, ma'am, honest," Winnie begged.

"He's the one whut said it—not me," Ralphie supplied, backing away from his former friend.

Max's eyes swept the crowd. They all appeared more interested in seeing some gunplay than in having a breed and a foreigner taken down a notch. "Calamity, even in this godforsaken place, we can't just shoot them without giving them a sporting chance. What say we allow them to draw first?" he suggested calmly.

"Why not?" she replied through gritted teeth, uncocking the Yellow Boy and lowering it to her side.

Max slipped his Smith & Wesson into its holster so smoothly, neither man could follow the movement.

Winnie started moaning. "Oh, shit, oh, shit, this is bad, Ralphie."

He was not telling the fat man anything he did not already know. "Lookee here, I kin make it up to the old Injun. I got me some cash money here from my last job." Ralphie pointed to his left pocket.

Max nodded approval as he very slowly reached down and pulled out a wad of bills. He waddled over to the old Indian, who stood with his arms crossed on his chest, ramrod straight and dignified in spite of the bloody evidence of his recent beating. But when the fat man began to search for a place to deposit the money, he found that his victim's buckskin leggings and leather vest had no pockets. Neither did the old man reach out for the bribe, but rather stared straight ahead as if the fat white man were invisible.

By this time, Ralphie was virtually sobbing in frustration and low rumbles of coarse laughter and catcalls had erupted in the crowd. Ralphie, Winnie and their semiconscious friend were apparently not well-liked in Tumbleweed. Then Winnie spied the old man's leather sack lying in the street beneath the horse's hooves. "Put it in his bag, yew turd," he hissed at the distraught Ralphie.

Taking his cue, the fat man lurched over to the horse and squatted clumsily down, seizing the pouch and stuffing the money inside it. He grunted as he struggled back to his feet, sweat running in rivers down his face. "We wuz only funnin', Granpop, honest," he said to the stolid Indian. "Yew keep yer horse. Yessiree." He looked pleadingly at Max.

"I don't know. Since the gentleman has made reparations for his unwarranted attack, it might be construed as murder if we shoot him and his charming fellows." Max casually turned his back on the men and whispered to Sky, "Love, you are facing more dead brain tissue than one could find on the laboratory slab at the London School of Medicine."

Sky's eyes never left the two quaking bullies as they began inching away, deserting their moaning friend still lying in the dirt. Then a grim smile spread across her face. "My, look at poor Ralphie. He's just committed an act of public indecency," she said.

Max turned to observe the stain at the crotch of the fat man's breeches as it moved down his leg with great rapidity, no doubt filling his scuffed, filthy boots. "All right, you two, pick up your companion and be gone," he commanded sternly.

"Well done, Limey," she said as the men each grabbed an arm of their downed friend and dragged him around the corner to jeers from the crowd. She turned to the elderly Indian man to ask if he was badly injured, but his dark fathomless eyes were fixed on Max, who had just removed his hat to wipe the perspiration from his forehead.

"Praise the Powers!" the old man cried as he pointed to Max. "The Pale Moon Stalker has come!"

Chapter Ten

The old man had spoken the words in a foreign tongue that Max did not understand. The Indian studied the white man with piercing dark eyes. Max felt peculiarly unnerved by the intense scrutiny. Turning to Sky, he asked, "What is he saying?"

"It's Cheyenne, but I only know a smattering of the language. He calls you the Pale Moon Stalker. It was your hair, that was what caused him to name you—almost as if he recognized you."

"That might not be good. Lots of men recognize the Limey. Usually they're not friendly. Can you communicate with him?" he asked.

"I'll try." She reached out to the tall old man, placing her hand on his arm, then said in halting Cheyenne, "I am called Sky Eyes of the Ehanktonwon, Grandfather. This is my husband, Max Stanhope. Who are you, and why do you call him Pale Moon Stalker?"

"I knew you were of the blood, even though it runs thin in your veins," he replied in Sioux that was far more fluent than her attempt at his language. "I am called True Dreamer and many times in medicine dreams I have seen this man with hair as pale as a cold winter moon. Among the whites, he is a hunter of evil men, is this not true?"

Sky nodded, not at all certain how the old man could know this or what it meant. "We track an evil man now," she said carefully.

"I know." True Dreamer's assurance appeared unshakable as he continued. "The man you stalk is the same one who has stolen my granddaughter Fawn. He comes from across the great waters, from the same place as the Pale Moon Stalker. I will guide you to where this evil one hides."

Sky's heart began racing. How could the old man know this . . . unless he truly had medicine dreams? She had known very few among her people with this gift, but had seen many charlatans over the years.

Sensing her confusion, Max interrupted. "What's going on, love?"

She shook her head. "Let me think." She asked True Dreamer, "How do you know where the man we seek is?"

"You have many questions, Daughter. But this is not the place or the time to answer them," he said, gazing at the remnants of the crowd staring at them. "I invite you and your man to share my campfire this night. Then I will explain many things that you wish to know."

Sky looked at Max and started to translate the invitation, but before she could utter a word, the old man said in clear but slightly halting English, "Pale Moon Stalker, I would be honored if you and your wife would come with me. I have . . . news . . . you will welcome."

Max and Sky exchanged startled glances before he said to her, "I repeat, what in flaming hell is going on?"

"He knows who you are—and that you and Deuce are both English. He's a medicine man among his people and he's had a vision about how to find our quarry. I think it's worth a try. Let's accept his invitation."

Max sighed, replacing his hat on his head. "Considering that every bed or pile of straw in this noisome town is crawling with vermin, sleeping under the stars once again holds considerably more appeal." He nodded politely to the old man. "We would be pleased to accept your kind offer."

As if expecting this acquiescence, True Dreamer grunted and swung onto the gruella with the effortless grace of a much younger man. "Come."

With that, he kicked his horse into a brisk trot, heading down the dusty street. Max and Sky mounted up and followed. The ride was brief, just a few miles outside of Tumbleweed. True Dreamer had chosen his campsite judiciously. It was well hidden from the trail and concealed by dense brush and scrub oak growing alongside a small, clear stream. Max had the feeling that everything the old man did was done judiciously.

Dusk fell like a silver-gray shroud as they dismounted. The old man had a fire laid, ready to light. A few meager possessions were arranged neatly on the ground. A brace of rabbits, freshly killed, hung suspended from one of the higher tree limbs. Had he been expecting them before he rode into town? Max noted a rifle, a Springfield breechloader, old but serviceable, leaning against the tree trunk. Why had he not gone to Tumbleweed armed?

The hairs on the back of his neck prickled in warning, but the man called True Dreamer started the fire and then went about cleaning his kills and spitting them on green twigs. Sky, apparently accepting the situation, pulled a sack of beans and a pot from their packhorse and started to prepare them. His stomach growled. Well, better to receive whatever news the medicine man had on a full stomach, he supposed, placing grounds in the tin coffeepot. He walked to the stream and filled it with water, then set it on the fire to boil.

After the old man chanted a brief benediction to whatever deity his people worshipped, they ate in companionable silence. In deference to her role as a woman traveling with "warriors," Sky took their dirty utensils and carried them to the stream to wash them, leaving her husband and True Dreamer alone by the flickering campfire.

When she returned, she was startled to see that Max had already retired to his bedroll and was soundly asleep. The wizened Cheyenne sat on the bare earth nearby, chanting softly as he wafted smoke toward the sleeper from a small dish directly above Max's head. The wisps True Dreamer fanned over Max smelled familiar to her—white sage, a healing plant used by her people as well as other High Plains Indians.

Without turning his head, he smiled and spoke softly in Sioux, "Now he rests undisturbed for the first time in a great long while." He stared with kindly eyes at the sleeping Englishman. The old man's face was burnished by the light of the fire, making his coppery skin seem to glow from within.

The hairs along Sky's arms and neck began to rise. "Max usually doesn't sleep this soundly," she said hesitantly. "You've drugged him." Yet, as she looked at Max's peaceful expression, she knew her voice held no condemnation. "You take much upon yourself, Grandfather."

He interrupted her by placing his finger to his lips, indicating she should lower her voice. "That is a privilege of the old. I would never do anything to harm the Pale Moon Stalker. He will save my granddaughter from the weasel-snake who holds her prisoner. Please sit. You and I must speak of many things while your man sleeps."

He gestured to the campfire several yards away, then arose with amazing gracefulness and walked over to it. They took their places facing each other across the fire. "He will awaken in the morning refreshed after happy dreams. Now he plays with an older boy . . . his brother, perhaps. The dark warriors will not return this night."

Sky gasped. "What do you know of these dark warriors?" she asked quietly, her heart hammering.

"The Powers have shown me that he was a soldier of the Great Mother Queen who rules across the waters. He wore a red coat . . ." His eyes stared beyond the flames to where Max slept, as if seeing another time, another place.

Sky shivered, knowing that she was truly in the presence of

a great medicine man. She said nothing, but waited for him to continue.

"The Pale Moon Stalker led his soldiers in a battle against warriors whose skin was the color of your hair, Daughter. Again and again the dark warriors came, brave and fierce. Their numbers were like the leaves rolling across the ground in the time of the Hunting Moon . . . many more warriors than we had in the Valley of the Greasy Grass where we destroyed the Long Hair Custer. Your man had many fewer soldiers than Long Hair. Yet they threw back the dark ones time and again."

He closed his eyes for a moment, as if living that horrendous experience himself. "It was a fine battle with much bravery on both sides." Then he nodded and opened his eyes, fixing them on her as if waiting for her to speak, and knowing what she would say before she said it.

"To him it is painful, terrible. He cries out in his sleep." Her voice choked, remembering the way Max bolted upright in bed, the expression in his eyes so haunted by the past that held him prisoner.

"Yes, the past holds him prisoner," True Dreamer echoed aloud. "He sees so many dead, black and white . . . and he feels guilt. This is what calls up the dead warriors night after night. The very battle he won in the real world, he is losing in his dreams. It robs him bit by bit of his spirit, leaving only darkness. There is much darkness inside him . . . as there is in you, Daughter, stripping away what your first husband would call your souls."

"What do you know of my first husband?" she asked, dreading the answer, knowing her quest for vengeance went against everything Will had believed in. She had broken her pledge to him, made as he lay dying. Yes, there was great darkness in her soul.

"It is difficult for one such as you, pulled between two worlds, red and white. Do you think the Powers have shown me the Pale Moon Stalker's story and not your own? In dreams, I have seen you standing beside him. You guard him. It is a fitting honor for a Sioux warrior-woman . . ." He paused and smiled at her gently, adding, "Even if your blood is thin."

"I have lived among the whites and been educated in their schools to help my Ehanktonwon family."

True Dreamer nodded again. "You have done this with the aid of your first husband. He was a holy man among the whites with a good heart for our peoples . . . and he was killed by an evil one with the eyes of a weasel and a heart as cold as a snake's. Do you believe you sought out the Pale Moon Stalker to achieve the vengeance you call justice against this weasel-snake?"

She swallowed hard. Yet when she met the old man's eyes, she saw no condemnation there, only gentle patience. "We made a bargain . . ."

True Dreamer shook his head and smiled at her. "You are mistaken. The Powers, the ones your people call Grandfather Spirit, have brought you and the Pale Moon Stalker together to heal each other, Sky Eyes of the Sioux."

Sky's mouth was suddenly dry, her heart pounding as she digested what he was saying. Was it true? How else could he know what he did about her and Max? "Perhaps I have too much white blood to understand," she said hesitantly . . . but hopefully.

The old man sighed in resignation. "Yes, and your man is all white, yet the Powers that control our fate have woven a design. No mere human, red or white, can change it." His chuckle sounded rusty as he looked over at Max once more. "Right now your man's dreams have changed. He is with his woman. There is no more bargain."

She knew her cheeks were hot with embarrassment. Did Max dream of her . . . of them, making love passionately as they had done so many times since their supposed marriage of convenience? If the old man's visions were right about this . . .

He interrupted her unsettling yet wistful ruminations, saying, "Tomorrow you will convince your man to allow me to accompany you on your journey. When we enter a white man's village, no matter how large, I will know if the weasel-snake is there. Together, we will find him and rescue my granddaughter."

Sky stared into his dark mesmerizing eyes. "Yes, I will convince him," she said in a shaky voice.

"Good. But I do not think it wise to tell him the true reason I join you. He will not believe. You will think of another way." He chuckled again. "Women always can."

In the morning, Sky awakened to the heavenly aroma of fresh brewed coffee. A thoroughly rested Max poured a cup and handed it to her when she approached the fire. He already had beans soaking and bacon in the skillet ready to place on the fire. "Good morning, love. You must've been exhausted—or did that old medicine man keep you up with his yarns all night?"

She accepted the tin cup and swallowed gratefully. "Where is True Dreamer?"

"Probably at his morning toilet. I heard some splashing upstream as I was finishing a quick bath myself. Bloody cold water." Max smiled wryly. "When I first came to America, I shared the common British prejudice of equating soap with civilization."

"In other words, you believed all Indians lacked proper hygiene," she said, knowing he now knew better.

"Imagine my surprise when I found many actually break the ice on streams to bathe every morning, even in coldest winter."

Sky nodded. "Daily ablutions are part of morning rituals for plains tribes." As Max placed the skillet on the fire and turned the bacon strips, she sipped her coffee, mulling over how to explain True Dreamer's request to join them. Using subterfuge on a man as clever as Max would never work. He was the least gullible or malleable male she'd ever met. She would have to risk the truth.

"Max, True Dreamer wants to ride with us after Deuce. I think it would be a good idea." She waited to see if he'd object.

But he merely cocked his head and looked at her. "To what end, love? We'll bring his granddaughter to him after we've run our quarry to ground."

"We've not had much luck so far picking up Deuce's trail. Perhaps the old man can help us. He certainly has a vested interest in finding the killer he calls the weasel-snake."

"What form would this help take, pray?" he asked, studying her with keen green eyes.

As her brother would say, "In for a dime, in for a dollar." "True Dreamer says if we get close to Deuce he'll be able to tell."

Max continued turning bacon as he added the beans to the sizzling grease. "And you believe him?"

"As Uncle Horace would say, 'There are more things in heaven and earth than are dreamt of in your philosophy . . . '" She nodded. "Yes, Max, I believe him."

He sat back to let the beans and bacon simmer, sighing. "I don't know. He's spry, but bloody hell, he must be ancient. He'll hold us back, Sky." He did not dare say that the old man might get in the way if he had to protect his wife under fire.

"You watched him ride yesterday, after the beating he took in that awful town. He's strong as a bull and he has an excellent horse. He won't hold us back. In fact, I think he'll guide us directly to Deuce. He really is a powerful medicine man."

He looked at her, startled.

"I was skeptical at first," she admitted, plunging ahead. "But he knows all about us—about your nightmares."

Max sucked in his breath and cursed. "What of 'my nightmares'?" he asked with icicles in his voice. Damn, all those nights traveling from Leadville. He'd revealed as much as he'd feared he had, maybe more.

"I knew you had terrible dreams about a battle back when you were a soldier—but that was all I knew. He's seen everything, Max. The thousands upon thousands of what he calls dark warriors who keep charging the soldiers under your command . . . and how guilty you feel because so many men died." Her voice was hushed now, and she was almost afraid to meet his cold eyes.

He squatted in front of the fire and stirred the skillet's contents with swift, angry motions. She'd heard his raving—damn, bloody damn! Of course, how could she not have by this time? How often, he wondered, had she lived his own personal hell with him as they lay side by side since becoming lovers? He did not ask, only shoved the skillet away from the fire and sat back, waiting for her to continue. "There is more?"

Sky swallowed for courage. "Yes. He even saw into your dreams last night. He told me that you were with another boy."

"It was my brother Edmund. He was teaching me to play rugby." Some of the coldness left his voice. Then he remembered that he'd also dreamed about his wife . . . vividly. He picked up the skillet without looking at her. Had the old man told her that, too?

Encouraged, Sky continued. "He . . . he knew how Will died . . . and that I've broken my oath to him by seeking you out to kill Deuce."

Max almost dropped the skillet into the fire this time. He placed it on the ground and shook his head in amazement, brushing his hand over his eyes. "I guess he isn't a fake. I met a few genuine mystics in India. Frightening chaps. Saw them in Africa, too, different names, same strange powers."

She placed her hand on his arm. "Can True Dreamer come with us?"

He gave a weary chuckle without mirth. "Bloody hell, I'd be afraid to try stopping him."

As if on cue, the old man emerged from the brush carrying an old Springfield rifle slung over his shoulder. His hair was still wet from his bath. He deposited the weapon by his bedroll, then walked to the fire and squatted down effortlessly. "That smells good," he said in English, looking into the skillet.

Max stared at True Dreamer speculatively. "My wife tells me that you can help us find Deuce," he said simply.

The Cheyenne nodded, accepting a tin plate of bacon and beans that Sky dished up. "Thank you, Daughter." To Max he said, "Yes, Pale Moon Stalker. The Indian agent who has a trading post where my people get food and blankets, he has a good heart for us. Not like many others. He said to me the weasel-snake told him he was going to Texas."

Max sighed. "There is quite a bit of Texas, Grandfather."

Undisturbed by the Englishman's pronouncement, True Dreamer added with utter certainty, "He goes to a place called Fort Worth."

The Pale Moon Stalker smiled coldly. "Yes, that would be our Johnny's kind of place. A wide-open cow town with plenty of saloons, gambling halls and people who don't ask questions. To Fort Worth we go, to find a weasel-snake."

The flat terrain of the western part of the Indian Nations gradually gave way to rolling hills and then the Wichita Mountains cropped up on the southern skyline. It was a dry, brushy land dotted with large boulders and sparse plains grasses. The rivers in summer's heat were little more than rocky gullies gouged out during torrential spring rainstorms. Now all was still and dry. Even the rattlers barely moved while the buzzards seemed to circle more lazily than they had farther north.

The trio rode southeast, headed for the big muddy river whose runoff of rust-colored soil gave it the name of Red. Once they crossed it they would be in Texas. Whatever strange potions or medicine prayers the old man employed, they appeared to help Max sleep through the nights without fearful dreams. The travelers fell into a pattern of rising just before dawn and making camp in midafternoon to avoid the worst of the heat.

With the stubby bluffs of the Wichitas directly ahead, Max reined in his horse and casually removed his hat, wiping the sweat from his forehead with his shirtsleeve as he said, "Don't look up now . . . have you seen it?"

Sky and True Dreamer stopped beside him. She fought the urge to stare at the sharp ridge in front of them, but the old man grunted, dismounting calmly as he commanded her in English, "Get down from your horse."

"I take that as a yes," Max said, casually turning his horse so as to shield his wife while she dismounted and led her mare toward the trickling stream where True Dreamer stood. When he swung down and joined them, she gave him a puzzled look.

"What is there to see?" she asked, trying to look at the skyline without raising her head visibly.

"A flash of light coming from the top of that bluff," Max replied. "A glint of sunlight on a rifle barrel . . . or perhaps a spyglass."

"I wondered how soon you would notice it," the Cheyenne replied. "For an English, you have good eyes."

Max snorted. "Thank you, I think. This could be dangerous. McKerrish's money has a long reach." He looked at the old man, wondering if he would know about the incident on the train.

Sky disliked the way the men were ignoring her, but they had seen the spyglass and she had not, she reminded herself.

Then she remembered the other attacks on them. "It might not be McKerrish's men. We were attacked in Central Park and I was nearly shot outside St. Louis, remember?"

Max nodded. "Whoever it is, we're within range—at least for high-powered rifles. Interesting that they haven't opened fire."

"Perhaps they're bad shots, waiting for us to draw nearer," she replied.

"How far from here to there?" he asked True Dreamer.

"Four or five arrow flights," the old man replied.

Max sighed and looked at Sky for an explanation.

"Eight hundred to a thousand yards," she said.

"So, the question is how do we get near enough to catch them without having them open fire." He looked at the old man, again wondering how long he had known about the ambush . . . if it was an ambush.

Before anyone answered him, three shots rang out in rapid succession, echoing down from the bluff. "Get down!" he hissed at Sky, shoving her behind a rock pile by the side of the stream as he yanked his rifle from its scabbard and knelt protectively in front of her.

But True Dreamer stood calmly. "It is finished, I think," he said serenely.

Max cautiously moved to his skittering horse and removed a glass from his saddlebags to see what was going on above them. Damned if he was not starting to trust the old man's intuition! Once he swept the ridgeline, he muttered, "Flaming hell, would you look at that? There are three of them. One appears to be a woman."

Sky seized the glass from him and peered through it. "It's the woman from St. Louis and her helpers!" she said excitedly, observing the small female figure wearing a sand-colored pith helmet and English riding breeches. "She must be English. Jodhpurs in the Indian Nations, for heaven's sake!"

As if he had orchestrated the whole bizarre event, True Dreamer said, "She is an English, yes." But he never looked at the horizon.

Max did, taking the glass from his wife and peering through it. "This I have to see." The woman had been joined by two small brown men who could have been southwestern Indians but for their goatees. As the trio stood on the ridgeline, the woman removed her pith helmet, revealing close-cropped pale blonde hair almost the color of his own. She raised a large revolver and fired three more shots into the air, waving them to come forward.

Max looked at True Dreamer. "Should we trust her?"

"If she wanted us dead, we would be feeding the beaked ones circling above even now."

"Then let us accept her invitation . . . with all due caution," he replied, holding his rifle across his saddle as he mounted.

"We should thank her. She may have saved our lives—mine for the second time," Sky said, already swinging onto her horse.

Both she and her husband noted that the old man had never even readied his rifle.

They rode slowly toward the bluff, Max in the lead, using brush and rocks for cover as they climbed a twisting trail to the place where the Englishwoman and her men had stood. When they crested the hill, they saw a sight that caused even Max to turn pale. "Bloody hell!"

Sky fought her rising gorge as she looked down.

True Dreamer only made a grunting sound of approval.

Chapter Eleven

$\mathcal{D}$on't look at them!" Max said tightly to Sky, but she could not stop staring at the two men sprawled on the rocky soil. Their throats had been slashed so completely that they had been decapitated, the heads lying several feet from the bodies. Blood soaked into the already red earth, darkening it in ever widening circles.

"There's a note pinned to the back of that one," she said, pointing to the corpse on the left.

Max quickly dismounted and pulled it free, then read aloud, "Lord and Lady Ruxton, you are being hunted. Please have a care. I have an interest in your continued good health. It's signed with a single initial, 'R.' Looks like a woman's flowing handwriting."

"I never saw her before that day in St. Louis," Sky said, looking questioningly at Max. "She knew our title. She is English." Then she shifted her attention to the serene Cheyenne who sat on his horse, as unconcerned as if nothing out of the ordinary had happened.

Sensing her unasked question, the old man said, "The Powers do not reveal everything to me, child. I only know the woman means you no harm."

Max knelt, examining the weapons the men had been preparing to use. "These chaps were professional marksmen. This is a Ballard rifle, the Pacific model, I would say. Either .44-100 or .45-100 caliber. The range is about a thousand yards. And both rifles have telescopic sights on them."

"They were going to shoot us any moment," Sky said in a choked voice.

"No, it was not fated to be so," True Dreamer replied.

Now Max stood and examined a tripod with a small instrument on it standing near the edge of the bluff. "This is a wind gauge. Very expensive. Whoever employed the dead men has decided to spend considerably more since those pathetic thugs in New York and St. Louis failed."

"Or, it could be McKerrish," she said, turning her head when a swarm of flies began to feast on the open cavities of the dead men's necks.

"I doubt it. We didn't run afoul of him until we were leaving Colorado, but this mysterious Englishwoman and her deadly companions rescued you in St. Louis."

"Who were those little men?" she asked. "If not for the mustaches, I would've guessed Apaches."

"Better than Apaches," True Dreamer said. "They move like spirits. Leave no sign. Very powerful medicine." Again, he grunted in approval.

"Think of them as Apaches from hell," Max replied to both of them. "They're Gurkhas, the world's most lethal swordsmen. From Nepal. They've served the British Crown as mercenaries for generations. This gory mess was done by their favorite weapon, the khukuri, a large curved knife capable of separating a man's head from his neck with a single slash. It's said once a Gurkha withdraws his khukuri, it must drink blood—if not the enemy's, then the owner must slash himself to feed it before he sheathes it again."

"That's barbaric," Sky whispered in horrified wonder. "But I'm glad they're on our side."

"So far," Max replied cynically. "Let's ride."

True Dreamer had already turned his horse away from the carnage and headed back down the trail.

* * *

They reached the Red River the next afternoon. Surveying the wide, fast-running water, Max eyed his wife and the old man. "Crossing could be rather chancy."

"Why is the water so high? It's been dry all the way here," Sky said.

"One good cloudburst to the northwest would serve," Max replied. "I imagine the water's no more than four or five feet deep in most places, but the current's swift enough to knock a rider from a horse. We'll need to take some precautions. Tie a line from saddle to saddle so if one of our horses stumbles, the rider will have something to hold on to."

He dismounted and dug a length of rope from one of the packs on their spare horse, wishing desperately that there were a few sturdy large trees nearby to which he could secure a line, but the vegetation was brushy and low growing. In the far distance across the vast river, he could see a lone oak standing, a good hundred yards from shore. *A fine lot of good that'll do us.*

Ever since Edmund had drowned, he'd had an intense dislike of lakes and rivers . . . especially ones swollen by recent rain. "I'll lead. Sky, you come next, True Dreamer, if you'd be so kind as to take our packhorse and follow?"

The old man nodded calmly, as if he crossed treacherous rivers on a daily basis. He accepted the rope that Max handed him, twisting it about his wrist and securing the end of it to the gear on the packhorse.

They set out, the horses kicking up the soft mud and rocks in the shallows as Max led the way, slowly. "At least it's too shallow to have sawyers or huge clumps of driftwood and debris like the Missouri," Sky said.

"Keep trying to assure yourself, love, but hold tight to that rope," Max replied grimly. They'd made it just past the middle of the river when his horse suddenly stumbled, almost pitching him headfirst into the water.

"Max!" Sky cried out, releasing her grip on the safety rope to urge her horse closer to him.

He kept his seat and tried to calm the frightened animal as it thrashed. "Stay back," he ordered his wife, but just as he uttered the words, her horse went down in the same trough, tossing her into the swift current. Hearing her scream almost froze him, but he yanked fiercely on his horse's reins, letting go of the rope as he turned downriver. His big buckskin lumbered after Sky's bobbing head, but she was moving far faster.

The old man held the rope and reins to their pack animal. He began chanting a prayer as he watched Max throw himself in frustration from his horse and swim furiously. Releasing the packhorse so that it headed toward the Texas shore, True Dreamer kicked his mount and turned it downriver after his friends.

Sky struggled to stay above water. Normally she was a strong swimmer, but the current was so powerful as they approached a narrowing bend in the river that she could do little more than thrash helplessly. When she saw Max behind her, she renewed her attempt to reach the shore, fearful he would drown trying to save her. She made little headway, but he closed the distance between them with agonizingly exhausting strokes.

Finally, she was pushed against a large boulder jutting from the riverbed and she held fast to it until he reached her. He flung his body over hers, holding them both against the rock. His hair was plastered to his skull and his breathing was labored. She could feel his heart pound as he shielded her from the fury of the current.

"We . . . have to . . . make it . . . to shore," he gasped out.

Sky nodded her understanding. "I'm ready when you catch your breath," she said, finding her earlier panic subsiding. Her own death held far less terror for her than the idea of watching her husband drown trying to save her when she'd foolishly endangered them both.

At length, he said in a far stronger voice, "Hold tightly to my belt. I think I can walk from here if the current doesn't knock me down . . . or there aren't any more sudden drop-offs. Whatever you do, don't let go."

They pushed off the boulder with Max leading while Sky held fast to him, trying to keep her own footing on the rocky, uneven river bottom. The water was well above Max's waist and came up to her breasts. His greater body weight served them well until he stepped into a trough and lost his balance, knocking them both into the current once more. He seized her arm and raised it, saying, "Lock your hands around my neck," as he started to swim.

If only the river were not so muddy and the bottom so obscured, they might have found shallows, but it was a deep murky rust brown filled with whirlpools and eddies. In their struggling, neither of them saw the old Cheyenne on his gruella, plodding carefully toward them—until the end of the safety rope struck Max across his shoulder. Sky grabbed a hold of it, crying out, "Max, hold on to the rope!"

Seeing True Dreamer reining in his horse twenty feet from them, holding the line taut, Max twisted the rope around his arm and held Sky tightly. Ever so slowly, the old man pulled them toward the shore until they reached knee-deep shallows. Holding on to each other, they stumbled through the water with soaked boots and moccasins impeding their progress each step of the way.

As soon as they reached the shore and a dry, grassy piece of ground, Max pulled her down. "Sit and catch your breath," he said, coughing, as he dropped to his knees.

True Dreamer dismounted a dozen yards away and his gruella ambled over to where the packhorse was grazing. When he drew near them, he nodded his approval. "We should camp here this night, I think," was all he said, then bent down, starting to gather dry brush for a fire.

"We owe you our lives, my friend," Max said.

The old man merely nodded.

Sky smiled and said, "He would only tell you that the Powers intended this to happen." She reached up and caressed his jaw. "You risked your life to save me."

"I'm your husband, Sky. What else would I do?" he asked simply, suddenly overwhelmed by the intensity of his love for her. Would it frighten her if he told her how he felt? Was she still in love with her priest—or at least, haunted by him? They remained on the road to revenge, he reminded himself. Killing men was something at which he excelled. Loving a woman . . . that was another matter, entirely new to him.

Sky saw his eyes darken, not with the hard, dangerous glitter of the past, but with another emotion that was more difficult to read. Impulsively, she raised her face to his and kissed him softly. "Thank you, husband," she said softly.

His face broke into a smile as he lifted her shiny plait of soaking-wet black hair. "You'd best loosen it and brush the Red River out. We'll need to change into dry clothes, too." He planted a swift kiss on the tip of her nose, then stood up and walked over to the packhorse to unload their gear from the waterproof canvas.

Sky sat, dreamily unplaiting her hair and then pulling off her moccasins as she watched Max. He was the most splendidly handsome man she'd ever seen . . . and he was hers—at least until Johnny Deuce was dead. What then? He said he wanted theirs to be a true marriage. Could they make it work? She didn't know, but was certain of one thing. She desired him with a desperation that went far beyond gratitude.

The flames of the campfire died down low and a brilliant tapestry of stars filled the vastness of the sky above them. They feasted ravenously on a brace of rabbits True Dreamer had shot while they made camp. After the meal, as she washed up the tinware, the old man announced that he had need of time alone for the Powers to speak to him. He took his sleeping gear and rifle and vanished in the brushy grass and shrubs lining the riverbank, leaving them alone.

Max made up their bedrolls side by side a distance from the fire, all the while watching her at her simple chore. Then he looked down at his hands and realized he was trembling. This went far beyond mere lust. He wanted her so badly he ached with it. *Bloody lovesick schoolboy!* Yet he could not feel angry with himself for what he felt.

Sky could sense that he was watching her. When she turned and looked over her shoulder at him, their gazes met across the flickering firelight. Gone was the harsh, dangerous gunman. This was her lover, her love. She put down the last plate, letting the tinware dry on the riverbank. Then she stood up and walked slowly toward him.

He knew his heart must be clearly visible in his expression. At least, he hoped that it was as he waited for her to round the campfire. Her hair, loose around her shoulders, gleamed like polished onyx and the soft buckskin tunic she wore molded to her lush curves. He knew she wore nothing beneath it. His breathing accelerated when she knelt in front of him, hands outstretched.

He took her small hands in his much larger ones and drew her into his embrace, burying his face in her hair as he murmured soft, indistinct love words against her throat. Her head tipped back, allowing him full access to the pounding pulse at her collarbone. His tongue dipped there, laving it while her fingers dug into the soft cotton of his shirt, feeling the hard muscles of his upper arms and shoulders. Then she slid her hands between them and began unfastening the shirt, splaying one palm against his thundering heart.

Max shrugged off the shirt, then reached for the fringed bottom of her long tunic, commanding hoarsely, "Raise your arms, love. I want to touch your satin skin."

Eagerly she complied and he pulled the buckskin garment off her. Her flesh glowed like gold in the firelight. His hands traced the curves of her body with loving delicacy, beginning with her breasts, kissing a trail down from them to her flat belly. In turn, she ran her fingers through the pale hair on his chest, following its narrowing course to the waistband of his breeches. Quickly she unfastened the fly and tugged them down his narrow hips, all the while gasping with the pleasure his tongue, lips and hands were giving her.

"I can't wait, love," he said raggedly, pulling away to shuck off the moccasins he'd worn and kick away his denims. He pressed her backward onto the bedding, covering her body with his own, feeling her open to him, her thighs splayed, inviting his invasion while her hands clawed at his back.

"Yes, oh, yes," was all she could answer as he positioned himself and plunged deep inside her in one long, hard, life-affirming stroke. Sky arched up to meet it, eagerly rolling with each succeeding thrust, rubbing her breasts against the sweet abrasion of his chest hair. One hand cupped his head, feeling the soft curling hair. She drew his mouth to hers for a ravishing kiss, hungry, rough, not stopping as they rolled across the bedding until she was on top, riding him in wild passion.

Looking down at him, she marveled in some dim, distant part of her mind at the sheer male beauty of him, limned pale silver-gold in the rising moon's light. *This is my husband and I love him!* But then her body took over, leaving her mind far behind as they rolled again, off the bedding, onto the soft cool grass . . . and the sudden rush of culmination swept over her.

Max muffled her cries with his mouth, drinking in her ecstasy, reveling as her body clenched around his, driving him toward the brink. He slowed, wanting to make it last for her, but her own passion drew him closer, closer until he could withstand her unconscious wiles no longer. When she arched up, her arms tight around his shoulders, her mouth joined with his in that same unendingly furious kiss, he tumbled past the abyss, spilling himself deep inside her.

Panting and spent, they lay on the grass for several moments. Sky could feel his fingertips caressing her cheek and knew he was staring down at her. She opened her eyes and met his gaze, trying to read by the flickering firelight what lay behind those dark green eyes. She waited for him to speak, only returning his gentle caress by running her hand up and down his arm.

"This is habit-forming, m'lady," he said at last. "I'll never get my fill of you, Sky. Will you stay my wife when all this is done, I wonder? Hmmm?"

She blinked, her mouth gone suddenly dry. How should she answer? Her heart cried out yes, but her guilt over Will made her shy away from making a commitment, especially to the man she'd sought out to perform the task she could not do herself. "Max . . . I . . ."

"Shhh," he murmured softly, cradling her head against his chest. "Your hesitance speaks for itself. Let us wait and see what our Cheyenne friend's Powers have planned for us."

The Powers have brought you and the Pale Moon Stalker together to heal each other, Sky Eyes of the Sioux. True Dreamer's words echoed in her mind as she lay beneath the bedroll, enveloped in Max's embrace. He slept soundly, at peace for the moment. But she stared at the starry, starry night, searching for answers . . . wondering if what the old man had told her was true, hoping that it would be so.

After another two days of hard riding, they reached Wichita Falls, a small rail town that had been founded a scant few years earlier but now bustled with life, and the seemingly inevitable violence of the frontier. When they passed a telegraph office, Max reined in and said, "Wait for a few minutes. I'm going to send a wire to London."

"You want to see if our mysterious Englishwoman and her Gurkhas have any connection to dear cousin Cletus?" Sky asked.

A harsh white grin slashed across his mouth as he dismounted. "Just so. Also, it never hurts to keep abreast of Cletus's latest peccadilloes, which might just provide us some idea what mischief he's about."

"Are you also going to wire the Lorings about McKerrish?" she asked shrewdly.

"Another enemy to watch. Yes, m'lady, I am."

"Good. I'll send a wire, too. No sense letting Clint and Delilah worry about where we are."

"We're supposed to be in San Francisco," he replied.

Sky shrugged. "I'll think of some reason for the detour to Texas."

Sitting silently through this conversation, True Dreamer then added, "Women can always think of a reason for any matter." Sky gave a snort of female irritation but Max chuckled in agreement. "I will guard the horses," the old man said placidly.

Having "borrowed" the gruella from his reservation when he went in search of Fawn, he knew many men would never return prime horseflesh taken from the unwary as he intended to do. But he chose not to share that information with the Stanhopes for the present.

After sending their wires, Max and Sky rode down the town's Main Street with True Dreamer, following the directions of the telegraph operator to the closest livery stable, with a hotel directly across the street. The smell of newly cut wood and fresh paint filled the air, although most of the buildings were modest. Everything seemed new and clean. Most of the citizens, probably only a few hundred, seemed to be sober merchants, businessmen and farmers. Sky could only hope there would be no drunken gunfire to awaken Max's nightmares here.

When they reached the livery, they dismounted and entered the dimly lit interior. "Rather shoddy compared with the rest of the town. Perhaps we should look for another," Max said, smelling stalls that had not been mucked out in some time.

"This will be sufficient. I will remain with our horses and sleep beneath the stars behind the building," True Dreamer said.

As he spoke, a tall, lanky man with an improbable paunch ambled in from that very back door. His weathered face indicated that he'd lived either hard or long, perhaps both. From between the empty spot where his front teeth should have been, he spit a noisome slug of tobacco. It landed directly in front of the Cheyenne's moccasins. He said without preamble, "I don't take to no Injuns hangin' 'round my stable . . . less they's hangin' fer real." He smiled at his own supposed witticism, then added, "This here's a white man's bidness."

Max stepped closer to the foul-smelling fellow, the hard green light in his eyes deadly. "We'll make it worth your while. The rate for a room at that estimable establishment across the street," he said quietly.

The livery owner, who according to the sign out front was named Baldy, took a step backward at the menace emanating from the foreigner. "Lookee, here, mister, I cain't rightly do thet. My bidness'd be hurt, havin' a redskin hanging 'round." As he spoke, his eyes swept curiously over Sky, as if wondering if she, too, might be bad for business.

Max felt a brief surge of shame, which immediately gave way to rage at the way this piece of offal was looking at his wife and his friend. His eyes glowed in the dim light as he reached for Baldy's skinny throat. "I might be forced to hurt something far more precious than your 'bidness,' you bloody ignorant—"

"My son, please let me take care of this matter," True Dreamer said, placing a restraining hand on Max's arm. "Do not soil yourself by touching this one. I have ways to make him suffer for his bad manners."

Baldy snorted, still keeping an eye on the dangerous-looking foreigner who wore a low-slung gun as if he knew how to use it.

After his quiet pronouncement, True Dreamer reached inside the sack slung over his shoulder and removed a gourd rattle. He threw back his head and let out a hair-raising cry. "Yeey Yah Ho!" Continuing the ominous chant, he began to shake the rattle and shuffle to and fro in front of Baldy, who backed off, his sunken eyes now widening with even greater alarm.

When the Cheyenne shook the rattle directly in front of his crotch, he gulped and asked Sky, "What's he doin'?" as if under the assumption that her "Injun" blood would enable her to answer. Or perhaps he was too frightened of the white gunman to say anything to him.

Sky noted with satisfaction that Baldy's complexion was turning as red as that of his nemesis and even in the relatively cool interior of the stable, sweat poured down his battered face. Turning from him as if he were some insect, she asked True Dreamer, "What medicine do you make, Grandfather?"

"Daughter, I place a curse on his man-lance. It will grow crooked and bend at the end like an old man's walking stick. His woman already refuses to lie with him. He now pays to share the blanket of a young Mexican girl who cooks food in one of the white man's feeding lodges. Even for money she will not want him when I finish my medicine." With that, he resumed his chanting and rattle shaking.

Baldy, meanwhile, looked as if he were about to crumple onto the filthy straw-covered dirt floor. Once again, True Dreamer's visions about others had hit the mark. Max suppressed a grin, but exchanged a look with his wife, who merely nodded her head in understanding, as if to say, *Just wait . . .*

"Who's that ole bastard been talkin' ta 'bout me?" Baldy choked out breathlessly. If Earlene found out about Rosita . . .

he shuddered. The foreigner wouldn't have to shoot him. His wife would.

"I'd watch my tongue if I were you," Max said. "We just arrived in town. The old man, my wife and I have spoken to no one. True Dreamer is the most powerful medicine man I have ever seen."

Now it was Sky suppressing her amusement as she said earnestly to the chanting old man, "Grandfather, the Powers might take offense that you use the gift they have given you to do such grievous harm. The Everywhere Spirit created us all and wishes for us to increase. If you curse this man's 'lance' so that it cannot be used for its proper purpose, surely you might offend the Powers."

Max watched as she actually wrung her hands while True Dreamer ceased his performance and listened to her supplication. He appeared lost in thought for a moment. Baldy, meanwhile, was swaying back and forth, too frightened to speak. His shirt was drenched with sweat.

At length, the medicine man sighed. "You may be right, Daughter. But there are times when the workings of the Powers confuse this old man. Why did they make so few of the True People and so many whites? Why do they allow the whites to breed like prairie dogs?" He signed once more and closed his eyes. "Sometimes I think the Powers did not carefully think out the Grand Design."

Sky's hand flew to her mouth. "Grandfather! That is blasphemy!"

Max had to bite his lip to keep from laughing now and suspected part of the reason for his wife's hand over her mouth was to hide her own suppressed laughter. She mimed horrified shock even better than she did trembling anxiety.

"W-whut's . . . uh, whut's he gonna do? Yew gotta stop him . . . p-please!" Baldy croaked to no one in particular.

Then True Dreamer spoke, but not to his victim. "You are right, Daughter. I must not bend his lance. I will simply curse him with the great burning stone itch." He resumed his shuffling, chanting and gourd rattling.

"Awe, now w-whut's th' burnin' stone itch?" Baldy asked Sky, who seemed the one to be reasoning with his enemy.

But it was Max who replied, "Your bollocks, man, your bollocks. I saw him do it to a couple of nasty chaps up in the Nations. Not a pretty sight. They were digging at their crotches like a couple of hounds scratching fleas, crying and begging True Dreamer to remove the hex . . . but he simply rode away, leaving them to suffer." Max gave a shudder as if truly recalling such a spectacle as he watched an utterly convinced Baldy start digging at himself.

"L-listen, yew kin stay here—no charge, all right—for f-free—jest stop thet rattlin' and s-spell s-settin'!" the liveryman pleaded as he flattened himself against the stall bars. "Make 'im stop!" he begged Max and Sky, looking from one to the other.

We're without shame! What a musical hall act this would be! Max forced his expression to remain stern and serious. "Grandfather, you really should stop before it's too late. Can you not sense that this miscreant has seen the error of his ways?" he asked, knowing Baldy had no idea what a miscreant was. As for the Cheyenne, Max wouldn't bet on it.

True Dreamer stopped and looked at Max. "Do you think so, my son?"

"Yes, sir, I do," Max averred solemnly.

"Good." With that abrupt pronouncement, the old medicine man stuffed his rattle back in his sack and picked up the reins of their horses, leading them toward the open corral behind the stable.

Once True Dreamer had left the stable, Baldy peeled himself from the splintery support of the stall and gathered his composure, swallowing several times before he was able to speak. "No hurry 'bout payin' me fer th' horses. Jest head on over ta th' ho-tel and git yerselves comfortable." With that he scrambled out the front door of his own establishment and toward the nearest saloon.

"The pair of you could teach Clint Daniels a thing or two about the art of the bluff," Max said to Sky.

Fixing him with a level expression, she asked, "What makes you think it was a bluff . . . white man?" Then she burst into laughter.

Chapter Twelve

After spending a relatively comfortable night sleeping in a bed, Sky and Max awakened at dawn, refreshed after so many long, dangerous days of hard riding. They rejoined True Dreamer at Baldy's, ready to continue on their quest. Unsurprisingly, the old livery owner was nowhere to be found. Reading the rates posted on the stable sign, Max left the proper amount of money for boarding four horses overnight and they set out.

Sky looked over her shoulder at the sun spreading red, gold and orange streaks across the western horizon. As they rode southeast toward Fort Worth, she said, "That vile old wretch is probably suffering a monumental headache from overindulgence."

True Dreamer merely grunted agreement, but Max chuckled grimly. "No, I suspect he's still passed out dead drunk in that bloody saloon. It will probably take him three days to sober up and repent the cheap whiskey. Then he'll revert to being precisely the same flaming bastard he was before."

Remembering the way the hotel desk clerk had looked at her, then back at Max, before reluctantly handing over a key, she knew her husband was right. Only fear of the lethal-looking gunman had kept the clerk from refusing to allow her a bed in his establishment. "Hatred of red people is deeply ingrained in whites. At times, I wonder if that will ever change," she said pensively.

"Hatred of all people who are different from us is a peculiar gift of the white race," Max said bitterly.

Sky knew by the hard, distant expression on his face that he was recalling his life as a soldier . . . and the dark warriors he had killed in Africa. "That isn't entirely true. Many of my father's people fear and distrust those different from themselves. Within our village, my father became a great chief, but at gatherings of the Sioux Nations, there were others who hated him for his white blood."

Max nodded. "Your family has been torn between two worlds all of your life." He could not help wondering if part of her attraction to Father Brewster had been his willingness to be a bridge between red and white for her. Would she ever speak of him once Deuce was dead? He vowed not to let the priest's ghost haunt their marriage. Sky belonged to him now and he would never let her go.

But when are you going to tell her about that damned codicil? The thought popped up suddenly, and he realized he'd pushed it to the back of his mind. Sooner or later he should share that devious provision of Harry's will with her, but if he did, would she ever believe he really loved her for herself alone?

The old Cheyenne interrupted his troubling revery. "The Powers did not intend for people to hate. No tribe, red or white, lives in peace. We all have much to learn." As he spoke, his penetrating gaze moved from Max to Sky, as if reading what lay inside their hearts.

He knew them better than they knew themselves.

They pushed hard for Fort Worth, no one speaking of what they would find there. Would Johnny Deuce really be there? And what of Fawn, True Dreamer's young granddaughter? By this time, Deuce might have traded her off to another perverted drunk. Or beaten her to death. If the old man knew, he chose not to share his counsel with Max and Sky. Yet his serenity appeared unshakable.

Considering all else that preyed on their minds, they took comfort in that.

The weather turned hot even for July on the Texas plains. Heat shimmered in undulating waves over the flat, treeless horizon and the vegetation appeared as desiccated as the bleached skulls of dead coyotes and other varmints they passed along the trail. After the third seemingly endless day, they saw a patch of true green, distinct from the gray green of mesquite and the yellow prairie grass surrounding them. The trees at the base of a rounded hill appeared like a mirage in the distance.

"Water ahead," True Dreamer said through cracked lips.

Shaking her canteen, which was almost empty, Sky breathed a sigh of relief. Although they'd filled several extra containers before leaving Wichita Falls, the water tasted brackish. Not to mention that the supply was running low.

Consulting a rough map he'd purchased in the town, Max said, "It must be a small tributary of the Trinity." Removing his hat and wiping the sweat from his forehead with his arm, he consulted the western sky, where the sun hung evilly like a malevolent yellow eye. "We're making good time, but there's no sense in pushing the horses until they drop."

True Dreamer grunted his agreement. Sky peered ahead, as if expecting the green promise to vanish in the hot desert wind. "Even if the water is alkaline or muddy, at least it will be running fresh," she said.

"Dreaming of a bath?" Max asked with a faint smile as she kneed her mount to move at a slightly faster pace and pulled ahead of them.

"She dreams of many things," the old man said.

Max's head turned toward his companion. "Oh, and what can you tell me about her dreams? I would dearly like to know."

"Every man wishes to understand women. No man does," was the enigmatic reply.

The stream was small and shallow, but the water was obviously spring fed, sweet, clear and cool. Sky jumped from her horse and knelt beside the edge, drinking eagerly once she'd tasted it carefully. The setting was lovely with the creek partly shielded by a dense copse of hackberry bushes. Overhead shinnery oaks and cottonwoods rustled in the hot wind as if inviting wayfarers to stop at the oasis.

"Watch you don't founder yourself," Max said as he led his horse to join hers where it drank greedily.

True Dreamer slid from his gruella and watched as it and the packhorse joined them. Then moving upstream, he joined Sky and Max in drinking from the stream.

She sat back on her heels and looked at Max with a smirk. "Watch out yourself," she said as he shoved his whole head beneath the water and then raised it up, shaking his hair as droplets flew around him. Sweaty and bearded, in severe need of a haircut, he looked so splendidly handsome that her heart skipped a beat. She was glad his eyes were closed so she could enjoy watching him for a moment without his being aware.

The old Cheyenne disappeared with his rifle after quenching his thirst. On foot, he walked into the thick vegetation downstream in search of game for their dinner. Beans and smoked pork became a tiresome diet after days on the trail. While their hunter was gone, Sky slipped away from Max, who was busy building a fire and setting up camp.

She walked upstream, carrying soap, her comb and a fresh change of clothes. After about fifteen minutes of following the twists and turns of the stream, she found it widened into a small pool at one sharp bend where the water was trapped by a rocky bank. "Perfect," she murmured to herself, stripping off her clothes and wading carefully into the icy cold.

She sank beneath the water and then reached for the soap, washing sand and red soil from her hair and body. The pool was too small for swimming, so she squeezed the excess water from her long tangle of hair, preparing to comb it dry while she sat on the edge of the bank.

Max watched her spine arch as she pulled all that dripping ebony splendor over one golden shoulder and twisted. Her raised arms revealed the sweet curve of a breast, its rose-brown nipple taut from the chill. He could warm it with his mouth. She stood waist deep in the shallow pool with water lapping at the navel in her flat belly. His breath caught when she started moving slowly toward the rocks at the edge of the pool, gradually revealing the curves of her hips and those long, luscious legs.

Shadows cast by the trees and bushes danced in mottled patterns over her skin. She intended to let the warm dry air do the work of the towel she'd brought. He stood frozen as she placed the white cotton over a rock and then sat on it to begin plying her comb. With every stroke, she raised her arm and arched her back. Sky was far more elegant and graceful than any noblewoman he had ever seen posing before a mirror in an English manor house . . . and over the years of his misspent youth, he'd observed more than his share of them. They posed. She was utterly without artifice, unaware of his presence.

Was he playing the voyeur? Most certainly. Max grinned and began stripping off his clothes as he called out, "Anyone there besides jackrabbits?"

She turned, a startled expression on her face. Just then a shot rang out from True Dreamer's rifle. "Well, one less jackrabbit to bother my tranquility here," she replied as he emerged from the cover of bushes and trees.

Another shot rang out in the distance. "I do believe dinner is on its way . . . but we have time. He'll not hurry back," he said as he walked into the pool and submerged himself. "Toss me that soap, love?" he asked.

"You'll smell like roses," she warned.

"I think I'll soon smell of you anyway. Better than you smelling of my sweat." She tossed the smooth soap and he caught it in one hand, watching her watch him as he lathered his upper body and head. Then he dunked beneath the water to finish his bath.

"You always assume I'll fall into your arms," she said, almost crossly. Were her feelings that transparent? Sky knew they must be, but his troubled expression surprised her.

"You are my wife, love," he said gently.

"But what's happened between us . . . it wasn't part of our agreement."

"No, only securing my inheritance and killing Deuce were," he said flatly. "I have yet to fulfill my end of the bargain."

Sky paused and moistened her lips. "Max . . . what if I said . . . what if I didn't want you to kill him anymore—that I only want to rescue True Dreamer's granddaughter?"

The soap slid from his nerveless fingers. He bought time scanning the clear water to retrieve it, then faced her as he walked to shore. "Are you saying you'll give up your vendetta?" *Will you give up the ghost of your priest?* He wanted to ask but did not quite dare yet.

"I'd be risking your life—and breaking my oath if I have him killed." Her eyes were hidden by her lashes, but he sat down beside her and took her chin in his hand, tipping her face up to his.

Max studied the depths of those huge blue eyes and what he saw robbed him of breath. "Oh, Sky, does it mean you can let go of the past and be my wife?"

She did not look away this time, her fingertips caressing the back of his hand. "I have so much guilt over Will . . . the way he died . . . that we couldn't have children, that I find you so . . . so . . ."

A wistful smile barely touched his lips. "So bloody irresistible? I'm not a saint, Sky. Far from it. I'm nothing like Father Will. At first I feared that might be the attraction."

"In some ways it was . . . but not how you think," she said hesitantly. "He was so large and self-conscious about his size, a great bear of a man, almost afraid to touch me . . ."

"Nightshirts in the dark?" he asked carefully, not wanting to know more than she was willing to share.

"Yes, but it was more than that . . . he was so afraid of hurting me that he held back . . . passion. I never knew passion before."

"And I made you feel as if you'd betrayed him a second time when you discovered it with me."

"How perceptive you can be. That's true, but there's more—things I've never told you about my past, things he knew."

Max held his breath, afraid to break the spell as he waited for her to continue.

"When I told you about the way Clint became my foster brother, I left out some painful memories. The soldiers he killed to earn his name, they raped me and my sister. I was a child . . . like Fawn."

Max took her in his arms and rocked her gently. "So Will was afraid he would bring back that terror on your wedding night . . . and every time after?"

She nodded in his embrace. "He was too good for this world . . . for me."

"No, love, the finest man on earth isn't worthy of you, least of all me. I've done many things in my life that were selfish, bad, even cruel. But I do love you, God help me, I do."

She looked up into his eyes and felt the sting of tears. "I love you, too, Max."

"I've wanted to hear those words for so long, but I was afraid . . ."

She placed her fingertips over his lips. "You are a fine and honorable man, only in a different way than Will was. You're willing to defend an old man against his enemies and rescue a child—"

"Somehow, I doubt True Dreamer has ever required help he could not readily conjure up. But if we're going to save Fawn from her captor, I'll still probably have to kill Deuce to do it."

Sky shook her head. "Stop trying to paint yourself as a villain. If Deuce won't let her go, his death won't be on either of our consciences now. The important thing is that we aren't seeking revenge. You and I are free."

"Are we now?" he murmured as he bent down and took her lips in a soft kiss that quickly escalated into mutual passion as they sank to the ground by the side of the clear tranquil pool . . .

The next morning, they rode with the dawn once more, watchful for another appearance by the mysterious Englishwoman and her companions, or more ominously, for any more killers hired by Cletus, McKerrish or whoever was behind the unsuccessful attempts on their lives. After a long day of hard riding, they easily crossed the narrow ribbon of brackish green water called the Trinity River and entered the cattle boomtown of Fort Worth.

Sky looked about as they rode down a dusty street. The various businesses along the way indicated that it must be Main Street. Although it was neither as large or noisy as Leadville, it was still a good-sized place. But True Dreamer had said he would be able to sense Johnny Deuce's presence no matter how large the white man's village.

Long wooden sidewalks lined the bustling streets. It was late afternoon on a Saturday and everyplace seemed to be preparing for the weekly visits of cowhands ready for a celebratory toot before the Sabbath. In truth, if Fort Worth was typical of most cow towns, there would be many more saloons than churches—and few inhabitants sober enough to attend worship on Sunday morning anyway. Although no church steeples were visible, she charitably decided that might be because they had entered from the wrong direction.

When Max reined in beside the red-striped pole of a barbershop doing a brisk business, she and True Dreamer followed suit. "I realize you require the services of a barber, but this is hardly the time," she said to her husband as he dismounted.

"No better place to learn where our boy might be—or at least where the worst saloons and bordellos in the city are situated," he replied. "Wait here while I learn what I can inside."

Within a few moments he reappeared. "If we continue heading down Main south toward the stockyards, we'll eventually come to an area rather colorfully called, 'Hell's Half Acre,' the brothel, gambling and drinking center of Fort Worth. I've been warned that decent citizens who wander in there seldom emerge with their skins intact."

"Just the place for Deuce to hide out," Sky said.

True Dreamer grunted agreement.

As they rode along, the rows of grocery, seamstress, pharmacy and other shops seemed fairly neat and prosperous. The town appeared to be a frontier city in the making. A general store advertising cowboy clothing for all ages caught her eye. Sky was certain whatever garments Fawn had worn when Deuce kidnapped her would be far beyond repair. Once she could gauge the girl's size, she would buy some boy's shirts and pants for the long journey home . . . if Fawn could withstand the ride.

She shuddered and cursed Jonathan Ducelin Framme more vigorously than ever she had when she intended his violent death. *Please, God, let the girl be alive!* She comforted herself by looking at True Dreamer's profile. The old man appeared relaxed and confident. That gave her heart to continue.

The farther south they went, moving slowly to avoid wagons, carts and other horsemen, the more unsavory the buildings and people looked. They rode by a saloon perhaps appropriately called The Cowboy's Lament, what passed for a cheap hotel and several very run-down boardinghouses and saloons. All had peeling paint, baking under the merciless rays of the setting sun.

From the second-story porch of one establishment, a woman with vermillion lips and dead black hair called out to Max, "Come on, honey, yew air the purtiest man I ever seed. Do ya fer free—but not the Injun," she quickly added.

The old man ignored her as if she did not exist.

Sky glared up at the whore with a deadly grin. "This 'purty' man is my husband," she called back, patting the .38 strapped to her hip.

The whore's head popped behind the filthy red curtains and the window slammed shut.

"I do believe we're approaching our destination," Max said grimly.

"We are near the weasel-snake," True Dreamer confirmed.

"Then it might be best to stable the horses and proceed on foot." Max pointed out a livery on the right side of the street. The sign proclaimed: HORSES AND MULES STABLED. BEST PRICES IN TOWN. IRV WATSON, PROP.

"Let's hope we have better luck with this place than the last one," Sky muttered to Max. "I don't feel up to another performance and I don't think True Dreamer does either."

"We will not be troubled," the old man said as they dismounted.

A man of middling years came ambling out to greet them. "Whut kin I do fer ya?" he asked with a friendly smile.

"We want to stable four horses for the night, perhaps for several days, mister—?" Max inquired.

"Name's Irv Watson. I own this here place. Two bits a day fer each horse. I make that ta be a buck," the man replied.

"Fair enough, Mr. Watson." Max offered his hand. After they shook, he gave the livery owner the money. "This is my wife, Mrs. Stanhope, and our friend True Dreamer. We're looking for a man named Johnny Deuce. Have you heard of him?"

A cautious light came into the man's pale hazel eyes. "Yew a friend of that one?"

"Quite the opposite," Max replied grimly.

"Good. Little bastard's mean as a snake—oh, beg pardon, ma'am," he said to Sky, blushing to the roots of his thinning brown hair.

Sky smiled and nodded, saying nothing, excusing all. Deuce was here! That meant Fawn was, too.

"Deuce shot up a young drover t'other day. Nice kid. Knowed him since he wuz a tadpole. Ever'body in town talked 'bout how the gunman pushed Billy ta draw. Never had a chance. Last I heerd, Deuce wuz hangin' 'round the Acre, drinkin' an' gamblin' purty steady. Yew might ketch 'im now, if'n yew look."

Silently, the old man handed the reins to the gruella and packhorse to Watson. Max and Sky handed over their horses as well, but she removed her Yellow Boy from its saddle scabbard first. The owner led the four animals inside the big livery.

"We can trust this one," True Dreamer said. "Now, you will go to a whiskey lodge with two red poles in front of it. He is there and Fawn is nearby."

To that startling pronouncement, he then added, "I would like to see the weasel-snake taste your justice." He shrugged philosophically. "But red men, whites and whiskey do not mix well. My presence would bring more trouble on you. Go and do what the Powers have ordained. I will seek out my granddaughter."

"You know where she is?" Sky asked.

"A big lodge called Excelsior," the old man replied. "I will find it."

"But if we know the hotel, then we don't have to confront Deuce."

True Dreamer shook his head. "Think, Daughter. If we try to leave the room of a white man with his prisoner, will no white man protest? Will the weasel-snake allow us to ride away in peace once he learns who has taken her? He will pursue us all . . . and everywhere he goes, death follows."

Sky looked at Max, who sighed and nodded. "He's right, love. If we let him go, we'll have more than McKerrish and whoever in England wants us dead setting ambushes. How much do you believe our mysterious protector and her Gurkhas can handle? Once we return True Dreamer and Fawn to their people, what would stop Deuce from stealing her again—or another girl?"

"He preys on the weak. There is only one way to deal with such a one," the old man said quietly.

Max stared at Sky, willing her to understand. "I want to bury the past as much as you, but I've thought about it for days. If I'd tracked him down after he shot Remy—a horse—he would not have been alive to kill that young boy Watson told us about—and who knows how many others in between? This is no longer our vendetta. It's something that has to be done to protect our friend and his people as well as us."

Sky looked into his eyes, trying to decide if he was right. "It's taken me so long to let go . . . can you . . . when this is over, can you let go of your past, too?" she asked.

"The dark warriors will soon rest, Daughter," True Dreamer answered for Max, eliciting a flash of anger from the Englishman.

Before he could say anything, she turned to the old man. "Then that is enough." Facing her husband, she said, "Let's do what must be done."

Max pushed the brim of his hat back on his head and sighed, uncertain whether he had just won or lost a battle. "Find Fawn. I'll handle Deuce," he said to both of them.

"I refuse to let you face him alone," she said stubbornly. "I'm your backup, Max."

He smiled wistfully. "You forget that I'm still the Limey. I can handle Deuce by myself. Go with True Dreamer. His

granddaughter will need a woman's touch." His tone indicated that the matter was not up for discussion. "Do you understand, love?"

"Yes, Max, I understand," she replied.

She stood with True Dreamer as her husband walked down
the wooden sidewalk and turned the corner. "Now, follow
your man," the old Cheyenne said.

Sky looked at him, startled. "How did you know—"

He smiled. "You understood, but you did not intend to
obey."

She nodded. "Go find Fawn. We'll be along as soon as we
can."

He grunted, watching as she slipped around the corner;
then he headed down the street, taking back alleys so as not to
raise unwelcome attention.

Chapter Thirteen

$\mathcal{M}$ax approached the first saloon he encountered after entering what he could see was obviously Hell's Half Acre. The Bucket of Blood in Denver looked like an exclusive English gentleman's club compared to what surrounded him here. Some of the gaudily painted shanties were as large as Drago's place, but their wood was blistered from the merciless sun and wind. Boards on the sidewalks, even on the buildings, were missing or hung askew. Broken windowpanes left large, jagged shards of glass sticking out of the frames, dangerous for the unwary who happened to stumble through them. Drunken cowboys and other denizens of the district ground up the glistening grit that had fallen beneath their dusty boots.

He entered the Cow Palace and stood with his back to the wall while his eyes adjusted to the dim light of newly lit rusty lanterns hanging from nails on the crude plank walls. The bar was a scarred ancient ruin of what had once been good wood, too stained and gouged to tell what variety. Men in trail gear drank alongside of those wearing the stained clothes of workmen. Even a few in rumpled suits slugged back whiskey.

After sizing up the place and making certain Deuce was not present, he moved to the bar and inquired of the bullet-headed man serving drinks, "I'm looking for a bar with two big red pillars in front of it. Do you know where I might find such a place?"

Several snickers greeted the request, made in a precise English accent.

"Who wants to know?" the barman asked, eyes narrowed suspiciously.

Max tugged his hat forward on his head again, blocking the lantern glare, then placed his hands loosely on his gun belt. "Mostly, I'm called the Limey."

The drinkers around him went silent and the bartender backed up a step. "Look, mister, we don't want no trouble. Place yer looking for, it's called the Burning Pillars. Corner of Calhoun and Grove, 'cross from the Waco Tap." He gestured out the door to the left.

"Obliged," Max said. After giving each of the men at the bar a level stare to make certain none of them had delusions of grandeur sufficient to draw on him, he turned and walked out the swinging doors.

Like True Dreamer and Sky, Max decided the alley offered a safer approach to his destination, now that he had it fixed in his mind. He crossed Rusk Street and came out on Calhoun. Looking down it, he could easily see the gaudy crimson pillars that gave the saloon its name. Like most of the Acre, they were in need of a fresh paint job. "So now, get the job done," he muttered to himself.

From her hiding place across the alley, Sky watched his hard green eyes grow cold as ice. She shivered, feeling responsible for this. In seeking justice for a dead man, had she done a terrible thing to a living one? What if this was the final straw that destroyed Max's soul? Was that what had happened to her brother all those years ago? She could never let Max go through such pain. Already he had enough to deal with. But then she remembered what True Dreamer had said.

The dark warriors will soon rest.

Did that mean they would disappear from Max's dreams— or that Max would die, ending his nightmares altogether? No, True Dreamer would not have sent Max to his death, she assured herself. But neither had the old medicine man stopped her from following her husband. Sky hurried after him, seeing the Burning Pillars just as he paused to look inside. How could she help without breaking his concentration?

The swinging doors groaned in protest when he pushed them open and walked into the large room. Men sat playing cards at tables scattered helter-skelter around the room, as if rearranged nightly during bar fights. Ladies of the line leaned over the shoulders of several, whispering advice, or other things. A few who were not engaged with customers noticed the tall striking man with the cold green eyes the moment he stepped inside. They smiled in invitation.

One called over the babel of voices and a tinny piano, "Hey, handsome, I got somethin' you'd like real good."

The long line of men drinking at the bar ignored the comment. The bar top ran the length of the room and was recognizably mahogany. Overall, the place was less seedy than the preceding one. Max spotted Deuce almost immediately. The other men kept their distance from him on both sides, talking among themselves. Even in a place as depraved as Hell's Half Acre, Jonathan Ducelin Framme drank alone. Perhaps it was by choice, but somehow Max intuited that it was not.

Ostracized in America just as you were in England, eh, old chap?

Before Max could voice his thought, Deuce leaned forward to engage the bartender in an argument. The gunman was a scant five foot five in high-heeled boots, slight of build, the wiry type that could be quick as lightning—or a rattlesnake when it struck. He remembered True Dreamer's name for Deuce. Weasel-snake. It fit. His bony shoulders were hunched up almost to his oversized ears. He shoved a glass at the big man behind the bar, who shook his head.

While Max sized up the room, Sky slipped in the back door and concealed herself in the shadows beneath the staircase leading to the bordello on the second floor; she held her Yellow Boy ready to shoot if necessary. Her heart pounded. *Please, my love, be careful!*

"I told you, old man, I wish to run a score. I will pay when

I have sampled enough of your swill." Deuce's voice was a surprising baritone, rumbling deeply across the noisy room.

Old or not, the barkeep was having none of it. "An' I tole yew, Deuce, ya gotta pay fer ever' drink when I pour it, jest like ever'one else. Now, it's time ta pay up."

Max approached Deuce, who turned when his adversary said in equally cultivated British tones, "The man's right, Johnny boy. It is time to pay up. Right now."

Deuce placed the shot glass on the bar, his thirst forgotten as he looked at his countryman's harsh face. If he was afraid, he gave no indication of it. Rather, a feverish excitement leaped into his pale gray eyes. "Well, my old friend Stanhope. You have traveled quite some distance to, ah, renew our acquaintance."

Max shrugged. "What are a few hundred miles to collect on a debt, Johnny?" He paused, then added, "Oh, and by the by, I am not your friend nor ever have been."

Deuce laughed, a rumbling, ugly sound deep in his narrow chest. "No, I imagine the Limey can claim as few friends in this benighted land as can I. But as to the debt you have come to collect . . . I do believe the only thing you will collect this evening is a bullet."

"I wouldn't count on that," Max said calmly.

The crowd at the bar, sensing the animosity between the two gunmen, began to back away. The barkeep ducked down and crawled on all fours from the far end of his post to watch the show.

Sky could hear the deadly undertone in Max's voice and knew he was poised, ready to fight. But so was the evil little man facing him. The hatred radiating from both antagonists swept over the now silent room. She scanned the crowd, looking to see if anyone would go to Deuce's aid and was relieved when there were no takers . . . at least not yet.

"Ah, but I *do* count on that. You see, old chap, the last time you caught me when I was a bit under the weather." He gestured with his left hand to the whiskey glass sitting on the bar. "I am much faster when sober . . . and you have the grave misfortune to have come upon me while I am yet quite unafflicted."

"I did not just happen on you, *old chap*. I've been hunting you. Do you, by the by, recall a young priest up in Yankton country about a year ago? Father Brewster was much beloved by my wife's people. And you shot him in the back when he rescued a young girl whom you were beating."

A hostile murmur went up around the room at the mention of backshooting a priest.

Deuce sneered. "She was just a filthy little wog, an Indian—and her protector was what the Americans quaintly call an 'Injun-lover.'" He appeared pleased when some of the outrage subsided.

Sky flinched, tightening her grip on the rifle in her hand. Oh, how she ached to shoot him herself—not in the back as he'd done to Will, but to call him out and blast him face-to-face! True Dreamer had been right. This was a rabid animal who would keep on killing until someone stopped him. But if she interfered, she might get Max killed in a crossfire. Sky bit her lip and waited in silence.

"Oh, and you're not an 'Injun lover'?" Max parried. "Then why do you have an eleven-year-old Cheyenne girl locked up in your hotel room right now? Is she the only female you can force to do your perverted bidding? You like to whip young girls, don't you, Johnny? It really doesn't matter if they're red or white. In fact, that's the reason you were run out of England—for abusing the daughter of a member of parliament."

Now the murmuring grew hostile, turning against Deuce once more.

The little killer smirked evilly. "You were forced to flee our beloved homeland in disgrace as well. Oh, I heard the rumors about your tawdry affair with an older—and very

married—viscountess. I understand your uncle was quite upset when you left university and joined the army."

"I did so to keep from killing her husband, a brave if foolish old man who felt constrained to defend the honor of a
woman who possessed none," Max replied tightly. "Killing
him would've been on my conscience. But killing a child-
abusing weasel-snake such as you . . ."

Sky suppressed a gasp of shock. No wonder her husband
did not want to speak about why he'd broken his uncle's
heart by leaving England.

Now, Deuce pushed away from the bar, his narrow, pockmarked face red with fury, pale eyes slitted, glittering like
those of a rattler ready to strike. "You bloody wog-loving son
of a bitch!"

He reached the pearl-handled Colt at his hip and cleared the
holster, but he was not fast enough. Max's Smith & Wesson
slug smashed into his chest, sending him sprawling along the
bar, clawing at the scarred edge, as if desperately trying to hold
on to life. His gun discharged into the floor, splintering the
whiskey-soaked wood a few feet in front of Max's boots. Then
it fell from his hand and clattered across the rough planking.

Deuce dropped to the floor immediately after it, lying flat on
his back with one arm hanging over a spittoon. The stain on
his chest blossomed deep red. Sky swallowed her gorge, remembering how similar spots had spread across Will's back
when Deuce had emptied his hidden gun into the gentle giant.
Something impelled her to step out from behind the stairs, uncocking the Yellow Boy as she walked over to where Deuce lay.

Max's expression hardened when he saw her, but she ignored him. Instead of moving to his side, she knelt next to
the dying man. He coughed blood and looked at her with
partially focused eyes. "Who . . . ?" He coughed again.

"I was Father Brewster's wife," she said quietly. Her words
echoed in the silent room as if it were a cave.

Deuce's lips twisted into a grimace. "Pray for me then," he gasped.

Sky could not tell if the words were a sneer or a plea. Perhaps it did not matter. Nothing she or anyone else could do would spare Jonathan Ducelin Framme the pangs of hell. His eyes glazed over and the last breath left his body. She stared at the dead man for a moment, then stood up and walked over to Max's side.

"You never could get the part about obeying correct, could you, love?" he asked her, cursing the dead man for what he had revealed.

"I couldn't leave you to face him alone. True Dreamer agreed that I should follow." This was not the time to discuss Deuce's accusations.

Then the room erupted in tension-purging noise and laughter.

"So, the leetle snake backshot a sky pilot. Pitchforks in hell must be extry sharp fer the likes of the Deuce," a gambler sitting at a front table said, spitting in the general direction of a cuspidor.

"Damn, 'magine Deuce kilt by another Englishman," one cowboy hiccupped.

"That there's the Limey, you fool," his companion corrected him.

"Hellfire, I heerd o' him up in Colorado," an old man said. "He's a bounty man. I knowed thet little bastard musta had a price on his haid." He took a tentative step toward Max. "Ya come to collect a re-ward, Mr. Limey?"

Before Max could reply, the first drunken cowboy, a kid barely old enough to shave, eyed Sky and asked, "Hey, Mr. Limey, who's the Injun gal? She don't look like the one you talked 'bout. Too growed up."

"Yeah, an too purty," another chimed in.

Max pinned the inebriated boy with an ice-cold stare and

the room went silent again. "This is no 'Injun gal.' This is a lady . . . and my wife."

The quiet was broken when an elderly man got up from a table in the back of the room and took off his battered Stetson, revealing a shock of thick, white hair. He said in a gravelly voice, "How do, Mrs. Limey."

That occasioned a spate of nervous shuffling and hat tipping. Holding her Yellow Boy rifle and standing beside the dangerous bounty hunter, Sky and her husband made a formidable-looking couple. Several of the braver men followed the old man's lead, although in less courtly terms, tipping their hats and saying, "Howdy, ma'am." "Hullo, Mrs. Limey." "No offense intended, ma'am."

Sky nodded tersely and turned sharply toward the door. Before following her out to the street, Max said, "If the town marshal wants to question me, I will remain in Fort Worth for the next few days. He will find me at the Excelsior Hotel."

The white-haired old man scoffed. "No cause fer the marshal to be mixin' in. Ya done a civic duty, Mr. Limey, shootin' thet bastard."

Max touched the brim of his hat. "I'm obliged, sir. I've always aspired to be a good citizen."

He caught up to her half a block down the street. "Bloody hell, Sky, you could've been killed! I don't care what True Dreamer said, you should not have been in that saloon."

She looked at him with anguish. "I wanted to kill him so bad I could taste it—to yell at him and open up this." She raised the Yellow Boy. "But I knew if I did, you would be in greater danger. True Dreamer was right. That man had to die before he killed another human being."

He touched her cheek gently. "It's over, Sky. Can we begin again?" *Now that your priest can rest in peace.*

Sky knew what he was asking. Slowly, she nodded. "Yes, Max, we can," she said gravely, not wanting to ruin the moment by asking about his affair with a married woman. But it explained much about why he had never wanted to return home.

A relieved smile broke across his face and all the coldness she'd seen in his eyes when he faced Deuce evaporated like morning fog. He was no longer the Limey, but the man she loved now . . . her husband, the one with whom she would spend the rest of her life. She placed her hand over his arm and they resumed walking down the street.

"We'll have to find out where the Excelsior is," he said, looking for someone to ask.

"I only pray what Deuce did to Fawn can be undone," she murmured. In her happiness to have Max safe and alive, she'd momentarily forgotten the awful plight of their friend's granddaughter.

"True Dreamer didn't appear worried. I imagine he'd be in the best position to know," he replied, hoping to reassure her, although he had a fair idea about what a depraved creature like Deuce was capable of doing.

They received directions to the hotel and walked the short distance to a ramshackle clapboard structure that appeared ready to fall down from neglect. When they entered, the clerk took one look at Sky and sneered. He was Ichabod Crane come to life, tall and emaciated with an exceedingly large Adam's apple that bobbed at the base of his scrawny neck.

"I don't rent to Injuns, even if they's only breeds," he said, looking at Sky's buckskins and exotic coloring as if she were some creature in a carnival sideshow.

Max's expression became glacial. "Nor would I subject my wife to a night in this sty, but I do require the key to Johnny Deuce's room." Without further warning, he reached across the desk and grabbed a handful of Ichabod's shirtfront, pulling the man halfway across the counter. "Give me the key to his room—now!"

The clerk began to sweat, squirming in Max's less than

gentle grasp. "Listen, mister, I cain't give you his key. He's snake mean and real particular." A quick glance in Sky's direction indicated to them that he knew about the Indian girl in the room. When Max gave another twist to his filthy shirt, cutting off blood flow to his head, he quickly gasped out, "H-he s-said seven was his l-lucky number—"

"Well, it wasn't his lucky number today, old chap. I just killed him. Now, if you think seven is your lucky number . . ." He released his hold on the clerk, who shrank back against the wall, terror etched on his bony face, Adam's apple bobbing like a cork on rough seas.

"Hell, no! Here's the damn key," he choked out, seizing the key from its slot and throwing it at Max, who caught it with ease, left-handed.

Max gave the key to Sky. "We probably don't require it. I'd bet True Dreamer's found a way to reach Fawn, but she'll need a doctor. I'll fetch one."

Sky bit her lip and nodded, turning toward the rickety stairs as Max asked the frightened clerk where the nearest doctor's office was located. This time he got no argument.

"Onliest one who might treat 'er's named Aaron Torres. Over on Calhoun Street," Ichabod replied.

As soon as he walked outside the hotel, Max looked down the street. Drunken cowboys and locals staggered from saloon to saloon celebrating Saturday night. No good. Then he saw what he was looking for—a young boy, obviously a townie, dressed in shabby clothes as if he worked in a stable or smithy's place. Most importantly, he appeared sober.

He pulled a wad of money from his pocket and motioned to the lad to approach, knowing the flash of the bills would catch his eye. "Do you know where Dr. Torres's office is?" he asked.

"Shore do, mister," the boy replied eagerly.

Max tore a five-dollar greenback in two and gave the boy half of it. "Fetch him to the Excelsior Hotel for me and you'll get the other half. Tell him there's a badly hurt girl there."

The youth sprinted down the street after pocketing his partial treasure. Max returned to the hotel, certain the boy would bring the doctor if he had to beg. He'd probably never seen that much money in his life. Max hoped Sky and True Dreamer would have Fawn reassured by now. The thought of the girl being dead or so badly injured that she was beyond medical help did not enter his mind.

The old man would have known.

He waited in the hotel lobby, knowing that another white man with an English accent was the last thing the girl would want to see or hear. As to this Dr. Aaron Torres, well, he would damn well treat an Indian child or he'd be in need of a doctor himself!

Max paced in the lobby, considering how he could explain to Sky about Cynthia. Bloody hell, he owed his wife an honest account of that, if they were to build a lasting marriage. But as for his time in Africa . . . no, he owed no one that much. Pushing the ugly memories away, he looked over at the desk. The clerk had deserted his post. He could hear the man muttering from behind a door that probably led to his private quarters.

Within five minutes, the boy returned with a tall, slim man carrying a small black bag. He was younger than Max expected, with an aristocratic bearing, neatly barbered golden blond hair and eyes as green as his own, although far softer, kinder.

The Englishman handed the boy the other half of the torn bill and watched him scurry away. "So, you're the physician?" he asked, still not certain what to expect when he told this elegant man who his patient would be. The question came out more harshly than he intended.

But the doctor nodded, meeting Max's gaze calmly, not the least intimidated. "Yes, I'm Dr. Torres. I understand there's a young girl here in need of my services. Please take me to her at once."

"First you have to understand one thing. She's Cheyenne, eleven years old, kidnapped by a sadistic white man who abused her."

"And you expect me to refuse to treat her because of her race?" Torres asked, looking at Max intently.

"I feared you might, considering how everyone else around here feels about '*Injuns.*'"

"I'm a Sephardic Jew, mister—?"

"Stanhope, Max Stanhope." He felt like a fool. "You understand what being an outcast is about, then."

"You could say that. My family has endured unreasoning prejudice in the New World for four hundred years, and in the Old for well over a millennium. Please take me to the girl."

"She's upstairs in room seven. My wife and her grandfather are with her. I don't know how badly she's hurt—but I do know what Johnny Deuce is capable of," Max said, gesturing toward the stairs. "Would you please tell my wife that I'll be along as soon as I locate a telegraph office and send a message?"

"It's Saturday night in Fort Worth. That may take a bit. But somehow I believe you'll find a way," Dr. Torres said with a fleeting smile as he began to climb the stairs.

Max crossed to the door behind which the clerk cowered and pounded on it. "Where is the telegraph office?" he demanded. He did not say please.

When she'd approached the door to room seven, Sky had heard True Dreamer's soft chanting. He must have climbed the back porch and somehow entered by the window. Perhaps Fawn was able to drop something to aid his climb? Sky had hesitated to barge in so for several minutes she'd stood uncertainly in the hallway. Finally, gathering her courage, she turned the lock and stepped inside the darkened room.

One small kerosene lantern cast a flickering glow over the shabby quarters. The bed was narrow, its sheets gray and filthy, smelling of sweat . . . and blood. A rickety wooden chair sat in one shadowy corner and a washstand with a chipped pitcher and basin atop it was next to the window. On the bare wooden floor, the old man had laid out the blanket he'd carried over his shoulder when they left the livery. That was where Fawn lay, held in her grandfather's arms.

Although he did not stop his soothing chant, True Dreamer nodded to Sky as she quietly closed the door. She knelt facing them and took one small hand that reached out to her and patted it. Fawn looked up at her with large, beautiful brown eyes and managed a smile. "You are Sky Eyes," she said. "Grandfather has told me of you."

"Your grandfather is a very great medicine man," she said softly, somehow not surprised by the child's calm self-possession. It was probably what had allowed her to survive Deuce.

Angry red weals from a riding quirt crisscrossed Fawn's hands, arms and legs. A torn, ragged tunic revealed that Deuce had plied his whip viciously enough to shred it in places.

"I'll bring cool water to bathe her wounds," Sky whispered to him. He nodded, still chanting.

Blinking back the burning tears in her eyes, Sky took the pitcher and walked down the back stairs to where a pump sat in what passed for a courtyard. Although rusty and neglected, it grudgingly gave a burst of water that proved clear and clean. Sky murmured a brief prayer of thanks and returned quickly. True Dreamer ceased his chant and said to her, "You will care for her until the white medicine man comes. I must make my own medicine." He touched the small pouch that hung on a leather thong around his neck. "I will be back soon."

Shortly, Sky could hear his chant resume and smelled the sweet aroma of burning white sage wafting through the open window. Fawn inhaled deeply and drifted off in an exhausted slumber. She was so small, so frail. Why had this unspeakable evil been visited upon a child? Very slowly and gently, Sky took her knife and cut away the remnants of the tunic. It was beyond repair. By the time she had undressed the child and applied cool compresses to her injured flesh, she heard a tap on the door, followed by a man's voice.

"I'm Dr. Torres. May I come in?"

He sounded gentle, but when Sky opened the door, she was startled by how much he resembled Max. His hair was a darker gold and his eyes a lighter green, but they could certainly have been mistaken for brothers. She gathered her wits and ushered him inside. "Please, she's been horribly abused," she said.

Wasting no time, he nodded at her and strode across the small room to where Fawn lay. He knelt beside her, opening his black leather bag. "Your husband asked me to tell you he'll be along as soon as he sends a telegram."

"Thank you, Doctor," she replied, watching him check the girl.

"You've applied cool water. That's good. But some of these cuts and bruises have been caked with old blood." He poured out the pale pink water and poured fresh into the basin, then added a powder from a small bottle. "We'll have to soak the crusts away, then disinfect all areas where the skin's been broken."

Sky heard him mutter what sounded like an oath in some foreign tongue as he viewed the savagery visited on the girl. His touch was incredibly deft and gentle as he examined Fawn's injuries. Then he gave Sky instructions about how to use the poultice he'd made. As they worked together, she asked hesitantly, "Has she been . . . that is, did the man who whipped her . . ."

"Violate her? From what I can tell, no. That's not unusual when men abuse young girls. He's probably impotent and vents his fury in this sick way to compensate."

"Not any longer. I watched him die today," she replied coldly.

"Good," was all the doctor said, continuing to work. "Would you be so kind as to find a clean sheet? This blanket's too heavy to use as a covering."

"Yes, at once," she replied, heading for the door. On the way she picked up the Yellow Boy. Let that scrawny clerk say one word and she'd apply the same treatment to him as she'd done to Zebulon McKerrish!

A chastened Ichabod quickly fetched a whole stack of clean sheets and handed them over without a word of protest. Something in the "breed's" eyes utterly terrified him. He'd heard the cries of the kid Deuce had brought with him. He did not want to know anything more about it, whether the gunman was dead or alive.

Sky returned to room number seven with the linens. After cleansing all Fawn's wounds, Dr. Torres applied a pale yellow salve and explained to Sky how it should be used during the following days as the patient began to heal. "I smell white sage and some other herbal sleep remedies," he said when they had covered Fawn with the sheet.

"You know about white sage?" she asked, amazed. Most white physicians scorned Indian herbal remedies.

Torres stood, looking down at the old man in the yard below, tending a small fire that wafted through the window. "My family has studied medicine for generations in Spain and Italy, now in America. We've found many plants, some common, some rare, that have proved useful in a variety of ways. I've practiced on the White Mountain Apache Reservation for a number of years. When I finish a new course of study here, I'll rejoin the doctor who's taken my place."

"Then the Apache have cures similar to ours." The physician nodded. Sky digested that, then asked, "Do you believe in spells and chants as well?"

"There are many things modern medicine has yet to learn.

I wouldn't discount anything until I observed it. I take it the old man is kin to Fawn?"

. "True Dreamer is her grandfather. He's been following her since she was kidnapped."

Before the doctor could reply, Max tapped on the door. Sky rushed over to open it. "Fawn's asleep," she said softly. "Come in."

"Can't, love. I'm afraid I have to go with a deputy marshal to answer some questions about killing Deuce."

Chapter Fourteen

Sky's expression hardened into fury. "They can't blame you for killing that—that thing!"

Max pulled her into the hall. "I'm sure it's only a formality, love. The deputy tracked me down at the telegraph office. I imagine that vile clerk downstairs did his civic duty and told him where to find me."

"No wonder he was so obliging when I asked for clean sheets. He was waiting for them to arrest all of us," she snarled.

"I'll have this straightened out in no time." He gave her a brief kiss on her forehead. "Oh, if there is any trouble, just ask our friend out back what we should do to fix it, eh?" He squeezed her arm reassuringly. "Fawn will be all right. So will we, so don't worry."

Max walked down the stairs to where a stocky man of medium height and more than medium girth waited patiently. Deputy Marshall Harry Kruger. "I thank you for letting me speak with my wife, Deputy. Now, shall we get on with it?" Max asked.

"Like I said, no real problem. Nigh onta a dozen witnesses come forward to tell me whut happened at the Burnin' Pillars. That mean little runt Deuce drew first. Clear self-defense. Howsomever, Marshal Courtright has ta ask ya a few questions, that's all."

Max almost laughed. "Isaiah Courtright—Longhair Jim?"

The deputy chuckled at the longtime nickname of his boss. "Yep, the very same."

"Damn, I thought he'd be dead by now."

Deputy Kruger laughed, pulling on the end of his mustache. "Mr. Stanhope, he said the 'xact same thing 'bout you."

"All things considered, I imagine it was a reasonable assumption," Max replied dryly as they walked out of the hotel lobby.

"You see here, Mr. Stanhope," the deputy explained, "Fort Worth's come down with a bad case of civic outrage. Couply weeks ago, a little whore got herself kilt in the Acre. Might not a raised many eyebrows, but the fella who cut her throat nailed her to an outhouse door. Mayor an' county prosecutor are plumb bound and determined to clean up the Acre onc't 'n fer all."

"So Marshall Courtright figures that when the word gets out that the infamous Limey shot a man in a gunfight, he'll need to give the high muckety-mucks a full report," Max supplied.

Kruger nodded. " 'Sides, ole Longhair Jim tole me, 'Harry,' he sez, 'you tell that Limey ta git his towheaded ass down to my office, 'cause it's been a blue moon sinc't we split a bottle and swapped some lies.' "

Max sighed. It was going to be a long night.

When he returned to the hotel, the clerk informed him that his wife and "the others" had departed for fancier digs. He could find them at the Bonhomme House about a dozen blocks away. Obligingly, now knowing how dangerous it would be to anger the Limey, Ichabod gave precise directions to Max. It was nearing midnight and the Acre was in full swing as he made his way past endless saloons and bordellos, ignoring the blatant cat-calls of local ladies of the line, almost drowned out by men's oaths and the joyless noise of tinny pianos.

The warm night air did little to sober him up. Damn, why did the marshal have to be Longhair Jim? He needed a clear head to talk with Sky. Still half drunk, he saw the gleaming white frame two-story edifice with a sign proclaiming, BON-HOMME HOUSE, GUESTS WELCOME. He checked at the desk and was told that the womenfolk were in room twelve. He wondered if True Dreamer had left his granddaughter in the care of Sky and camped outside again, but figured he'd find out soon enough. If this clerk had any misgivings about the "guests" being Indians, he showed no signs of his prejudice.

Max managed to climb the stairs, only stumbling once. He located room twelve with no trouble in the dim light, but when he reached the door, he took a deep breath. Lord, he must smell like a distillery. He was surprised that Sky had not charged into the marshal's office to fetch him back. The image of her confronting Longhair Jim by jamming her Yellow Boy in his gut made him smile.

He opened the door quietly. A single light burned on a table across from where Fawn slept. Sky sat stiffly on a cushioned chair beside the lamp, staring at him. True Dreamer was nowhere to be seen. "How is she?" he whispered, looking at the child.

"She will recover," Sky replied in an icy voice.

"Love, I'm sorry about the way you learned of my past . . . for being so late—"

"I don't care if you committed adultery with every noble-woman in England, or if you and that marshal talked—or drank—all night," she said, smelling the whiskey from across the room. It even penetrated the scent of white sage coming from the small brazier that sat beside Fawn's bed.

Before he could digest her angry remark, she stood up and thrust a telegram at him. "W-what's this?" he said idiotically.

"The answer to your wire to Jerome Bartlett. It arrived shortly after you left with the deputy. Your solicitor is a very efficient man. Read it," she commanded coldly.

Squinting in the pale light, he skimmed the contents of the wire. "Damnation, Phillip has drowned in some kind of accident. Never had a chance to know him all that well, but he was a decent fellow. And young. Jerome will let us know the circumstances as soon as the investigation is complete." He frowned and cursed at the second paragraph. "Cletus has dropped out of sight. Bartlett urges us to be wary," he said, looking up at her.

"Read on." Her words dripped icicles in the warm room.

He did so and his hand began to tremble. Every ounce of blood seemed to drain from his veins. As if Deuce's revelations were not fat enough on the fire, Jerome now had to be a chatty bastard as well. The solicitor said that it would have been better if Cletus had been the one to die instead of their cousin. He then cautioned Max that the codicil to Harry's will regarding their marriage was still in force. Had he and his wife succeeded yet in starting a family?

He looked down at her set expression. "Sky, love, I can explain—at least I hope I can if—"

"That codicil you never told me about. It says you have to get a child on me in order to stop Cletus from inheriting the fortune. Do I have it right?"

His shoulders slumped. "Harry wanted to see me settled, but that doesn't mean I—"

"I don't want to hear any more. Not tonight," she whispered fiercely as she stood up, none too steady herself. "It's been a long, terrible day. I can't handle your glib explanation, Max . . . even if you were capable of giving one. True Dreamer and I will take turns watching over Fawn. He's gone to the stables to check on our horses now. Dr. Torres says she should be able to travel in a couple of days if we use a wagon. I've booked you a room down the hall." She thrust the key at him.

"Don't do this, Sky, love, please," he said, knowing he was begging now and not giving a damn.

"Get some sleep, Lord Ruxton. I have a feeling you're going to need a clear head in the morning." With that, she shoved him out the door and closed it behind him. He stood in the hall as the lock clicked from inside. It sounded sepulchral in its finality.

Well, what had he expected? Sooner or later he would have had to tell her about Harry's damnable will. Her reaction now was the very reason he had been too cowardly to do it. But her finding out this way was so much worse. If he'd at least tried to explain after he realized how much he loved her . . . but he had not. "Now I'll never know," he muttered thickly as he walked down the hall.

He opened the door to another room, with a single bed, furnished as comfortably as the one Sky and Fawn occupied. Moonlight filtered in from the window on one side. He did not even bother turning up the gaslight. God, the empty bed looked bleak and lonely. There were things he, too, could not handle after this terrible day.

Max closed the door and went downstairs, headed back to the Acre, in search of a barrel of rotgut whiskey.

Sky sat, staring woodenly at the closed door after Max left. Tears silently trickled down her cheeks. She could forgive his boyhood indiscretions, but this . . . this . . . *Why, oh, why, Max? Why did you deceive me so cruelly? Do you really hate Cletus that much? Was your vengeance worth it?* Of course, that was assuming he gave a damn about her and had not been using her only to fulfill the stipulations of his uncle's will. She could be with child right now! A mixed-blood wife and child to deal with and to make matters even worse, Cletus on his trail hiring gunmen to kill them all.

The irony of it only brought more bitter tears. In the morning she would have to decide what to do. They had to remain together to see True Dreamer and Fawn safely back to their home. They both owed the old man and innocent girl that much. After that . . . she rubbed her burning eyes, uncertain of what she should do, too exhausted to think about it any longer.

When the old Cheyenne entered the room, he found her asleep in the chair. He could see that she had been crying and knew the white man's message from the singing wires must have occasioned it. He and Fawn had both learned to speak English from a white man on their reservation who had married a Cheyenne woman and chosen to live with them. But Fawn had also been taught to read and write by the government agent they called Good Heart. True Dreamer had felt he was too old to master what came so easily to his granddaughter. Now he wondered if that was the reason the Powers gave him no indication about what troubled Sky Eyes and her man. No matter what had happened, he knew they were fated to be together.

Confident in that, he let Fawn sleep and lay down beside her bed to rest himself.

The next morning Max awakened, miraculously in the hotel bed he'd rejected the night before. He lay half across it, fully clothed. Even his boots remained on his feet. He rolled over and sat on the edge of the mattress, holding his aching head in his hands. What a bloody tangle he'd made of their lives. But at least he had an idea that might redeem himself in Sky's eyes.

Before he began drinking himself into utter oblivion last night, he had managed one important task—rescuing the remittance money Deuce had hidden in his room at the Excelsior. Sooner or later that vile clerk would've gathered nerve enough to search for whatever the dead man had left behind. The wastrel Englishman had gone through at least half of it, but Max had added a generous amount to the saddlebags he'd found beneath the bed. Now he had to put his plan into action.

He stood up on shaky legs and paused until the room righted itself before he proceeded to the mirror and looked at himself. Not a pretty picture. Sighing, he noted the bellpull. This certainly was a giant step up from Deuce's filthy hidey-hole in the Acre. He rang for hot water and set to work repairing his appearance. As he dug his razor from his own saddlebags, which Sky had put in the room last night, he considered that he might just cut his throat while shaving and save her the trouble of divorcing him.

After a bath, shave, change of clothes and several cups of hot coffee, he began to feel marginally human. When he opened the door of his room, he heard Sky and True Dreamer talking down the hall. She was going to buy some boy's pants and oversized shirts made of soft cloth to replace the destroyed tunic, as well as some kind of footwear for Fawn. After he heard the sounds of her footfalls fade down the stairs, he approached the old man, who turned as if expecting him.

True Dreamer smiled and beckoned him. "Come, meet my granddaughter, whose life you saved."

"Are you certain she'll want to meet another Englishman?" Max asked dubiously.

The old man grunted impatiently. "She is not foolish. She knows the difference between a good heart and a bad one." With that, he opened the door and stepped inside, making room for Max to follow.

Fawn was seated in the bed with the covers pulled up to her neck. One ugly red weal marred an otherwise lovely little face with strong, straight features. Max hoped the mark would not leave a scar. It appeared superficial. As to the wounds inside . . . only time would tell. He smiled at the girl as the old man made introductions.

"Child, this is the warrior I have told you of, the Pale Moon Stalker. He destroyed the weasel-snake and restored our honor."

She nodded politely, her large luminous eyes round with wonder and a bit of apprehension, when her grandfather added, "He, too, is an English. They are not all evil."

Max swept his hat from his head with a courtly flourish.

"It is a great honor to meet the granddaughter of my friend True Dreamer."

The girl's eyes widened even more as she began to speak rapidly in her native tongue. Her grandfather interrupted with a patient smile, admonishing, "Do not be discourteous, Fawn. You speak Pale Moon Stalker's tongue."

She flushed becomingly. "I meant no insult, Pale Moon Stalker, but I have never seen hair such as yours before. It is beautiful. You walk always in pale moonlight, gleaming like a ghost spirit guiding people on the Hanging Road to the Sky."

Now it was Max's turn to flush. Lord save him from girl-ish infatuations! "Er, well, when all's said and done, it is only hair. It confers no special powers. Among my people it's quite common."

"Oh, no, Stalker," Fawn said impulsively. "I have seen many whites and none look like you. You are beautiful. Sky Eyes has good fortune to have you for her man."

"I think Sky might not agree at present," he replied wryly.

"Then she is foolish. If she throws you away, I will have you if—"

True Dreamer interrupted her infatuated outburst while hiding a smile behind the hand covering his mouth. "Fawn, you should not speak so of a brave warrior-woman who has aided us. Besides, Sky Eyes will never let this one go."

If only that were true. Max took heart. Did the old medi-cine man know how this would end for them? He watched as the child lowered her head under the rebuke. "I am sorry, Grandfather. You speak true . . . but I do not understand how a wise woman like Sky Eyes would leave such a man as this."

Desperate to redirect the conversation and escape from his adoring new charge, Max turned to True Dreamer. "I have something we must discuss, regarding the return journey to your home," he said, patting the saddlebags carelessly slung over one shoulder.

True Dreamer nodded, then turned to Fawn. "We must

speak of our journey home, child. Only remain quiet until Sky Eyes returns with gifts for you as she promised."

The girl nodded, but Max could feel her gaze on his back as he walked through the door. Once out in the hall, he said, "It might be safer to talk about this in the privacy of my room."

The old man followed him down the hall and into the single room without making a comment on the peculiar sleeping arrangements Sky had made. Max opened the saddlebags and pulled out the money, saying, "This belonged to the weasel-snake. I found it beneath the bed in his room last night." He pulled out the fat bundle of greenbacks. "He has no use for it now."

"But, my son, we have no use for it either," True Dreamer replied.

"Ah, but that is where you are mistaken, my friend. This," he said, shaking the cash, "is better than lifting Deuce's scalp. Fawn will need to ride in a wagon for several days of the long journey. First, we will use it to buy that wagon and mules to pull it. Also last night at the whiskey lodge where Deuce died, I found an old man, a drover. With this money I can pay him to help me select and drive a small herd of cattle back to your people."

True Dreamer considered this for a moment, then grunted. "You are not only brave but also wise, Pale Moon Stalker. There is much hunger where our people are forced to live. The spotted buffalo will feed many hungry bellies through the next winter."

"That isn't all. I took the weasel-snake's gelding and the pony he obtained for Fawn and moved them to Watson's livery. As far as anyone is concerned, they belong to us now."

The medicine man beamed with pride. "My son, truly you are a great warrior. You have captured an enemy's horses and seized his weapon," he said, pointing at Deuce's Winchester, which Max had also taken from the room the previous night.

"And you have not only destroyed him but also now possess all of his wealth. You have counted so many coup that you would be a great chief among our people."

The approbation soothed a bit of the pain caused by Sky's angry rejection. He would find a way to win her trust. He simply had to, but for now, there were other matters to attend. "There is one question I must ask, Grandfather. I mean no insult, but those men in Tumbleweed accused you of stealing the gruella. Sir, did you, ah, count coup by taking it?"

"No, I did not, although I can see why you might think that," True Dreamer replied, choosing his words carefully. He appeared to grope for the proper explanation in English, then continued, "When I learned Fawn was taken, I needed a good horse to pursue the weasel-snake quickly. I took the one I ride from my friend the trader, Campbell. He is known among our people as Good Heart. In return I left my talisman in the stall so that he would know who took the gruella. He will trust me to return it. This I know."

Max sighed in relief. At least they wouldn't be greeted in the Nations by a federal marshal waiting to take them to Fort Smith to face the "Hanging Judge's" justice! "You are fortunate to have such a friend. When you return his horse, you will have the weasel-snake's to ride in its place, and his new rifle with which to shoot rabbits. It is only right since Sky and I could not have found him so quickly without your aid."

The old man nodded. Then some imp made him say, "Come, let us tell Fawn the good news."

There was nothing for it but to follow True Dreamer back to the girl's room. As her grandfather explained all of Pale Moon Stalker's valorous deeds to the child, she gazed at Max with rapt awe. "I will even have that pony to keep as my own. You are very generous, Stalker," she said coquettishly, again shortening his name, making it sound more familiar.

Max simply smiled at her, then said to the old man, "I have to go now, to meet the drover who'll help me buy the cattle.

Do you think that you and Sky can help him herd them all the way back to the Nations?"

"They will not be as wild as a herd of half-tame Indian ponies. I have managed those many times. So has Fawn—and your wife, I think."

"Excellent," Max said, eager to get about business now that everything here was settled. He was not quite ready to face his wife yet. He feared she would veto his accompanying them on the trip, but knew once she found out about his plans for the cattle drive, she could not accomplish it without him. Still, it would be wise to allow time to cool her temper.

He started to leave, but when he looked at Fawn and she said good-bye shyly, he impulsively bent down and kissed her hand before leaving the room.

The girl blinked and looked down at her hand while her tall warrior walked away. She would not have been half as delighted if he'd given her a ten-carat diamond ring. "Grandfather, he kissed my hand!" she exclaimed when her voice returned.

The old man grunted. "White men are strange. Especially English. To kiss a woman's hand . . ." He shook his head.

"Sky, this is Bronc Bodie," Max said as she sat sipping coffee in the hotel dining room. She turned, startled, not expecting her husband to approach her so soon after the ugly scene late last night.

"How do, missus," the white-haired old man said, doffing his hat respectfully as he stood beside her table. "You might remember me from the Burning Pillars saloon." His face reddened as he recalled the drunken crowd's reaction before the Limey had identified the woman carrying the rifle as his wife.

"Mr. Bodie, Sky Stanhope," Max continued smoothly, hoping she would be willing to hear out his plans before walking out in an icy huff.

"Yes, I do remember you, Mr. Bodie. You were most

chivalrous." She looked up at Max, puzzled by this unexpected development. She had just returned with clothing for Fawn, who was sleeping. True Dreamer had insisted that Sky should eat breakfast downstairs. Now, she realized that he had arranged this meeting with Max before sending her here.

"If we might join you for coffee?" Max inquired politely—too politely. He knew Bodie was wondering what was wrong between the two of them. "I have a plan to help our Cheyenne friends and their people in the Nations."

Sky nodded to two of the empty chairs around the small table. "Please, Mr. Bodie, Maxwell."

Regal as old Victoria. Butter wouldn't melt in her mouth either, Max thought as they sat down. "Mr. Bodie is a drover, a man who—"

"I know what drovers do, Maxwell," she cut in sharply, tapping her spoon nervously against the saucer beneath her cup.

"I've used Deuce's money to buy a wagon and mules so we'll have a safe way for Fawn to travel, but also, with this gentleman's help, I've purchased a couple of dozen cattle to drive back to the Nations. That will provide their people with meat through the winter."

She looked at Bodie. "Do you believe you, along with a woman, an Englishman and an old Cheyenne can drive over twenty head of cattle across the Red and into the Nations?"

"Reckon we might lose one or two, ma'am. But, I done drove bigger herds with less help all the way up to Montana Territory," he averred.

As she digested this, Max breathed a sigh of relief. In spite of her denigrating remark about "an Englishman," she had not refused outright. She understood how much good this would do for True Dreamer and Fawn's people. And it would buy him time . . .

"Very well. I imagine we can make it without too much

difficulty, barring interference from our old enemies," she said, looking pointedly at Max.

"If Cletus hires more thugs, we'll have to watch our backs and hope the mysterious Lady R is doing the same," Max said.

Sky turned to Bodie and asked, "Would you please excuse us, Mr. Bodie? My husband and I have a personal matter we need to discuss. We could meet for dinner here this evening, say about six, to iron out the details about the drive, if that's all right with you?"

Bodie rose and gave her a polite bow. "Be my pleasure, ma'am."

When he walked out of the nearly deserted room, Sky returned her attention to Max. "Taking the cattle to the reservation is a fine way to use Deuce's money. I commend you for it."

Noting the level, precise tone of her voice, he waited for the other shoe to drop. "Thank you. However, I hear a 'but' in there someplace." He scarcely dared to breathe, waiting for her to say he should not go along with them. "You know we're in danger from bushwhackers. Not only Cletus's inept thugs, but possibly McKerrish, too, and he's a lot more dangerous. I have Steve watching him. We'll know before we cross into Colorado whether he plans any trouble. I doubt he'd try killing us in Fort Smith's jurisdiction. Even his money can't buy a federal judge such as the fabled Isaac Parker."

"It isn't just Cletus and McKerrish that worry me," she said calmly. Far more calmly than she felt, sitting with his intense green eyes watching her like a puma ready to pounce on a crippled deer. "Has it ever occurred to you that the person behind the attempts on our lives might not be a Stanhope?"

"Surely you're not still suspicious of Jerome Bartlett?" he asked.

"Surely I am. Think, Max," she said intently, forgetting to use his full name. "Ever since we were married in Dakota Territory, every step along the way from New York to London, then back to St. Louis and into Colorado—and even from here, whom have you wired our every move to? Who else knew our itinerary so well as to be able to hire assassins to wait for us?"

"But for what reason?" he asked as doubt began to niggle. "Not Jerome. He's been Uncle Harry's solicitor for forty years. I trust him implicitly."

"Just as I trusted you?" she snapped back before biting her lip. This was not the time to discuss his betrayal.

"Touché, love. I should have told you in London, but—"

"Don't, Max, please. I can't deal with that now. Our first priority has to be Fawn and her safe return home." She remembered when she and her sister had been raped by the bluecoats and rescued by Clint. Without the love of her family, she would never have survived the shame and anguish. Clearing her throat, she went on. "All of the Stanhope fortune is handled by Bartlett, is it not?"

"If he'd ever stolen a penny, do you think a businessman as shrewd as my uncle would not have found out?" he retorted, seeing the gulf between them widening.

"Perhaps he waited until he had an absentee client. Note, there were no attempts to kill either of us in London. But who back there would question our deaths on this wild frontier? Bartlett could rob that little sot blind if he inherited. No one would be the wiser. He may already have chanced skimming money from the accounts since your uncle's death. As far as I've observed, you're not a great deal more attentive than your cousin when it comes to financial matters."

When she sat back, Max smiled at the unflattering comparison. "Ah, a double touché." Sky's cool expression did not change. He looked out the bay window of the hotel at the busy street, mulling over her reasoning. Jerome certainly had moved up in the world. Could his elegant new office and fine tailored clothes be because he was handling business affairs for that wealthy widow . . . or could there be a more sinister reason? "I suppose I could have someone in London investigate discreetly," he said reluctantly.

"Perhaps your friend Steve Loring can help. He appears to have business dealings practically everywhere," she suggested.

"Is this what we're reduced to, love? Stilted, polite conversations having nothing to do with our marriage?"

"At least I'm being polite, m'lord. You've seen me when I'm not."

He knew she did not refer to smashing McKerrish in the mouth. No, she was thinking of the diatribe that had sent his cousin stumbling from the Ruxton city house. "I was very proud of you that evening, m'lady," he replied, his eyes turning dark now. "But make no mistake. I am not Cletus."

Chapter Fifteen

By the time they rode out of Fort Worth, Fawn was recovering both physically and mentally. Dr. Torres had given his approval for her to undertake the arduous journey provided she ride in the wagon for at least the first few days. He remarked on how well her skin healed. For all the ghastly beatings she had endured, with his skillful stitching and the herbal salves, she would have no visible scars.

If her keen fascination with "Stalker" was any indication, her mind had not been damaged either. She feared no one and faced each day with renewed joy. "Will I be able to help with the cattle?" she asked Sky that first morning as the men herded the wild-eyed steers from the stockyard and up the busy street. She was standing up, holding on to the covered frame of the small wagon as Sky drove it behind the cattle. Before she could reply to the girl's question, they were interrupted by a loud, braying voice.

"Never seed a red-skinned wrangler afore," one drunken cowboy called out as he hung on to a lamp pole at the edge of the sidewalk, watching True Dreamer skillfully cut off a straying steer.

Sky calmly pulled the wagon to a stop, cocked the Yellow Boy and sighted it directly between the eyes of the commentator. "Funny, I've never seen a white-skinned polecat either. Where I come from, we shoot *pole* cats."

He backed away from the pole, his bloodshot eyes nearly popping from their sockets. "I-I never meant nothin', honest, m-ma'am," he stuttered as he scuttled clumsily around the corner into an alley, tripping over his own spurs.

"Would you have shot him?" Fawn asked from inside the wagon.

"Unfortunately, no. The white man's law would hang me if I killed a man just for being stupid," she replied.

Fawn giggled. "He looked very frightened, like a rabbit chased by a bobcat."

After caring for Fawn the past week, Sky realized how much she wanted children. If she and Will had been able to have them, a girl nearly Fawn's age could be her own. What had been a dream so long denied with Will now made Max's betrayal all the more cruel. He wanted to give her a child, but only to keep Cletus from inheriting the Stanhope wealth.

But he says he loves you, a self-torturing inner voice reminded her. Did he? Sky honestly had no idea. If only he'd explained the codicil to her before she fell in love with him. But when would that have been? As she looked back now, she was forced to admit she had probably fallen under Maxwell Stanhope's spell the first time he removed his hat and she saw that incredible face and the silver-gilt hair framing it. The Pale Moon Stalker. True Dreamer had certainly named him right.

She once again slapped the reins and the recalcitrant mules began moving. Just then, Fawn interrupted her self-pitying reverie. "I do not think Stalker is used to herding cattle," she said with a giggle.

A smirk tilted Sky's lips as she watched Max unsuccessfully attempt to prevent a steer from climbing nimbly onto the boardwalk in front of a saloon. "No, it would appear he is not," she replied while Bronc twirled his lariat and caught the would-be imbiber around the neck, dragging it from the swinging doors back to the street.

"Move along, doggie. You ain't got the two bits for a drink anyways," the old drover said with a chuckle.

The steer rejoined the herd as if nothing had happened while Max yanked hard on the brim of his hat, a nervous gesture Sky knew meant he was agitated. "Herding animals is quite a different matter than hunting them," she said to Fawn.

"But Stalker is a great hunter of evil men. Grandfather says his deeds are sung across the land in the white man's newspapers. I wish we had some of those newspapers at the trading post while Mr. Campbell was teaching me to read," she said dreamily.

Sky sighed. *Eleven years old and already another of Max's conquests. How does he do it?* But one glance at his lean, muscular body and chiseled features explained it all. She forced her eyes to stare straight ahead as they followed the small herd out onto the open plain stretching in front of them. This was going to be a very long ride indeed.

By the end of the day, it had become painfully obvious to Max that he was an utter failure as a drover. Although a superb horseman and tracker, he had never had occasion to acquire the cutting and roping skills required to hold a herd together. He watched Bronc and True Dreamer calmly kneeing their horses in intricate maneuvers to outflank frisky steers. Their lariats flew with artless precision, always landing around the necks of the ornery critters.

"Flaming hell, for all the good I'm doing, I might as well be herding cats! Two bloody old men! They're riding circles around me, literally," he muttered to himself when yet another wily steer slipped past him. Bronc headed it off and used his coiled rope to shoo it back, calling to it in whatever damnable mooing language cattle spoke. "I don't suppose French or Zulu would work," he groused, hating to look incompetent in front of Sky.

At least she was laughing. But not *with* him—*at* him. He was not, however, losing face with Fawn, who had made a point of sitting with him when they stopped for their midday meal, peppering him with questions about his life in England.

"Do they select English lords the way we choose our chiefs, from the bravest and wisest warriors?"

Max smiled. "Nothing so sensible. Titles are passed on from father to eldest son."

"Even if someone else is braver or smarter?" she asked, incredulously.

"I'm afraid so," he said with a shrug.

"Perhaps that's why Maxwell became a lord," Sky could not resist saying. Her already foul humor had not sweetened after six grueling hours trying to control a pair of incredibly strong mules. Her shoulders ached as if her arms had been ripped from their sockets.

"I became a lord by pure chance. I'm the last Stanhope male still alive, save for one cousin," he said aloud to Fawn. Then he stood up and moved across the campfire to his wife. "A situation you might wish to alter for both of us, eh, love?" he added lightly, kneeling behind her to massage her tense muscles. "You're going to be too sore to drive by morning."

She pulled away. "I'll manage. I'm used to handling jackasses," she replied, getting up and dusting off her breeches, anything to escape his touch. How well she remembered those long, callused fingers caressing her bare skin, the heat and scent of his body pressed to hers . . . no! She would survive this drive, one day at a time and not think of the past.

After they made camp that night and ate supper, Sky climbed into the wagon to sleep with Fawn. Max spread his solitary bedroll on the far side of the campfire. No one commented on why husband and wife did not share blankets. But everyone knew something was seriously amiss between them.

The next morning, Max's prediction about Sky's shoulders came true. Rolling over in the wagon, she bit her lip to keep from crying out and awakening the sleeping child. The pain was horrible and when she tried to raise her right arm, it simply refused to do her bidding. She felt the burning muscles quiver, then let the arm drop uselessly.

"I have some of the salve Dr. Torres gave me. Perhaps it will help," Fawn offered. She had awakened and sat quietly behind Sky, watching her friend struggle.

"That heals skin, Fawn, but I don't think it will help with muscles. I'll just have to work out the pain." Gritting her teeth, she pulled herself up and began to don her buckskins. She was sweating by the time she finished the simple task.

Fawn, too, had put on one of her new loose shirts and slid into a pair of boy's pants, securing the waistband with a length of rope. The store had no belts small enough for her. "I will cook breakfast."

"You're not strong enough," Sky admonished. "Just set out the cooking utensils on the wagon gate for me. I'll start the fire."

The men, who took turns watching the herd and sleeping under the stars, were awake and hungry. By dint of sheer will, she managed to light the fire and stir up a batch of biscuits before putting on the coffee.

"Mmm, smells good, ma'am," Bronc said as she pulled a tin of golden brown biscuits from the hot coals at the side of the fire and replaced it with a skillet filled with sliced bacon strips.

"I think the coffee's done. Will you test it, please?" she asked the old man. As he did so and gave her a thumbs-up, she asked, "How did you get the name Bronc?"

He laughed. "Come out West from Illinois. My folks was farmers 'n I wanted to be a broncobuster. Seen 'em in a traveling rodeo that passed by our town when I was a tadpole. Read all them penny novels 'bout cowboys 'n such." He stopped and chuckled.

"What happened then?" Fawn asked from the wagon gate where she was arranging a stack of tin plates.

"Oh, I bluffed my way into a job busting wild horses, right

enough. Busted both legs, my collarbone 'n an arm, too. 'Fore I had to give it up, I done busted everything but my peck—, er, pardon me, ma'am," he said, red-faced. When Sky only smiled, he continued, "That's when I got the handle, 'Bronc.' My being so bad at it, bronc busting was plumb hazardous for my health. Then I heard about a big cattle drive from Texas up to Montana Territory. Signed on. By that time I could sit a horse right well—long as someone else broke him first. Been drovin' beeves ever since, but the nickname stuck."

"We're grateful you agreed to help us," Sky said with a smile, offering him a jar of honey to go with the biscuits she'd piled onto a plate.

"I'm gettin' too old to take them Montana winters. Texas is hot as—'pardon, again, ladies," he interrupted himself, blushing once more. "Let's just say it's hot. But I'm fixin' on spending the rest of my life hereabouts. Drovin' beeves to the railheads in Kansas is as far north as I'll ever ride."

"You are a fine rider," Fawn said solemnly. Good horsemanship was a matter of honor among her people.

"It takes more than good riding to make a drover. You got to think like them beeves. Keep one step ahead of 'em," Bronc replied.

"It would appear that I am incapable of thinking like a steer," Max said wryly as he walked into camp. "I spent half the night chasing down strays with insomnia."

"What is in-insomnia?" Fawn asked him.

"Not being able to sleep," Sky supplied, as she and Max exchanged an understanding glance. Perhaps it was a good thing he stayed awake on night turn, rather than face his "dark warriors" once again and awaken the whole camp.

He seemed to understand her thoughts, for he quickly returned his attention to Fawn. "I hope you slept well in the wagon."

"Oh, yes, thank you. But Sky did not. I heard her tossing

and trying to find a way to rest that did not hurt her shoulders. They are very painful," she said, watching Sky struggle to lift a large iron skillet from the fire.

Max nodded as he stood up and quickly walked over to Sky, wrapping his larger hands over hers and helping her with the simple task. "I told you this would happen."

"I'll manage. I was raised doing camp chores far more arduous than cooking," she replied, relieved when he removed his hands from hers and stepped back.

"You never drove mules," he argued.

"You never drove cattle," she countered.

He snorted. "That is readily apparent to everyone . . . with the possible exception of my young admirer," he added with a rueful chuckle.

"She commented on it this morning, too," Sky volleyed back.

"Her infatuation does have its merits. She gave away how badly you're hurting. Let me drive the bloody wagon. I can do the cooking and you, according to Grandfather, learned to drive wild ponies when you were a girl in Dakota Territory."

"How on earth . . ." Her voice faded away. It was true. "I imagine there's no point in asking him how he knows that," she said.

"None whatsoever," Max replied cheerfully.

"You can barely make coffee. I'll drive the wagon." Her voice indicated the discussion was closed.

Max gave up when True Dreamer dismounted from the fine buckskin gelding he had "inherited" from Johnny Deuce. "Try talking some sense into her hard Sioux head," he said to the old man, then walked over to his horse and began rubbing it down after the night's exertion.

The Cheyenne only chuckled slyly and helped himself to bacon and biscuits. "You are a fine cook, Daughter." As he made the comment, he watched Max curry the buckskin he had ridden with strokes hard enough to rub the hair off the restive animal's hide.

Later that morning, they drew in sight of a shallow, rocky stream similar to the one with the pool above Wichita Falls where Sky and Max had bathed and made love. Sky was too exhausted even to think about that passionate interlude. She tugged on the reins as the mules smelled freshwater and picked up their normally desultory pace. "Whoa! You wretched, stubborn, ugly—"

Her diatribe was interrupted when the lead mule yanked its reins from her hands, causing the wagon to career on two wheels, then bounce wildly across the sagebrush and rocks toward the water. From behind her Sky could hear Fawn's pained cry as she was slammed against the side of the wagon, but Sky could not spare time to look back. She had to get the team under control before they overturned the wagon.

Max saw the team bolt from a distance, but the lowing of the cattle drowned out Sky and Fawn's cries for help. He yelled to the other men, then turned his horse as he kicked it into a full gallop to head off the mules. If only he could grab the leader's reins—or, if need be, jump on its back and yank the bit directly until it stopped.

Then his mouth went dry and a cry froze in his throat as he saw his wife preparing to leap from the bouncing driver's seat onto the mule. "No Sky!" he yelled as loudly as he could.

She could be trampled! He whipped his reins across his horse's neck frantically, leaning low as he closed in, praying she would hear him before she did something suicidal. Then her head jerked suddenly around and she saw him a second before jumping. He could see her call his name as he raced beside the team. Reaching out, he wrapped his fist around the lead mule's harness and yanked so hard that the headstall and bit cut through his heavy leather gloves and drew blood.

"Hold on tight!" he yelled to Sky and Fawn.

His painful grip did its work. Gradually, the wild team began to slow. By the time Bronc and True Dreamer reached them, Max had the wagon stopped. He kept his agonizing hold on the headstall where it joined the bit, having the satisfaction of seeing he was not the only one bleeding. The dumb brute had cut its mouth before giving up the crazed dash.

Without relinquishing his hold, Max walked the team to the water and allowed them to drink. Then, he dismounted and looked up at Sky and Fawn, peering from behind her. "Are you injured?" he asked.

"Oh, Stalker, we are not hurt. You are the one who is bleeding!" Fawn cried.

But Max and Sky did not hear her. Their gazes were locked on each other. Both of them were pale and frightened. He spoke first. "Now, will you let me drive these damnable animals?"

Prying her fingers from their death grip on the remaining set of reins, Sky tied them to the brake and set it, then climbed down. "Thank you for saving our lives," she said quietly. "Now, let me see your hand. I'm certain that's a nasty cut. It'll require stitching."

"Which you will doubtless enjoy," he replied with a fleeting grin that turned into a grimace when he removed the glove and blood poured across his palm.

"I can't see how you're going to handle those mules with your hand in this condition," Sky said as she prepared to stitch the deep cut across his palm.

"I've had worse and fired a rifle," he replied.

Both of them were acutely aware of each other, afraid to touch, yet knowing that they had to do so. They could feel everyone watching them as she laid out the medical supplies and struggled to thread the needle. Max could see her hands tremble, but she finally succeeded in hitting the eye and tied off a knot on a foot long piece of thread.

"I hope that's more thread than you'll require for a couple of stitches," he said as True Dreamer poured the stinging disinfectant over his hand. He stifled an oath of pain out of consideration for Fawn, who sat nearby, watching her brave "Stalker."

"Would you rather I had to stop before the cut's closed and rethread the needle?" she asked crossly.

"Here. Drink this. For pain," the old Cheyenne said, handing Max a small vial of some horrid-smelling liquid.

"Thanks just the same, but I fear the pain of tasting it would be worse than the pain from the needle." He thrust out his hand toward Sky. How soft and gentle those small, golden hands were. How well he remembered their feel against his skin. He focused on those erotic memories to blot out the sharp stabs and tugging of flesh he knew were coming.

Sky bit her lip in concentration, forcing her hands to be steady. He was a man who survived by using a gun. Without his right hand, he would be helpless. She could not afford to be clumsy. The wound must heal completely. Now that Grandfather had washed away the worst of the blood, she saw that the cut was not as long as she had first feared. *Three, four stitches, perhaps five.* She extended his arm across her knee and set to work.

Fawn watched his stoic acceptance of the pain in awe. "He is so brave, Grandfather," she whispered. "I would be content to be his second wife," she added hopefully.

"Hush, child. He does what he must . . . just as his warrior-woman does. And she will not share him," he added sternly, although he hid a faint smile from the girl. She, too, was brave, surviving the weasel-snake as she had. Her spirit remained strong. He thanked the Powers for that great blessing.

Now all he had to do was make certain the foolish English and his equally foolish woman recognized that their love was fated to last.

★ ★ ★

They spent the afternoon by the stream, resting their horses and the mules. The following morning, they set out once more, this time with Max driving the supply wagon with Fawn in the back. After his encounter with the Englishman, the lead mule's sore mouth made him somewhat more tractable. Considering how wickedly his hand throbbed, Max was grateful. He wore the heaviest pair of leather gloves they had with their supplies and a heavy pad over his palm, but it took all his concentration to hold the team steady.

No wonder his slender wife had not been able to control these powerful beasts. It took considerably more upper body strength than she possessed, and Sky was hardly a fragile belle. He watched her ride, admiring the way she cut off a steer before it could stray far from the herd. She was a natural on horseback and skilled at herding. She was skilled at many things, he thought. There was no way he could lose her and bear it.

So, he simply resolved that somehow he would find a way to prove that he loved her. He could renounce the title, but that would do no good. Max would be left offering her the prospect of living a dangerous and uncertain life as the wife of a bounty hunter. Scarcely an appealing prospect—or any way to help her people. After everything he had learned about the plight of the Ehanktonwon, not to mention the other tribes in the Nations, Max wanted to use his uncle's vast wealth to benefit as many as he could.

Fawn broke into his reverie, asking, "May I sit on the seat beside you, Stalker?"

He looked over his shoulder at the girl's hopeful face and sighed. "Are you certain you won't injure yourself? Dr. Torres said to wait another day or so."

"I am fine," she pronounced with the resilience of youth. "It has been a week since the weasel-snake hurt me."

Her matter-of-fact words startled him. But then, what did he know about Indian children—or English children—for that matter? He'd been the youngest in his family and always a bit of a loner, even as a boy, especially after Edmund died. He extended his hand and held her arm as she climbed over and sat beside him. "Hold on tight. Watch you don't fall off. We cannot afford to stop and pick you from a prickly cactus," he teased.

Fawn rewarded him with a giggle. "I will not fall, Stalker. I am strong."

"Yes, you are," he agreed. Lord, what this child had survived would have reduced many adults to blubbering bedlamites!

"Then I would make a fine second wife for you . . . in a year or so. I would do as Sky Eyes asked me and cause no trouble," she added dutifully.

When he had recovered his breath, Max replied as calmly as possible, "In a year or so you will be twelve. Even if white men were allowed to take more than one wife—which they are not—the woman would have to be at least sixteen or seventeen."

Fawn pouted. "That is very old. And having only one wife is very foolish." Then another thought struck her. "You could come and live among our people. There, a great warrior like you can have as many wives as he wishes!" Pleased with her solution, she beamed up at him.

He swore to himself and stared at the lead mule. Trading places with it was beginning to hold singular appeal, but in spite of himself, Max could see humor in the situation. With a teasing smile, he said, "Once you return to your people, there will be many fine young warriors growing into manhood. All of them will want you. You would be very sorry being stuck with an old man such as I. In a few years I shall grow so creaky, my bones will sound like Grandfather's gourd. Sky will have to help me stand up and sit down. Englishmen don't last as long as Cheyenne warriors such as True Dreamer."

Fawn digested this for a moment, then shook her head stubbornly. "Grandfather is very strong. He has good medicine, but he would share it with you if you were part of our family. Then your bones would not rattle like an Englishman's."

They both burst into laughter.

From horseback near the end of the herd, Sky could hear the musical tones of Fawn's soprano and Max's baritone blending. *He would make a good father,* that inner voice whispered once again.

Already scorching, the weather turned even hotter the next day. Awakening after spending a cramped, sweaty night in the wagon, Fawn announced, "I do not want to spend another night in here. It would be much better for us to sleep under the stars and feel the cooling night breeze."

Mopping perspiration from her forehead, Sky nodded, but before she could reply, the girl stated the obvious. "Then you can share Stalker's blankets once more. That will be good."

Sky's fingers froze on her thick plait of hair, which she was going to pin up to keep its warm weight off her neck. Her mind raced for explanations. "I have night riding duty. I'd only awaken him when I returned," she blurted out.

"He does not sleep well when he is alone. I have heard him cry out in the night several times, even though he sleeps far from the campfire. He misses you, I think."

Sky knew his nightmares were back. She had asked True Dreamer to dose him with more of his sleeping potions, but the old man simply gave her a lecture about her place at Max's side. "A wife is the best sleeping potion for a man," were his final words.

"My being there won't stop his nightmares, Fawn. Besides, there'll be little sharing of blankets the way you mean. With you, Grandfather and Bronc in camp, we would have no privacy. No, I'll sleep beneath the wagon with you."

Fawn sighed. "Sometimes I think I will never understand white people. Stalker should not allow you such freedom— and you should not want it," she added.

Freedom. The irony of Fawn's words struck Sky as she made up their bedrolls that night beneath the wagon. She knew the old drover must wonder why she and Max slept separately, although he was far too polite to mention it. True Dreamer scowled disapprovingly at her, while Fawn chattered away at Max as he prepared their dinner that night.

She watched him stir a bubbling pot over the fire. Because he could not help out on night turn watching the herd, he had inherited the cooking chores. And he was dreadful. This morning he'd made biscuits so leaden, Bronc claimed he broke a tooth on one. Even the coffee, which he had normally been able to make well enough, was full of grounds. Everyone had to strain it through their teeth. Having survived many a harsh trail experience, Bronc said that such "chawin'" was always required in Texas, even when one drank water.

The stew was a conglomeration of beans, bacon chunks, some wild onions Fawn had gathered and a rabbit True Dreamer had trapped last night. The meat was either greasy or stringy, the onions horribly strong and the beans had not soaked long enough to lose their crunch. But they were all so hungry from the day's hard work, they ate without complaint.

When she climbed into her bedroll next to Fawn, Sky felt as if the three men all watched her, Bronc puzzled, the medicine man disapproving, and Max . . . she was not certain what he felt. Anger? Embarrassment? Or sadness. She dared not look across the fire into those deep green eyes or she'd be lost. After they delivered their friends safely home, paid off Bronc and were alone—then they could sort their marriage out.

If it could ever be sorted out.

She lay staring up at the sky, listening to Bronc humming in the distance to the herd. Fawn and her grandfather were sleeping soundly. Bone weary after the long day, she knew she had only four hours to sleep before it would be time for her to take her turn with the herd. Yet sleep eluded her. She rolled over and had just begun to drift off when a loud cry rent the night air, eerie and terrible.

"Preeesent! Fire! Fire, dammit, fire, you bloody young fool! No!"

Chapter Sixteen

Sky threw off the light sheet and leaped to her feet, flying around the flickering embers of the fire and off into the distance, far from the others, where Max sat, staring into his own personal hell. True Dreamer raised his head, nodding approval when he saw her pass. Fawn started to get up, but he whispered softly to her, "Do not trouble yourself, child. Sky Eyes knows how to heal the Pale Moon Stalker."

When she lay back down, he rolled over and waited, smiling to himself. The couple's journey would be long . . . but the Powers had given him a vision. He knew now how he could aid them in finding their way.

Sky knelt in front of Max and placed one hand on his chest, feeling his heart thud furiously. His yelled commands ceased the instant they made contact. With her other hand, she took his raised arm, the one cocking the imaginary pistol, and gently lowered it, while crooning softly to him, "It's all right, Max. The past can't hurt you. Lie back and sleep . . ."

She pressed against his chest and he leaned back, drawing her with him. Sky lay over him for several moments, feeling the steady cadence of his breathing. He was sound asleep. So was the rest of the camp. But when she attempted to slip from his side, his arm wrapped around her shoulders and he held her fast against him, turning them on their sides. His warm breath brushed the nape of her neck as they lay spooned together the way they had so often slept.

It felt so natural. Was he faking this? No, he would never

intentionally reveal his nightmares this way. Nor did she feel an erection probing between her legs. He was truly asleep. Her presence had driven the dark warriors away. True Dreamer was right about the power she had to heal her husband. Perhaps that was fated to bind them together in this marriage, no matter what Max Stanhope's original intentions had been.

Too weary to think straight, she closed her eyes, but then heard the soft footfalls of the old Cheyenne. He drew just near enough so she could hear him say, "I will take your place with the cattle this night. You are where you belong now. Stay there."

With that, he returned to the campfire.

Is this where I belong? Sleep claimed her and she sank into its welcoming embrace.

Max came slowly awake, feeling the first faint light of dawn seep beneath his eyelids. Then he inhaled Sky's unique scent and felt the warmth of her soft body pressed to his side. She lay with one arm across his chest, her head nestled against his shoulder. A soaring joy filled him as he opened his eyes and watched her sleep. But then he considered how she'd come to be there and memories of the nightmare crowded out his contentment.

She must have heard him. Flaming hell, the whole camp had probably heard him, including the steers. It was a miracle the dumb brutes hadn't stampeded. That was why she'd come to him—to shut him up. And that crafty old Cheyenne was complicit in seeing that she stayed. Without checking, he knew the old man must have taken her night turn riding herd. *So she could ride herd on one raving mad Englishman.*

He looked at her lovely face, peacefully asleep. But he could see the dark circles beneath her eyes and knew she was exhausted and had not been sleeping much better than he. "Ah, Sky, love, how will we untangle the mess I've made of our lives?" he whispered, placing a kiss on the tip of her nose as he gently lifted her arm and slid away. As camp cook, he had to restart the fire and begin making breakfast.

After spending years on the trail, he was used to fending for himself. Cooking simple food for one person or two was easy enough, but cooking for five seemed disproportionately difficult. He managed to wreck virtually every meal some way or other. Perhaps he was just too worried about his marriage to concentrate, he thought as he pulled on his boots and trudged off to gather firewood.

Sky felt the absence of his warmth and rolled over in time to watch him stride away from camp. Would he assume that she had returned to him for good? Or, would the realization that she'd gone to him because of his outburst make him angry and defensive as it had after they'd left Leadville? "There's only one way to find out," she muttered to herself and sat up to face the dawn.

No one mentioned her absence on night duty, or where she'd spent that time. If Bronc figured it out, he was too much a gentleman to say anything. Sky could tell that Fawn knew, as well as her grandfather. Mercifully, the loquacious child for once kept quiet. Max said nothing to her as they ate breakfast and broke camp . . . but she could sense his speculative gaze on her as she rode away with the steers.

Just as they were skirting a small town to avoid trouble with unfriendly white men, a gaudily painted wagon appeared on the trail directly ahead of them. "It's a medicine showman. A snake oil salesman, or I miss my guess," Bronc said, turning the steers so as to avoid a collision.

"That man has no true medicine," the old Cheyenne said with a grunt of displeasure.

Sky approached the wagon, which did indeed say, DOCTOR ADAMS' MIRACLE CURES AND OTHER AMAZING FEATS. A rumpled, dusty man with a round face and keen dark eyes smiled broadly. He had a narrow mustache perched above a set of improbably white teeth, and held a cigar clenched in one of his meaty fists. Perched on a bar beside him at the front of the wagon was a tiny monkey dressed in a red satin cap and vest.

"Good afternoon, my dear young lady. Would you or your companions be interested in curing saddle sores, gout, boils, disorders of the intestines or social diseases?"

Suppressing a smile, Sky replied, "No, we're not afflicted by any of those things." *Although, if Max continues to cook, 'disorders of the intestines' might soon be a problem.*

Bronc and True Dreamer reined in beside the wagon as the man was climbing down, waving a bottle. Max pulled up their wagon and Fawn immediately jumped down, her eyes growing large as she looked at the monkey, then the fantastical circus pictures painted on the sides of the strange man's conveyance.

"It is a house on wheels," she said in wonder. "And a strange animal who wears clothes!" She turned to Max. "Have you ever seen such a one, Stalker? Is it magic?"

"It's a monkey. From Africa, Fawn, but not magic, I'm afraid."

"This here's a circus wagon," Bronc explained. "You have a show for the young'un here?" he asked.

"I might. But first, I know you have been on this long weary trail for many days. You must try this fine elixir to help you sleep and grant you renewed vitality to face each day." He produced a bottle of some dark liquid and offered it to True Dreamer. "You, sir, appear to be most in need of revitalization."

The old man grunted and uncorked the bottle. He wrinkled his nose and shoved it back to the salesman. "Ugh! That is poison, not medicine."

Undaunted, the fat man pressed the awful-smelling bottle on Bronc and Max, both of whom blinked at its foul odor. "Smells like skunk piss," Bronc whispered to Max. " 'Nough to make yer eyes burn."

"Or blind you if you drink it," Max replied.

Overhearing their less than flattering comments, the showman said, "Nonsense. It's quite safe." To demonstrate, he took a deep swallow and wiped the back of his hand across his mouth. "Aah, the elixir of life itself. Are you certain you don't wish to buy—"

"Do you have a show to entertain the little girl?" Sky asked impatiently. She had seen the disappointed look on Fawn's face when the salesman had ignored Bronc's request and Max explained that the monkey was not magic. The little animal studied them with his head cocked but remained at his perch on the wagon seat.

A crafty look came into his owner's eyes as he sized up the group. "As I said, I might . . . if you can afford a buck for it."

Max reached into his pocket and tossed a silver dollar at the salesman, who caught it deftly. "Very well. Let's see the show."

"Will the monkey perform tricks?" Fawn asked.

"Better than that. He will perform them with the aid of his personal assistant," Adams replied as he waddled around to the back of the wagon and raised the tailgate, propping it open and folding down a stage, complete with curtain. A thin bark sounded from behind the curtain. "Voila! Al Kazir, the Wonder Dog!" With that, he pulled the curtain open to reveal a small shaggy dog of indeterminate color and breed, which sat up on his hind legs, begging for a treat.

"Oh, how sweet," Fawn exclaimed.

"He don't look like no Al-kasser to me," Bronc said dubiously. "Just a cute lil' ole mutt."

The salesman fed the dog a tiny bit of hardtack from his pocket, commanding him to stay. When he fetched the monkey from its perch, they noticed the reason the little animal had not moved before. Its leg had been chained to the post. Adams freed it and let it climb on his shoulder as he sauntered to the miniature stage at the back. "This is a most remarkable animal from darkest Africa. Zulu, you may begin."

Sky caught the involuntary flinch from the corner of her eye and looked at Max. His face had suddenly turned the color of bleached clay. Zulu. The fierce tribe he had battled in southern Africa. She felt the urge to offer comfort, but stood still, afraid of what Max might do if he realized she had seen his reaction.

Fawn watched in rapt awe as the nimble little monkey turned backflips and cartwheels, tossed its satin cap in the air and caught it. To the girl's utter glee, it then tossed the cap to the dog, which caught it in his teeth, then did a dance on its hind legs before walking across the tiny stage to lay it at Zulu's feet.

"And now, ladies and gentlemen," Adams said with a grand flourish, "I ask you, have you ever seen a monkey or a dog who could count?"

Fawn shook her head and the adults joined in. She was obviously enjoying the show immensely.

"Zulu will turn flips. Each time he completes a series, Al Kazir will scratch the corresponding number with his paw. One," he said to the monkey, who turned one backflip and looked at the mutt. The dog's right front paw made a single scratching motion on the stage. Fawn clapped her hands delightedly.

"Three," Adams said and the monkey complied. So did the dog, who then looked at his owner, hopeful for another treat, but the fat man rewarded the monkey, not his other performer. "Seven," he commanded and the monkey turned seven times. But the dog made a whining sound and sat back. "Seven," Adams repeated through gritted teeth, almost biting off the end of the cigar clenched between them. He pounded the stage and the monkey leaped onto his shoulder, screeching angrily. The dog looked at him with sad eyes.

"Perhaps that is too high a number," Fawn ventured.

"Worthless mutt's counted as high as twelve," Adams said with an oath.

"No need for cussing in front of womenfolk," Bronc said in a warning tone, but Adams ignored him, intent on his glaring contest with the dog. "Seven," he repeated again, moving his hand in his pocket.

"He hides the food," True Dreamer said quietly to Max. "His heart is not good for the dog."

As if on cue, the mutt whined again and tried to lick Adams's hand. The man withdrew his other hand from his pocket and punched the little dog sharply across the muzzle. "Now we'll see who's boss. I run this show," he muttered as the monkey screamed and jumped up and down on his shoulder.

"They suit, don't you think?" Max said tautly to Sky.

"Do not hurt the dog," Fawn pleaded, tugging on the man's hand as he tried to raise it for another blow.

"That's it, folks. Show's over," he said, shaking the girl's hand off as if she were a leper.

He shoved the dog off the stage onto the floor of the wagon behind it. They could hear it land with a thump and a yelp. Then Adams started to raise the tailgate, but Max interrupted him. "How much for the dog?" he asked.

Adams turned, shoving the back of the wagon closed, his eyes narrowed in crafty calculation. "This is a highly trained animal from Arabia. Zulu and I could never think of—"

"How much?" Max asked again, this time crowding the fat man's space, looking down into his perspiration-soaked face.

"I couldn't accept anything less than fifty dollars, hard currency," he said, wheedling. The monkey screeched its approval as if happy to get rid of its competition for treats.

"You're amusing enough to go on the stage in a music hall, old chap. Five dollars, hard currency," Max replied. "And that is my final offer."

Something in his cold green eyes made the snake oil man back up and raise his hands protectively. "Lookee, mister, I spent a lot of time training that mutt—"

"It would appear you've wasted your time. I suggest you

take the money before I start seeing how many backflips *you* can do."

"Now, see here—"

"One," Max said quietly.

Bobbing his head in nervous assent, Adams hastily agreed. "All right, five dollars it is." He reached out one pudgy hand, palm up.

"First the dog," Max said.

Adams turned around angrily and yanked down the tailgate. Leaning over as much as his belly would allow, he grabbed the dog by the scruff of his neck and threw him on the ground. "There's your damned mutt. Now give me my money," he snarled over the shrill noise of the monkey.

Fawn rushed over and picked up the rail-thin dog. "Oh, he is shivering," she said, backing away from the fat man with the piggy little eyes.

"Take it and leave quickly, old chap. Any more theatrics from you and I shall turn you over to the tender mercies of the young lady's grandfather. He is a real medicine man who could do things to you that would make backflips seem tame." Max shoved a greenback into the fat man's suit pocket. True Dreamer fixed the snake oil man with a penetrating stare that was even more frightening than the Englishman's.

It was not "hard currency," but Pythagoras Adams was not inclined to argue. He waddled to the front of his wagon and clamored up, stumbling in his haste to get away. With the monkey still screeching from his shoulder, he whipped his horse into a fast trot and vanished down the road.

Both men looked down at Fawn and exchanged a smile when she said, "He does not look like an Al Kazir to me, whatever that is. What should we name you?"

Sky knelt beside her and patted the dog, whose tail thumped happily. "Before we do that, I think we should get him something to eat. He looks starved."

"Probably how he trained the poor critter," Bronc said.

"Thank you, Stalker, and you, Grandfather, for rescuing him from that bad man," Fawn said before she followed Sky to their wagon in search of food for their new charge. "Can he ride in the wagon with me?" she asked Sky.

"I don't see why not, do you, 'Stalker'?" Sky asked with a grin.

He smiled back at her. "No reason at all." Turning to Fawn, he said, "Before you name him, consider carefully. He looks to me to be a rather special dog."

"Of course, Stalker," the girl replied solemnly. "That is our custom. Our people always choose their own names by how they act or something they do, or visions they see. I will do the same for this one."

The mutt did not receive his name until they stopped for the night. Max set a fire and set about making dinner as the other adults bedded down the steers. By the time they returned to camp, tired and hungry, they could scent another culinary catastrophe. The pot of beans and fatback did not smell too bad, but something was definitely burning.

They found Max muttering to himself as he squatted beside the coals, fishing burned biscuits from a tin, inspecting each one and tossing those with black bottoms behind him. "There's one. Two." He replaced several passable ones, then threw out another. "Three. Four . . ."

By the time he reached ten, Fawn, Sky and the two old men could contain their laughter no longer. "What's so flaming funny?" he asked, throwing biscuit number eleven with a wicked snap.

"He can count—when he wishes to do it," Fawn said between giggles.

Behind his back, the dog made a scratch in the dirt each time he called out a number and threw away a burned offering.

"Snake oil fellow said . . . he could count . . . up to twelve. I betcha . . . he can go clean up ta . . . twenty," Bronc got out between guffaws.

"He appears quite proficient at mathematics," Max said, glaring at his laughing tormentors.

"I think we should call him Numbers," Fawn announced.

Max scowled at the performer, who sat, intently waiting for further direction. "All right, Numbers, shall we test precisely how high you can count?" he asked, picking up another tin of burned biscuits. He threw one to the dog, who sniffed it and whined, but did not eat.

That night Sky knew everyone was waiting to see whether she would again sleep with her husband. To give her a push in that direction, Fawn invited an eager Numbers to sleep with her beside the wagon, shoving Sky's bedroll to one side to make room. She calmly picked up the roll and carried it away from the fire, but not to where Max had tossed his. If his nightmare returned, she would be close enough to reach him quickly, yet far enough away to preserve her pride . . . and peace of mind.

How long would it be before they again gave in to the simmering sexual attraction that had begun when they first met? It was his nightmare that had occasioned the consummation of their marriage in the first place. This was not the time to resume a relationship that might yet end sadly.

Max stretched out beside the fire, sipping coffee, this time not filled with grounds, thank heavens. In spite of the debacle with the biscuits, the meal had been palatable. He was progressing as a cook, but an utter failure as a husband. Over the rim of his cup, he watched his wife make up her bedroll. As much as he despised the humiliating dream that would not let him go, he had been grateful last night that it brought Sky to him. He knew it was the first restful sleep either of them had gotten since she'd read that damnable telegram from Bartlett.

And here she was, intent on keeping her distance. He debated walking over and dragging her to his bed. Bloody hell, she was his wife. He had the right to at least lie by her side. She was due to take the first night turn with the cattle. He watched her swing up on her horse and lope out to the herd. What should he do?

Fawn and Numbers were already sleeping soundly. He smiled at the child and her dog, then noted that Bronc was snoring with his usual buzzing gusto. But the old medicine man sat cross-legged on his blanket, back ramrod straight, face turned up to the starry night sky. Was he making some kind of new magic? Communing with his Powers? True Dreamer had watched the interaction between him and Sky ever since the rift began. The old man's calm confidence gave Max hope. But nothing so far had turned out the way he'd imagined it might. Sky still kept her distance, polite yet remote.

What the flaming devil does he expect me to do?

Go to her. The words intruded in his mind so suddenly, he splashed coffee into the dust as he jerked his body around, looking once more at the silhouette of Grandfather's straight back. Could he enter another man's mind? Max felt the hair along his neck stand up. Well, it was not as if he hadn't already seen True Dreamer's power demonstrated.

Quietly, he tossed the dregs of his coffee out and got up. He walked across the open ground toward the distant shadows of the cattle. He could see his wife and her horse outlined against the night sky. Moving slowly so as not to set off the cows as they grazed, he approached her. "Hello," he said when he was close enough not to have to raise his voice to be heard.

Sky turned and saw him standing in the moonlight, that pale hair gleaming brighter than the full moon itself. "What are you doing out here? You'll spook the herd."

"They seem calm enough to me. Get down, Sky. We need to talk and this is the only place with privacy enough."

She did not move. "What we have to settle can wait until after we leave the others behind."

"Is that when you plan to leave me behind, too, love?"

"I-I don't know. I need time to think things through." Her voice sounded defensive and she knew it. But he was the one who had betrayed her! Why should he make her feel guilty?

"Until we find out who's trying to kill us—oh, and deal with McKerrish as well—I don't think we can afford for you to be off by yourself. We have to stay together."

"We are staying together, Max. We're just not sleeping together."

"We did last night." There was a darkness in his voice.

"That isn't what I meant and you know it," she snapped.

"Raving out loud from a damnable nightmare is scarcely the way I would choose to win you back," he replied, his voice tight, low. "But having you with me . . . lets me sleep," he confessed.

"If you're trying to lure me back with guilt, it won't work." A steer bawled at her sharp voice.

"Best have a care or I could be trampled in a stampede," he said, drawing closer.

"Don't tempt me."

"That would solve the problem for you, wouldn't it? You'd have no choice to make. You'd be a widow again."

"What a perfectly horrid thing to say!" This time several of the steers started to move restlessly. "Look, Max, this isn't going to work. We can't talk now."

"Then meet me by that cottonwood when you're relieved," he said, pointing to the only tree of any size, located on the opposite bank of the muddy creek they'd camped by.

"And if I don't?" she asked, swallowing when he stood directly beside her, his hard green gaze fixed on her face.

"Then I'll bloody well drag you kicking and screaming. And no one shall say me nay, madam."

She watched him stalk away and rubbed her aching head. If only she weren't so tired and filthy, she might be able to think straight. Maybe the accumulating layers of trail dust were clogging her brain. But arrogant as his statement was, she did know Maxwell Stanhope. Limey or Baron Ruxton, he was a man of his word. Worse yet, everyone around that campfire would probably cheer him on, blast them!

Should she go to him . . . or refuse and take the consequences?

Chapter Seventeen

$\mathcal{M}$ax waited beneath the shadows of the cottonwood, so weary that sleep should have claimed him, but too tense for it to be possible. Instead, he paced. Would she come? What would he say to her? "This is the last time I listen to voices inside my head," he muttered, tossing away a dry blade of grass he'd been chewing on. How long had it been? He looked at the moon, judging how high it was. Bronc must have relieved Sky by now.

He thought about his threat. Could he actually humiliate them both by tossing her over his shoulder and carrying her through the camp as if she were his possession? That would solve nothing, only alienate her more. He pounded his fist against the rough bark of the cottonwood and cursed. "Bloody hell!" He'd broken open the stitches she'd sewn on his hand. He was an idiot. But then, wasn't that a congenital condition of besotted men?

Certainly his father had never been so afflicted. But Harry had. Of course, Lodicia had never behaved the way Sky did. From all reports after her death, she'd been a proper English lady. A wry smile strained at his lips when he considered how his uncle would have handled a wife as headstrong and independent as Sky Eyes of the Ehanktonwon.

He was in the midst of wrapping a handkerchief around his hand when he heard a soft rustling noise and looked up. She walked deliberately toward the tree, as if going to her own hanging. "Defiant to the bitter end, eh, love?" he murmured as he waited hidden in the shadows. *Let her wonder if I'm the one who decided not to talk.*

Sky's mouth felt as if she'd swallowed a tumbleweed whole. What if he were back in camp, laughing at her? After the embarrassment she'd caused him by refusing to share his bedroll, he might believe this served her right. Max was a proud man. Sky had not intended to hurt him, but she was willing to admit—to herself, at least—that she feared she would succumb to his touch if they spent any time together.

When she reached the tree, she stopped, trying to penetrate the darkness beneath it. Then his voice. "I won't fall on you like a ravening wolf, Sky."

"Considering the threat you made out there"—she gestured toward the herd—"I might have reason to doubt that."

"I said I'd drag you to my bedroll, not that I'd rape you, love. I've never forced a woman in my life."

"You've never needed to, Max. Women flock to you adoringly. But I have been forced . . . and it . . . it made my first husband afraid of frightening me . . ." Her voice trailed away. She had not meant to dredge up those painful memories. He already knew about the bluecoats.

"You've always felt guilty for enjoying something with me that you never shared with him, haven't you?" His tone was softer now. "I had hoped we were past that, but I see I was mistaken."

"It's more complicated than that."

"That's pretty complicated, already. Father Will's ghost has been hanging over us since the day we met. I thought once you asked me not to kill Deuce that Brewster had been laid to rest."

"He has—or, he was until I found out you needed a real marriage to fulfill your uncle's will. You made me love you . . . and then . . . and then, after I shared all my secrets with you, I learned what you should have told me the day we made our bargain."

"I didn't know then, Sky. I honestly believed I required a wife in name only, a marriage that could be annulled, that I could walk away from. I found out about the codicil when I first spoke with Bartlett in London."

"Then why didn't you tell me in London?" she asked, wondering whether or not he was speaking the truth now. No, she knew Max would not lie.

"I was afraid you'd ask for an annulment and find another man to avenge Brewster." His voice was bleak. "Don't tell me you would not have done. I know you well, love."

Her shoulders slumped. "Yes," she said in a small voice. "I probably would have bolted. But not because of Will . . . although I didn't know that my grieving for him was over then. Now I realize that I was using him as an excuse . . ."

"For what?" he prompted, stepping closer to her.

"When you made your impulsive offer in Bismarck, you had few choices and little time. I was convenient. But I have mixed blood. I was raped. I'm scarcely the kind of woman you would have picked had circumstances been different."

"You are exactly the woman I would choose. The only woman I want—strong, maddeningly willful, intelligent, beautiful, passionate." He reached out and placed his hands on her shoulders, willing her to believe him. "What's past is past, love. I'm not cut out to be a lord. My life is here, not back in English society. I know who you are . . . and I love you for it . . . all of it."

Sky trembled. "Yes," she choked out, "you do know everything, I suppose. I've shared my past, but you've held back so much."

"I can explain about Cynthia—the viscountess. I was twenty and she was a decade older when—"

"She took advantage of you?" Sky interrupted bitterly. "I honestly don't give a damn about the peccadilloes of your youth, Max. It's the foundation of our marriage that concerns me. Can you blame me for believing the worst when I read that telegram?"

"To hell with the will! I'd give every penny of the money to Cletus if I thought it would win you back—but how could I support us then? Continue my life as a bounty hunter? And what of your people? I want to help them. The inheritance would be an incredible blessing—for them and for True Dreamer's people."

"How noble," she said coldly. Was he telling the truth? She honestly did not know. Her own insecurities, bolstered by a lifetime of prejudice as she was caught between red and white worlds, made her vulnerable. She could no longer trust her own judgment.

"The only reason I want our marriage to continue is because I love you, Sky."

"And because I hold your nightmares at bay?" When he made no response, she persisted. "Do you love me enough to tell me why you have them? Why you resigned from the army and scorned a Victoria's Cross? Why you became a bounty hunter?"

His arms dropped from her shoulders and he stepped away, turning his back. "You ask too much. You've admitted it took you months to realize that you were ready to start over . . ."

"And you aren't ready to share painful memories with me as I did with you. You said the past is past, Max. Then why can't you let it go?"

"I have . . . but, God above, it won't let *me* go," he said in a strangled voice.

"Then the only way to break free is to trust me with it," she pleaded.

He stood and watched her walk away, holding his bleeding hand against his chest, hoping the throbbing physical pain would take his mind away from the anguish twisting his soul. But nothing could do that.

When he finally returned to camp, he was amazed to see Sky sitting on his bedroll. "What are you doing here?" he asked, not daring to hope.

In an equally soft whisper, she replied, "You can't hold the nightmares at bay without me. Besides, everyone treats me as if I'm a traitor or a fool for staying away. We will sleep together until we reach the reservation . . . but sleep only—is that clear?"

A tight smile spread across his mouth. "Always dutiful, Sky . . . even if you're coerced by a couple of old men and a child. I'll settle—"

"You're bleeding!" she said louder than she intended, but only Numbers stirred. After giving them a quick inspection, the dog lay back down beside Fawn.

"I may have opened the stitches. It's not bad."

Sky jumped to her feet and led him to the low embers of the fire, stirring them into fresh flames. She unwrapped the handkerchief and the bandage beneath it. "I'll have to clean it off before I can tell if it requires restitching. How did you do it?"

He gave her a bitter smile. "Pounding on the tree trunk while I was waiting for you."

She snorted in disgust and walked silently to the back of the wagon to get her medical supplies. Were all men idiots?

His hand did not require restitching, but she wrapped it tightly after disinfecting it and giving him a whispered tongue-lashing. Then they slept side by side, too exhausted to stay awake in spite of the unsatisfactory conclusion of their conversation.

In the morning, Fawn and True Dreamer smiled broadly when they saw the placement of bedrolls, assuming the arrangement would continue permanently. Even Bronc appeared relieved that whatever was troubling husband and wife appeared to be settled.

They continued north and forded the Red River without incident. After all his years as a drover, Bodie knew a place around the bend from where Max, Sky and True Dreamer had made their almost deadly crossing. Burkburnett was a few miles out of the way, but the current was slower and the streambed more level.

A day later they lost a steer. After it placed one hoof in a prairie dog hole and broke its leg while evading Sky's lariat, Bronc shot the animal to put it out of its misery. Everyone did their share of the work, butchering and salting down most of the meat to preserve it, and they only lost one day.

They reserved enough fresh beef to last for several days. Max applied himself to making a roast with dried vegetables in the Dutch oven that night. It turned out fairly well. "You can be my trail cook any day, yer lordship," Bodie said, wiping his mouth and going back for seconds.

"It is a gift from the Powers," True Dreamer intoned.

Sky and Fawn chuckled while Max glowered at the old medicine man.

The trip through the reservations was slow, complicated by various jurisdictions and "officials" who demanded tolls to let a herd of cattle cross their land. Usually, Max was able to buy them off cheaply. At one place, a white marshal, who had strayed far from his town limits, tried to extort ten dollars a head from a man he thought was simply a "dumb Injun-loving foreigner."

Once he learned the funny accent belonged to the infamous Limey, he quickly backed off and rode away with Numbers barking furiously at the heels of his galloping horse until he disappeared over the nearest ridge. The little dog, which had put on considerable weight since changing owners, continued to dance, count and generally delight them all, but most especially Fawn.

Max was particularly happy because the more attention she paid to Numbers, the less time she had to think up ways to devil him about becoming his "second wife." Her healing had progressed so fast that not a mark was visible on her face, arms or legs. Everyone was grateful for she was a lovely and loving child.

As the little group sat around the campfire on the last night before reaching the Cheyenne reservation, Fawn fed her pet bits of meat from her plate. Max smiled and said, "Have a care there, before he grows so fat and you so skinny, no one will recognize you, or that he is indeed a dog and not a pig ready for roasting."

Numbers barked in protest and turned in a circle on his hind legs, waiting to see if that might earn him another sliver of beef, but Fawn defended his honor. "No one will dare touch Numbers. He is far too clever and he does not look like a pig!" Then another thought occurred to her. "Do you think I am too skinny, Stalker?"

He had to grin. *Well, old boy, you brought this one on yourself.* "No, I was only jesting, Fawn. You are just right, not too thin at all."

She brightened, placing her empty plate on the ground. Numbers's tongue busily polished it clean before she could utter a word. "That is good. If you ever change your mind, I promise that I won't get too skinny to be your second wife."

Sky choked back a laugh and looked at her husband as if saying, now what are you going to do? True Dreamer's mouth curved in what might have been a grin but he maintained his composure.

"Lil' gal sure does have a one-track mind when it comes to her plans for you, Max," Bronc said with a guffaw.

Max looked at Fawn's face, ignoring the others. After a moment, he said, "Young lady, are you jesting with me?" He waited a beat, then added sternly, "Tell the truth now."

"But I am not a lady, Stalker."

"One day you will be," Max said and suddenly realized he had meant that as a promise. Yes, one day when she was ready, he would return for this wonderful child—if he lived. He might not have a wife, but by God, he would have a foster daughter to love. Then, his head snapped up, and his eyes locked with True Dreamer's. The old man nodded, and slowly both of them smiled.

Fawn sighed dramatically, completely unaware of the silent exchange that would shape her future. "Well, after Sky and"—she paused and glanced over at the old medicine man—"Grandfather explained to me about white men's foolish customs, I decided it would not be a good idea for us to marry. But it is great fun to tease you," she confessed with a sly grin. Then her face became solemn once more. "Besides, it was you who told me that you would soon be too creaky with age to be a good warrior."

This time Sky laughed out loud. True Dreamer and Bronc joined in while Numbers began barking happily.

Max spilled the cup of coffee he was holding. "I was jesting about how soon I would creak, Fawn! It won't be—for at least a year or two," he quickly added when he realized he might just dig himself a deeper hole if he didn't remove his foot from his mouth and close it immediately.

"You're a quick-witted devil, m'lord," Sky murmured as she handed him her dirty dinner plate for washing. "I have first turn with the cattle. Have fun in the kitchen."

"You'll pay for your saucy insolence, m'lady," he called after her. Suddenly, he felt more certain she would not leave him . . . or was he only deceiving himself with wishful thinking during a moment of shared laughter.

When they drove the herd into the small, impoverished Cheyenne village beside a stout log trading post, around seventy or eighty men, women and children came out to greet them, exclaiming joyously over Fawn's miraculous return. Although Max and Bronc could not understand their language, the sentiment was clear enough. One old woman wrapped her arms around the little girl and allowed tears to slide down her leathery cheeks. Several children around Fawn's age jumped up and down, crying out what must have been her name in their language.

A group of older men gathered around True Dreamer, gesturing to the cattle and the strangers who accompanied them. "I imagine he'll have quite a tale to tell before the day is done," Max said wryly.

"That ole feller could spin tales till all the snow melts on Pikes Peak. 'N not a man alive'd doubt a word he said," Bronc commented.

"You and he will both be heroes now," Sky said to Max.

Preoccupied, he looked past the crowd of Cheyenne to the large log building situated by a stand of cottonwood trees several hundred yards away. A tall, rangy man, slightly stooped with age, climbed down from the front steps with a wide smile on his face, raising his hand in a friendly salute to True Dreamer as he called out his name.

"My friend, Good Heart, I am happy to see you once more," the old Cheyenne said as the people around him parted to admit Clyde Campbell. The Indian agent wore a shaggy handlebar mustache and his curly gray hair hung to his shoulders. Clear brown eyes peered from beneath a set of thick dark eyebrows. When he spoke, the unmistakable burr of the Highlands was in his deep voice.

"I dinna ken how you could find the lass. I was a fool to doubt," he said, bending down to give Fawn a fatherly hug.

"We have so much to tell you, Mr. Campbell," she said excitedly.

"Aye, that I can see," he replied as he looked at the three strangers and the herd of cattle that had accompanied True Dreamer and Fawn home.

"I have returned your fine pony, Good Heart. I am sorry you were not here when I had to borrow it," True Dreamer said to the agent as he motioned to the gruella tied to the rear of the wagon.

"Dinna fash yourself, my friend. After I returned and was told Fawn had been kidnapped, I found your talisman in the stall. I ken why you had to take the beastie."

True Dreamer grunted. "I hoped you would think this."

"I have coffee on the stove at my post. Please, join us," Campbell offered Max, Sky and Bronc.

"We best get the beeves settled down first, Max," Bronc said, gesturing to a few patches of green alongside the small stream behind the trading post.

"I do believe he's right," Max said to the trader as he offered his hand with a wide smile. "We've struggled to get them here all the way from Fort Worth. Is it all right if we loose them by the water's edge?"

"Aye, that would be fine," the Scot replied as he shook Max's hand. "Are the cattle yours?"

"No, they're the property of this band of Cheyenne, courtesy of one Johnny Deuce, now deceased," Max replied.

Campbell chuckled. "For a Sassenach, you are a bray laddie, then."

"This is Pale Moon Stalker, the one I saw in my vision. He and his warrior-woman saved Fawn and returned our honor."

"Otherwise, I'm called Maxwell Stanhope and this is my wife, Sky. That tough old drover is Bronc Bodie."

"I am Clyde Campbell, the agent for the Cheyenne," he said, shaking hands with Bronc and bowing politely to Sky.

Within a quarter hour they had the cattle grazing peacefully. Fawn went with the women, disappearing inside a crudely patched teepee. True Dreamer spoke briefly with several of the leaders, but then joined Max, Sky and Bronc as they walked up to the post.

The agent's abode was a combination of general store,

trading post and official place of business between the Bureau of Indian Affairs and the various Cheyenne bands living in the surrounding area. The place was dimly lit and disorganized. Shelves holding canned foods, bolts of cloth and blankets had many empty spaces. The pungent smell of tobacco filled the air, but fresh coffee wafted over it.

"As you see, the Great White Father in Washington could teach a Scot a bit aboot frugality," Campbell said sourly, offering his guests seats around a battered oak table in the small back room that served as his bachelor's kitchen.

"Good Heart does battle to get food and blankets for us, but it is hard to make greedy men give what we have been promised," True Dreamer said.

"Aye, but I am not done yet. Before winter, I will make another trip East." He handed a letter with the official seal of the Bureau of Indian Affairs on it to Max.

Skimming it quickly, Max said, "You've found a friend high on the pecking order. This should get your allotment on its way."

"But only if I have someone here to run the post while I am gone. I dinna ken who I could trust."

Max and Sky exchanged a glance before she said, "We would all vouch for Bronc to take care of this place—that is, if he's willing?" she added, looking at the white-haired old man.

"Think you could stand a winter this far north, old chap?" Max asked.

Bronc nodded. "Save me a long ride back to Texas. Not much work for a busted-up old drover anyways." He looked at Campbell to see if he was interested.

"Dinna fash yourself, Mr. Bodie. I would be happy to offer you a job—permanently, not just for a month or two. I am no the best housekeeper, as you may have noticed," he said with a wry grin. "Riding from village to village, dispensing what I have of food, blankets and medicine leaves little time for aught else. The pay isna much but there is a second bedroom and your meals would be part of the compensation."

"Sounds like a real fine deal. Onliest problem I see is understanding what you're a saying half the time," Bronc replied, offering his hand, which the Scot shook enthusiastically.

Then he asked, "Can you cook?"

Bronc shrugged. "I reckon I'm a passable trail cook. Good as some others I seen," he could not resist adding as he tipped his head toward Max.

"I managed not to poison any of you," Stanhope replied as the others laughed.

That night the whole village celebrated Fawn's safe return. One young woman shyly offered Sky a well-worn but still beautiful deerskin tunic worked with quills and beads in intricate designs, explaining that it had been her grandmother's. Although Sky knew such a precious gift should remain with this impoverished family, she also knew that refusing it would be considered most ill-mannered.

She accepted it graciously and offered in return a necklace that Will had given her when they were first married. She'd carried it with her for the past bitter year. Perhaps it would bring happiness to her new friend that Sky herself had not found. With help from the other Cheyenne women, they plaited her hair in two long shiny braids, interlacing the black tresses with beads and bits of copper ornamentation.

Max, too, wore gifts from Fawn's grateful family. In exchange for the gold pocket watch he'd carried since arriving in America, he accepted a pair of butter-soft moccasins, a buckskin shirt and a beaded headband that gave him a wild, rakish appearance. He wondered if this was how Clint Daniels looked when he was Lightning Hand of the Sioux.

Along with Bronc, who had also exchanged gifts with their new friends, they took their place as guests of honor beside

True Dreamer and Fawn. The drumming and dancing had just begun when Campbell came strolling toward the large bonfire, carrying something that glittered in the firelight.

"You returned my horse. I return your powerful medicine," he said gravely to True Dreamer, handing him a heavy brass medallion. It was ancient and engraved with strange pictographs that obviously were very important to the old Cheyenne.

True Dreamer accepted the necklace with equal gravity and placed it around his neck to words and nods of approval from the people. "The Powers have blessed us but have still more to give," he said, looking at Max and Sky.

In the firelight, his eyes seemed to glow as if he was receiving a whole new vision. Sky felt the hairs on her nape prickle. Looking over at her husband, she sensed that he, too, felt the same thing.

Fawn introduced her new friends to everyone. Sitting with the old women while the younger people danced, Sky learned that the little girl had lost her mother and father in a smallpox epidemic when she was four years old. Her only immediate kin was her mother's father, the great medicine man and one of the tribal elders. But she was surrounded by loving people who would care for her. Still, Sky hated to part with the child.

You only wish she were yours. You, who may never have children of your own. She could not help looking across the flames to where Max sat with Campbell, Bronc and True Dreamer. What had the medicine man meant when he said the Powers had more to give them? She had no idea what would happen when they rode away the next day.

Someone from England still wanted them dead. Cletus? Or Bartlett? She was certain it was the solicitor, but until they found the answer, she and Max would be forced to stay together. As to what would happen once that riddle was solved, she had no idea. Would McKerrish seek vengeance for his humiliation? She shivered, wondering if their mysterious Englishwoman would come to their aid, but somehow doubted it. Fawn interrupted her troubling reverie, sitting down beside her and giving her a hug.

"I will miss you very much, Sky. Will you and Stalker come to visit us one day?"

Sky somehow managed to smile reassuringly. "Yes, of course we will. And in the meanwhile, I will send books so you can continue your studies. Mr. Campbell will help you with them."

"That would be wonderful. Good Heart is a fine teacher, but he has only old newspapers and a few primers for those children who wish to learn about the white people. I want to study England," she added impishly.

"I'll send you a book of English history," Sky promised, hugging the child, missing her already.

When the fire began to die down and all the children were fast asleep, Max approached his wife, saying, "We've been given an honor by True Dreamer and the other tribal elders—their finest lodge to sleep in tonight. We couldn't refuse their hospitality, could we, love?"

Chapter Eighteen

That old schemer won't give up, will he?" Sky said with a sigh. They had been so busy since arriving at the village, she'd given no thought to sleeping arrangements. Max shrugged, his face inscrutable by firelight as he bent down and offered her his hand. She almost refused, but realized they were being watched by many of the late revelers. Rather than fuel gossip and cause Fawn more worry when she heard it, Sky accepted his hand.

When they touched, a frisson of heat tingled down her arm and radiated through her body. It was one thing lying beneath the open skies with other people around, but quite different sleeping together in the privacy of an isolated lodge. Reading her thoughts, he said impatiently, "I won't fall on you and rip off that lovely old tunic, Sky."

"You know it wouldn't be a matter of force, Max." She slipped her hand from his, afraid to look into his eyes as she walked beside him toward the shelter that might prove her undoing. *No, it won't!*

After they'd passed a dozen or so lodges, the old woman who'd been the first to hug Fawn stepped in front of them. In broken English Bright Leaf held up a ceremonial cup decorated with brightly painted designs and said, "Good medicine to help sleep. Thank you from us . . . for Fawn."

Beaming with pleasure, she offered it to Sky. How could she refuse? Sky took the cup and sniffed the cool liquid. Its scent was slightly tangy, some herb she did not recognize.

Gingerly, she tasted. It was sweetened with honey. After taking several swallows, she tried to hand it back, but Bright Leaf shook her head.

"Now your man drink. You give?" She made a gesture indicating that Sky should hold it for Max.

"A love potion?" he murmured, taking a sip.

The old woman merely grunted, urging him to finish it. When he did so and returned the cup to her, she smiled broadly, revealing several missing teeth. "Sleep good tonight," was all she said, scurrying off.

"Any idea what that was about?" he asked his wife.

"Perhaps a fertility drug. It didn't taste familiar. Or, it might just have been some of that stuff Grandfather put in your food the first night we met him. You had good dreams that night."

"So I did," he said thoughtfully as they approached the small edifice. He held open the leather flap that served as a door. "M'lady?"

She ducked her head and stepped inside where a small fire leaped from the pit in the center of the circular space, its wispy smoke traveling up to the opening at the apex of the roof. In spite of the summer heat, the night was cool . . . but Sky was beginning to feel a strange warmth stealing over her. As soon as she felt Max's body heat close behind her, she stepped quickly away and felt her head spin.

He steadied her with one hand. "Watch you don't fall," he said, his speech slightly thickened. "What the hell was in that drink?"

"I feel tipsy," she said, suppressing an absurd urge to giggle. She did not move away from him this time.

He looked at her in the soft firelight. "We certainly had no alcohol tonight. Good Heart doesn't allow it on his watch."

"No, he doesn't."

They stood looking into each other's eyes, drawn irresistibly closer . . . closer. "That chalice—or medicine bowl—or whatever it was, did the drawings on it mean anything?"

"I didn't get much of a look at them. Wild flowers . . . a bee . . . oooh." She started to laugh in earnest now.

Max was not amused. "If we've just been poisoned, I scarcely think it's a laughing matter."

"You were right," she said, stifling her laughter.

"About being poisoned?" he asked, incredulous.

"No, about it being a love potion. The bee travels from flower . . . to flower . . . to flower . . ." She stepped closer and raised her arms to encircle his neck. Her eyes closed as she tipped her face upward to his.

He could smell her sweet essence, feel those soft, lush curves as her breasts pressed against his chest. He was suddenly stone hard and desperate to make love. But not this way! They'd both been drugged. That crafty old medicine man had put Bright Leaf up to the trick. *I'd bet my bloody barony on it!*

"It won't do any good to fight it," Sky whispered, having drunk considerably more of the concoction than he.

He could feel her pelvis wriggle against his lower body and sweat broke out on his forehead. "You'll hate yourself in the morning, love," he managed to say through gritted teeth.

"Let the morning take care of itself," she murmured, feeling his erection against her belly, able to think of nothing else. She kissed him, probing at the tight seam of his lips until he opened them and returned the caress with savage hunger. When she began unfastening his fly, he unlaced her tunic, then reached inside and cupped her breasts. She felt his hands working their old, familiar magic and cried out against his mouth with the pleasure of it.

This time it was she who took his hand and pulled him down onto the neatly laid out bedroll. She knelt before him and pulled the loosened tunic over her head, laying it beside the bedroll. Her body gleamed like pale, polished bronze in the firelight. The night darkness of her plaited hair contrasted with her skin, one braid lying enticingly over a breast. He had never seen such perfection in a woman, never imagined one to equal his Sky.

All he could think of was joining their bodies, holding on to her forever. When she reached over and started unlacing his buckskin shirt, he quickly yanked it over his head, then kicked off his moccasins and shucked off his breeches. There would be nothing between them but love this night.

Sky looked at the patterns of dark tan and white skin on his lean, powerful body, tracing with her palms the gleaming hair on his chest in its arrow descent to the hard jut of his staff. When her palm encircled it, he made a low guttural sound and pressed her back onto the bedroll, covering her body with wet kisses. She spread her legs and pressed her thighs against his hips, encouraging him to drive deep inside her.

Max could not have stopped if lightning struck the lodge that very instant. He felt her arch toward him and sank all the way inside her. She was wet and slick and tight, so perfectly right for him that he stopped, glorying in the sensations overwhelming him. Her breath hitched at the ripe fullness of his body inside hers, stretching her, driving her mad with desire. When he began to withdraw and then plunged back, she locked her ankles behind his back, urging him to stroke harder and faster.

The wild ride was fierce and sweet. Perhaps it was something in the drug, but it seemed they were both insatiable that night as passion consumed them. By the time they finally reached culmination, the fire had burned to pale embers and they lay, locked together, sleeping soundly in mindless contentment.

They could not hear the soft chanting emanating from True Dreamer's lodge at the opposite side of the village. . . .

When she awakened the next morning, Sky looked at her husband, who lay beside her, his green eyes studying her as he propped up his head with one hand. "I broke my word," he said quietly. "But I'm not sorry. Are you?"

"No. Like so many other things, this was fated to happen." She grew pensive. "I have never felt my Sioux blood so strongly before," she said with a tiny smile.

"Fate and all that?" he asked, relieved that she was not angry.

"Fate named True Dreamer. It wasn't the drink. It was some spell he cast, although the drink was most probably a fertility drug."

He swallowed. "Sky, love, if . . . if it worked, would you be angry then?"

She felt his eyes studying her and considered his question. "When I sat beside Fawn last night, I wished she were mine. I've always wanted children . . . for awhile, I dreamed of having your children . . . but not this way. Not to fulfill the terms of a—"

He cursed and rolled over. "I want *you,* that bloody accursed will of Harry's be damned! What must I do to make you understand?" He sat up and combed his fingers through his hair in frustration.

"We're trapped for the moment, Max. Until we can stop whoever it is who's trying to kill us."

"You haven't answered my question." He sounded accusatory and knew it, but was powerless to stop his feelings of loss and hurt.

She looked away, unable to bear the intensity of his angry green eyes. "I don't know, Max. I honestly don't know."

With that choked admission, she slid from the blanket and pulled the tunic over her head. He watched in silence as she lifted the flap and walked from the lodge.

Sky hugged Fawn, promising to return for a visit as soon as possible. She did not say whether or not "Stalker" would come with her and the girl did not ask, simply assuming they would be together. Sky wondered if Fawn as well as the rest of the village knew about the machinations of the crafty old medicine man and what he had done last night. She saw the old woman who had given them the "ceremonial drink" smiling knowingly at her while True Dreamer approached Max.

"You must leave and search for the evil ones who wish you ill. May the Powers guide you safely on this journey. I give you this powerful medicine for protection." With that he removed the gleaming brass medallion from his neck and placed it over Max's head.

Knowing that it was considered exceedingly impolite to refuse a gift, Max still felt he must protest. "But this is your medicine. You are the one who should wear it to protect and guide your people here."

True Dreamer shook his head. "When you no longer have need of it, you will return it, just as I returned the gruella to Good Heart. I will survive without it as I did when the Powers sent me to you."

Max felt the old man's dark, penetrating eyes bore into him and knew he must not refuse the protection offered. "I thank you. And I will return this," he said, looking down at the heavy brass disc hanging over his chest.

The old medicine man grunted his approval and turned his attention to Sky. "I must speak privately with you before you leave," he said, ushering her to his lodge, which was only a few yards away.

Sky followed, wondering if he intended to ask her about the spell he'd cast last night, further complicating what was already an impossible tangle of emotions. "Grandfather, about last night—"

His sense of urgency when he turned to face her made her stop. "That is not important. This is. Hear me now. You must never allow Pale Moon Stalker to remove the medicine symbol, awake or sleeping. When the time is right, you will return it to me. Then you will no longer have need of it. Do you swear this?"

Almost mesmerized by his vehemence, she nodded. His request must have something to do with the attempts on their lives. "Yes, I swear, but how will I know when the time is right?" she asked, praying that it would not be when she removed it from Max's dead body.

His harsh expression turned into a warm smile now. He beamed at her, only saying, "You will know . . . and you will know what must be done."

Long after their fond farewells to their Cheyenne friends, and to Bronc and Clyde Campbell, True Dreamer's words echoed in Sky's mind. How would she know when the time was right? And what should she do then?

Max noted her troubled expression, but was loath to inquire about it, assuming that it had to do with their lovemaking. Finally, after they had ridden in silence for over an hour, he could endure it no longer. "What did True Dreamer say to you?"

She stared at the brass disc hanging suspended from his neck. "That you must never remove that talisman. It will save your life, I think." *I pray.* "Asleep or awake, it must stay with you."

He grimaced. "It's heavy and uncomfortable. I'll have a green chest within a fortnight," he added in a teasing tone.

"You won't have to wear it indefinitely," she replied, "only until we stop the men who are after us."

"Do you honestly believe it will protect us?"

"You've seen what True Dreamer can do. What do you think?" she asked angrily. "I swore to him I would see you kept it on and I won't break my word."

He digested that. "He is a truly powerful man . . . but that does mean you'll have to remain by my side, perhaps for a considerable while," he added thoughtfully, grinning at her.

When he smiled at her that way, Sky felt her heart turn

over. Without making a reply, she kicked her mare into a brisk trot and pulled ahead of him.

They spent the days on the trail following a cautious routine, watching every time they approached any arroyo or hillside that might mean ambush. They shared standing watch at night outside the perimeter of the campfire, caring for the horses and doing the cooking and clean-up chores. What they never shared was a bedroll. Sky always laid hers carefully on the opposite side of the fire from his.

They spoke little, except when it was necessary for their mutual safety. Max's nightmares still stalked him. Although Sky would soothe him when it happened, she would quickly withdraw when the dark warriors released him. Every passing day, his hard-edged green gaze pierced her with increasing anger. The smiles of earlier times that had melted her heart had now vanished.

And Sky knew it was her doing. She felt alternately guilty, bereft, then angry herself because it was he who clung to his need to avenge his brother by thwarting Cletus even though she'd given up her need to avenge Will. He was the one who had deceived her and refused to speak of his earlier life. Then a sudden thought occurred to her. She had a new understanding of True Dreamer's cryptic words about the brass medicine disk . . . but what if she was mistaken?

Looking over at her husband's harsh visage in profile as he rode slightly ahead of her, she felt her heart lurch. No matter what happened, she would always love him. At this point in their relationship, it was a bittersweet knowledge, but a tiny flicker of hope filled her.

Yet she said nothing.

A sudden rainstorm struck as they were climbing a gradual slope in the narrow strip of no-man's-land below the Colorado border. They took shelter beside some boulders at the foot of an upcropping of red rock and huddled together beneath their rain slickers, trying to keep the cold downpour from soaking them. The horses stood, restive at the lightning flashes and roll of thunder, but they were well trained and did not bolt.

"I think we'll have to spend the night here," Max yelled at her over the din.

"We've hours of daylight yet," she yelled back.

"Traveling will be too treacherous once the rain stops."

His reply was reasonable. Sky knew that the vicious storms passed quickly but soaked the thirsty earth until it was a quagmire of slippery mud. The ground ahead of them was rising at a steep grade. One of the horses could stumble and break a leg. Grudgingly, she agreed, although it would mean another day on the trail before they could reach Pueblo and the railroad back to Denver.

As they expected, the storm vented its fury and passed them by within the hour. They made a wet, muddy camp at the base of a series of rocky hills covered with scrub oaks and sage. Sky laid out their clothing and footgear on the underside of the rain slickers, to hasten the drying so they would not have to be packed up damp the next morning. Then she tended to the horses and staked them so they could find graze in a patch of short prairie grass. Max went in search of enough dry wood to make a small, smoldering fire and then prepared a meager dinner of bacon, day-old biscuits and coffee.

After changing into dry clothes from their saddlebags, they ate in what had become their usual terse fashion, speaking only about practical matters of survival on the journey. "I'll take the first watch," he said, refilling his coffee cup.

"Do you think it's necessary?" she responded, stifling a yawn. "You look too weary to stay awake, even if you drank all the coffee in South America. No one's going to find us here in the middle of nowhere."

He took another swallow and grimaced at its bitterness. "Bloody hell, I detest coffee without cream! You're probably right, but I'll watch awhile until the fire dies down." He looked at the barely glowing coals, then pitched the black liquid over them, creating a sizzling hiss.

She looked up at the night sky. A few faint stars winked and the sickle of a quarter moon rose as scudding clouds obscured it. "If you think there's a need, wake me at two." With that, she lay on her bedroll, fully clothed as was their custom on the trail, and curled up, Yellow Boy at her side—also a habit she'd grown accustomed to following.

Max watched her sleep in the dim light as the last of the fire died. There were dark circles beneath her eyes and her face looked strained from the long, dangerous journey they had made from Denver to Fort Worth and back through the Nations. Was she carrying his child? It would account for her fatigue. But then, so would the awful tension that hung like an unspoken curse between them.

Lord, much as he wanted them to have children, he did not want it to happen this way. She would always be bound to him and he would never know if she would have stayed out of love and trust, instead of duty. Then an even more disturbing thought occurred to him. What if she was carrying his baby, but left him anyway, without telling him? Would Sky do such a thing? He honestly was not certain anymore.

If only Harry had known what his damnable codicil had wrought, he would never have had Bartlett draw it up. Max laid his head in his hands and sighed. That was when he heard the soft snick of a gun hammer being cocked.

Max looked up too late to draw his Smith & Wesson. Two tall Indians dressed in an odd mix of buckskins and calico shirts stood on opposite sides of the camp. One held an old Henry lever-action repeater on him, motioning for him to toss his weapon out of reach. Carefully, Max withdrew the revolver and did as he was bidden.

Sky, who had come awake at the soft thud of his Smith & Wesson landing in the dirt, reached for her Yellow Boy. She stopped when she saw the second man's Springfield breechloader aimed directly at her heart. The trackers stood in stone silence, while the clumsy footfalls of a man unaccustomed to this kind of rough country drew nearer.

"Cletus?" Max called out, unbelievingly.

"It's Bartlett," Sky said.

"You're getting a tad careless, considering the fearful reputation you have in this godforsaken wilderness, Maxwell, old coz."

Both of them froze in disbelief as Phillip Stanhope materialized out of the darkness, his silver-gilt hair glowing like a halo in the moonlight when the clouds cleared away. He was dressed like their missing guardian Englishwoman in jodhpurs and a white linen shirt, with a ridiculously high crowned hat shoved back on his head. But there was nothing ludicrous about the Enfield Mark II service revolver strapped to his left hip, butt forward.

"But you're supposed to be dead!" Sky blurted out.

"Dead?" he echoed, startled. "As you can see, I am quite alive. Hullo, Max, Sky," he said as politely as if inviting them in for afternoon tea, tipping his hat and sketching a bow for her. "You know, it has been the very devil keeping track of you, what with you haring about this wretched wild country hither and yon."

Max said calmly, "I presume you and Cletus arranged your death so you could pursue us."

Phillip appeared affronted. "Max, I see I've overrated your intelligence considerably if you'd believe for a moment that I would throw in with Cletus. The drunken sot had no more sense than a hedgehog."

"I note you speak of our cousin in the past tense," Max said, desperately holding on to his aura of calm indulgence until he could formulate a way to escape.

"Quite correct. I had assumed Bartlett would wire you of Cletus's unfortunate demise, but now I can see dear old Jerome was rushing his fences a bit."

"He told us you had drowned and Cletus had vanished,"

Sky said, communicating silently with Max that she understood the longer they kept Phillip talking, the better their chances were to find a way to outsmart him.

Phillip chuckled. "And so, you believed it was poor, stupid Cletus who attempted unsuccessfully to have you killed in New York and St. Louis. But after those professional marksmen failed—they came highly recommended, by the by—I grew quite frustrated. That's when I decided it best to handle matters directly."

"You killed Cletus?" Sky asked.

"It was really quite simple. I sent him word the trout were voracious at the family lodge in Scotland . . . and that the liquor cabinet was unlocked. Then I announced to my servants that I was departing to purchase draft horses in the Low Countries. It was simple to detour on my way abroad and drown him, making it appear an accident. Some local constabulary must have discovered his body and thought it was mine. I did note the wretch had borrowed my fishing gear and favorite deerstalker. The little toad always was a thief," he added with a sniff.

"I imagine Jerome has discovered the truth, now that the body's been returned to London for burial," Max said.

"No harm done. 'Twas a natural mistake and I do have a handsome alibi. I will arrive home from my trip to the continent only to be greeted by the shocking news that all the remaining Stanhopes, save I, have predeceased me." He tisked, smiling guilelessly.

"But you must have had help from Jerome Bartlett. How else would you have known our itinerary?" Sky asked.

Phillip was amused by his own cleverness now. "Your husband was assiduous about telegraphing his every move to his trusted solicitor. Unfortunately, what neither Max nor Jerome knew was that I bribed his clerk, Hampton. Not only did I have word of your every move, but of that damnable codicil to Uncle Harry's will. That, alas, made your death imperative as well, my dear lady," he said with a regretful sigh.

"You've never been to America, much less out West before," Max said. "How did you know to hire Shawnee to track us across this rough country? We're following no trail."

"Ah, that was ironic. I read the accounts of your exploits in the Eastern tabloids. You have, on occasion, employed them. Why not I? And more recent scandal sheets trumpeted your killing a desperado in Fort Worth and driving a herd of cattle to that beastly amalgam of savages quaintly called 'the Nations.' These most efficient men met me at the train in Garden City, Kansas. By the by, the place is neither a garden nor a city. Americans possess the strangest sense of humor."

He's so pleased with himself, so self-inflated. Sky's thoughts whirled.

There has to be a way to distract him. Max edged closer to where his rifle lay, partially hidden in the darkness. He hoped the Shawnee could not see it. Sky's Yellow Boy was closer to her, but he was afraid she would attempt something that would get her killed before he could figure a way out for them. He casually leaned back and looked up at Phillip as if seeing him for the first time in his life. "All for the title?" he asked, not really giving a damn.

"That is an added perk, but it's only a barony. No, the money our dear uncle chose to bestow on you is far more enticing. I was not at all sorry about Cletus, but I do sincerely regret the necessity of killing you. You, dear coz, were the best of the Stanhopes. I was almost as proud of your heroism at Rorke's Drift as Uncle Harry." He turned to Sky. "And you are one of the most beautiful and intelligent women I have ever met. Yes, I am indeed very sorry to see such a remarkable woman die."

He sighed and raised his hand as a signal to his men.

That was when Sky saw a flash of steel, followed by a spurting fountain of blood.

Chapter Nineteen

The Shawnee dropped to the ground, his head tumbling in the opposite direction as it was cleanly sliced from his neck. His companion's fate was identical and occurred at the same instant, leaving Phillip Stanhope frozen with his hand on the butt of his Enfield revolver. A rich contralto voice spoke from the darkness. "Take your hand off your weapon, Phillip," the woman commanded sharply. "I will not repeat my request."

Both Max and Sky seized their rifles, but did not raise them as Phillip complied with the woman's demand. He refused to look at the decapitated bodies of his trackers, instead staring straight ahead into the darkness. Max smiled grimly. *I imagine his agents reported back to him precisely how those professional shootists he hired died.* Their mysterious Englishwoman had once again come to their rescue.

She materialized from behind Phillip, a Webley trained levelly on him as she approached the dying campfire. Phillip had to know her Gurkhas were close enough to end his life as mercilessly as they had that of his Shawnee. She was a petite woman with a cap of gleaming silver-blonde hair a shade darker than the Stanhopes'. Although the pith helmet was nowhere to be seen, she still wore English safari clothing, a light tan shirt, brown jodhpurs and high boots.

"Please, m'lord and lady, would you be so kind as to lay aside your weapons?" she requested courteously. Her precise diction left no doubt that she was an English aristocrat.

Sky shot Max a glance and he nodded. If this woman had wanted to kill them, she could have let Phillip's Indians do the job for her. They both placed their rifles on the ground.

"Thank you," their guardian angel replied as she stood with her weapon trained on Phillip. To him she said coldly, "You would be most wise to remain absolutely still."

Through everything he had not moved or uttered a sound. An expression of incredulity was frozen on his face. It was apparent that he recognized their protector . . . and that her appearance boded ill for him.

She asked Sky, "Would you please throw some of that wood near you on what remains of the fire? Additional light would be most welcome."

Sky did as she was asked and the dying embers quickly reignited into small but bright flames, illuminating the grisly scene surrounding them. Phillip had been wise not to look at the work of her Gurkhas. Apaches from hell, Max called them. How right he was! Now they materialized, one on either side of Phillip. Although he was more than a head taller than the two little brown men, their menace made them appear Goliaths. Without command, they knelt and tossed the heads away from the camp into the brush, then dragged the bodies into the darkness as easily as if the Shawnee had not weighed half again as much as they did.

The Englishwoman faced her enemy. His face was white as bleached bone. Her eyes gleamed with triumph when she looked up at him.

"Well, Phillip, we meet again . . . for the last time."

His voice sounded strangled when he responded. "Bloody hell, Ronnie, I thought—"

"You thought you had escaped punishment because it's been so many years," she concluded in a harsh tone. Sparing a glance for Max, she continued. "Your adoring cousin omitted one vital thing from the recitation of his murderous brilliance. It was he who drowned your brother. Not Cletus." Her words were icy and clipped.

The truth of the accusation blazed across Phillip Stanhope's face.

Max sucked in his breath and Sky gasped as they stared at him. When Max reached for his Smith & Wesson, the Englishwoman said, "No, Lord Ruxton. Though I understand your need to avenge Edmund, mine is greater. I have prepared for this moment nearly half my lifetime."

Still trembling, Max released his hold on his revolver. "Why is your claim greater? Edmund was my only brother."

Now Phillip laughed, a hollow, ugly sound. "You honestly don't remember her, do you? She was your brother's lover."

"Lord Ruxton was just a boy then. There is no reason he should know me, but yes, Edmund Stanhope was my first, my only love . . . and you took him away from me."

"I was certain Cletus did it—or at least, stood by and let my brother drown. He was found nearby . . ." Max's voice faded as he realized he'd blamed a weak, foolish man for a diabolical evil.

"Cletus was foxed. His father hid his drinking problem until the old man died," she replied. "Cletus could have done nothing, worthless creature that he was," she said to Max.

"But then, how—"

"Did you know, in addition to his other crimes, dear Phillip attempted to rape me? One day . . ." She paused and took a breath, then resumed speaking in an eerie, calm tone. "One day when your brother and I had arranged a tryst by the river, Phillip happened upon me while I was waiting for Edmund. I was a petite girl and he was already a tall man. Edmund arrived before he was able to do more than tear my frock." She glared at Phillip. "He thrashed you within an inch of your life, did he not?" she asked.

Phillip did not answer, only stared at her with cold, dead eyes.

"When Edmund died less than a week later, I knew the drowning was no accident. We often swam in the river. He knew every rock and current for miles and he was a strong swimmer. I would have killed you that day, so great was my grief and rage, but my father found me in his gun room loading a pistol. He packed me off to his sister in India, who was married to an English colonel."

"And now you're going to let your wogs kill me." Phillip finally spoke in a detached voice.

"I should allow my friends the pleasure for that filthy remark . . ." She shrugged.

"What do you intend?" Phillip snarled, now all pretense of civility stripped away.

"I am going to give you some options. None are particularly good, but they are what I will allow." Each word was precisely clipped off. "I propose that you and I have a duel right now. If you kill me, you can run for your life. I've instructed Jai and Javeen to let you go and wait until dawn before they begin to track you. They will take Lord and Lady Ruxton's horses and weapons and leave them three miles away when they depart."

"Then I'll have your hellhounds and the Limey both trailing me," Phillip said tightly. "Not much of a choice."

"No, it is not. But if the fabled Limey finds you first, he'll just shoot you. If Jai and Javeen do, I have instructed them to kill you . . . slowly." She peered into the darkness, as if giving a signal.

Sky shuddered when both Gurkhas reappeared and nodded stoically, replying in unison, "Yes, Lady."

"What if I do not choose to duel with you?" he asked warily, knowing the answer.

"Why then, Jai and Javeen will begin right now. You have just had a demonstration of their skill with the khukuri." She smiled. "It is time to make a decision, Phillip."

"A duel it is, Ronnie," he said, attempting a boldness he did not feel.

"Most wise, Phillip. You may draw your weapon whenever you wish. I will not attempt to aim my weapon until yours is out of the holster." She lowered her Webley and held the heavy piece loosely at her side.

The only sound in the camp was the crackling of the wood on the fire, which had caught quite well. The duelists faced each other, motionless as carved idols. Phillip radiated hatred and fear. Ronnie appeared icy calm, assured.

With blurring speed Stanhope pulled the Enfield from its holster and almost had it leveled when the .455-caliber slug from Ronnie's revolver hurled him backward into darkness . . . both temporal and eternal. She put the revolver to her lips and blew the smoke from the barrel, then slipped it into the military-style holster on her left hip, snapping the flap closed. Without instruction, the two little men dragged the dead man into the brush where they had deposited his Shawnee trackers. After they did so, the small woman seemed to sag slightly.

"Javeen, would you please retrieve our mounts and pack animal? Jai, please make some coffee. I believe an explanation is owed Lord and Lady Ruxton, considering that I have made them my stalking horse to flush out Phillip."

As the two Gurkhas went about their business, Max rose from his bedroll and pulled the saddle he'd been using as a pillow closer to the fire. "Please, Lady Ronnie, sit down," he offered.

"We owe you our lives," Sky said as she moved closer to the diminutive blonde woman.

"You are both most kind. Thank you for your understanding, Lady Ruxton."

"Please call me Sky."

"And you must call me Ronnie," she said to both of them with a weary smile.

"You look familiar, but I can't place where or when I've met you. I thought I knew most of Edmund's friends," Max said.

"You look like brother and sister," Sky blurted out, then sat back embarrassed.

"Well, my dear Sky, we almost were." She turned to Max. "If Edmund had lived to marry me, I would have been your sister-in-law," she said with a pained look in her eyes. Then it vanished as she continued. "I am Andromeda Beaumont. My mother chose my given name but Papa detested it almost as much as I and shortened it to Ronnie. By the by, he is the Marquess of Cargrave."

"Yes, I remember now. Falconridge, one of your family estates, marches with Ruxton land," Max said. "Your mother, Cassiopeia Beaumont, was a dear friend of my aunt Lodicia."

" 'Twas my mother who bestowed the blonde hair along with the traditional wretched naming of daughters after constellations." When Ronnie smiled, she looked like a beautiful elf. "The last time I saw you, Maxwell, you were a boy home from Eton, all arms and legs. Now, you look so much like Edmund . . . or as he would have looked, had he grown to be a man." Her expression turned melancholy once more as she stared into the flames.

To distract her from such sad thoughts, Sky asked, "How long did you remain in India with your aunt's family? It must have been a grand adventure."

Ronnie smiled once again. "Oh, it was that, indeed! My uncle Anthony was commandant of an outpost beneath the shadows of the Himalaya Mountains to the far north, bordering Nepal. Jai and Javeen scouted for his regiment. When I kept slipping away to ride and hunt in the dangerous countryside—a fit of rebellion for being shipped so far from home—my uncle assigned them to be my protectors. They have taught me much and we have become friends, traveling across India, Africa, indeed around the world. I have seen things few Englishwomen could ever imagine. One could say mine has been . . . a colorful life." She paused, considering whether or not she should volunteer more.

"But all the while, you were preparing to exact vengeance for Edmund," Sky said quietly. What strange tricks the Powers could play, she mused, feeling Max's gaze on her and knowing that he understood what the two women shared.

"Yes, my favorite aunt back in England kept me apprised of Phillip's life while I was abroad. When I was of age and came into an independent living, I hired an agent to watch your family, Maxwell. Phillip had said that day when Edmund thrashed him that he would 'have it all eventually' . . ."

"And you knew that he wouldn't stop after killing my brother. Cletus and I would have to die as well for him to inherit," Max said.

She nodded. "I must confess I followed your career with more than mild interest, from the Victoria Cross in Africa to becoming the Limey in America. But when I was informed that your uncle had died and you were heir, I knew it was time for me to take action. Once you reached London, my agents found out you had married. Then the possibility of an heir made it even more imperative that I stop Phillip before he not only had you murdered, but your wife as well."

"He certainly tried. Numerous times. We are greatly in your debt, Ronnie," Sky said.

Ronnie scoffed. "Scarcely anything to thank me for, considering I was using you as bait. But Phillip kept employing incompetents until those two shootists in the Nations. He did not come after you himself. But I deducted that if I foiled him enough times, I would force him to deal with the problem personally."

"You were right. And you dealt with him amazingly well. I would hate to go up against you, Ronnie," Max said, shaking his head.

Sky could not resist adding, "I would place my bet on Ronnie."

For the first time, they heard the Englishwoman laugh. It was a rich, musical sound, deep and hearty, matching her voice, belying her diminutive stature. "Considering everything, I think that unlikely, Sky."

Max shook his head. "All these years, I've clung to the notion Cletus had allowed Edmund to drown or deliberately killed him. Incredible."

"It is over now," Ronnie said with finality. "The two of you have your whole lives together ahead of you. Think of the future and be cheered." If she noted the uneasy exchange between husband and wife, she did not acknowledge it, but rather yawned daintily and said, "Would it be a great imposition for us to pitch a camp nearby so we can get some rest?" Then she looked at the bloodstains darkening the ground and added, "It might be best if you became my guests. Jai and Javeen can have everything prepared shortly, away from . . . this."

Sky nodded, remembering the ghastly executions of the Shawnee. "Yes, that would be very kind of you."

Max had a great deal to say to his wife, but it would have to wait until they were alone. He assisted the Gurkhas, picking up bedrolls and leading horses several hundred yards away. Sky and Ronnie efficiently packed their coffeepot, tinware and food supplies.

When Sky reached the brightly burning fire, she could see that her bedroll had been laid out beside Max's. Without protest, she lay down and fell instantly asleep, spooned against her husband.

The next morning, they awakened to find the camp deserted. But a note lay beside their bed, weighted down with a small rock.

"Damn bloody Gurkhas move like ghosts," he muttered, picking up the missive.

"So does Lady Ronnie, apparently," Sky said, wiping sleep from her eyes. "What does it say?"

He read aloud, "My dear Maxwell and Sky. Please forgive our unannounced departure, but I so detest good-byes. My companions and I have never seen your magnificent Southwest. I do believe such an environment would suit Jai and Javeen. Also me since I am certain life in England would prove far too confining. Wish us Godspeed as we do you. Your friend, R." Then he looked up, saying, "There's a postscript asking that I not send Phillip home to be buried in the Stanhope family plot. I would never contaminate hallowed ground by doing that. Let the buzzards and coyotes feed on him."

Sky nodded, understanding. "I'll rekindle the fire and make coffee. We should reach Pueblo in two more days if we ride hard."

When she arose and began picking up kindling, he walked over and placed one hand on her arm. "First, we must reach an understanding, Sky. I suspect Ronnie left us alone because she could sense we required privacy."

She tossed the kindling into the fire pit and looked up at him, afraid of what he was going to say. *Are you afraid he'll say he loves you . . . or that he doesn't need you any longer now that Cletus is dead?* "What understanding, Max?" she managed to get out.

Max knew he was treading on very thin ice. He dropped his hand from her arm and walked away, combing his fingers through his hair, pacing restlessly as he gathered his thoughts. *Say precisely the correct thing, old boy, or she'll walk away . . .*

Sky watched him and icicles began to form around her heart. Now he was probably worried that she might be carrying his child when he no longer needed a wife. He was too honorable a man to simply walk away. No, not Maxwell Stanhope. He'd stand by her. But she could not bear that. Her courses were not due to begin for another two weeks. She would not be able to set his mind at ease until then.

Moistening her dry lips, she said quietly, "You need say

nothing now, Max. I understand that you don't require a wi—"

He spun around and scowled at her fiercely, stopping her. "Bloody hell, Sky, I'm trying to think of the right words and you break in to tell me what I do and don't 'require'!" He let loose a volley of curses and stalked over to her until they stood with only inches between them, glaring at each other, wide blue eyes and hard green ones revealing the same desperation.

"You're too dutiful to leave me, I know, but if—"

"Will you stop interrupting me, woman! Have the common decency to allow me to tell you that I love you and I won't give you up." His fists were balled at his sides and he towered over her.

Sky refused to back away. She sighed and placed one hand on his arm, startled to find he was trembling. "You do need me . . . at least for now. Save for True Dreamer's herbal sleeping potion, I am the only one who can hold your nightmares at bay."

"That is an insult," he snapped. "First you accused me of wanting you as my wife only to thwart Cletus. Well, bloody hell, the bastard's dead! I don't need you for that—and I don't want you as a damnable sleeping potion either. I—"

"You want to take care of me because I may be pregnant," she blurted out.

Now he was so angry his eyes glittered like green glass, just as they had that first day they met in Bismarck. "At least you have a high enough opinion of me not to think I'd leave you alone to fend for yourself and our child. I suppose I should be honored," he sneered. This was not going any better than he had feared it would. In fact, it was going far worse.

"We'll know in about two weeks whether or not we must test your honor, m'lord," she said coldly. "In the meanwhile, let's try to be civil on the arduous trip to Denver while we return the horses to the Lorings and retrieve our possessions."

Max sighed and nodded. There was nothing left to say . . .

at least until he knew whether or not fatherhood was impending. Damn that old Cheyenne and his meddling! He had not even considered that his wife would think carrying his child was yet another reason to believe he did not truly love her. But once they knew for certain, either way, he would keep Sky Eyes of the Ehanktonwon as his wife!

They fell back into the routine they had established when they left Fort Worth, quiet civility, shared camp chores, sleeping separately. Although they had no reason to fear an ambush now that Phillip was dead, Max remained cautious. When Sky caught him studying the horizon of the looming Sangre de Cristo Mountains with a spyglass, he explained.

"McKerrish has a far reach in Colorado. I doubt he'll find us before we leave the state, but it's best to be watchful."

"I thought you wired Steve Loring to investigate McKerrish," she replied, scraping dried beans from a plate as she cleaned the last of their breakfast utensils.

"I did. As far as he's been able to find out, the old man's holed up on his ranch southeast of Denver. Nursing an infection of the gums. No sign that he's plotting any retaliation."

"I hope his whole mouth rots," she said, clapping two tin plates together and stuffing them in the cook bag on the packhorse.

Max chuckled grimly. "If it does, you can claim sole credit, m'lady."

They followed the Arkansas River for a couple of days, then neared a small town that was what Max judged to be a day's ride from the railhead. In spite of the gritty work done by the Colorado Fuel and Iron Company in Pueblo, the surrounding area was cattle country with thick, tough prairie grasses feeding large herds of what Bronc fondly referred to as "beeves." Max could see why the region east of the Rockies had made men like Zebulon McKerrish rich. He was glad McKerrish's spread lay over a hundred miles to the north.

"Tomorrow we'll reach Pueblo and the train to Denver," he said, studying her drawn, exhausted face. "Best we spend the night here."

"I can make it for another couple of hours," Sky said stubbornly.

"Well, the horses can't. And as for me, I would like to sleep in a bed tonight. If a train's leaving Pueblo when we get there, I'd prefer to climb aboard posthaste."

"You're still thinking about McKerrish, aren't you? I thought you said he was recuperating at his ranch."

Max shrugged. "Why take unnecessary chances? We can spend the night in . . ." He squinted at the weathered sign beside the river and read, "Welcome to Clean Sweep, Population two hundred seventy-one." Except the number one had been crossed out and a zero substituted for it. "Some poor chap must've been swept away recently."

"Or just simply shot," Sky said, looking at the clapboard buildings that lined several wide, dusty streets. She could see a corral and livery and several saloons. It was just like dozens of other towns they had stopped in on the trail to find Johnny Deuce. She rubbed her eyes, thinking that the quest seemed long, long ago, even though it had been only a matter of months. She was bone weary, but her exhaustion had less to do with their time on the trail than with the tension between her and Max.

She knew he was watching her, wondering if she was pregnant. Ever since they'd left the Cheyenne village back in the Nations, he had been solicitous beyond ordinary British courtesy. Irrationally, that irritated her, most probably because it meant she might have to face the fact that she was indeed carrying his baby. *Oh, Max, what will we do then?* If it was so, she would never know whether he had chosen to make their marriage permanent because of love or duty.

Even more irrationally, she desperately wanted to have his child. Her first husband had been sterile, but she, too, might be barren. After all the times she and Max had made love, she had not conceived. For some reason he felt the fertility drug the old Cheyenne woman had given them might make a difference. Considering the power of True Dreamer's medicine, it might be true. But her Sioux family had taught all young girls about the physical changes in a woman's body during pregnancy. Sky knew she exhibited no symptoms. Of course, not every woman experienced them.

But she was exhausted—was that not a symptom? She looked over at Max's drawn, haggard face and knew he was every bit as bone weary as she. No, their tiredness was simply because of all they had lived through. Max broke into her troubling reverie as they rode down the Main Street of Clean Sweep.

"Are you off gathering wool, love? I asked you if that hotel would suit? It looks as good as we'll find in this metropolis."

"What? Oh, yes, I don't care," she replied distractedly, looking up at the two-story building badly in need of a fresh coat of whitewash. Hung from the front balcony was a sign proclaiming, THE GOLDEN PROMISE HOTEL.

As they reined in, Max grunted. "It appears to be neither golden nor does it hold any discernable promise, but the windows are washed and the front steps swept—in accordance with the town's name. One might hope for clean linens, eh?"

A youth in shabby clothes emerged from the front door, sauntering toward the livery next door. When he caught sight of Max and Sky and their fine horses, he quickly approached. "Want them horses taken care of, mister? Me an' my brother, we own that there livery. Nice-lookin' horses. We'll treat 'em real good." He stood by, watching them intently.

"That would be fine," Max said, fishing in his pocket for coins as he dismounted. "And you are?" he inquired as he handed the boy the money.

"Name's Sam'el Broom," the lad replied, eagerly accepting the gratuity.

"Your name fits rather well with the town's name," Sky commented with a slight smile.

The boy nodded, studying Max with round eyes. "Yep, most ever'body's a Broom hereabouts. That's why the town's called Clean Sweep."

Max and Sky dismounted and led the three horses inside the livery, which smelled of a mixture of fresh straw, hay and manure. They quickly removed their saddlebags and weapons, and several items from the packhorse, then handed the reins to the lad as an older man who bore a striking resemblance to the lanky youth appeared.

"This here's my brother Davie Broom."

The elder Broom offered a callused hand. "Pleasure, mister . . . ?"

"Stanhope. Max Stanhope and this is my wife," Max replied as they shook hands. Neither of them commented on her Indian blood. Rather, both focused on Max. He could sense their wary curiosity and it made the hairs on the back of his neck prickle in warning.

He dismissed the intuitive warning. His English accent had often elicited curiosity. *I'm growing paranoid.*

As they walked out of the livery and climbed the steps to the hotel, Sky said wistfully, "Do you think we might be fortunate enough to have hot baths before dinner?"

"One can hope," he replied. "I'm more interested in food."

Sky looked at the shabby street and said doubtfully, "Don't expect Delmonico's."

"I am so flaming tired of beans, anything else chewable will suffice." He was pleased to see her face actually break into a wide smile for the first time in days.

They entered the lobby, a small place devoid of any amenities but at least clean and orderly. A skinny young man sporting muttonchop whiskers, doubtless to make him appear older, hurried from behind the desk in his eagerness to greet them. "I suspect there are vacancies," Max murmured to Sky.

"Can I help you, mister, missus?" the clerk inquired.

"Is the livery next door trustworthy?" Max asked.

"Sure is. Them boys who run it are my cousins. I'm Zeke'l Broom."

Again Max noticed that when he spoke, the townie's eyes almost glowed with excitement. Now his guts began to clench. Perhaps stopping here had been a mistake . . . but if not here, where? "Would you be so kind as to let me sign the guest register?" he asked.

Eager and excited as a puppy dog, Zeke'l Broom hopped over to the desk and swiveled the dusty ledger around so that Max could sign . . . and check who else might have registered earlier. The ledger indicated no recent entries. Perhaps he was mistaken.

Unaware of what Max was doing, Sky asked, "Do you have hot baths available on the premises?"

The clerk swallowed, but made no reply. Instead, he stared goggle-eyed over her shoulder. She could hear the creak of the floorboards as another person entered. When she turned, relief washed over her. The young man was probably several years younger than she and very well dressed in a fine three-piece suit of brown wool, a boiled shirt and well-polished cordovan shoes. Atop his well-barbered light brown hair a bowler hat perched at a jaunty angle. He would have looked at home in the financial district of New York. Then she sensed Max stiffen as he faced the newcomer.

Did he know the dude? Before she could inquire, the man swept his hat from his head and made a gallant bow to them both. When he did so, his suit jacket fell open and she noticed the hand-tooled leather holster and double-action Colt Lightning inside it.

The holster was strapped down.

Chapter Twenty

Smiling cordially, the young man nodded and said, "Mr. Stanhope, Mrs. Stanhope, good day to you both."

Sky suppressed a slither of fear. She watched Max lean casually against the registration desk and say, "You have us at a disadvantage, sir."

"My name is Taylor, Mr. Stanhope, and I fear I'm on an errand that will not make you or Mrs. Stanhope happy. Mr. Zebulon McKerrish is outside in the street and he wishes to have a word with you . . . and your wife."

"How did that scum know we were here?" Sky snapped, white-hot anger replacing the coiling dread in her gut.

Max shook his head at her while keeping Taylor's gun hand clearly in sight. "Ah, m'lady, we must strive to maintain the ceremony of civility, please," he said calmly. "Nonetheless, sir, my wife poses an interesting question."

"I'm not offended by your choice of words, ma'am," Taylor said, glancing at her while still keeping close watch on Max's slightest movement. "As to how he located you, sir, the answer is simple—since you're the famous Limey. Your gunfight with another Englishman in Fort Worth was written up in newspapers and word circulated as far north as Pueblo." Taylor shrugged. "McKerrish figured you were heading back to Denver, where your friend Steve Loring resides. He sent out scouts to cut your trail before you reached the railhead in Pueblo."

"And they reported back to him. He wanted to be here in person," Max said in a deadly cold voice.

In that same tone, Sky said, "So, the old pig wants to talk, does he? I would've thought after I rearranged his stable-yard mouth for him, he would be afraid to open it around me again."

Taylor's boyish grin widened. "A fine piece of work you did there. Mr. McKerrish had to have his gums slit open and all his teeth—the ones you left him—removed so he could be fitted for dentures." He laughed, never taking his eyes completely off Max. Then he gave a perfect imitation of McKerrish's twangy drawl, saying, "Gaudammitahell! Tryin' ta eat steak with these here gauddamned chompers is like tryin' ta chaw straw through a picket fence!"

"Quite amusing. You're a most talented young man, Mr. Taylor," Max said, not amused at all.

"Just Taylor, Mr. Stanhope. I dearly hope you are correct . . . or I will not live to see the sunset."

"McKerrish wants more than just talk, does he not?" Max asked, watching the keen assessment in the young gunman's eyes.

"He intends to have you and your wife killed . . . especially your wife." He did not look at Sky as he added with what sounded like genuine regret, "When I took this assignment, I did not know it involved a woman."

Max's gut tightened as he envisioned what an animal like Zeb McKerrish would do to Sky. He tamped the disorienting thoughts down and asked coldly, "And if we refuse to meet McKerrish in the street?"

"He and his men will come in here and kill you both," was the matter-of-fact reply.

"And anyone else who gets in the way?" Sky asked, knowing the answer.

"Regretfully, that is true," Taylor replied.

Max knew she was thinking of Will Brewster and what happened when innocent people got in the way of crazed killers. "If we were to slip out the back and attempt to avoid a fight, what would happen?"

Taylor smiled, bemused. "I'm certain you know the answer."

"So, there is someone—or ones—out back, waiting for us." It was not a question. Taylor made no attempt to answer, but his very silence indicated what they all three knew. A cowardly bully such as McKerrish would have come with a small army to seek his vengeance. "It would appear your employer has left us no way out of this but to fight, would you not agree?"

This time Taylor replied. "There is no way out." Then he smiled in admiration. "You are establishing in front of this witness"—he gestured to the trembling clerk—"that you have been forced into this fight. Very clever . . . if you survive to worry about the legal repercussions. Now, if you will excuse me, I'm afraid I have to get back to Mr. McKerrish. He is a very impatient man."

Max raised his left hand. "Please exercise a bit of patience yourself, Taylor. What if you and I were to settle things right now? If you can kill the Limey, your asking price will at least double, perhaps triple." His tone was as genial as if they were discussing the weather.

Sky's heart, already racing, now nearly ceased beating as she looked at the young killer. If he shot Max, she would kill him. Taylor never spared her a glance. It was as if she had become invisible. Only he and the Limey were present.

Taylor studied Max for a moment. "I considered that very fact when Mr. McKerrish made me his offer, which was why I volunteered to come in here and relay his message. But he made it very clear that . . . such enterprise on my part . . . would be punished most severely. If I take you, I'll never live to profit from the honor."

"And you're quite certain you could," Max prodded.

Taylor flashed a boyish smile. "I know you think killing me would lessen the odds out there . . . but the only way to learn if that's true has been taken out of our hands."

Sky spoke through cracked, dry lips. "Why not side with

us if you're so good? We'll pay you three times whatever McKerrish promised."

For the first time in several moments, he glanced at her and again sighed. "Mrs. Stanhope—begging your pardon— although I've since learned that Zebulon McKerrish is so vile that coyotes wouldn't piss on him, I have taken his money. We shook hands over the deal. As I said, I didn't know a woman was involved, or I would have refused. But a deal is a deal and I've already made it." He shrugged regretfully.

"All right, Taylor," Max said with resignation. "You may inform your employer that we will be out momentarily."

After the young gunman backed out the door and crossed the street, Max turned to the terrified clerk cowering behind the desk. "How many of them rode in? The truth!"

"S-s-six," Zeke'l stuttered, his eyes almost rolling back in his head, all thoughts of the thrill of seeing an actual shootout gone now that he was faced with the reality of the two ice-cold gunmen he'd just watched face off.

"Sky, love, who's out there with Taylor?"

She stepped carefully to the window and looked out. "McKerrish and another hard-looking man in range clothes. He looks like another hired gun," she replied, trying to remain as cool as her husband.

"And where, pray, are the other three hidden?" Max asked the clerk.

Zeke'l shook his head. "I dunno, honest, Mr. Stanhope! They rode in a couple hours ago 'n went into the saloon. Word spread they was looking for an Englishman named Stanhope 'n his In—his wife," he stuttered, correcting what could have proven to be a serious mistake. "I never seen what went on after that, I swear!"

Max fixed him with a chilling glare, then turned to Sky. "Taylor told us they had the back covered. My guess is one's on the roof above us, overlooking the rear door. The other two could be anywhere nearby."

"Probably one's in the livery to make sure we can't reach our horses," Sky said.

Max nodded. "Yes, but even if we could, they're too tired to outrun McKerrish."

Casting a scornful glance at the clerk whose cousins had been so eager to stable their animals, Sky said, "I imagine Samuel and Davie figure on owning three pieces of prime horseflesh in a few minutes."

"If you're right about the livery, that leaves one gun either on the rooftop here or hidden across the street," Max said as he peered through the window at the wide dusty expanse, its boardwalks now utterly deserted.

"Do you have a plan?" Sky asked as she pulled a box of ammunition from her saddlebags and stuffed extra .44 Henry cartridges in the pockets of her buckskin shirt.

"First I take out the one watching us from the back. Then we slip into the stable and look for the second fellow," he replied, checking the action on his Winchester '76 and stuffing his own pockets with .45-70 cartridges from his saddle-bag. "That will bring McKerrish and his other minions rushing to join the fray. Our only hope is to fight a running battle, using the buildings as cover," he said grimly. "Pick them off one or two at a time."

"All right," she replied calmly. "But we both go after the one on the roof together, then head for the livery." He considered until she quickly added, "That's the only way we can cover each other's back."

Before he could reply, McKerrish's ugly braying voice echoed from across the street. "Whut's holdin' yew up, red nigger? Got nothin' ta say now?"

Sky yelled out, "How are those chompers working for you, Zeb?"

"Yew'll know real soon, slut, when I'm a takin' a chaw off'n yer tit. Then yew kin tell me how they's workin'. After I kill yer squaw man, I'll shoot yew up jest 'nough ta leave somethin' to play with fer a piece."

"You mean after your hired hands kill me for you, don't you, Zeb?" Max yelled out. Zeke'l had vanished beneath his desk, but Max dragged him out by his shirtfront and demanded, "How can we get to the roof from here?"

His eyes bugging out, the clerk said, "Up the s-steps. T-third f-floor p-porch out b-back has a l-ladder up. Mr. Stan-h-hope, k-kill 'em. Ain't nobody gonna b-blame ya."

"Stall McKerrish for a minute, then run like hell after me," Max said to his wife.

As he began to take the steps at the side of the lobby two at a time, quiet as a panther, she yelled out the front door, "You're a real ladies' man, Zeb. Do you always have to have two men to hold a woman down for you?"

With that she took off after Max while the cattleman's infuriated voice cried after her, "Yew ain't gonna be in any shape fer me ta need any holdin' down, bitch!"

Max saw the narrow ladder from the porch to the roof as he eased out the open doorway. He heard Sky's soft footfalls coming up behind him and made a quieting sign to her with his hand, then slipped out and tested the first rung. It made no sound. He leaned his rifle against the wall and drew his Smith & Wesson, starting to climb while Sky waited at the bottom of the ladder with her Yellow Boy cocked and ready to fire.

But he had miscalculated. Just as he made it halfway to the roof, a shot rang out from the second-story window of the building across the alley. It barely missed Max, who dropped cat quick back onto the porch. Sky raised her rifle and took aim at the glint of the gun barrel, then saw a man's head appear through the curtains. She fired. His rifle discharged into the air as he pitched backward.

"One down, five to go," she whispered to Max.

"Follow me," he hissed, holstering his revolver and grabbing his Winchester before climbing over the edge of the porch rail. He shinned awkwardly down the support post to the second-floor porch. By the time he'd climbed over its rail, pausing to cover her, she was down the pole after him. "I'll jump, then catch you after you toss me the rifles," he said, handing her his Winchester as he looked at the dusty earth a dozen feet below. Sounds of curses and pounding boots drew nearer. "Pray I don't break anything."

With that he dropped to the ground and caught his rifle, then hers, tossing them at his feet. When he raised his hands to catch her, Sky did not hesitate, but followed him, landing in his arms. They grabbed their rifles and took off running for the livery, where Max could see a man's head sticking out the back door. Without breaking stride, he fired from the hip and the head vanished inside. He cursed and flattened himself against the back wall of the livery, inching forward, Winchester cocked.

Sky was right behind him, but when he crouched low and ducked into the dim stable, all he saw was the blurred silhouette of the shooter running toward the front, yelling, "They're in here, Mr. Ze—"

Max fired his Winchester and the gunman pitched forward into the street. "They'll expect us to make a run for it," he said as he yanked open a gate and led the skittering horse inside the stall toward the back door, then swatted it on the rump.

Realizing his plan, Sky did the same with a second horse, which followed the first down the back alley in a mad stampede.

"Slip into that stall and wait," he ordered, crouching inside the opposite stall, resting his rifle barrel on one of its rails. The other horses nickered in terror, penned in, kicking against the slats of the gates.

One man rushed in. Neither McKerrish nor Taylor followed. When the gunman looked toward where Sky was hidden, Max yelled. As the killer's gun turned toward him, he fired. "Three down, three to go," he said over the noise of the panicked horses. Then he shoved her toward the front of the livery.

When they neared the front door, they each flattened themselves against opposite sides of the wall. Max made a sign for her to remain still and watch the back as he looked out and scanned up and down the street. Taylor and the other professional were not foolish enough to rush their fences. McKerrish was too cowardly. That third man might still be inside the saloon or up on its rooftop across the street. That worried Stanhope. But then, so did Taylor. The kid was no fool.

If he could only kill McKerrish, it might end. But how? Then an idea presented itself. "When I fire, cry out my name and act as if you've been hit and I'm not here," he whispered to her, raising his revolver with the barrel pointed to the ground.

As soon as he fired, Sky screamed over the frantic nickering of horses, "Ahhh, Max! Where are you?" She followed that with moans as he quickly replaced the spent round in his Smith & Wesson and holstered the weapon.

"Bitch, I tole yew I'd make yew crawl!" McKerrish's triumphant laugh came from her side of the livery.

The instant she heard him, Sky dashed to the loose wooden plank wall and peered through a knothole. She could see, even smell his filthy body. Her Yellow Boy ready to fire, she positioned it carefully and pulled the trigger. McKerrish's tall, lanky figure stumbled backward and then dropped.

"Your employer is dead, gentlemen. I suggest you leave while you are still able to walk," Max called out with confidence he was far from feeling. It could not be this easy.

That was when Taylor peered around the corner of the saloon across the street. "Very fine ploy, Mr. and Mrs. Stanhope. I applaud your acting ability, but I'm afraid I have a job to finish."

Sky returned to Max's side and started to raise her rifle, but he pushed the barrel down. "No, if you miss or even graze him, he'll duck into that alley. It's not worth the risk. At least now we know where he is. I'm going out—"

"No!" she hissed.

"Yes. While I start out, I'll keep him talking. The boy likes drama. You watch for any sign of that last man. Apparently they both feel a professional obligation to see this through," he said.

"Taylor wants the reputation of killing you, nothing more."

Max shrugged. "Perhaps, but first we have to know where his companion is."

"I think I know," Sky said, firing her rifle at the figure who had just slipped inside the back door. She heard a grunt, but after her own performance, could not risk rushing to investigate. She flattened herself against the wall and listened. Nothing. After what seemed like an eternity, a tiny rustling noise caused one of the horses to start nickering again.

They both waited, listening closely. The bright sunlight pouring in the front door hid them in shadows but left the man in the stall exposed if he tried to step out for a shot at them. It was a standoff.

Then Taylor's voice taunted again. "I'm losing patience, Mr. Stanhope. After we complete our rendezvous, I give my word I will not harm your wife."

Max dared not reply lest he reveal his exact position to the man in the back of the stable. Understanding that, Sky set down her rifle. Because of the cramped close quarters, it would be easier to use a revolver. She withdrew her Merwin & Hulvert from her holster and moved from the door, slipping quickly between the lower rails into the first stall.

Seeing what she was doing, Max started to do the same from the opposite side, but then he heard Taylor's voice growing closer. He probably was slipping from one doorway to another, too cagy to completely expose himself. Max dared not leave the deadly young man unattended.

Sky used the uneasy nickering of the horses to cover her movements as she crawled beneath the bars of the next stall. Two more to go. It was difficult to see out the gate without risking being shot. She was almost certain she'd hit her target, but did not know how badly he was hurt. When a horse in the stall across from her nickered, she slipped between the gate rails into the third stall and stroked the pinto confined there until it calmed.

No sign of motion from the back. Good. But outside, Taylor was becoming more vocal. "I know a man such as you, Mr. Stanhope, wouldn't hide behind a woman."

Sky knew time was running out. Soon Max would step out to kill or die protecting her. She had to do something, fast. Standing up, she peered over the divider into the next stall, where a bay horse shook his head nervously. She seized a pitchfork leaning at the rear of the stall, barely able to reach the handle. Carefully raising it until she had a good grip on it, she prodded the horse's rump. When the big bay reared up, she shoved the gate to his stall open with the fork. The horse lunged out and headed for the back door.

Using the diversion, she slipped from the pinto's stall and edged closer to where her target had gone down.

Max yelled, "Sky, no, dammit!" and whirled to fire as soon as he could see the gunman.

But Sky was ahead of him. The man had been crouched against the back wall of the last stall. When she heard him cock his revolver, she opened up, firing from the cover of the stall's partition. The distance was ten feet or less. One of his bullets grazed her ribs but her .38 found its mark. She pumped four shots into him and watched as he slid down the wall.

Turning around, she saw Max silhouetted in the front door. "All right, young Taylor. All your companions and your employer are dead. You have earned your money. Walk away. Now."

"You know I won't do that, Mr. Stanhope." Taylor laughed. "I do believe I'd rather face you than your wife. I'm certain those last four shots were hers."

"As you wish," Max said quietly.

As Sky ran down the aisle of the livery and out the front door, two shots blended together. She looked at the two men still standing in the street thirty feet apart. Her heart hammered as she clutched the Yellow Boy she'd seized in her headlong rush. Max lowered his Smith & Wesson. For a moment Taylor seemed frozen, but the hand holding his Colt Lightning had also lowered. Then the revolver dropped from his nerveless fingers and he crumpled.

Sky watched her husband walk toward the man he had just shot, who now lay stretched out on the ground. Max knelt and stared down at the dying young man, shaking his head as he did so. Max appeared unscathed. She ran into the street after him and heard the dying gunman's last words to Max.

"I . . . was . . . actually faster."

"Yes, Taylor, but it's accuracy that kills," Max said softly. Then he heard Sky running to him and stood up to embrace her. "You're hurt!" he said, seeing the blood seeping from her side.

"He just grazed me," she said, burying her face against the familiar curve of her husband's shoulder and neck. It felt wonderful to be held. They were both alive. They had survived in spite of the odds! Then Max suddenly shoved her roughly away from him and drew his Smith & Wesson with blurring speed, firing toward the right side of the livery.

Again two shots went off almost as one, but this time it was Max's bullet that missed. McKerrish had crawled to the boardwalk, bloody and dying, yet filled with enough hate to stand and raise his single-action Colt. He'd intended to shoot

Sky in the back, but he had hit her husband instead when Max pushed her out of the line of fire. Sky raised her Yellow Boy and fired into McKerrish's face, hitting him squarely in his false teeth and knocking him to the ground. She kept shooting until the rifle clicked on the empty chamber. Then she ran to Max, who lay flat on his back.

"Oh, please, God, please, don't let him be dead," she prayed as she threw down her empty rifle and dropped to her knees at his side. He did not move and his eyes were closed. "Max!" she screamed, frantically searching his chest for blood beneath the burned bullet hole in his buckskins.

Suddenly his eyes fluttered open and he looked up at her. "Always . . . check . . . to be certain they're . . . dead, Sky," he said, grimacing in pain.

"Oh, Max, I thought you were dead!" she cried.

"Rather . . . glad to . . . say I'm not . . . for whatever . . . reason," he replied.

She looked down once more at the round hole in the center of his buckskin shirt. Then she knew. With trembling hands, she unsheathed the skinning knife on her left hip and carefully slit his shirt down the front. "Oh, thank you, God! Thank you, Everywhere Spirit! Thank you, True Dreamer, you and the Powers of the Cheyenne!" All the while, she laughed and wept at the same time.

The brass medallion that the old medicine man had insisted Max wear "until the time was right" had a large bulge directly in its center filled with the lead of a flattened .44-40 slug from McKerrish's Colt. It had stopped the bullet from killing her husband. She clutched it in her hand, raising it so Max could see.

"Well, I'll be damned," he rasped breathlessly.

"Eventually, m'lord, but not today," she said between teary gulps of air.

A crowd began to gather, materializing from the storefronts,

saloons and other buildings up and down the street. One of
the first to arrive was Zeke'l Broom, who said, "I s-sent for a
d-doctor."

"Your cousin?" Max asked.

"No, sir, Mr. S-Stanhope, sir. Dr. Abraham Broom is my
uncle."

"Good. Let's . . . keep it . . . in the family," Max replied,
then passed out.

Davie Broom and his younger brother Sam'l came running from their livery with a detached door panel to use as a
stretcher. Several men stepped forward from the crowd and
placed the unconscious Limey on the wooden carrier as they
talked excitedly among themselves, practically ignoring his
wife.

"I knowed I's right, Jake. This here's the Limey, that
Britisher what shot them men down in Trinidad, like I's
tellin' you 'bout."

"Heerd he walked into a saloon in Benton last year 'n shot
one fella, then clubbed the dead guy's partner stupid, 'n drug
'em both off for the re-ward."

"Think McKerrish's gun hands is wanted anywheres?" a
third townie inquired.

Sky followed behind them as they made their way to the
Golden Promise Hotel. She had broken the fifth command-
ment. Killed three men, tried to kill three others. But now all
she could think about was that Max had survived. Grandfather's medicine came from a merciful God, whatever name
men, red or white, chose to give him. She would ask forgive-
ness for what she had done later.

You will know when the time is right.

Suddenly as the townsmen carried Max through the doors
of the hotel, she realized what True Dreamer had really
meant by those cryptic words . . .

Chapter Twenty-one

Max felt as if one of Cass Loring's biggest mules had kicked him directly in the chest. Bloody hell, it hurt to breathe. That was when he felt the thick bandage wrapped around his upper body. He could feel that he had nothing on beneath the sheet covering his lower half. Blinking his eyes, he tried to think. The room spun in dizzy circles. He could see that he was in a hotel bedroom, sparsely furnished, unfamiliar. But it was not a jail. And the woman asleep in the large overstuffed chair at the foot of his bed was his wife.

A sense of contentment washed over him. They had come through the nightmare alive and she appeared unhurt. He could see a narrow strip of gauze wound around her ribs through the sheer night rail she wore, although her thick hair curtained her lush breasts. He studied her beautiful face by the light of a flickering kerosene lamp. The dark circles under her eyes that had worried him on the trip seemed to be gone.

Then he noticed the white lawn had ridden up her slender legs, showing off the curves of calves and slender ankles. He feasted quietly on her loveliness for several moments. Had not True Dreamer's talisman been meant to save his life because they were fated to remain together? Just then, she stirred, raising her head and meeting his gaze.

His smile was wobbly from the painkilling narcotic as he rasped, "Where did you get that fetching little frock?" The effort of speaking brought a grimace of misery.

Sky was up and at his side in an instant. "From Neddie Broom."

"Another cousin?"

"No, an aunt. Dr. Broom's wife. She runs the hotel. They've both been quite kind."

"Now that the shooting's over," he said dryly, then realized that part of his difficulty speaking was caused by extreme thirst. "Might I have some water?"

Sky was already reaching for a pitcher and glass from the small table beside his bed. She poured and then very carefully lifted his head so he could drink. He felt the pain roaring through his chest and then realized the brass medallion that had absorbed the bullet must have made quite a dent.

"How do you feel?" she asked, lowering him back onto the pillows after he'd taken several swallows.

"Like a bull buffalo is sitting on my chest . . . wiggling."

"Dr. Broom says you have a severely bruised sternum." Just then a soft knock sounded and she walked to the door and opened it. "Yes, he's awake. Thank you, Mrs. Broom."

Sky closed the door and turned toward him with a large bundle in her hands. "What's that?" he asked warily.

"Another ice pack to take down the swelling," she replied matter-of-factly, placing the cold sack directly on his chest.

He sucked in a big gulp of air and immediately expelled it. "Flaming hell, that hurts!" he said, adding a string of guttural, breathless curses.

"It's supposed to," she said calmly, stroking his brow and planting a light kiss on his lips.

"You know, love, there are far pleasanter ways to relieve swelling than ice bags," he said after he caught his breath.

Sky looked down at the sheet covering his lower body. "M'lord, you are thoroughly incorrigible. But that is a truly impressive lodge pole you are . . . ah, erecting down there," she added with a tiny smile. "However, doctor's orders are for bed rest."

"Lots of ways to rest in bed, hmmm?" he whispered.

Sky shook her head. "If you try to use that 'lodge pole,' I guarantee you'll feel as if your buffalo has been joined by an entire herd. Rest." Her voice was stern now.

"How in hell am I supposed to rest when I awaken to see my wife's long, golden legs and then have her kiss me?" he asked in a surly tone.

Sky smiled broadly. "Grumpy and tepee building. You're on the path to recovery, I'm certain now."

"How long have I been asleep?" he asked, rubbing a bristly beard sprouted on his jaw.

"Since yesterday evening."

He blinked and looked out the window. "It's dark."

"Glad to see your eyesight hasn't been affected by your injury," she said dryly. "Yes, m'lord, it's nearly ten in the evening."

"Has the town marshal—"

"There will be no difficulty with the law," she quickly assured him. "McKerrish may have been powerful, but he was also hated and left no heirs, so we've been declared local heroes—by the marshal, Elijah Broom. I wired Jerome Bartlett about Phillip and explained everything . . . discreetly," she added.

"He'll be devastated to know how we've all been deceived."

Sky nodded. "I also wired the Lorings. Cass responded immediately. Steve is out of the city, but she'll track him down and he'll send his private car to Pueblo by day after tomorrow at the latest. If you rest properly and take your medication, you should be able to make the trip there in a specially sprung wagon that Hezekiah Broom has offered us."

"And he would be?"

"The mayor, of course. Now, would you like something to eat?"

His stomach gave a loud growl, answering for him. "I trust Mrs. Broom is a better cook than I?"

Sky smiled. "Any sentient being is a better cook than you, m'lord," she said with a chuckle. As he harrumphed, she added, "I'll fetch you a tray and your medicine. You need to rest and heal."

The meal was decent, a bowl of chicken stew with fresh vegetables, accompanied by a slab of freshly baked bread slathered with butter. She watched him eat, knowing every swallow was costing him dearly because of the pain in his chest. Just sitting up had been an ordeal. By the time he had finished the food, a fine film of sweat moistened his face. She tenderly wiped it with a cool cloth and then held up a spoonful of laudanum.

"Now, time for some rest."

"I don't need that. It makes me muzzy-headed," he protested, but when he tried to raise his arm to fend off the approaching spoon in her hand, the sudden pain in his chest made him relent. He took two teaspoons of the nasty stuff and allowed her to help him lie down. In moments he drifted into a deep sleep.

Sky watched through the night, dozing fitfully in the big chair, listening for him to stir. Near false dawn, she came fully awake when the old familiar nightmare began once more. She had been waiting for it. His voice commanded, "First rank, preesent. Fire! Second rank, preesent. Fire—"

"Max, wake up, darling," she said, cradling his head in one arm while she replaced his right hand on the mattress. She sat on the edge of the bed, careful not to bump his painfully injured chest as she crooned to him, "The nightmares are going to end now . . . forever."

You will know when the time is right.

Max slowly came out of his dazed vision of hell, blinking as he looked up at her. Bloody hell, his chest hurt. Had he been hit? Who would take over the command? Then he realized he was not in Africa, but America . . . held in the arms of his wife.

Sky could see him returning to the present. That was when she issued the command, softly. "Now, tell me about Rorke's Drift." She was relieved that her voice did not break. But would he answer? She could feel him stiffen in her arms. For several seemingly endless moments he did not speak. "Now, my love. It is time," she urged him.

"It was a missionary station . . . with a hospital. Located on the Tugela River . . . bordering the Zulu kingdom." He paused, going back to another time, another place. "It was late January . . . or maybe early February of '79. General Lord Chelmsford took an army across the border to confront the Zulu king. Damned fool thought to teach the benighted savages the superiority of *civilized* fighting men." He scoffed bitterly. "They taught him a lesson before he died . . . or perhaps he learned nothing."

"I don't believe you were like Chelmsford . . . ever," she said softly.

"I wasn't. At least not after what I'd already learned in service to the empire. I'd been seconded from my regiment as liaison to the Natal militia."

"Natal militia?" she echoed.

"Native and European chaps . . . free-roaming scouts, no spit and polish at all."

"They taught you to track," she said, understanding why he fit in so well here, was so good as a bounty hunter.

Max nodded, his eyelids heavy with the laudanum. "Yes . . . and that good men come in many colors, from many nations. But when Chelmsford was instructed to invade the Zulu kingdom, I was ordered back to my regiment and given command of a company in the Second battalion . . . Twenty-fourth regiment of foot."

"Is that a lot of men?" she asked, guessing it was.

"Eighty soldiers . . . I was ordered to secure the station at Rorke's Drift. When my men and I arrived, the place was already under the command of an engineering officer named

Chard who had twenty men building a bloody bridge—in the middle of a flaming war! Orders from central command . . . I'm surprised they didn't demand a gazebo as well."

He laughed and started coughing. She gave him a sip of water.

"There were about one hundred forty souls at the Drift . . . missionaries, a medical contingent . . . and wounded. Since Chard's commission was a few days older than mine, he was in charge . . ."

"But he was an engineer," Sky protested.

Max tried to laugh again, but it came out a hollow sound. "And a damned good one, luckily for us . . . the survivors, that is. That afternoon two riders reached us with word that Chelmsford had split his command. His smaller force of sixteen hundred men had been wiped out . . ."

"I had no idea of the scale of the warfare," she said, thinking of the thousands of Sioux, Cheyenne and Arapahoe who had sealed Custer's fate when he attacked them . . . and the slaughter of the Indians that had followed. "What happened after that?"

"The riders told us the Zulu forces were heading our way, flush with victory. Chard set the men to fortifying an outer perimeter, then a smaller inner redoubt that would serve as our last stand . . ." He grew silent, remembering the battle.

Sky sat patiently, waiting.

Finally, he started speaking again in a drugged voice. "The next afternoon, just as we were finishing the fortifications, a small troop of militia rode up and told us that right behind them was an army of four to five thousand Zulu. I don't think any of us expected to live through their attack . . ."

"And those men, they just left you?"

"They were no fools. They had horses and knew the terrain. Had no wounded to carry. They fled . . . can't say I blame them. We had only around a hundred able-bodied men."

"Forty or fifty to one!" she gasped out.

His eyes closed for a moment, but a small bitter laugh escaped. "We shared your consternation. Especially when the Zulu appeared, filling the ridge overlooking the station as far as the eye could see . . . thousands and thousands, slapping their short spears on their shields . . . it sounded like the roar of a dozen steam locomotives. The very earth shook . . . and they cried, '*Useto! Useto!*' Kill . . . kill . . .

"They climbed over the bodies of their fallen warriors to breach our outer perimeter, vaulting over the wall. We fell back to the redoubt . . . after that it was simply, 'First rank, preesent. Fire! Second rank, preesent. Fire! Third rank . . . '" He shuddered.

By now she was holding on to him, stroking his sweat-soaked face as he relived the bloody horror. It seemed that once the floodgate had been breeched, he could not stop.

"The noise was like a dozen cannon pounding inside my brain. Deafening. And the stench of blood . . . it was everywhere . . . we were bathed in it. Flaming hell, I shot men with the barrel of my revolver pressed directly into their flesh . . . I watched that flesh explode . . . but the brave fools kept coming . . . wave after wave . . . all through the night . . . Then for some reason, they finally stopped . . ."

His body was shaking. He made soft gasps that Sky knew were suppressed sobs. Hating what she had to do, she pressed him to go on. "What happened next?"

"With the dawn, we could see the full extent of the carnage . . . like some bloody madman's depiction of hell . . . so many corpses there was no way to begin to count . . . piled like cordwood, one on top of another . . . chest high in places. Some of the lads started puking . . . I ordered them to the outer perimeter. We had to climb over the dead to reach it . . . and all I could think of was all of those widows and orphans we had made . . . for the glory of civilization and the empire." His voice was bitter.

"And then the most bizarre thing happened . . ." He

paused again, shaking his head in wonder and confusion. "Up on the ridge surrounding us, they reappeared, thousands of them, as if we hadn't even touched their ranks . . . and they began to chant in unison. I know a bit of Zulu, but one of our native scouts explained that they were singing a song of praise . . . telling us that we were worthy warriors! All I felt was guilt . . . shame . . . disgust . . . bloody, puking disgust for what we'd done—been ordered to do—because of our stupid, arrogant government . . . may all bureaucrats rot in hell!"

He turned his head, but she could see the tracks of tears streaming down his cheeks. Using her hand, she forced him to face her. Softly, she said, "You don't understand. True Dreamer knew that you did not. I'm certain he could explain it better than I, but he charged me with the task . . . to banish the dark warriors from your mind forever."

He said nothing as she gathered her thoughts and continued, all the while holding him close. "You were not raised in a warrior culture, but you are a warrior, nonetheless. It would have been easier to understand if you had lived among the Zulu—or the Sioux. With them, young men do not expect to become old men. Life is hard. They and their wives and children know that a man can meet death during the hunt, fording a river, or in battle. Death is a part of life. Every day must end. Every life must end. Existence is one huge wheel. We are born, we live . . . and we die. We are part of the design that goes on after us. What matters is how we live while we are here."

"I lived by killing men who were defending their homes and families from invasion," he said stubbornly.

"You are not a Custer or a Chivington, Max! You and your men were warriors facing warriors. True Dreamer said that yours was a great battle with much bravery on both sides. The Zulu understood. That's why they honored you and allowed you to depart instead of killing you. The men in your nightmares aren't angry ghosts, but images of your own lack of understanding. There is no need for them to haunt you . . . ever again. Now . . . you will let them go. True Dreamer's talisman saved your life. And now, my love will free you . . . if you only believe what I have told you."

"You really do . . . love me?" he murmured. When Sky nodded, he could see that tears ran silently down her cheeks as well. He smiled weakly at her. "Crafty old medicine man . . . even more crafty wife. I love you more than life, Sky Eyes of the Ehanktonwon . . . m'lady."

When his eyes closed and he drifted off to sleep, she whispered, "I love *you* more than life, Maxwell Stanhope, m'lord." With that, she carefully stretched out alongside of him on the bed. They slept a deep and dreamless sleep.

Far to the south, in a lodge on the Cheyenne reservation in the Nations, True Dreamer stared into the embers of a small fire . . . and nodded in contentment.

Max awakened to find Sky curled against his side. A sense of deep peace pervaded his whole being, a feeling he had not had since Edmund had died. All his ghosts had been laid to rest because of this remarkable woman. As he gazed over at her with pure love shining in his eyes, her own opened and she smiled.

"Good morning, slugabed. I'm starving and I love you—oh, and did I mention that I was starving?" he added with a grin.

"I'll see what Mrs. Broom can do about breakfast," she replied, slipping from the bed. "While I'm at it, I'll inquire about that wagon—if the doctor approves of your traveling by tomorrow." She paused, then added, "Oh, and I love you, too."

He watched her remove her night rail and slip into her buckskins. All the while, he could feel his body hardening. "I need no physician to tell me that I am greatly improved."

Glancing at the "lodge pole" again rising beneath the

sheets, she chuckled. "I suspect by the time you spend a few hours bouncing in even the best sprung wagon, you'll not feel so 'exalted.'"

"There are other kinds of bouncing I'd be willing to risk right now, m'lady" he replied, loving the return of their old banter.

"I'll bring an extra ice bag to cool your ardor," she said, starting for the door.

Then he noticed the medicine medallion lying on the table. "You removed it . . . after we talked during the night."

"Yes, I did," she said simply. "True Dreamer told me that I would know when the time was right."

He nodded. "It's almost frightening, that old man's powers . . . and yours. We'll have to return his prized possession to him." He looked at her questioningly.

"Yes, when I see that you're mended sufficiently enough, we will." With that settled, she slipped from the room.

As she walked downstairs, Sky realized that it no longer mattered whether or not she was carrying Max's child. He was not bound to her by duty, but by love. After last night, she knew that he had never betrayed her. He trusted her enough to bare his innermost soul.

Fawn had been correct. She had been foolish for even considering "throwing away" such a man. Grandfather was probably right, too. She possessed too much "foolish white-man blood." Sky laughed like a young girl, free to love as she had never been before in her life.

That evening as she arranged pillows behind Max so he could sit up, she explained her feelings. "I knew I would always love you, but I didn't want to tie you to me with a child."

"I have wanted you for my wife since we were in London, even considering the possibility that you might not be able to have children. I should have told you then—Harry's will and its provisions be damned! I love you."

"You've told me now. That's all that matters. But I do want

your babies, Max. You were certain the fertility drugs and spells we fell under that night in the Cheyenne lodge had worked. Perhaps they did. It will be over a week before I can be certain."

"Just in case it failed, we can continue with due diligence to see that—"

"You are unbelievable!" she said, laughing as she kissed him.

Max did not release her, but cradled her head with one hand and deepened the kiss. Only a tap on the door announcing the arrival of their dinner prevented his sickbed seduction from going any further.

The following day Dr. Broom pronounced Max fit to travel in a wagon. He expressed amazement at Mr. Stanhope's recovery. But, as Sky had predicted, by the time they had spent a day in the wagon, her husband was in considerable pain and willing to accept laudanum so he could sleep that night. Early the next morning they reached Pueblo, where Steve Loring's private railcar awaited. So did several telegrams. Blackie Drago offered congratulations, saying he knew they'd track down Deuce. Steve reiterated in more detail that all legal ramifications regarding McKerrish's death had been settled and his guest suite awaited the weary travelers.

Additionally, Cass had taken it upon herself to inform Sky's family about their adventures and his injury. Of course, her elder brother demanded that as soon as Max recuperated sufficiently, he was to escort his wife to St. Louis for a visit. Rob had been incessantly pestering his parents with questions about when his famous English uncle would return.

Jerome Bartlett expressed shock and dismay at Phillip's actions and did indeed confirm that the body assumed by Scots authorities to be Phillip was actually Cletus. Sky felt guilty for suspecting the loyal family solicitor of malfeasance, not to mention attempted murder. Over Max's signature, she sent a letter, giving Bartlett full authority to handle all the baron's financial interests in Britain and appoint a new estate manager for the Ruxton lands.

When a Pueblo newspaper reported that the Limey had killed a dozen desperados in a street fight in Clean Sweep, Max went into a towering rage. "What did I use? A Gatling gun! A dozen men—bloody, flaming hell, weren't the six we faced enough for them!"

Sky shrugged, gently shoving him back onto the soft pile of pillows on the luxury railcar's bed. "Literary license. Oh, and Max, they're calling you 'Lord Limey' now." When he gave her a fierce glare, she suppressed her laughter.

As to what the Stanhopes would do with his very considerable fortune in America, Max and Sky reached an agreement. He wanted to spend it on her people and their new Cheyenne friends. Agreeing, Sky proposed not just feeding, clothing and schooling the people on reservations, but providing them with opportunities such as she had been given so they could survive in the white man's world.

They agreed to select the brightest among the youth and send them East to study medicine, law and government, either in fine colleges or by employing private tutors, as Clint had arranged for her. They both agreed that one of the first to be offered this opportunity would be True Dreamer's granddaughter Fawn, and they would serve as her legal guardians.

When they reached Denver, a much exhausted Maxwell Stanhope, the infamous bounty hunter known as the Limey, was willing to climb meekly into a large freshly made-up bed and take a midafternoon nap in the Lorings' guest suite. Thus began the arduous road to recovery.

Within the week, he refused any further laudanum, saying, "I'll become a bloody opium eater if you insist on forcing another spoonful of that ghastly tasting stuff down my throat!"

At the end of the following week, he was taking brisk

walks around the lavish grounds of the Loring estate. It was a quiet time for Max and Sky to spend talking about the past and their very different childhoods.

"I was ever a rebel, even before Edmund died. Always getting into trouble with my tutors. Received some good canings. University bored me, too. That was when I met Cynthia Warrington at a ball."

"She was married to a much older man and seduced you." Sky did not phrase it as a question.

Max sighed. "He was in Lords, a good man who had married a woman not worthy of him. Her reputation was quite dreadful, but he knew nothing of her many young lovers. I was but one in a string."

"The one unfortunate enough to be caught?"

He nodded. "He called me out. Bloody hell, Sky, the man was over three times my age and knew nothing of weapons. It would've been criminal to duel him."

"So, you took a commission in the army instead and left England behind."

"And, mercifully, Cynthia." He made a grimace of distaste. "But the circumstances of my departure hurt my uncle. For that I'll always feel regret."

"You made him proud of you, Max. Never forget that. And he loved you. He understood you all too well, which explains why he made that codicil to his will. He knew it would straighten out your life."

He sighed. "I led a reckless, dangerous life and, after my experience with Cynthia, I fear women came all too easily to me. Many of them. But I never knew what it meant to love one until I met you."

Sky knew he had never told another woman he loved her and the realization filled her with joy. But she felt constrained to confess, "I did love Will . . . in a different way. He was kind and protective, always concerned for me . . ."

"But you knew no passion with him," he said gently,

understanding what she was trying to say, relieved to have it out in the open.

"No, what I felt from those first moments in your Bismarck hotel room made me feel guilty . . . and attracted at the same time."

"The guilt's gone now." He did not make it a question, but needed to hear her answer just the same.

"I'm sorry a good man's life had to end that way, but, yes, I no longer feel guilty because I love you . . . and desire you."

He could see a faint flush stain her cheeks as she met his gaze. "Bloody hell, I was never so grateful as when we consummated our vows. Then I knew you could never leave me. You can't imagine how often I cursed that infernal bargain we'd made."

"I was afraid when we left the Cheyenne that if I was with child, you would feel honor bound to stay with me," Sky said as they approached the gazebo overlooking the carefully manicured landscape of the Loring estate.

He drew her inside and they sat down on the wooden bench running around the inside of the octagonal structure. "I suppose I should thank you for not believing me such an absolute rotter that I'd abandon you and our offspring," he said with the hint of a smile tugging at his lips.

"After what happened in Clean Sweep, I knew I'd been a fool, but I've told you about my lifelong insecurities," she said, raising his hand to her lips and brushing the knuckles with a kiss. "It would've been easier if you were a rotter. Then I could've simply left you."

"Rotter or not, I would never have permitted that, m'lady," he replied, pressing a kiss on her hand as they faced each other. "I would have followed you and dragged you back, kicking and cursing. Remember to whom you are making confession—the best man or woman hunter in America."

"And a most modest chap, as well," she said with a chuckle.

Max sniffed, affecting a very English air. "There are those who have much about which to be modest. I do not happen to be one of them."

His quip elicited a laugh from Sky. "I would punch you if not for your injury, you arrogant beast." Then the laughter left her eyes and she grew very serious. "There is something I must tell you."

"That you are carrying my child," he responded softly, framing her face with his hands. "I've wondered how long it would be before you shared that with me."

Her eyes widened with a combination of indignation and amazement. "But I've only just become certain. My courses are a week late and that's the longest I ever go before they start."

"I may not possess Indian blood, but True Dreamer and Bright Leaf convinced me that a higher power, by whatever name, wanted to bestow this blessing on us." He kissed her softly. "Never doubt how much I want you for my wife or how proud I am to have you as the mother of my children, Sky," he murmured against her face and throat as he continued to kiss her with growing ardor.

Sky returned his passion and soon they were locked in an embrace. Max's clever fingers had the buttons at the front of her yellow lawn dress unfastened and one hand slipped inside to cup her breast through her lacy chemise. She moaned, arching against the intense pleasure.

"They're growing," he whispered in wonder, lifting the other and teasing the nipple until it hardened and she gasped. "Ah, pregnancy does make them more sensitive."

"Just wait . . . until I'm . . . fat and shapeless," she managed to say.

"It won't alter my desire for you in the least." He renewed

his assault on her mouth, but when he tried to pull her closer and lean back against the hard wooden bench, a sharp pain from his injury made him gasp.

Sky blinked and pulled away, breathing hard, her blue eyes dark with passion . . . and embarrassment when she realized a gardener was busily raking leaves directly down the hill from them. And here she was, half undressed right out in the middle of the yard! "See, you lecherous man, what you've almost done," she scolded, sitting up and starting to refasten her dress.

"I know what I've almost done—rebruised my accursed sternum—and it's all your fault for denying me the past nights. What we require is a large, soft bed where you may play nurse and console your injured husband. Let us adjourn to that bed, eh?"

A smile curved her lips. "I could apply an ice bag to the appropriate place. That would cool you off, m'lord."

"And what then of you, m'lady? I doubt an ice bag would suffice."

"To bed!" they both said in unison as they stood up and hastened from the lovely wooden gazebo.

Sky was grateful that Cass and Steve were both at work. She and Max slipped past several smiling servants who knew what their dishabille foretold. Max locked the door to their quarters, saying, "The children will be home from school within the hour. I don't intend for you to complete your 'nursing' duties so quickly."

With that, he kicked off his shoes and began removing his shirt. It cost him some pain, but watching Sky unfasten that row of buttons on her dress, revealing her golden skin and the swell of her breasts was opiate enough to make him forget everything, even an aching chest. Then she pulled the pins from her hair and allowed the heavy tresses to fall around her shoulders like gleaming blue-black ink.

After quickly stripping her dress, petticoats and shoes off,

Sky approached him and placed her hands around his biceps. "Now, if I am to be your nurse, you must be a good patient and allow me to prepare you for bed."

"I place myself completely in your capable hands," he said, his voice raw, hungry.

Her breath hitched as she looked at his bare chest, still discolored by bruises, now turning greenish yellow. How close she had come to losing him! Very gently she feathered kisses across the hard muscles and crisp hair, savoring the sound of his heart pounding. Then she set to work on his belt buckle and unfastened his trousers. "Now, lie down," she commanded, guiding him until the backs of his legs made contact with the mattress.

Once he stretched out his long, lean body on the bed, she pulled his pants and undergarments off and tossed them aside, then gazed in wonder at him. "Pale Moon Stalker. Grandfather named you rightly. When I first met you and agreed to your devil's bargain, I thought you were the hardest, most dangerous man I'd ever met . . ."

"And now?" he asked hoarsely, loving the way her eyes wandered over his body, pausing at his throbbing erection.

"You certainly are hard," she said, running her hand up and down the length of his phallus as she scooted onto the side of the mattress. "But the only thing dangerous about you, m'lord, is that you make me desire you every waking moment."

"Perhaps you would care to act on that desire now . . . I'm a most accommodating chap," he said, his breathing accelerating as she caressed and cupped him. "Ah, such nursing care as I never received in hospital when I was a soldier!"

Sky took her time, enjoying having him lie still while she caressed and kissed every inch of his body, from his silver-gilt hair and chiseled facial features to his injured chest, bypassing for the moment his pulsing staff to run her fingers and tongue over the insides of his thighs. When he seized hold of her hair and tried to pull her up for a kiss, she pressed his shoulders against the pillows. "Remember, I am the nurse . . . you the patient," she admonished.

"I have little patience left in me, but too much of something else. I fear I'll burst if you don't act quickly, Nurse Stanhope."

"Well then, you vulgar lout," she said consideringly, standing up beside the bed. "Lie still and observe only . . . no touching until I give permission." She slipped off her chemise, then peeled her stockings and garters down ever so slowly, bracing one foot at a time on the edge of the mattress.

"My hand can encircle your ankle so easily," he said raggedly. She shook her head and placed her foot out of his reach. She loved the way he watched like the lobo wolf she had once thought of him as being. When she was as naked as he, she slid onto the mattress and carefully positioned herself over him, her knees pressed against his hips.

"Ah, medicinal relief at last," he sighed, cupping her derriere in his hands to guide her down.

Sky gently removed his hands. "You're spoiling my concentration. Please, allow me . . ." With that she began ever so slowly, brushing, teasing, rubbing the wet softness of her body against the head of his hard staff. Finally, she slid down the length of it, impaling herself until the fullness was pure bliss.

Max watched her eyelids flutter and her golden skin flush darkly. When she tipped her head back, her long straight mane of hair brushed against his thighs, eliciting a growl as he arched up, seating himself even deeper inside her.

That was all the urging she required. With a small moan, she began to rise and fall, riding him with splendid grace, completing him, completing her. As they gained speed and the intensity grew unbearable, she slowed down, biting her lip to regain control. "This cure . . . is going . . . to take . . . a . . . long . . . time . . . I fear more than . . . one session," she managed to whisper, bracing her hands on the pillow so she could bend down and kiss him without pressing against his injured chest.

"Capital, m'lady, capital," he murmured into her open mouth as he savaged her lips in a devouring kiss.

But Sky knew his pleasure was mixed with pain because of the deep bruising on his chest. As another peak neared for her, she rolled her hips and squeezed her thighs, pulling them both over the abyss. When she felt him swell and spill himself deeply inside her, her own body convulsed uncontrollably. She leaned on her elbows, not wanting to hurt him, yet not wanting to break their joining either.

Max threaded his fingers through her hair and caressed her back, kissing her face and throat. At length, when he caught his breath, he murmured, "I recall saying this would be far superior to those damnable ice bags."

As she rolled to his side, Sky's laughter was rich and infectious. "Now I know at least two remedies for keeping you under control—loving and ice bags!" She pulled the sheet over them and they lay side by side, dozing and sated as the sun arced across the sky toward the west.

At last he reached down and placed his palm against her still flat belly. "I want a daughter with long black hair and eyes the color of a Colorado sky, just like her mother's."

"We shall see," she said dreamily, "because I think we'll have a son with his father's silver-gilt hair and dark green eyes."

"I don't think that's likely, love," he said cautiously.

"You don't want a son?" she asked incredulously. "Just because you don't care about the title—"

He interrupted her with laughter. "No, that is, yes, I certainly want a son. What I meant is that the likelihood he'll have blond hair is slim."

"My father is half white and my mother was a Swedish blonde. My Ehanktonwon brother has pale tan hair and gray eyes. I will have my little replica of you, m'lord."

He gave her a lopsided grin. "Just so I have my little replica of you, m'lady, I will be content."

★   ★   ★

Far to the south in the Nations, a young girl awakened suddenly from a dream. She had fallen asleep by the side of a shallow pool shaded by a cottonwood tree. She sat up and looked into the water, sorting out the remnants of her vision. Grandfather had told her the gift from the Powers would be passed. But in spite of his assurances, she had not dared to believe that she would be chosen.

As she gazed raptly into the still water, she knew that he had spoken true. Closing her eyes again, she looked up through the rustling leaves of the tree and felt the golden warmth of the sun touch her eyelids. The dream-vision shimmered in her mind with startling clarity. A half smile spread across her face.

The wishes of both Stalker and Sky would be granted. Then the tiny smile morphed into a mischievous grin. The Powers did like to play tricks, sometimes even on those who were favored. A daughter would be their firstborn, made in this very village, and she would have hair as dark as a raven's wing. The boy child would have hair like the pale moon's silver-gold light. But the girl's eyes would be green like her father's and the boy's eyes blue like his mother's.

Her laughter echoed like clear sweet chimes across the pool. When she looked down at the still water again, hoping for a glimpse of her own future, the vision vanished like the mists at sunrise. Grandfather had always told her that the Powers did not permit a dreamer to see his or her own future. But she knew that, when it was time, something wonderful and exciting would happen that would change her life forever.

Fawn stretched out in the soft grass and drifted back to sleep . . .

Betrayed by the girl he loved, disgraced before his commander, wounded in battle and left for dead, John Murray thought he'd hit his lowest point. But the sweet touch of a lover he'd never thought to see again taught him that no matter how far a man falls, with the right woman at his side, he can always stand tall.

Fallen
by
Cindy Holby

Aberdeen, Scotland, 1773

A fine mist fell. John Murray could not help shivering in his shirtsleeves as he stepped out into the damp gray gloom of early morning. A shudder moved down his spine as his eyes fell upon the post planted in the middle of the courtyard at Castlehill. The ground around it was trampled, torn, and filled with the muck from the mix of rain and free-flowing blood. Ewan Ferguson's blood. No comfort for him there; his blood would soon join it.

Was she watching? His blue eyes scanned the ranks of his peers, all standing at attention in the despicable weather, all surely cursing his name because they were given orders to rise early this miserable morning and watch his punishment.

Where was she? Surely they would force her to watch since it was her fault he was here in the first place. Surely they had made her watch her brother's lashing, as it was his fault that two men now lay dead.

There. He saw her. She stood next to the general with her chin held high and her shoulders squared as if she had just handed down the sentence herself. In some strange, turned about way, she had. Luckily for her, the general was magnanimous in his show of mercy. She was a woman, after all, and nothing more than an instrument in the treachery of her clansmen.

Her hair was plastered down against her head instead of the usual mass of springy curls that framed her face like sunlight. This morning it seemed darker than its reddish blonde, whether from the rain, or the doom and gloom that hung over the courtyard, he could not tell. Her dress was stained dark with blood and the neckline gaped open, torn by him in his haste the afternoon they were together. Of course she would have had no way to mend it, so it hung open, teasing him, tormenting him, just as she did the first time he met her. She had gotten into his head that day, damn her. She had no choice but to live with the state of her dress since her hands were tied before her. Even though the distance between them was great, he could feel her deep brown eyes upon him. That gave him a measure of satisfaction. A small measure, but it was something to hang on to.

If only they would lash her also. Did she not deserve it? Was she not as guilty as her brothers and her father in the planning and the plotting and the betrayal?

John looked at her. Isobel. Izzy. It was her fault. He trusted her with his life, with his soul, with his heart and she had betrayed him.

Fallen

Coming early next year.